Before reading this book visit our website: <u>angelcomehome.com</u>.
Click on the
'Bios' link for the theme song and the introduction to the story.

"Many people who are open to animal communication and a deepened connection with nature say that it is like a sense of coming home, of suddenly knowing ourselves, and all our relations in a more expansive way - in a way we always knew but somehow forgot. As we allow ourselves to sense with our bodies, hear with our heart, and see with our inner vision, we begin to experience the world in a very different way. How do we begin our journey? Often, it is not where we are going but what we find along the way that holds the key to our true adventure. It is frequently the diversions and the strange circumstances that lead us to the most extraordinary places - heartfelt, humorous, amazing, sometimes barely believable."

Dawn Baumann Brunke,
Animal Voices, Telepathic Communication
in the Web of Life.

(published by Bear & Company/Inner Traditions, 2002.)

Photographs by Ryan Hadlock

Angel Come Home

a love story

BY

STUART R. WISONG

First Published in the United States of America
by Stuart R. Wisong and Ryan C. Hadlock, 2007

Second edition published 2008

Third edition published 2008

Fourth edition published 2008

Fifth edition published 2010

Sixth edition published 2013

Establishing the "Angel Come Home Living Legacy"
benefitting domestic animal welfare organizations
through donation of its profits after taxes in perpetuity

ISBN 978-1-60461-050-5

Cover photo by Ryan Hadlock

Illustrators: Denise Brown and Carol Adams

Book Design: ad-cetera graphics
www.adceteragraphics.com

Communicate with the Author.
I welcome your questions, comments and ideas for a sequel to
Angel Come Home - A Love Story.
www.AngelComeHome.com

Dedicated to my mentor
Ryan Hadlock
and
our devoted companions
Angel and Baby Angel

Author's Note

*A*ngel Come Home – A Love Story, is a deeply moving tale. You will laugh. You will cry. It could change your life forever.

Although this story is fiction, much of it is taken from actual experience. Many of the events, places, and people are real.

Our story is rich in adventure, kindness, truth, hope and love. It is not only for those of us who share our home with a fuzzy companion, but also for anyone who enjoys reading about love-lost and love-found.

Angel Come Home - Living Legacy

*P*roceeds from the sale of this book are benefitting many Humane Societies and other Domestic Animal Welfare Organizations throughout the United States.

If your organization would like to receive funds from the proceeds of this book, please visit our web site: **www.angelcomehome.com**

Introduction

I've been writing all of my life, transferring my thoughts into words, whether by keeping a journal or by creating imaginary characters who came alive on paper. It was my youth's private journey. Writing is one of the ways I make sense of life.

In my freshman year of high school I wrote an essay, "We Are the Gods of Our Pets." I discovered that an affectionate bond exists between our pets and ourselves that transcends every emotion with no limit to its dedication or devotion.

While attending college, one of my professors, Dr. Holsinger, encouraged me to use my imagination by writing each day. She would say, "Stuart, don't let the day go by without putting your thoughts on paper in a new and imaginative way. If a musician must practice each day to perfect a skill, so must you."

My journey as a writer began on that day. I wrote short stories, mysteries, comedies, speeches, and poems. I wrote about my parents, friends, teachers, and more importantly, my feelings, my deepest, most private feelings.

The idea for this story began five years ago when we took our companion to Europe. Spending the summer traveling throughout the cities and villages of Italy, Germany, France and Spain with our small fluffy dog added an additional level of adventure. Traveling with a canine is like traveling with a movie star, both are constantly attracting attention. People in every country wanted to come close, to ask questions, and to touch her. Come along as Angel and Brad tell their story.

Portsmouth

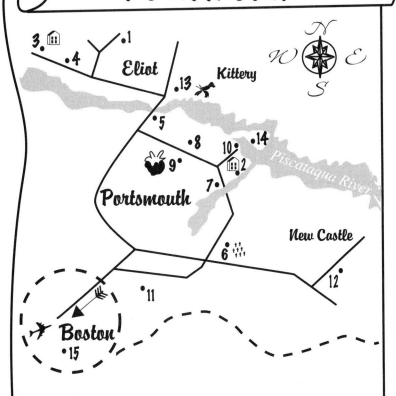

1. Tidewater School
2. Brad's House
3. Pine Tree Farm
4. Eliot Library
5. Memorial Bridge
6. South Cemetary
7. Mill Race/Mill Pond
8. Prescott Park
9. Strawbery Banke
10. Audrey's House
11. Portsmouth High School
12. Ice House Ice Cream
13. Warren's Lobster House
14. Peirce Island
15. Boston Logan Airport

Paris

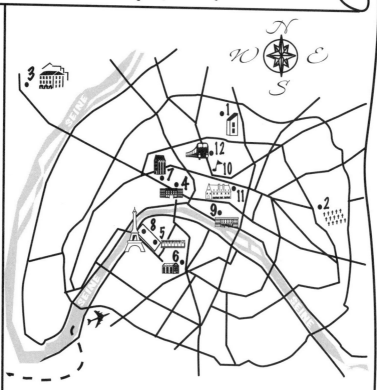

1. Sacré Coeur
   Madame Noblesse's
   Rooming House
2. Cimétiere du
   Père-Lachaise
3. Chateau Domaine
   (20 miles from Paris)
4. Embassy Row
   (61 Rue du Cirque)
5. Colonade
6. Hotel du Danube
7. Hotel Moulin Rouge
8. Eiffel Tower
9. Louvre
10. Paris Opera House
11. Count Beauchamp's
    Mansion
12. Rue Saint-Lazare
    Train Station

Chapter 1

The Rescue

His leash locked in a fallen tree branch, a small dog lay cold, frightened and alone. As he struggled, his collar tightened around his throat, muffling his cries for help.

A squirrel, having eluded the imprisoned animal, jumped into a chestnut tree then looked back at the unfamiliar creature held securely in the brush. A curious, white furry dog came forward and leaned over the frightened creature.

"What did you find?" A man's voice called out.

Stepping over the fallen branch, he saw his dog licking a puppy's face.

"Lie still, we'll have you untangled from this mess."

A couple with a child walked quickly down the path. Hearing a man's voice, they pushed their way through the brush and came over to where he was standing. "Hello, we've been looking all over the cemetery for my daughter's dog. Have you seen our Yorkie?"

"Yes, my dog found him." The man wrenched the offending branch from the tree trunk and threw it to one side. The little dog was gently placed into the child's waiting arms.

"We've been searching everywhere. Thank God you found him."

Consoling their pet, the mother removed the collar and massaged the Yorkie's neck.

"Would you and your dog please join us for lunch? We have plenty of food in our picnic satchel."

The entourage pushed their way through the brush and back to the path leading to the lake.

"Every year we come to South Cemetery to visit my mother. It's so beautiful here with the lake and rolling hills. Won't you join us? Look what I'm carrying! In all of the excitement we forgot to leave the flowers for Nana's grave."

"Thank you for the invitation, I know my companion does also." The man and his white dog followed the young family as they walked toward the lake.

With the blanket and picnic cloth spread across the grass, the lady looked up and said, "In all the excitement we haven't

introduced ourselves. My name is Karen and this is my husband, Allen, and our daughter, Emma, and you are?"

"My name is Brad Kennedy and this is Angel my best friend."

"Are you the Brad Kennedy from Portsmouth, the one who writes all those travel books?" Allen asked.

"Guilty."

"Are you here visiting a relative also?"

"No, I'm gathering historic information for an article that will appear in the next issue of *Accent* magazine."

"Didn't you write a novel recently? I heard you interviewed on the "Sam Adams" radio show. You traveled to Europe with your dog."

"Yes, that's true."

"Why did you take your dog with you?"

Karen tugged on her husband's sleeve, interrupting him. "Don't bother him with questions. Let Brad finish his sandwich."

"I don't mind. I always like to discuss my books. They're like my children."

Emma sat on the cool grass holding the two furry animals close to her, feeding them pieces from a large pretzel. "Did you train your dog to find lost animals?"

"No, I didn't train her. She was born with special gifts. She not only rescues animals, she also rescues people."

He could see the look of bewilderment on Emma's face. Brad sipped his coffee and beckoned Angel to come. As she rested her head on his leg, she looked at him with her all-knowing eyes. "Angel, should we tell the story to our new friends?"

With Angel spread comfortably on his lap, Brad began.

"When Angel came into my life, I had no idea of the incredible journey we would be taking. I'll always remember that crisp New England autumn day…

Chapter 2

Angel's Adoption

*A*pale blue October sky, sprinkled with white clouds, carried the promise of fair weather. Even though the wind was cold the sun's rays warmed my two-story 1840 colonial home nestled on the bank of the millrace leading to South Mill Pond. Although it looked like many other historical homes in Portsmouth, New Hampshire, there would soon be one remarkable difference; an angel would be coming to live with me.

As I stepped from the shower, I heard the phone ring. Grabbing my robe from the back of the door, I crossed the hall to my office and picked up the receiver. As I glanced through the skylight, I saw a pair of seagulls glide by, wings touching.

"Good morning, Brad speaking."

"Hello. Mr. Kennedy, this is Mrs. Luna," said a pleasant voice on the other end. "You called about the puppies for adoption? Would you like to come over today? I have three left, two girls and a boy."

"Yes. I can be over in twenty minutes. Will that be convenient?"

"That would be fine, dear. I'll have my little Maltese family ready for you. Once you get acquainted, you can make your choice. Now, give yourself plenty of time. Each puppy has a different personality you know. You'll want to choose the one that suits you."

"Of course, Mrs. Luna."

"Now, you have our address and the directions?"

"Yes, I'm familiar with Eliot. I attended the Tidewater School as a young boy. I'll see you in a little while. Thank you Mrs. Luna."

Every town has its show-time, that one month of the year when nature is at its best, when townsfolk all across New England are putting on their storm windows or raking their leaves, beaming with satisfaction and thinking, "Ours is the best town in the U.S. of A!" October is surely that time in Eliot. Throughout the village, maple trees are lit in flames of red and crimson. The wind brings a crisp apple smell from orchards near by as the whispering pines along the river lean toward the north.

I observed the swift current of the Piscataqua River as I drove over the old Memorial Drawbridge that connects New Hampshire with Maine. I could see the Portsmouth Naval Shipyard sprawled to my right while rural Kittery, Maine, lay ahead.

After driving only a short distance, I saw a sign that read, "Welcome to Eliot." Following Mrs. Luna's directions, I turned left at the fork and continued along a winding country road that hugged the side of the river. Ahead, I saw a kaleidoscope of homes, dating from the seventeenth to the twentieth centuries. Many had generous lawns, still green under the autumn leaves recently fallen from native oak, maple and birch trees.

Traditional New England farms dotted the landscape, some resisting "modern-living" by continuing to grow organic crops on a modest scale. A few barns, weathered by the long New England winters, had been reincarnated as antique shops while others were doing their best to simply remain standing.

Reaching a sharp curve in the road, I could see the William Fogg Public Library, named after the visionary pioneer who donated the land and the building to the people of Eliot. This handsome Greek revival building stands on top of a knoll, commanding an extended view of what old-timers say is the center of town.

Here the road separated. One road went northward, and the other, known simply as "Old Road," turned to the west and continued along the river, just as it has for over three hundred years. Native Americans wearing moccasins traveled this road when it was nothing more than a deer path through a dense forest.

As I continued on, my car hugging the gentle curves, dipping slightly, and then rising once again, I finally turned off the road observing a sign that read "Pine Tree Farm." The curving gravel driveway made a popcorn sound as I drove toward the top of the hill and parked next to the barn.

A pair of mourning doves flew past my car as I looked toward a rock retaining wall covered with alyssum. "It's a haven of restful tranquility," I thought. "I can't imagine a more peaceful place to raise dogs."

Just as I closed the car door, a woman, perhaps in her fifties, appeared from around the side of the barn, dressed in jeans and a flannel shirt. "Hello there," she said warmly, extending her hand. "I'm Mrs. Luna. You're right on time. I hope you didn't have any trouble finding us. She laughed. "I've got three eager puppies who are looking forward to meeting you. Right this way." As we entered through the back doorway, the screen door slammed behind us.

"Please excuse the noise. We have to make sure the doors close good and tight. We can't have the little ones wandering outside." Mrs. Luna's eyes were bright with love for her little charges.

The aroma of bread, fresh from the oven, filled the kitchen, reminding me of my childhood years. Those were the golden days, the days in my grandmother Simon's kitchen as she made her Challah bread. Its twisted shape mirrored her grey hair, braided into a halo on the top of her head. Mrs. Luna reminded me of her.

"Would you like a slice of my freshly baked bread?" Mrs. Luna fairly sang the words as she walked over to the table where five loaves of hot bread sat cooling.

"Sure, how can I refuse!"

After handing me a large slice of buttered bread, Mrs. Luna said, "You just make yourself comfortable, dear, and munch on that while I get the puppies and their mother and father. The mom's name is Precious. The dad is Iggy. Don't let Iggy intimidate you. He likes to growl, but all you have to do is scratch his back and he'll be licking your hand."

As she opened the door to the adjoining room, three furry, white, rabbit-like creatures dashed toward me, followed by a pair of very proud parents. I assumed the puppies were happy to see me until I realized they were lunging for the piece of bread still in my hand.

"Hey, whoa! Okay, which of you are girls?" I crouched down to get a better look at the pups.

"That's right, you wanted a female. I'll put the male in the baby pen with the toys so you can get to know our girls."

Both puppies looked identical, but on closer observation, it was clear that one was smaller and more delicate while the other was larger and more robust. As I sat on the floor with the two puppies, I tried to get the smaller one's attention. Each time I held her she managed to squirm away.

The larger puppy took every opportunity to snuggle up next to me, resting her head on my arm. After half an hour of gently pushing away the larger puppy, my resistance was overcome by her persistence.

"Mrs. Luna, I came here to choose a puppy, but one of your puppies has chosen me. I'm going to take the larger female."

While filling out the adoption forms, I noticed my puppy gazing at me. A minute ago she'd been playing about the room, and now she sat motionless. I had a feeling she was trying to tell me something.

"Mrs. Luna, this puppy is talking to me with her eyes. I feel an emotional connection flowing between us."

"What you're feeling is a long legacy of love and devotion."

I continued to glance periodically at the puppy, as I read the adoption papers. "Mrs. Luna, this puppy seems more like a cat. Why is she sitting so quietly? Are you sure she's healthy?"

Mrs. Luna took a seat on the rocking chair across from me. Her eyes lit up. "Oh, she's healthy all right. She's the strongest and healthiest of the litter. She was always the first to grab her meal and the last to leave. I've been raising Maltese puppies for ten years, Mr. Kennedy, and I've got to tell you, this girl's different from the rest." Mrs. Luna hesitated a moment. Looking over her shoulder as if she expected some unseen person to be listening, she leaned forward and placed her hands on her knees and whispered.

"Mr. Kennedy, I don't much go to church. But I say my prayers. I hope you won't think I'm imagining this, but this puppy can read your thoughts." Mrs. Luna hesitated, observing my look of surprise. "I can see you need some convincing."

"Just listen to this... The other day, I couldn't find my car keys, and I had this doctor's appointment. I kept going all over the house looking in the same places, thinking I might have overlooked them the first time. Well, this little puppy stays right behind me when I walk from room to room. I thought she wanted to play, so I turn around to pick her up, but she ran toward the bathroom. So, I followed her. When I get into the bathroom, there she is, sitting on the floor, looking up at the sink. I'm thinking, that's odd, but I don't have time for this. As I started to leave to continue my search, I heard a whimper, and I turned around and there, on the sink, were my keys, right by the soap. The minute she saw me pick them up, she turned around and dashed into the kitchen and plopped herself down next to her sister. This little Maltese is like no other I've ever had. Just look at those eyes staring at you. She's telling you all kinds of things. You just need to listen."

For a moment neither of us spoke. We just looked at the puppy. Somehow I knew we were both hearing the same voice in our heads. There she was, my new responsibility. Those two brown eyes gazing at me.

Hi, I'm twelve weeks old. I'm finally adopted! When you said you wanted a girl, I knew I had a chance. I'm kind of a tomboy, actually – I act a lot more like my brothers. I sure hope you live in a quiet house – there's too much barking here. I know I talk a lot but I have a lot to say.

I started getting concerned when I saw my brothers and sisters leaving. I'm glad it's my turn.

The people who came here to adopt us seemed to have an image of the kind of companion they wanted. That was fine with me. I knew exactly the kind of person I wanted.

One lady said, I've heard females are more affectionate, another said, I don't want a male puppy because they lift their leg and pee on things. Maybe you should know I lift my leg a little, but not all the way like my brothers. Squatting like my sisters just doesn't come naturally to me.

Today, Mrs. Luna told us a man was coming at one o'clock to adopt one of us girls, that we should look our best. I didn't know what she meant – I've always stayed clean, except for that day when I stepped in some poop. Then I didn't smell so good!

When I heard you were coming, I decided I wasn't going to play coy like my sister. I knew you were going to pick either her or me. I was disappointed when you picked up my sister, but I was relieved when she kept walking away. You wouldn't have wanted her if you knew what I know. She wets on everything and whines most of the time. She's just fur and bones… never got enough milk. It was either too cold or too hot. She was never satisfied. I'm the strongest of all the puppies. I was always the first one to nurse, and I wouldn't let go until my mum got up and walked away. I love living here with Mrs. Luna, but it's time for me to have my own home. I know you'll take good care of me. I hope my new home will be a tub-of-love.

I glanced across the room at Mrs. Luna as she continued to rock back and forth, a broad smile creasing her face.

After I completed the adoption forms, I said to Mrs. Luna, "You have a loving place here at Pine Tree Farm. These puppies are very lucky."

Sliding the adoption papers under my arm, I gently picked up the three pounds of silky white fur.

Mrs. Luna kissed her favorite puppy on the nose and brushed away a tear with the edge of her apron as she held the screen door for us. As I carried my treasure-of-puppy-love down the driveway, I saw Mrs. Luna standing by the kitchen window.

Just as we reached the car, Angel turned and looked back toward the house. On the window seat near the kitchen door were Iggy and Precious, looking through the glass at their little girl. Precious started to howl and Iggy gave several low growls.

Goodbye Mum. So long Dad. Thank you for a good start in life. Mrs. Luna, I love you.

Hmmm. I wonder where we're going. I've never been on the other side of the fence before…

❧

Two days after I adopted Angel, some close friends, Mark and Kathleen, came by to see the new addition to my family. "She's beautiful," Kathleen said. "What's her name?"

"Her name is Angel."

"How did you choose the name, Angel?"

"I didn't choose the name, she told me her name."

"Sure, and did she tell you what zodiac sign she was too?"

"You think I'm joking, don't you? Let me tell you how it happened and then you'll understand…

"After arriving home from Pine Tree Farm with Angel, I placed the adoption papers on my desk and took her into the kitchen. I placed her in the window seat with her bowl of food while I sat down at the kitchen table and began to eat the lunch I had prepared. After she'd finished eating, she put her head down on the cushion. Looking over at her, I said, 'What should I call you?' She looked up quickly and stared at me. I thought she would look away in a few seconds, but she didn't. She didn't even blink. As I continued to eat, I'd glance over, but she just kept on gazing at me.

"Now, this is where it gets hard to explain, and I don't fully understand it myself. I asked the question once again. 'Hey little lady, what should I call you?' As she continued to stare, I found myself distracted by the cumulus clouds slowly forming in the distance. Magically, a shaft of sunlight broke through the clouds, illuminating the area all around her. I had to look away for a few seconds because the sun was so intense. When I looked back, I saw directly above her, a beam of light dissolving into a kind of mist. I thought it was from the moisture on the window, but when I looked more closely, I saw that it wasn't. All the while she didn't move. She just kept gazing at me.

"What should I call you? What name would you like? I found myself asking her again. I laughed when I realized that I was playing a mind game with my pet. I started to get up from the table and then I saw her turn around, put her paws on the windowpane and look up toward the clouds. As she held that position I heard myself say, 'Your name is Angel.' I raised my voice and repeated, 'Your name is Angel! Right?' I sensed her agreement as she wagged her tail. So – Angel you are."

Later that evening, I was reading on the patio and I thought I would call Mrs. Luna and tell her what happened. Angel was lying on her side in the grass, all stretched out comfortably, as I dialed my cell phone. The phone rang a few times and then I heard her cheerful, familiar voice. "Mrs. Luna, I have a little news to share with you, but first I want to make sure of something. You didn't happen to name your last litter of dogs, did you? 'What? Could you repeat that? So, you're saying you did give a name to one of the girls? … And what did you name my puppy? … I see. Yes, I think it's a perfect name for her. When I hung up the phone, I stood in disbelief. This is what Mrs. Luna had recounted."

"Mr. Kennedy, remember Precious, that's the mother? It was time for her to deliver her babies and I was there to help as usual. The moment your puppy was born, I realized something was wrong. I picked up the lifeless form and held her in the palm of my hand. As I put my ear to her chest, I didn't hear a heart beat, and I couldn't feel her breathing.

"The pup's mother looked at me as if to say, 'Can you do something for my baby?' I took a warm washcloth from the kitchen counter and rubbed her vigorously. The poor lifeless thing just lay there. Suddenly, I saw the puppy's tail move. When I brought her to my ear I heard a faint heart beat. As I continued to stroke her, the heartbeat grew louder. After I was sure that it was beating strong, I placed the breathing newborn next to her mother so that she could be fed.

"When I turned out the light, I noticed the fireplace casting an orange glow on the nursing puppies. There was a white light around one of them. I was so tired; I thought I was imagining things. The light would glow brighter and then fade. Walking closer to the litter, I saw the puppy whose life I had saved. She looked much whiter than the rest of the litter. That's when I heard myself say, 'Hello Angel.'"

"I contemplated what Mrs. Luna had told me. As I looked at my white fluffy puppy sleeping on the lawn, so serenely angelic, I thought of the picture that hung on my bedroom wall when I was a child. There were two children crossing over a bridge. The bridge had several slats missing and there was a raging stream far below. Standing nearby was an angel watching over them.

"As I sat looking at Angel lying on the grass I thought, Angels come in all forms - not just in robes and wings - there are some angels with fur and a tail."

A white stream of jet vapor five thousand feet above South Cemetery hung in the sky as Emma and her family listened intently to Brad's story.

"And after Angel told you her name, what happened next?" Emma asked.

"Yes, please continue with the story," Allan and Karen encouraged.

"Well, the first part of the story is just as I experienced it but now the adventure begins. And you may find some of what I tell you hard to believe. So, I ask you to suspend your doubts and let your imagination take flight."

This is the story of Brad and Angel and their incredible journey.

Chapter 3

Rainbows Make Me Happy

T he ornate Westminster clock began to chime its familiar melody, comforting when followed by six gongs. Hearing the seventh, Brad felt anxious. It was Monday morning, and after a week's vacation from teaching, Brad had lingered a few minutes too long before rising. Now he was late. He had arranged to leave Angel with Audrey, his dog sitter. He hoped to have a few minutes to visit before he left her.

Audrey Bierhans was a woman who had spent her life in the service of others. Even though a stroke had sapped a great deal of her energy, she carried on unabated.

Brad felt protective of Audrey, as he did all of his friends, but Audrey had a special place in his heart, and in Angel's too, which became apparent the minute they were introduced. Audrey had fallen in love with Angel, and the feeling was mutual. Brad felt reassured to know Angel would have a caring friend to look after her while he was teaching at Portsmouth High School.

Now he was at Audrey's kitchen door feeling embarrassed about being late. Time never seemed to cooperate for Brad. He had a clock in every room, yet he was rarely on time. "I'm like the white rabbit in Alice in Wonderland," he'd explained. "I'm late, I'm late, for a very important date. That's my theme song," he'd laugh.

It wasn't that Brad disregarded the importance of being on time; he just never managed to internalize the passage of time. Somehow his thoughts always drifted away into some imaginary place where adventure lay around every corner. "You're not only the white rabbit. You're a Peter Pan," his friends would say.

Hurrying to Audrey's with Angel in one arm and a briefcase full of corrected exams in the other, he rang the doorbell with his elbow. Audrey began laughing when she opened the door.

"Let me help you." She pushed the storm door open wider and reached for Angel. "Come to Audrey." Angel looked up, giving her chin a quick lick, then snuggled into her open arms.

I missed you Audrey. When is lunch?

"I'm sorry. I know I'm late."

"Don't you worry about us. You go on to school. Angel and I'll be just fine, won't we, little one? I'll give her a treat to distract her when you close the door."

Could I have two treats instead of just one?

"I always feel like I'm in the Indianapolis 500, racing my students to the finish line, at the 7:30 bell. Thank you, Audrey. I can't thank you enough."

"Yes you can, and yes you have. Now hurry."

Audrey stood on her porch holding Angel as Brad drove away.

At the end of the school day, Brad pulled into Audrey's driveway and hurried to the back door. Angel, hearing his car, hopped into the chair by the window, barking her welcome.

Hey, Brad! I've been waiting for you. I met a new dog in the neighborhood through the fence in the back yard.

"I'm sorry, Audrey, I know I'm late. I told you I'd be here by four. I'm sorry!"

"If you're late I hadn't noticed. We've been having a great time. It never entered my mind to look at the clock. Just now, we were sitting in the living room having a private conversation, just us girls. Those two big brown eyes of hers! The way she just stares! She talks to me with her eyes. Dogs have so much to tell us!"

I am talking all the time. You just have to listen. I even know some four-letter words, but I never use them.

"Angel does talk to me! In fact, she wanted me to buy a gift for you." Reaching in his pocket, Brad withdrew a small package wrapped in tissue paper and held it in the palm of his hand for

Audrey to unwrap.

"They're crystals."

"Yes, there are two, one for your home and one for ours. There were several hanging in the windows at Pine Tree Farm where she was born. Angel likes rainbows.

Rainbows make me happy. All those bright colors make me feel warm inside.

"That's wonderful," Audrey said. "I'll hang mine in my living room window. It will catch the morning sun."

"I was planning to hang ours in the same place, for just the same reason."

Audrey took Angel's leash from the hook by the kitchen door and attached it to her halter. "Remember to say your prayers, Angel."

"Goodbye, Audrey. Thank you for everything," Brad leaned over to hug Angel's favorite friend.

"Thank you both for the thoughtful gift." Audrey waved goodbye from the open kitchen door.

See you tomorrow Audrey. Thanks for everything.

Angel pranced away across the lawn with Brad.

Chapter 4

❧

Angel Of Mercy

*T*hree years had passed since Brad had taken the drive to Pine Tree Farm. Brad and Angel had settled into the normal routine that every family with a dog understands. "Come here Angel. Let's go over your daily schedule." Angel looked attentively as Brad stretched out on the carpet bracing his head with his hand. "Jump right in with your feelings." Brad began; "Let's see…

"There's feeding twice a day."

That's enjoyable.

"Occasional trips to the vet."

Not enjoyable.

"A bath twice a month."

Tolerable.

"Daily back scratching."

Ecstasy.

Angel rolled over, paws extended.

Remember my tummy rubs.

A warm breeze drifted across the pond outside the window of Brad's saltbox style home by the sea. Bright beams of sunlight reflected off the water illuminating the ceiling with specks of white dots.

The crystal prism hanging in the open window, swayed back and forth sending streams of rainbow-colored light bouncing across the room like a large iridescent fan. A bundle of white fur sprawled in the middle of her puffy bed captured the rainbow and became a vision in Technicolor.

"Angel, do you want to go for a walk?"

Instead of responding to his voice, Angel slowly turned her head toward the window. Brad knew she had heard him, yet she seemed preoccupied with the prism that was swinging slowly back and forth like the pendulum of a clock.

Angel walked toward the rainbow that appeared on the carpet and looked at Brad. He sensed Angel's voice as he had so many times over the past three years.

I have something to tell you. You have to understand what I'm saying.

"What are you telling me, Angel? What is it?" Brad's thoughts flew back to the day he first saw Angel, the day she came into his life, the first time he felt her mystical energy. Now, here in his living room, he was struck by the profound sense that Angel was communicating. Taking a few steps toward her, she finally broke eye contact and began staring at the crystal that was identical to the one that hung in Audrey Bierhan's window.

"What are you telling me, Angel?"

Angel stared at Audrey's house. A feeling deep inside Brad was transforming into thoughts that were now words waiting to be spoken.

"What is it? Has something happened, where?

Next door. Audrey needs us.

Brad followed Angel's gaze across the yard to Audrey's house. He pulled back the curtains and looked over into her sun-filled cottage garden. A tangle of wild roses straddled the white picket fence between their two properties. A newspaper lay unclaimed on the front step.

"Audrey's an early riser. I've never seen her leave her paper outside after seven." Brad turned from the window and saw Angel by the front door with her nose pressed up against the scant space between the door and the door frame.

Something's happened to Audrey.

"Let's pay Audrey a visit, Angel."

As he opened the door, she dashed out across the lawn, her long white tail flying behind her like a thoroughbred racehorse. Reaching the gate that separated their property, she jumped up, pawing the wood as if trying to reach the latch.

"Hold on! I'm right behind you!"

Angel ran to the front door with Brad close behind. After ringing the doorbell and knocking several times, Brad tried the doorknob. The door was locked.

Angel, sitting anxiously at his side, barked sharply, as Brad looked down at her.

Come on, hurry! I know the back door's unlocked.

"Okay, let's try it," Brad said. Racing around the side of the house, Angel ran up the steps of the back porch and placed her paws on the door frame and scratched frantically. Brad, breathing heavily, turned the doorknob; it was unlocked.

He had barely pushed the door aside when Angel dashed past him, across the blue tile floor of the kitchen and into the living room. A rainbow from Audrey's crystal, laid a path of blue and purple light across the floor where she lay unconscious.

Brad knelt down beside Audrey as Angel circled around her,

whimpering and licking Audrey's hand and cheek.

Is she going to be all right?

"I hope so, Angel. I sure hope so."

Shortly after dialing 911, the paramedics arrived and began to administer CPR. Angel lay across Audrey's chest. As the paramedics gently placed Audrey onto the stretcher, Angel walked over to Brad and waited anxiously.

Let's go! Audrey needs us!

Brad shouted to the ambulance driver, "I'll meet you at the hospital!"

It wasn't long after their arrival before a doctor came looking for Brad in the waiting room.

"Are you Mr. Kennedy?"

"Yes. When can I see Audrey?"

"Her rabbi is with her now. You can see her in a few minutes. Mrs. Bierhans has had another stroke. Your timing made all the difference. Another ten minutes and we couldn't have saved her. Um – excuse me, what's that dog doing in here?"

"She's the one who 'made the difference,' doctor. She knew Audrey was in trouble and she led the way."

"Well, under those circumstances, I guess we can make an exception. And what is this little angel of mercy's name?"

"Her name is Angel, doctor. She's my Angel."

Thank you, Brad. It's my job.

Although fall, winter, and spring, brought new adventures for Brad and Angel, each summer a trip to Europe was planned without Angel. Leaving her was becoming more difficult, and since airline pet travel to Europe was becoming more accessible, Brad made tentative plans to take Angel with him the next time he traveled abroad.

Brad was encouraged when his books increased in sales at all major bookstores, and there was additional income from renting his home for the summer while he traveled to Europe. Clearly

early retirement was looking like an attractive option. "I could turn my avocation into a full-time career that much sooner," Brad told a friend.

It was Friday in the seaside town of Portsmouth and Brad's workday at school was over. As he biked home along South Street, he met one of his favorite people crossing Marcy Street near Sanders Olde Fish Market.

"Hi, Peggy. Enjoy the Press Room jazz Tuesday night?"

"It was exceptional, you should have been there. They had Gypsy-Jazz-Night and the musicians were incredible."

"Call me next Tuesday to remind me." Brad jumped from his bike and walked along with Peggy.

"Peggy, I need your advice."

"Whoa… just a minute! Every time I give advice to my friends I find out that they do just the opposite. I suppose there's some kind of message there, but I'm not sure what?" They both laughed.

"So, how can I help you?" Peggy leaned against the fence that separated their homes.

"I'm thinking about early retirement, devoting full time to writing. I could travel as much as I want and write my travel books. According to my travel agent friend, the off-season traveler can get some great bargains on cruise lines, airlines and hotels. She said that people are traveling more during the off-season. I think there should be an off-season travel book and I'm just the guy who can write it.

"That's terrific, Brad. You could take Angel with you."

"Yea, I like that idea. You know, Peggy, I'm going to be the friend who takes your advice. I'm going to write full time. This is going to be my last year of teaching." Brad put his arms around Peggy.

"Now, will you help me pack?"

"Wait a minute. I give advice, not maid service."

Chapter 5

The Literary Worm

*A*fter twenty-five years of teaching, Brad's days in the classroom were coming to a close. The calendar reminded him that there were only a few days left until his teaching career would end.

One Sunday afternoon while passing the Athenaeum on Congress Street, Brad saw a friend and his dog seated at Popovers, a coffee shop in downtown Portsmouth. "David, I see Joey's wearing his Boston Red Sox sweater I got for him." Brad stroked David's companion with affection while Angel snuggled next to Joey. Brad knew David had recently retired from teaching and he wanted to get his feelings about the big change in his life. "How do you like being unemployed?" Brad sat down with two cups of cappuccino.

"I thought I would enjoy sleeping in every day and kayaking, but you know, I miss the feeling of accomplishment. And I never thought I would say this: I miss the kids. Don't tell anyone I said that," David laughed.

Brad knew what David was feeling. He was also struggling with conflicting emotions. Although writing full time was what he wanted, he would be leaving the profession he loved.

"You know David, when I was young I wanted to write, but being an optimistic-realist, I knew there was a possibility I might never be able to earn a living with a journalism degree. I knew I had to be practical. Being a writer usually means part-time work – and that could mean part-time eating. You've heard of the term 'free lance writing?' That's an accurate name for the job, very little money. And the competition is unreal. Whether you're submitting to a newspaper, a magazine, or writing a book, steady work is always scarce. I needed a full-time job, a job where I could use my brain. A teaching credential was the best choice. Looking back, I have no regrets.

"When I retire, I'll have plenty of time to focus on my second passion, writing travel books. It's a big step for me. I'm a little scared. I remember my father saying, 'Son, don't let fear of the unknown stand in your way of moving on. Remember, life is pure gold and time a thief.'"

Angel and Brad waved goodbye as they strolled down Pleasant Street. Joey strained on his leash indicating his desire to follow Angel for some play activity. "So long David. Bring Joey over next week."

After emptying his desk, Brad filled the last of several cartons with files and accumulated memorabilia. His colleagues at Portsmouth High had given him a farewell luncheon earlier in the day, and now, the room seemed lonely. The parking lot outside his window was as empty as the classroom.

Looking around the room, Brad envisioned some of his students. He wondered if Shannon would take his advice and make the grades of which she was capable. Brad encouraged her to take school seriously even though her friends challenged her to simply "hang out" and not worry about grades.

He remembered Greg, whose parents refused to treat him like a young adult, planning his future career, regardless of his interests or his ability.

After making his decision to take early retirement, he began to look forward to the last day of school with as much anticipation as his students – yet the finality of his decision, as he locked the door for the last time, made him realize that he could never use his classroom key again.

Closing the trunk, he climbed into his car and drove the two and a half miles to his home. After pulling into the driveway, he hesitated. "I'll leave everything in the car until tomorrow. I can decide what to keep and what to discard later," he thought.

He stood by the gate looking at the barn-like structure across the road. With its narrow gable and faded paint, it resembled an 18th century schoolhouse. It would become a reminder of his teaching days during his retirement years.

Brad cut across the yard to see Audrey, who had rallied from her ordeal, and was again providing doggy daycare for Angel. Audrey stood by the open kitchen door watching Brad walking toward her. "Just because you're retiring, I hope this doesn't mean I have to retire as Angel's nanny." As always, Angel raced to the door to see if Brad had arrived to take her home. When she saw him standing in the doorway, she ran past him toward the gate in anticipation of her dinner. "Wait Angel," he shouted. "Come back here! Stay. I'll be just a minute!" Angel returned reluctantly and sat by the open door of Audrey's kitchen as Brad explained to Audrey how he would be spending his time in retirement.

"I intend to be just as busy writing as I have been teaching. I don't want Angel feeling that I'm neglecting her when I'm stuck at my computer most of the day. I would like to continue the present arrangement if that's all right with you. The hours may shift a little – I want to sleep in for awhile."

"Well, just don't forget, young man, the early bird catches the *literary worm*, you know."

Chapter 6

The Party Is Here

*I*t was two weeks since Brad packed away his classroom materials, and with no school bells to monitor his daily schedule, Brad relied on self-motivation to tell him what time to begin his writing day. After spending five straight days working at his computer, Brad thought today looked more like a biking day than a working day.

After a quick breakfast he changed into his biking gear. Angel ran toward him dragging his helmet from the mudroom.

You'll need this. Remember the spill you took the last time we were on wheels?

"Thank you, Angel. You look after me as much as I look after you."

It's my job remember?

A few minutes later, Angel hopped into her bike trailer, and they set off for a six-mile loop around Newcastle Island.

Stopping at the beach and later the Icehouse for ice cream, Brad and Angel noticed that a picture of Angel had been placed over the back of the counter with all the other regular Icehouse customers. "Hi, Mr. Kennedy. Hi, Angel," said the girl behind the counter. "One small butter pecan coming right up, and a broken cone for Angel, right?"

Thanks, Amy. The cone's all I want. Ice cream's not good for dogs.

"Thanks, Amy. So, have you decided what you're majoring in yet?" Amy had been one of his favorite students in his American history class.

"Yep. Can you guess what?" Amy winked.

"American history?"

"You bet!" She put the finishing touches on his cone and handed it through the window. "I want to be a teacher, just like you."

Brad couldn't have asked for a better retirement gift.

As the sun hung low over the ocean, Brad turned the final corner onto South Mill Street when he spotted a green and orange sign attached to his fence announcing, THE PARTY IS HERE!!

"What's this?"

Two cars pulled up and parked alongside the rusting chain-link fence overlooking the South Mill Race. Car doors slammed, first one, then another, as conversations intermingled and shouts of recognition were exchanged between friends.

"Hi, John! Hi, Joni!" Brad heard Peggy's familiar voice calling to them. "I'm really glad you could make it. You must have found a sitter for your baby," Peggy laughed. This was a standing joke between friends. John and Joni's "baby" was a hundred pound black poodle.

Larry, Adrienne and Marian piled out of the second car. Elida and Burt lived three doors down and were arriving on foot.

Brad unloaded Angel from her bike trailer, turned around and stood gaping as she ran to welcome the group that was strolling up the walk, arms loaded with potato chips, wine, beer, soft drinks and the makings for a barbecue.

"Surprise!" they shouted.

Brad shook his head. "You guys! You better believe I'm surprised. How did you do this without me knowing?"

"It was Marian – a born party planner," Ryan said, throwing his arm around Marian's waist.

"Any excuse for a little merrymaking! Quick – open the gate. We've got some serious grilling to do!" Marian unwound Ryan's arm and pushed him forward.

All of the guests headed for the patio in the middle of what was commonly referred to as a "pocket garden" in the South End of Portsmouth.

"Well, honey, look who's come to see us!" Shirley said to her husband, Jay. Brad had to laugh at the sight of two of his favorite people casually sprawled on his lounge chairs as if they owned the place. Obviously they had come over early; the barbecue coals were already glowing.

"I'll have the city send you the property tax bill next month since you obviously have squatter's rights," Brad joked.

"Have a seat, Brad," Jay laughed. "It's all yours, my man." Jay ushered him to one of the lounge chairs.

"We knew they'd be having a party for you at work," Adrienne commented, "but we couldn't let you retire without a civil ceremony as well. I'm throwing in a couple of birthdays too, since I never remember to send you a card."

Marian pulled out a gift from her tote bag. "Open this first. You'll need it." Inside the box was an apron that proclaimed "Retired & Busier Than Ever" and a chef's hat. Brad put both on and headed for the grill where hamburgers and hot dogs were already sizzling.

"Outta the way. Chef comin' through!" Brad took his place at the grill, pushing, prodding and flipping the patties. A few minutes later, Marian and Ryan approached him from behind.

"We took a vote, honey. You're being transferred to salad." Marian took the spatula from Brad's hand and handed it to Norbert.

"Salad? This sounds like a demotion, which of course reminds me of my Army days. Do I get to keep my stripes at least?" Brad took the package of organic mixed greens Marian bought at the Farmer's Market and emptied the contents into a large salad bowl on the picnic table.

Angel stationed herself where the smells of food were the strongest, right next to the grill.

I'd like to place my order now. Just brown the meat on both sides for two minutes.

"Brad, how does Angel want her hamburger?" Ryan shouted across the crowd as he looked down at Angel's big brown eyes staring back at him.

I like this guy. Rare please. And hold the onions, tomato and mayonnaise, and the bun too. Just a burger will do fine!

The aroma of food, the sounds of laughter and music all mingled and drifted through the patio.

During a break between songs, Pam began the singing of, "For he's a jolly good fellow, for he's a jolly good fellow." Most were off-key, "which nobody can deny!"

"Okay, that's enough." Brad reached for his cycling helmet and tossed it toward the group singing the loudest. Ryan caught it in midair.

"Speech, speech," Ryan and Marian shouted in unison. Someone lowered the music as ongoing conversations dissolved into whispers.

Brad reached down and picked up Angel, who had come trotting over to see what all the shouting was about. Standing next to the small fountain, surrounded by his friends and holding Angel in his arms, he began, "As you are aware, I'm now officially retired and you know what that means."

"Yeah, it means you got your last pay check and you'll be eating TV dinners from now on!" Ryan interrupted. Laughter erupted around the patio.

"Beans!" Pam shouted as she looked at Marian. "Didn't you tell me you had plenty of great recipes for beans, Marian?"

"I'll never get through this speech if you keep interrupting. Do you want the short speech or the long one?" A groan came from the audience.

"As most of you know, I've decided to write full time. My publisher's been happy with the books I've turned out while working during the summers, so I submitted a proposal for a new project that they're very excited about. It will be about my experiences while traveling through France."

"Hasn't he already written a couple of books on France and Italy?" Burt whispered.

"Well, that's what he does best," Sally answered.

"But France with a twist," Brad continued, lifting Angel up so everyone could see her.

"This time I'm taking Angel."

What, me? In France? I get to go to France? New sights, new sounds

– and plenty of new smells!

Angel began to lick Brad's chin.

"I think she likes the idea," Brad laughed.

The garden lights went on automatically. Like fireflies, a soft glow illuminated the patio and the house on South Mill Street. Brad's friends began to say their goodbyes with hugs and hand shakes.

Marian picked up Angel and kissed her on both ears. "I'm giving you a kiss on each cheek. You'll be getting a lot of these in France. You're going to have to learn French also, you know."

Ah, so you think I don't know French, do you? Brad parle français to me all the time. Merci beaucoup, ma chérie.

Placing the little Maltese on the grass by the gate, Marian looked down at her and grinned. "I remember the first time I held you on my lap. You were just a puppy and you peed on me, you naughty dog! And I didn't even like dogs. Is that why you peed on me, Angel?" Marian laughed. "You take good care of Brad for me. God knows he needs someone to look after him."

You don't have to worry about that. I'm his best friend. I always look after him. That's my job.

As the last guests drove away, Brad watched them make the narrow turn on Mechanic Street, their tail lights disappearing into the darkness. Standing by the open gate, holding Angel, he noticed a pair of sea gulls flying over the house.

"Look Angel." Brad lifted Angel's chin toward the sky. "When you see two sea gulls flying together, it means good luck on your next journey. That's an old New England saying."

I knew that; I was born in Eliot, Maine.

While they stood in the warm night air, and watched the gulls trailing across the sky, Brad recalled a poem he had once given to someone very special. "We are all angels with one wing. We need each other to fly." Brad whispered in Angel's ear.

Hmm. I like that.

"It was for Adeline. You remember Adeline?" The question was purely rhetorical because Brad had a habit of confiding in Angel.

Angel looked up at him.

Yes, Brad. I remember you telling me about Adeline. I wonder where she is right now?

"She was my first love. It seems like a lifetime ago."

Chapter 7

Dog On Board

With signs of the impending journey all over the house,
Angel became both anxious and hopeful.

*Brad always leaves me at home when he goes on a trip to collect
information for his travel books and magazine articles. I'm glad he's
taking me, but I like staying with Audrey, too. The first time she took
care of me, she hid treats around the house for me to find. It only took me
a week to teach her that trick.*

*Brad told Audrey not to leave me in the garden alone. He was afraid
I might be kidnapped. Somebody named Elizabeth Browning – Brad
always refers to her as "the famous poet" – had a little companion named
Flush who was kidnapped. She paid the ransom and got him back.
Elizabeth Browning traveled and wrote about France. Brad said he
might take me to France! He says I'm really going to love it because the
French give their canine companions the royal treatment.*

*Yesterday, when I came into the house, I found Brad's luggage lying
on the floor of the living room. I sniffed the unzipped black vinyl bags.
Brad has never taken me on a business trip, but when we travel for fun,
I have everything I need in my collapsible kennel. It's pretty basic: black
vinyl pouch on the side that holds several packets of food – that's all I
need, except for water.*

*Brad's got a great sense of humor. He actually asked me if I wanted
to go or stay home with Audrey. Who's he kidding? I saw him filling out
the forms from the French Consulate.*

*He even made a passport for me from one of his old ones by pasting
my picture over his and placing my paw print where a signature would
go. That should get a laugh from the customs people.*

*There will be many new sights – and smells! It's a big decision,
leaving all this comfort and security, but I'd rather go than stay. The last*

time Brad went to Europe, Audrey stayed here with me, and although I know she loves me, my heart will always be with Brad. Sometimes when he goes off for a few hours and I'm home alone, I won't drink any water until he comes back. I don't know why I do that - some primitive instinct canines have I guess.

❈

The next morning, Brad and Angel arrived at Boston's Logan Airport long before their flight was scheduled to depart, only to find that it was delayed due to poor weather. While Angel relaxed next to Brad in the boarding area, she noticed several people pacing back and forth. Some shouted into cell phones, others tried to contain their children. One couple was seated, leaning against one another, asleep.

The worst part of a long-distance flight is the security checks and flight delays. They can make everyone anxious and sometimes angry. But if you think that's tough, put yourself in my place! Here I am, traveling in a black bag with a mesh screen for air circulation with only a limited view – of feet! Can't use the toilet, so I have to go into my "hold-mode" until we get to our destination. Think about it! I'm not complaining, just asking for a little sympathy.

An announcement came over the loudspeaker. The flight would be taking off in five minutes. Grabbing his laptop in one hand and Angel and her travel case in the other, Brad quickly headed for Gate 12. Thinking he had more time, Brad had wandered to the far end of the terminal. Now he raced, dodged and maneuvered his way back through the airport like a veteran quarterback.

The flight attendant at the gate grabbed Brad's ticket as he hurried down the ramp. With the roar of the jet engines; they were lifted into the sky, banking over Boston before heading out across the Atlantic Ocean.

Angel laid quietly in her carrying case under the seat in front of Brad. A seven-hour flight can get pretty boring for people; for Angel, after an hour of looking at shoes, sleep was the only answer, that is until she smelled food. This caused her to squirm around in her travel bag making soft whimpering sounds.

"You won't like this food," Brad whispered. After he'd given her a bite, she agreed.

I'll stick to my dog food. Hmm...I wonder if we're flying first class or coach. It doesn't make any difference when you're a dog flying in a travel bag. The space under the seat is the same. Since there isn't anything to do, I guess I'll sleep some more.

After flying for several hours, Brad quietly slid Angel's travel case out from under the seat, opened the bag and placed her on the empty seat next to him. The touch of his hand was reassuring for Angel after her long wait in darkness. When the steward came down the aisle, Brad put his 49ers sweatshirt over Angel until he had passed.

I know why Brad hides me. It's because I'm not human. If I could only speak! I could hire an attorney and sue for some civil rights for dogs. But for now, I'm keeping quiet.

Angel stretched out, luxuriating in her newfound freedom with Brad's comforting hand. An hour before landing, however, she whimpered. She was hungry. In a matter of seconds, the steward was at Brad's side. "You'll have to put your dog back in the case, no argument."

All I wanted was a snack and some of that great-recycled air everyone else gets to enjoy.

Brad gently guided her back into her travel bag and slid it under the seat in front of him. Angel resigned herself to the requirements of modern air travel, and went back to sleep. A few minutes later a stewardess who stood a head taller than the steward, destroyed the droning calm.

"Sir, the airline *was* not notified that there would be a dog on board."

"The airline *was* notified that there would be a dog on board," Brad countered with as much self-possession as he could muster.

"I have no record of your dog. We could be fined heavily for bringing a dog into France without prior notification. Did you tell the agent? We were not notified."

Brad's answers were calm and poised. "As I told you, I did

notify the airlines. I have all the necessary papers. They were issued by the French consulate in Boston." Unzipping the pocket of his laptop carrying case, Brad produced the official papers.

I had my rabies shot. Tell her that.

Angel had a rug's eye view of the big lady as she did her tiny pirouette, snatched the official-looking documents and disappeared down the aisle.

In a few minutes she was back looming over them once again, announcing loud enough for the entire flight to hear, "The captain will speak with you when we land." Angel became apprehensive.

Brad, this is scary. Are we going to prison? I'm getting this mental image of you sitting in a French prison, and me, I'm locked up in a kennel, lying on a dirty towel with no night-light. I've never stayed in a French kennel. I've never stayed in an American kennel. If I have to go, I'll go obediently. But I insist on a private room. Also, breakfast should be served at seven and dinner no later than, let's say, two thirty, with two snacks in between. I prefer my music classical or jazz, and I am allergic to dust, wheat products and Dalmatians. I'll need an air purifier, and oh yes, did I mention a night-light?

Angel didn't have long to contemplate her fate. The flight steward announced that all passengers should fasten their seat belts. The plane was preparing to land.

Where's my seat belt?

As Brad and Angel disembarked from the plane, two security police in blue uniforms met them. One said in heavily accented English, "Follow me, monsieur."

Directly behind the security police was the pilot of the 747 in a wrinkled grey uniform. "I'm sorry, sir, but the French take this very seriously. You cannot take a pet on a transatlantic flight in the cabin."

Oops, that means I should have been in the cargo section.

Lifting Angel from her black case, Brad held her close to him.

The two French airline security officers gestured for Brad and the captain to follow them. Brad whispered into Angel's ear, "Don't worry, Angel. We won't be separated."

The entourage descended a long flight of stairs, and entered a room with a low counter, behind which two men sat, each with decorative brass glittering on their shoulders and chests. The two officers who had escorted them leaned over the counter and spoke in rapid French, each one seemingly overlapping and repeating what the other said. One of the men behind the counter asked to see Brad's papers.

There was a lot of conversation and a lot of animated gesturing. Suddenly, the commotion stopped, and the papers were stamped several times with a seal of approval.

"Everything is in order monsieur." Angel felt the officer's hand on her head as he inquired, "So, what kind of dog is this?"

"She is an American white-haired hunting dog. She catches white rabbits on the sandy beaches of Naples, Florida." Exasperated from the annoying incident, Brad was being flippant. Angel nuzzled next to the inspector's hand.

He's just kidding. Come on, Brad. Let's get out of here before they change their minds and lock us away.

"Welcome to Roissy Charles de Gaulle International Airport," Brad whispered into Angel's ear.

Chapter 8

Lunch For Two

*O*nce outside the terminal, Brad hailed a taxi to take them to the office of the Renault Car Leasing Center.

Brad signed all the papers for his rental car and they were on their way.

Even though Brad knew the peculiarities of Paris traffic, he had forgotten the complex patterns of the streets. Following the directions the auto dealer suggested and consulting a map of Paris, after fifteen minutes of driving, Brad knew he wasn't making any progress toward his destination. The streets looked like pieces of a puzzle. Each time Angel looked out the window, she saw the same buildings.

Brad, we must be going the wrong way. We've been around this block three times.

He knew, except for the grand boulevards, most of the streets of Paris were never planned. They were the remnants of paths from ancient peasant-village life during the 12th century.

He remembered an old French riddle, repeated often by Parisians. "What is the similarity between a shattered mirror and a map of Paris?" The answer, "each consists of hundreds of fragments with no order or design." Brad always enjoyed a challenge, for he knew from experience that driving in New York is all one-way. London is daunting, driving on the left side. Boston is a parking lot with the "Big Dig." But then none is as challenging as Paris.

After a while he realized he was in the center of Paris, entangled in a web of traffic as far as he could see. Tail lights pulsated on and off as vehicles inched forward. At one point, with traffic at a complete standstill, Brad glanced at the hotel brochure, rechecking the address of the Hotel du Danube.

After several wrong turns, Brad, by chance more than design, drove up to the Hotel du Danube.

Paris is an expensive city. But this hotel was a bargain, according to the guidebook. The Hotel du Danube had been in the same family for three generations. Monsieur Corroyer ran it quietly and considerately while his mother held court "with charm and generosity." Their service was said to equal the best of Paris hotels.

At the entrance stood a grey-haired distinguished looking man in a black suit with shoes so shiny that Angel caught a glimpse of her own reflection in them. "Monsieur, I will take your luggage."

As they made their way to the entrance, Angel stopped in front of the revolving glass doors.

Whoa! This looks like a giant slicing machine. I'm not going to be the first American dog to be cut in half.

Refusing to go forward, Angel pulled on her leash "Come on Angel. Okay, I'll carry you."

Brad placed Angel on the cool marble counter. While he waited for hotel assistance, he looked around the lobby. Out the window he noticed the traditional neighborhood grocery store across the street with boxes of colorful fruit and vegetables displayed on the sidewalk. The scene reminded Brad of a Renoir painting he saw in the Portland, Maine, Art Gallery.

Directly across the narrow street was a 19th century apartment building with windows that faced the hotel. Art students attending the Parsons Paris School of Design, only a few blocks away, regularly sketched its elaborate Art Nouveau facades. It was a reminder of the golden age when conspicuous consumption was an expected characteristic of the rich. Only the wealthy carried large stomachs and full wallets. This was an era when the classes were distinctly divided and everyone knew their place.

The celebrated French architect, Castel Beranger, interviewed by Vogue magazine in 1898 described the facades as follows: "Columns on either side of the entrance resemble tree trunks with branches twisting and turning toward the second and third floors.

Two balustrades support twelve cantilevered balconies with floral wrought iron railings, each one connected by highly polished bronze figures of forest nymphs."

The Hotel du Danube was far less grand than the elegant apartment building across the street. Nevertheless it attracted a most discreet clientele of distinguished world travelers who expected service, privacy and fine cuisine.

Walking from the registration desk through the lobby, Brad was surprised to see a late 19th century gilded cage elevator in pristine condition. He pushed the ornate lattice gate to one side and encouraged Angel to follow him. But she hesitated, examining the antiquated means of transportation.

This looks rather tenuous for vertical travel. Could we use the stairs?

As he opened the door to their room, Angel dashed in and began sniffing every object.

No dogs or cats stayed in this room. There's no odor, except cleaning solution.

Brad opened the side pocket of his carrying case and pulled out a travel-size can of dog food. Emptying the contents into a small dish, Angel sat poised, eagerly waiting for her first meal since her flight from Boston.

This is my evening meal of chicken and vegetables.

Hesitating, Brad reached for the phone and spoke to the desk clerk.

What? What are you waiting for? I always have the same thing, three times a day. I'm not complaining – I'm used to it. It's predictable and it feels good in my stomach. When I grab something off the street or someone gives me a piece of weird food off of their plate, I usually throw up an hour later.

"Hello, may I have the hotel restaurant? I'd like to make reservations for lunch. I have a companion of the canine variety. Do you allow dogs in your restaurant?"

"Mais oui! Of course!" came the enthusiastic response. "Nous avons un menu spécial pour la chienne."

"Angel, we will be eating together in the dining room, and they have a 'companion menu' for you."

Chapter 9

Bon Appetite

T he hostess greeted Brad and Angel as they approached the dining room.

"Good evening monsieur. Have you a reservation?"

"Yes, I made a reservations for two under the name Kennedy."

"Mais oui, I see. Would you introduce me to your lovely companion?" She leaned over and patted Angel.

"Of course, I would be delighted." Brad noticed a name embroidered on her blouse.

"Mademoiselle Ramage, may I introduce Angélique. Angélique, this is Mademoiselle Ramage." Angel's feathery plume-like tail waved a friendly greeting.

"Enchanté, Angélique! We are so delighted to have you and your friend dine with us aujourd'hui. We hope you will find everything to your complete satisfaction."

The dining room was remodeled in the 1930's art deco motif. Two dining levels gave the impression of spaciousness with a grand staircase that led to an elevated dance floor of turquoise and silver. The upper level was bordered by a highly polished chrome railing while twelve alabaster columns punctuated the perimeter of the room. The effect was one of casual elegance. A major French Designer magazine had recently called the creation one of the best in Paris. Everyone recognized the signature style of Lauren Nurisso.

Taking his seat, Brad placed Angel on the chair next to him. Shortly, a waiter arrived with two menus and placed one in front of Brad and the second before Angel.

This is the first time I've eaten inside a restaurant. I could get used to this!

*I can't read this menu, but what ever you order, I promise to eat –
as long as it has meat in it.*

"Okay, Angel. You have your choice of calves' liver, boiled
chicken, venison or buffalo stew. They all sound delicious, but
your stomach is used to chicken; I don't think you should have
anything different until we've been here for a while.

After a brief conversation with an attractive couple seated at
the next table concerning their Bichon Frise, the waiter placed the
two entrées on the table. "Bon appetit, monsieur et mademoiselle
poochie."

Angel finished her meal quickly, then looked longingly at
Brad's half-eaten entrée, a confit de canard.

"You eat too fast, Angel. Don't expect me to give you some of
my duck."

But I'm still hungry.

"Sorry, my friend. You won't make me feel guilty with those
big, sad eyes this time."

As he glanced around the room, Brad noticed two other dogs
dining with their companions, a very elegant Pekinese and a
studious cocker spaniel. A third, a German shepherd, too large for
a chair, sat on the carpet eating from a large plate filled with steak.

Sharing mealtime here with Angel seemed the most natural
thing in the world. Brad could enjoy her company as he had done
so often in their home.

"Health standards in French restaurants are as stringent as
restaurants in the United States, and the French welcome dogs.
Why shouldn't our companions be permitted to dine with us in
the United States?" Brad thought. As he pondered this question,
he noticed Angel looking at the German shepherd.

*That German dog over there has a lot more meat on his plate than
I did.*

A slight whining murmur began to grow and resonated from
Angel. Brad, squinting his eyes, shook his head, "No…!"

Angel had made a faux pas. With a guilty expression, she
lowered her head, and glanced over at Brad.

"That's much better." Brad praised.

I'm sorry; I'll do better next time.

After a brief stroll around of the hotel's garden, Brad and Angel returned to enjoy their private space in the hotel room.

Decorated in olive-browns and blues with an oval mirror over the fireplace, their room reminded Brad of the living room of Gwyneth Wykes, the famous British actress now living in the small village of York, Maine. Her traditional, "afternoon teas," attended by many of the literary personalities of both New Hampshire and Maine were becoming a coveted social event throughout New England.

Brad looked in the oval mirror and saw the reflection of the ornate apartment building across the street. It captured the ambiance of Paris like a 19th century photograph.

He pulled a pillow from the bed, placed it on the floor by the opened window, and called Angel.

"You can make yourself comfortable on this while I'm gone. I must take care of my writing responsibilities. Here's your blue ball, Angélique – vôtre boule bleu."

Great! I get to have the place to myself! I enjoy my own company. I know some dogs don't, but I do. Brad thinks I need to be kept occupied with a toy, so he got a blue rubber ball a year ago. It's got this round hole. Brad puts a few food pellets inside. I entertain myself by pushing the ball until the food pellets come out. Pretty cool! I think Brad gives it to me so he won't feel guilty when I'm left alone. But he misses me as much as I miss him. Maybe I should get him a toy.

As the door closed behind Brad, Angel nosed the ball across the carpet and under the chair by the window. After all the pellets were eaten, Angel grew weary of the unrewarding empty plaything.

Looking at the pillow Brad had put on the floor, Angel wandered over and gave it a sniff. After an experimental wiggle, she curled her body into its soft surface and went to sleep.

A gentle breeze drifting through the window ruffled Angel's soft white fur as the sound of sparrows chirping outside lent a peaceful serenity to the room.

Suddenly the tranquility was shattered.

Chapter 10

Imminent Danger

S tartled, Angel heard loud voices. Shouting and screaming were sounds that were unfamiliar to her. Trying to interpret where the sounds were coming from, she stood on her hind legs and looked around the room.

The sound of breaking glass sent Angel bounding up onto the chair by the open window. She could see the apartment across the street. A man and a woman, both extremely angry, were quarreling in front of an open window on the fifth floor. The woman gestured excitedly, pointing toward the apartment door. Her angry words grew louder as they echoed through the window.

"I have given you too many chances. I know that you won't change!"

They need help.

Angel saw the woman push the man aside, yank open a drawer and throw her clothes into a suitcase. The man blocked the door as the woman shouted, "Va-t'en!" "Get out of my way!"

They're fighting worse than the two dogs in the park last Sunday.

As the shouting continued, the young woman pressed past the man, grabbed her luggage and went through the doorway into the hall, "Tu es un menteur! You're a liar!"

Soon quiet settled over the street once again as darkness dimmed the colors of the buildings outside.

Angel pulled away from the window ledge, curled up on the chair cushion, and placed her head on a small pillow.

Now maybe I can get some rest.

The street lamp outside the window flooded the narrow lane and buildings with a somber glow. The shop windows of the neighborhood market on the corner were now dark, only a small exit light illuminated the door. All the containers of produce had disappeared from the sidewalk, giving the once bustling corner a sense of loneliness. Only the slow stride of an overweight cat, circling and sniffing the cardboard box left by the curb, gave life to the streetscape.

Angel stood up in the chair to adjust her pillow, pushing it with her nose creating a depression in the center in which to lie. Satisfied, she glanced across the street where she had seen the young couple arguing. To her astonishment, the man she had seen earlier was now standing on the window ledge.

Angel, reacting instinctively to what she sensed as imminent danger, raised her ears, arched her back and planted her front paws on the windowsill.

You better get off that ledge before you fall.

A rumbling sound, growing deep within, came up through her throat and emerged as continuous, strident barking. Every muscle tensed for action, she focused intently on the man, balancing himself five stories above the street. Her loud barking continued to echo between the two buildings.

Go back in where you belong. People aren't supposed to be standing on ledges.

Distracted by her barking, the man on the ledge turned toward Angel. His incoherent state of mind tried to focus on the barking coming from across the street. Raising his wavering right hand to his lips, he gestured for her to be quiet. With her persistent, rhythmic barking, she held his attention, communicating her objection.

You shouldn't be out there! You might fall!

Angel's short sequence of barks, one after another, at the same constant volume, soon had the inebriated man mesmerized.

In his confusion, he failed to notice an elderly couple crossing the street below. Looking up to see what all the barking was about, the couple quickly turned toward the man on the ledge. Pointing, the woman shouted. "Young man, come down from there!"

Come down? That's not what you should say.

While the woman looked back and forth from Angel to the man on the ledge, her friend hurried toward the apartment building and knocked rapidly on the glass-paneled front door. The concierge, a woman of considerable age, pushed the curtain aside and peered through the glass, "What do you want?"

"Madame, there's a man on your ledge. Come see!" The man shouted.

The concierge, glancing over her eyeglasses that were balanced precariously on the bridge of her nose, stared intently at the anxious man outside her door. Slowly releasing the curtain she opened the door a few inches, as she repeated, "What do you want?"

"There is a young man standing on the ledge up there. Come out and see for yourself!"

"This had better not be a joke."

The concierge followed the man into the street. With her hand on the back of her neck she looked up toward the fifth floor and shouted, "Henri! Henri!" Raising her arm, she pointed toward Henri and turned toward the couple. "If this happens one more time, he will get his notice. Thank you, monsieur and madame, I will take care of this."

Henri looked down as the concierge walked quickly into the building. A few minutes later she could be seen at the window, persuading the distraught man to return to his room. All the while, Angel continued her persistent barking. Not until she saw the man return to his apartment did she stop.

Once again the street grew quiet. The light from the street lamp cast a golden glow across the hotel carpet and onto the chair in which Angel sat. Relieved that the crisis was now over, Angel yawned, closed her eyes and fell asleep.

The cars that were parked on the narrow street below had all disappeared. A light mist of rain illuminated by the street lamps, covered the sidewalk, reflecting the hotel sign like a watercolor painting.

With a newspaper suspended over his head, Brad walked hurriedly toward the hotel entrance. Satisfied with his interviews, he entered the hotel, and stopped at the front desk to check for messages. Seeing no one, he tapped the bell on the counter. The hotel clerk, speaking with another guest, excused himself, crossed the lobby, and stepped behind the counter.

"Oui, monsieur?"

"Do I have any messages?"

"Yes, monsieur, you have two messages. Here they are. Bonne nuit, monsieur."

"Merci bien, monsieur, et bonsoir à vous aussi."

Brad was expecting the first message. It read: "Send the first draft of your manuscript. I will edit and e-mail it to you in one week." Signed, "Kathleen Sullivan."

The second message was puzzling. He read it a second time while riding the elevator to the fifth floor.

Angel awoke to the sound of Brad's key turning in the lock. Lifting her head, she jumped down from the chair and ran to him.

"Hello, my little sprite. I have a note I want to share with you."

We had some excitement while you were gone.

Placing Angel on his lap, he read the message aloud. "Please don't leave your dog unattended. She disturbed the hotel guests this evening."

Brad looked down at Angel. "Could the dog in question be you?"

What did you say? I'm very tired. It must be jet lag.

Angel yawned.

"Angel, you've never barked before in a hotel room. What is your excuse?"

I have a very good reason. Right now I'm tired. Would you turn out the lights, please?

"I can't imagine what there was to bark about." Brad unfolded a lap robe and arranged it in a circle at the foot of the bed for Angel. "We'll sort this out in the morning."

Thanks, Brad. Bonsoir.

Chapter 11

Attempted Suicide

*A*fter his morning shower, Brad looked out the open bathroom door to see Angel rubbing herself along the edge of the sofa, first one side of her body, then with a quick turn, the other.

"I know what you're doing, miss," Brad laughed. "Dogs groom themselves that way. A lot less complicated than what I go through each morning."

These are the things a girl has to do to make herself beautiful. After all, this is Paris!

Leaving their room and crossing the hall, Brad held the door of the elevator, allowing a young lady with several packages to enter.

"What kind of dog is that?"

"She's a Parisian Fluff," Brad joked.

I haven't heard that one before. You keep coming up with new ones.

Having heard numerous people ask the same question prompted Brad's remark. "What kind of dog is that?" Devising humorous replies was his way of turning an annoyance into a form of levity.

Pulling on her leash, Angel indicated her impatience to take a before-breakfast stroll.

A warm breeze welcomed the early risers as they crossed the Rue Picot. Coming upon the little grocery store next to the apartment house, Angel lingered in front of several crates of fruit displayed on the sidewalk. Resisting the tug on her leash, she stopped in front of a basket of apples and took several deep sniffs.

"What is it Angel? Do you like French apples?"

I smell something else besides apples. It smells like fresh baked-bread, like Mrs. Luna made.

The grocer came outside of his shop with a black apron tied around his waist. As he stood in the doorway, he surveyed the morning shoppers. He noticed Angel sniffing the basket of apples.

"Bonjour, monsieur. Your dog smells the fresh bread that came in the basket this morning. I used it to move the loaves to the shelf inside the store. I don't know any dogs that like apples."

"That's just what I was thinking."

Show me the bread.

I'll have two apples, please," Brad said.

The grocer took a paper sack, held it with one hand and snapped it forcefully against his leg, opening the bag. He selected two red Fuji apples and polished each one on his apron before placing them in the sack. "That will be €1.25, s'il vous plait, monsieur."

As Brad placed several coins in the grocer's hand, he noticed a man leaning over the display of peaches. The man appeared preoccupied, distant. First, he choose a peach from the display, inspected it carefully, and then placed it back in the box. The man stared at the coins in his hand for a moment, then looked over toward Angel. She had been observing the man closely and pulled on her leash as he walked in her direction. Hesitating, he bent down and stroked her. "Thank you my little friend for helping me."

You should get a companion to watch over you.

The grocer, watching the man walk away, nodded at Brad and then pointed at the man who was now standing in front of the apartment building across from Brad's hotel.

Leaning closely, the grocer whispered, "Monsieur, did you hear what happened last night? That man tried to kill himself. He was on that ledge, up there, on the fifth floor." The grocer pointed halfway up the apartment building.

"My wife and I live above this shop. We went to bed early; unfortunately a barking dog awakened us. I looked out of our window and saw a white dog in that window over there in the hotel. I could only see the little dog's head and she was barking at something across the street." The grocer pointed at the man entering the apartment. "I saw that man standing on the ledge." The grocer swung his arms about, illustrating his story.

"There was a couple in the street talking to the concierge. The concierge went to the man's apartment and brought him inside. That little dog looked like your dog, monsieur."

"Excuse me, how much is this spinach?" A woman interrupted.

"Pardonnez-moi, monsieur. Au revoir. Au revoir, little doggie," Handing Brad his apples, the grocer smiled broadly at Angel, gave her a wink, then turned to his next customer.

"Madame, pardonnez-moi. You would like some spinach?"

Brad looked down at Angel, grinned, waved goodbye to the grocer and walked across the street to the hotel entrance. After giving Angel one last opportunity to sniff and leave her message, Brad crouched down, cupped his hands around Angel's face and looked into her eyes. "You're the white dog who was barking last night, aren't you?"

Yep, I did it. I told you I had a reason for barking.

"I'm very proud of you, Angel. What would we do without the devotion of our companions?"

Chapter 12

Le Château Domaine

B rad spent the next day visiting the Musée d'Orsay, Musée Marmottan-Monet and various historic buildings around Paris. His notes were transcribed and then e-mailed to his editor in Portsmouth.

A college student was hired to look after Angel during the time he spent in the Museums, although she was included in many outside activities whenever possible. The boat down the Seine was one of her favorites. The wind would carry the various smells of Paris for her to savor. Looking up at Nôtre Dame Cathedral, its tall spires seeming to touch the clouds, she barked approvingly.

Is this where Quasimodo lived?

When Brad returned to his hotel there was a message waiting for him from his agent suggesting he include a trip to the French countryside after his tour of Paris. "Visit places with lakes and forests, maybe a quaint village," the note read.

Brad asked the hotel concierge if he knew a village that fit the note's description. While the two men leaned over the maps and brochures, Angel looked on with anticipation. She sensed a change was imminent which meant another move from her temporary home was about to take place.

We're on the road again. What a great life for a dog.

The concierge looked over at Angel, smiled, and then went back to his desk to retrieve another map and several brochures. "Perhaps *this* is the kind of place you're looking for." Unfolding the brochure, he spread it before Brad. He pointed to a photo of a large château with several smaller pictures of a village near by. "There is a beautiful lake for boating, extensive gardens, excellent cuisine, and one of the finest wine cellars in France. Parisians and tourists have given Le Château Domaine their highest rating. My cousin worked there many years as chef. "

"I know this place. I saw it listed in a book I purchased at River Run bookstore, or was it Barnes & Noble? I like your suggestion. This hotel should be perfect. It should provide some good material for my book. Would you make a reservation for me right away?"

"Of course, monsieur."

It took Brad only a few minutes to complete his packing. Early in his writing career he decided that traveling light meant less time spent on packing and unpacking. "I think we'll take the train and return the rental car Angel, this way we can save some money and I won't have to drive."

Are we going first or second-class?

Their taxi pulled up to the curb at Rue Saint-Lazare train station. Designed to impress the traveler as well as provide an efficient means of transportation, it is a marvel of architecture and convenience.

Rebuilt in 1889 with a beaux-arts style facades, it was the first train station to be located in close proximity to a hotel thereby providing an efficient means of travel to the late 19th century Universal Exhibition. Brad recalled a famous painting of its interior by Claude Monet.

The station looked much as it did then except for the thousands of panes of glass that were covered with decades of smoke from coal burning engines. With the introduction of the diesel, and the glass panes cleaned, the sun shone white beams of light onto the people as they hurried along the train platform toward the waiting cars.

With his black vinyl luggage rolling along behind him, and Angel aggressively pulling her leash forward, they weaved through the passengers who were preparing for their journey to the suburbs of Paris.

Glancing out the window of their compartment, Brad and Angel saw a stationary train, identical to theirs, idling on the tracks.

With the rush of excitement and the anticipation of new

experiences, Brad retrieved a pad and pencil from his backpack and began to take a few notes while Angel sat on Brad's sweater looking out of the window.

The soft click, click, click of their moving train as they left the station seemed to be saying, "farewell, farewell, Paris.'"

Tall wooden fences that separated the train tracks from the streets and narrow lanes began to glide by. The formidable ornate buildings of the city slowly disappeared, replaced with rivers, meadows, and fields of sunflowers.

Brad preferred relying on public transport whenever possible. He knew that Europe's excellent train and subway systems were faster and less expensive than traveling by car. When arriving at his destination, he was alert and rested.

Public transit afforded opportunities for Brad to meet interesting people who would bring additional local color to his writing. Brad's travel articles and books were known as much for the characters he introduced to his readers as for the vivid descriptions of fascinating and often out-of-the-way tourist destinations.

One *New York Times* critic summed up Brad's gift for travel writing. "His books are word-pictures. The people he describes are nothing short of fascinating. I find myself wanting to know more about each one of them. I want to stroll the city with them, play a game of boules, drop by a pub or café and share a beer or a glass of wine with them. The characters Kennedy introduces begin to feel like new-found friends."

The locals responded to Brad's candor and his fluent French. He was at ease initiating conversations with people of all ages. Now that Angel was his traveling partner, people would often approach him to talk about their pets.

Rows of poplars lined the train tracks as a canopy of flickering sunlight danced across the passengers. Brad listened to the couple sitting across the aisle share their story of immigrating to France. As the picturesque homes with manicured gardens flashed by the window, the two men pointed to one of the houses, enthusiastically describing the similarity to their own. Laughter and smiles became more numerous once Angel entered their conversation, encouraging everyone to tell their pet stories.

Soon it was time to bid farewell. After shaking hands and the usual exchange of e-mail addresses, the couple departed at the next station.

While their conversation was still fresh in his mind, Brad wrote a few notes on his pad. Glancing up from his writing, he saw a sign dash by. He tried to remember the spelling and recalled the name Massignac.

When the train pulled into the station, a flurry of activity surrounded Brad as the passengers prepared to depart. Bags were pulled from the upper storage bins, baby strollers were prepared for their valuable passengers, each person smiling with anticipation as they jostled by Angel.

"Look at the cute dog. I thought it was a stuffed animal," one woman said to her child.

"Monsieur, can I pet your dog?" asked the little girl.

"I don't mind, but you'd better ask Angel first," Brad laughed.

The girl leaned over and very seriously asked, "Can I pet you?"

"Let her smell your hand first. That's the first rule of dog etiquette," Brad said.

That smells good. You've had some licorice.

Standing on the platform with Angel, Brad noticed a line of taxi drivers.

"Monsieur!" he shouted, waving to the nearest one. "Would you take us to Le Château Domaine?"

"Of course, monsieur, let me take your bags."

With a few quick movements the cab driver placed Brad's luggage in the trunk and was behind the wheel.

The taxi moved swiftly onto the narrow lane leaving the Massignac train station in the distance.

The intense July sun was tempered by the refreshing shade of the poplar trees that lined the road. Brad rolled down the window allowing the warm wind to rush through the car bringing with it the heady country fragrance of lavender.

Angel thrust her head out of the window, enjoying the wind blowing on her face, one of her favorite sensual pleasures.

There's nothing like having a face full of smells.

The taxi pulled off the main road. Following the lane that bordered a lake, they could see the hotel in the distance. A mystical reflection appeared in the water of the castle-like structure.

"Well, princess, there's your castle! "Brad said. As they drove around the lake, the road began to descend. The points of the turrets disappeared from view. Then, as the car made its ascent, the château appeared to rise out of the ground.

"Angel, can you see what's happening?" Brad said, impressed by the optical illusion, " The château is rising out of the land. It looks like Camelot."

The cab driver could see Brad's surprised look. "Monsieur, you are not the first to be astonished. Everyone has the same look on their faces the first time they arrive at the château. Several hundred years ago, when the estate was built, the architect designed the approach to the Castle by excavating the terrain in precise measurements to create the allusion that the estate is rising out of the ground like magic."

While the attendants arranged Brad's small collection of luggage on a cart, Brad placed Angel on the blue-carpeted entrance and walked into the grand lobby of Le Château Domaine.

Waiting to register, Brad picked out a postcard from the revolving rack by the counter. A picture of the château appeared on one side and its history on the other. "Le Château Domaine was originally built by Count Beauchamp du Domaine in the 18th century as a hunting lodge. Through the centuries, both the château and the acquisition of land were greatly enlarged. By the twentieth century, much of the land was sold to pay the taxes, leaving the estate with a lake and sixty acres of land. In 1955 it was opened as a four star hotel by Count Charles Beauchamp."

Brad slipped the complimentary postcard into his pocket and signed the hotel register.

"Let's go out and enjoy the grass and maybe a stroll by the lake before we settle in," said Brad.

Yes! I'd like to run through grass!

Angel pranced alongside Brad as he crossed the lobby. Stopping to take a piece of complimentary Lindt chocolate from a large crystal bowl, he saw an oil painting hanging over the marble fireplace.

"Wait, Angel. Look at this! What a beautiful painting. I've seen this painting in a book,"

Brad examined every detail of the canvas - the muted colors, the broad-brush strokes, and the relaxed pose of the couple in the composition. A small brass plaque on the wall beside the portrait read, 'Pierre-Auguste Renoir, "Confidences", a copy, circa 1873. The original is on display at the Louvre Museum, Paris.'

Pulling on her leash, Angel tried to get Brad's attention.

Look, Brad. Look at the petit chien, in the corner of the portrait? It's a Maltese! That's the most important part of the painting!

Brad continued to admire the Renoir masterpiece, as Angel tried to draw his attention to the dog in the painting. However, to Angel's disappointment he turned and walked toward the garden without noticing.

A series of opened doors, ten feet high, led to a long broad stone terrace. As they walked through the opening, Brad became aware of the fragrant blossoms of the linden trees off in the distance.

The broad expanse of emerald green lawn extending from the château flowed into the blue-green sparkling surface of the lake.

Angel, having been confined on the train from Paris was now pulling vigorously on her leash in eager anticipation of her playtime.

Come on, Brad! Let's go, go, go!

Angel gave another sharp tug on the leash prompting Brad to pretend to accidentally lose his grip.

"Hey, come back here!"

Angel raced down the stairs and across the wide expanse of lawn, her leash trailing behind as she ran around a statue of Vénus de Milo.

What happened to your arms, lady?

"Angel, wait!" Brad shouted.

Running along the hedge that leads to one of the three wings of the château, they saw a small sign over an iron door that read "Wine Cellar."

"Phew! I need a rest." Breathing heavily, Brad lay down on the cool grass in the shade of an enormous linden tree and looked through the branches at the dark-green foliage.

Sunlight streamed down, glistening on the edge of each blade of grass. Brad's knowledge of horticulture inspired his interest in the tree he was sitting under. It was the largest tree in sight and the closest to the château. Another tree, smaller, stood some sixty feet away. It was half the size of the larger one.

Brad examined both trees carefully as Angel trotted along beside him.

"I wonder why there's such a discrepancy, one tree is twice the size of the other. Perhaps the smaller tree was planted more recently."

Brad discovered a bronze plaque attached to the bench in front of the larger tree.

It read, "August 31, 1944. In Memory of All French People Who Resist Tyranny."

"I would like to know the significance of this plaque and the mystery of the two Linden trees," Brad said to Angel.

Angel shoved her nose into the grass near the trunk of the tree, sniffing vigorously.

"What do you think about all this, mon amie? You are the expert, always smelling the trees." Brad laughed as he stood up and brushed the blades of grass from his pants. "Well, shall we go now?" Brad began to stroll across the lawn toward the château.

When they reached the doorway of the hotel, Brad turned around and looked in the direction from where they came. Observing the tremendous difference in the two trees, Brad picked up Angel and whispered in her ear. "Are you going to tell me what your nose told you about the trees?"

It's a mystery that will be solved in time. You'll know the answer before we leave France, Dr. Watson.

Brad walked through the lobby thinking about the mystery.

Their room, decorated with 18th century furniture, graced the château for more than two hundred years. Every piece seemed well preserved for its age.

"Bonsoir, mon amie, it's time for all good dogs to rest on their laurels." Brad leaned over and scratched Angel.

"I must go to work. You relax little girl and I'll be back before you know it."

This room has memories stored in it. Some dangerous people used this room to give orders.

As soon as the door closed, Angel looked around for a comfortable place to take her nap. She chose a sun-lit location next to the veranda. A breeze blew playfully across her fur, as she lay stretched out on the cool tiled surface.

After a short nap, Angel circled the room, sniffing each item her nose could reach. Of all the puppies Mrs. Luna had for adoption, Angel was the most curious. Opening each trash can, she would thrust her body into its cavernous space, sniffing every item.

If there were any unfamiliar odors, she would move about, room by room, looking for its origin.

I smell food. Someone ate pretzels. There was a Golden Retriever in here yesterday. But there is another odor from a long time ago. I smell black leather boots. People who destroy used this room.

Angel wandered onto the terrace that over looked the glittering blue water of the lake. The sun, low on the horizon, reflected several sailboats gliding silently in the distance.

As Angel sniffed the cool breeze, she recognized a strong fragrance coming from the blossoms of the linden trees below.

Suddenly, Angel heard a voice coming from the adjoining terrace.

Chapter 13

The Count

S tanding on the terrace, sniffing the air, Angel detected someone. She listened intently and turned her head in each direction. A man's voice came from the adjoining terrace.

She walked over to the railing that separated the terraces and pushed her head through the tangled ivy. Angel saw a distinguished looking man in a wheelchair with a lap robe covering his legs. She could sense something was wrong.

He's not well. He is very sad.

A gold crest, embroidered on his jacket, lent an air of aristocracy. From the darkened room, a gentleman stepped forward to drape a shawl around the man's shoulders. "Je serai en bas, Monsieur le Compte, pour avoir mon repas. I will be downstairs having my meal. If you need anything before I return, call me."

The reflection of the sparkling lake eluded the man as he slumped forward, his eyes staring into his lap.

He looks so sad. Maybe I can make him smile.

Every summer Count Charles Beauchamp reserved the same suite at the château for one week. He was always seen sitting alone on the terrace each day.

Even though he was physically present, his thoughts would drift away to the secret memories of his childhood.

For the past fifty years, the same memories carried him back through the decades to one hot summer's day in August 1944, during the German occupation of France.

As a young boy, Charles lived most of the year in Paris with his parents. Arriving at the le Château Domain in late June, they would stay for the summer.

His father often told him of his family's royal heritage and the enormous responsibilities Charles would inherit one day, along with two estates. His father would say, "Your great, great grandparents were given this château and the entire village by Napoleon Bonaparte I, in 1810, for services rendered to the crown. This you must never forget."

Sitting in his wheelchair, under the warm rays of the sun, his shawl draped across his shoulders, he saw an image of himself as a young boy returning from an afternoon swim in the lake. The shawl became a towel, draped around his neck.

Raising his head, he looked beyond the terrace to the lake as his thoughts traveled back, back to a distant memory he had refused to share with anyone.

"Why do I revisit that day? I was only a child. Children should never have to live a nightmare that leaves them scarred for life."

As a boy of nine, Charles Beauchamp's days were filled with climbing, hiding and playing jokes on his parents. Recalling images from his past he was once again a child...

The young boy finished tying the rope securely to the terrace railing, threw his leg over the side, and lowered himself until his bare feet reached the gravel path below.

Suddenly, the images disappeared. Just as swiftly as his thoughts had come, the Count's memories fled as he sensed he was not alone.

Through the ivy-covered railing that separated the two terraces, Angel observed the Count. The old man saw something white just beyond the railing. "What is that?" Turning his chair, he peered in Angel's direction.

"Une chienne, Tu es une chienne!"

That is correct, sir – I'm a dog.

Clapping his hands, he called out in the high-pitched tone that people often adopt when communicating with their pets. "Viens ici, petite chienne. Viens ici." He extended his hands motioning for her to come.

Is this an invitation? Pour moi?

After squeezing through the railing, Angel gave herself a shake and trotted over to Count Charles. He started to reach down to touch Angel, but realized that his arthritis restricted his ability to bridge the distance between them.

That's okay. I can make myself taller.

Angel raised her paws, placing them tentatively on the Count's knees. When she looked into his eyes, she found them filled with tears.

"I had a dog with big brown eyes like you many years ago."

Slowly, he reached down and with great effort raised Angel onto his lap. "Quand j'étais petit, je n'avais qu'un seul ami. I was a boy and he was my only playmate."

Dogs make the best playmates, especially for lonely boys and girls.

"I've been burdened with memories for a very long time, not only in my head, but here in my heart. I want to share what's in here with you my little friend." The Count looked toward the sky as he tapped his chest.

Angel, stood on her hind legs and licked the Count's chin.

Charles scratched Angel's chin. Seeing her dog tag, he said, "Ah, so your name is Angel and you are from New Hampshire – I believe that is in the United States. Am I right?

Yes, we are far from our home in Portsmouth.

Off in the distance a sailboat leaned into the wind, its bough slicing through the white caps. The sounds of laughter that floated above the lake were in sharp contrast to the sadness Charles felt in his heart.

"Angelique, I have never told anyone what I am about to tell you. I know you will not tell my secret, ah, but you couldn't anyway, could you? You are an angel."

A slight smile appeared then vanished. Angel felt the depths of Charles' sadness. Trying to communicate her compassion, she rested her chin on his knee. "Un petit ange...", the Count said.

Charles looked up at the cloud that hid the sun's warmth. A chill pinched his shoulders causing a slight shiver as he pulled his scarf tighter to his chest. Angel sighed and curled comfortably into the folds of Charles' lap robe as he began to tell his story...

"I was born here at the château. From an early age I knew that we were not the same as the people in the village. When we drove through the streets, men would tip their hats. My father was of the nobility. We lived a quiet life here at the Château Domaine, every day was gentle and familiar.

"Even when the Second World War began we saw no signs of it until the occupation of France. One day a German general and fifteen of his soldiers arrived. They occupied our home, ordering my family to stay in the servants' quarters on the top floor of the east wing. We adapted to our new circumstance. My father never discussed the war or the occupation with anyone.

"It was exceptionally hot that August day - the day our lives changed forever. Quite unexpectedly I saw a white-haired woman pushing a handcart with what looked like bright pieces of the sun piled high. I had never seen anything like this before. My father explained that they were oranges imported from Spain, for the general. I knew the woman. Her name was Mme. Combier. Father had always treated her kindly. Many years before, when her husband died, father gave her a place to live on our estate. As they talked, I could hear everything. She told my father that her daughter worked at the city hall in Dijon, where the Nazis had established their command post. Her daughter overheard the Nazis say they would be coming to join the General's staff at our home by order of the high command in Berlin. She said, 'You must hide your most valued possessions. They are thieves and murderers.' She risked her life to tell my father. I knew this even as a child."

Chapter 14

The Confession

"*I* want to tell you what happened. I have lived with this secret all my life. Today, you will be the one to hear my confession, my little white angel.

"I was a precocious child, making up games to amuse myself. My favorite was called, 'SPY.'

"I would hide and watch everyone. Unfortunately I didn't have any playmates and my best friend, our dog, had died a few days before the General's staff arrived.

"The General said I reminded him of his son in Berlin and allowed me to come and go as I pleased throughout the house. However, when his office door closed I was not to disturb him.

"Every day I would run through his office, which was once my father's, to reach the terrace where my rope was tied to the banister. On this day, as on so many others, I lowered myself onto the garden path.

"When I reached the gravel walkway I ran into the shrubs where I had carved a tunnel. There I could hide and observe everyone. I pretended that I was a spy for France.

"From this hidden vantage point, I could see the front and side of the house and the door to the wine cellar.

"It was cool under the bushes, and I kept a little pad and pencil in an old cigar box. I took notes when I saw the soldiers pass by. I wrote down what they said. They spoke German, of course, but the General taught me enough to understand some of what they were saying.

"News reached us that the Allied soldiers were on the outskirts of our village. My father was hopeful that the war would soon be over, perhaps before the end of the month. As I sat crouched under my bush that day, I heard a commotion coming from the front of the house. A car had just pulled into the driveway. With great urgency, the soldiers started running about carrying luggage and guns.

"The General appeared at the top of the stairs. He turned around and looked up at the terrace where my rope dangled in the wind. I heard him shout, 'Auf Wiedersehen, my little friend.' I did not answer, but stayed where I was hidden. The General's aide opened his car door, and they sped away.

"A truckload of soldiers, followed by a staff car with Nazi officers crowded inside, disappeared in the distance.

"Suddenly, a tall man with brightly polished boots and a swastika on his arm ran past the bush and into the château.

"In a short while, father and mother came down the stairs followed by the Nazi officer who was holding onto my father's vest from behind his neck. Father and mother were looking down at the ground. They stopped in the driveway and I could hear every word the officer said.

" 'Everyone has left. You only have a few minutes to make up your mind!' The officer shouted at them."

Angel looked up at Charles, whose breathing had become more intense. Sitting up, she turned and nestled closer into his arms. This seemed to calm Charles and he resumed his story.

I'm listening.

"I heard my mother cry out, 'I told you we have nothing of value left. We had to sell everything to buy food.'

"I knew this was not true, because my father had hidden his valuable paintings, paintings collected by my great-great-grandfather and inherited by my father.

"The paintings were hidden in a small room in the wine cellar. The room was once used for storing potatoes, when we had them. Father and I wrapped the paintings and put them into the storage room. Then we emptied one of the wine racks and pushed it against the door. Afterwards, we returned all the bottles to the wine rack. The best wines were put on the bottom. The vinegar was placed where the outline of the door was more obvious. My father said, 'The soldiers may drink all of our wine but they will leave the vinegar,' and they had."

Angel continued to glance up at Charles. When she felt his heart rate increase, she would encourage him to slow down by licking his hand.

There is no rush, my friend. Take your time.

"The Nazi officer started screaming at my father, 'I can't give you any more time, old man!' Then he pulled a gun from his holster and pointed it at my mother!

"I thought he was going to shoot her so I pushed myself from the dark recess of the shrubs and ran toward him screaming, 'Don't Shoot! Don't shoot!' The Nazi officer was surprised to see me running toward him. I kicked at his boots and reached for his gun. Then he hit me on the right side of my head. I fell to the ground. Blood was dripping from my ear onto the dirt path. I heard ringing in my ear like church bells. My father's face was a mask of fear. He shouted, 'Stop! I have paintings, valuable paintings. I'll give them to you if you just go and leave us alone. They're in the wine cellar.'

"Father led the way, followed by the officer with his gun pointed at my father's back.

"After they entered the cellar, I struggled to get to my feet, pulled myself away from my mother and ran toward the cellar door wanting to protect my father. My mother tried to stop me, but I was stronger than she. Children can be foolish, but often they are as brave as adults.

"When I reached the door to the wine cellar, I could see my father and the officer. I crept very carefully toward them, and concealed myself behind the end of the wine rack.

"Father told the officer, 'The paintings are hidden behind this rack. But first we must empty it so we can move the shelf.'

"They began taking the bottles off the rack and piling them nearby. It was dark in the basement – the only light came from a dusty window. I could see my father's hands shaking.

"The officer had placed his gun in his holster while he prepared to lift the wine rack away from the hidden door. Taking the last remaining bottle from the rack, he threw it in the corner.

"I crept closer and was now only a few feet away from my father but he still couldn't see me. As I crouched in the darkness, I saw him reach into the pocket of an old coat that had hung on a peg in the basement for as long as I could remember. I saw him slip a black object into his right pants pocket, just before he grabbed his end of the wine shelf.

"The Nazi officer began to curse my father because the shelf, even though empty, could not be easily moved. 'I will take over now, old man,' the officer said, pushing my father aside in frustration. He grabbed a corner of the wine rack that towered above his head and began to pull it away from the wall. I could see his black boots dig into the dirt floor as he pushed the shelf. Suddenly the shelf crashed to the floor as the remaining bottles collided.

"At the moment the shelf smashed to the cellar floor, I heard several sharp pinging sounds like firecrackers. They echoed through the cellar, making my ears ring. To this day I can still hear the ringing in my ear.

"Everything was hazy because of all the dust in the air. When the air had cleared, I saw the Nazi officer lying on his back, his eyes staring at the ceiling. My father was standing over him, shaking, and crying."

Charles was silent, his pain as fresh as if sixty years – the weight of a lifetime – had never passed. Lifting Angel from his lap, he gently brought her toward his face so he could look deep into her eyes. Angel returned his gaze.

I understand your sorrow.

"Une petit chienne très étrange. Sera t'il possible que tu sois une personne qui porte la fourrure blanche d' animal?"

So you think I'm strange. Non, mon ami, I may look like a person in a white coat as you say, but I'm just a dog.

A smile of relief appeared on his face. Without realizing it he had addressed Angel in the French familiar form, leaving all formality behind.

The Count's personal aide, returning from his meal, walked through the suite and out onto the terrace. "How are you feeling?

I see you have company."

"Broderick, I am feeling better than I have felt in fifty years. I think this little dog has healing powers better than the pills you give me."

"As a matter of fact, it is time for your medications now, monsieur." Turning away, Broderick started to go into the suite.

"Wait, I am not feeling any particular need for my medication, Broderick,"

Broderick stopped and turned back, confused. Broderick had served as the Count's personal servant for over twenty years, and he was stunned to see and hear the change in the Count's demeanor. Retracing his steps, he looked down at Angel who blinked innocently in return. As he looked closely at the Count's face, he detected a slight, knowing smile.

Angel got up, stretched, reached up to give Charles a lick, then jumped down from the his lap.

I have to leave now. I don't want Brad to come home and not find me. He would worry.

Angel squeezed her way back through the wrought iron railing. From the other side, she poked her nose through the bars and looked at her new friend once more.

You won't be unhappy any longer, my friend.

"Bonne nuit, Angélique. Dors bien," Charles said softly. Turning his wheelchair, he looked around to see where Broderick had gone.

"Broderick, about the medications, just put them away, s'il vous plait. I'll let you know if I need them."

Brad had returned and was looking for Angel when she suddenly appeared by the French doors that led to the terrace. "There you are. I'm sorry you had to be alone so long. I'll take you out shortly."

Angel came through the doorway and greeted Brad with a soft bark, wagging her tail.

"And how have you entertained yourself, Angel? Have you

been a good girl? No barking, I hope."

No, there was no reason to bark. I made a new friend. Want to meet him?

Angel walked towards the French door, motioning with her body, hoping she could entice Brad out onto the terrace.

"Poor Angel. You've been indoors by yourself long enough. Let's go for a walk in the gardens."

Taking the leash from the table, he attached it to Angel's halter and started to lead her to the door. Instead of following him, Angel lunged for the French doors, wrenching the leash from Brad's hand.

"Angel! Where are you going? Come back!" Brad followed her out of the room, and found Angel sitting by the railing that separated the two terraces. She was facing the Count who had wheeled himself over to the railing. Angel looked up at her new friend.

I want you to meet Charles.

"Excuse me, monsieur," Brad said to the Count. "I apologize for the disturbance. My companion seems to want to introduce us. My name is Brad Kennedy." He held his hand over the railing toward the Count. "I am very pleased to meet you."

"I am Charles Beauchamp, the eleventh Compte du Domaine. I have had the pleasure of meeting your little friend. You have a very wise and beautiful companion. She appears to have human-like qualities and, perhaps, a bit of extra-sensory perception."

"It's interesting you should say that, Count Beauchamp. I have been thinking the same thing for a long time. She brought me out here so that I could meet you. Her name is – Angel," said Brad smiling.

"I felt as if I were in the presence of an angel, even before I read her dog tag."

"Then you won't be surprised when I tell you that she named herself the day after I adopted her. The word Angel simply appeared in my mind. 'Your name is Angel, isn't it?' That's just what I said to her." Brad recounted.

"Well, your Angel and I have been visiting for quite a while.

She opened my heart and made a place for herself. I know we shall always be friends. I would like you to have this." The Count held his card out to Brad as he pressed a button on the arm of his wheelchair.

Immediately, Broderick returned to the terrace. "Oui, monsieur?"

"Broderick, I am inviting Monsieur Kennedy and our little friend to lunch when next they are in Paris and I would like you to arrange for the best wine and a plate of pâté for Angélique."

"We would be honored to accept your invitation, Count Beauchamp."

That's a great idea. Especially the pâté!

"Until then, Count, adieu et bonsoir," Brad said, leaning down to pick up Angel's leash.

"Monsieur Kennedy, you must call me Charles," the Count insisted.

"Then you must call me Brad,"

"Bonsoir, Brad. Et bonsoir, Angelique!"

"Bonsoir, Charles."

As they reached the French doors, Angel paused, turned her head and looked toward the Count.

Au revoir, Charles, mon ami. See you in Paris!

The Count followed his little white friend with his eyes as he heard a voice whisper in his silent, right ear, "Au revoir, monsieur, see you in Paris."

"Au revoir, Angélique," said the Count, smiling broadly as he waved.

Feeling energized with a renewed optimism, Charles sat straighter in his chair than he had in years.

"Broderick, we will be leaving today for Paris. We will not be returning to the château. This is my last visit."

Chapter 15

A Course In Driver's Education

The next morning Brad stopped at the concierge's desk to inquire about his train reservation. "Monsieur, do you have my trip ticket to Paris?"

"Oui, monsieur. The train leaves Massignac station in two hours." The clerk handed the ticket to Brad as the porter approached.

"Monsieur Kennedy, your taxi will be ready to take you to the train station in one hour. I'll take care of your luggage."

After looking over the hotel charges, Brad handed his credit card to the clerk. When he pulled out his wallet, a business card fell onto the counter.

"Monsieur, you dropped your card." Pausing, the clerk examined the card lying on the counter. Correcting himself, he said, "No, I'm sorry. The Count must have dropped it."

"Actually, the card is mine. The Count gave it to me."

"You have met Count Beauchamp, monsieur? What a gracious man. He is the owner of this hotel you know, and several others. He comes here every year for only one week and sits on his terrace all day. He is a very unhappy man. The Count's family lived here during the war and left for Paris after the liberation. None of the family has lived here for over fifty years. Some of the old villagers say there is an unsolved mystery about this place, but no one will say anymore. It is a grand hotel though, do you not agree?"

"Oh, yes. It certainly is."

"I hope you found time for a tour of our wine cellar, monsieur. We are very proud of our excellent vintage wines."

I'd prefer another tour of the gardens where I can enjoy some excellent vintage grass.

Angel tugged on her leash. After Brad signed the charge slip, he looked at Angel. "I'll bet you'd like to get out in the gardens again." Angel wagged her tail in eager anticipation.

Stepping onto the broad terrace that extended the full length of the lobby, they surveyed the variety of topiary, each illuminated by the morning sun radiating through a low-lying bank of clouds.

The upper garden was a shower of white and red roses that cascaded over the granite embankment along the steps.

Brad enjoyed the many fragrances, ripe on the morning air, vying for his attention. Angel was equally drawn to them as she sniffed her way along the cobblestone border, pausing to "read" messages left by other dogs and leaving messages of her own.

There weren't many dogs today. French dogs don't smell like American dogs. Perhaps French dogs have a little wine in their water bowls. I smell traces of a fine Bordeaux.

At the lower end of the garden, bright crimson, orange, yellow and pink lilies leaned over the walkway. A multi-tiered fountain sprayed water on to an overhanging weeping willow tree branch, one of many that draped over the beautiful garden paths.

Angel forged her way along the path like a white snowplow until she came to the wide expanse of lawn. Lying on the soft grass, she burrowed her head deep into the carpet of coolness while Brad sat on a granite bench enjoying the vista that lay before him.

The dazzling green of the grass and the brilliant white of Angel's coat sent his thoughts back to the green and white flooring in Mrs. Luna's kitchen on the day he first saw Angel. As if on cue, Angel raised her head and looked up at Brad.

There he goes again, thinking about the day we met. Each time he thinks of that day, the story changes. I'm the one who remembers exactly what happened.

Actually, my story begins the day I was born. I had three brothers and an equal number of sisters. Dear old Mum – she had only six nipples, and seven puppies. I decided that I wasn't the one who was going to go hungry. That's the root of my obsession with food. I can't get enough!

In six weeks, I was the strongest in the family, except for Mum and Dad.

72

The lady of the house, Mrs. Luna, gave me more attention than the others. We hung out together. I could look into her eyes and know what she was thinking.

Every afternoon Mrs. Luna would pour a cup of coffee for herself and give me a special dog biscuit while we listened to her, "motivational tapes," she called them. I was the only one in my family who paid attention. All that affirmative stuff made sense to me. 'Go after what you want.' 'If at first you don't succeed, try, try, again.' 'Have goals.' 'Personality is number one.'

Those were my formative months and I was determined to make the most of my opportunity to be adopted. Mrs. Luna couldn't afford to keep all of us.

In a few weeks, there were only three of us left, two girls and a boy.

I would always listen carefully when anyone came into the house to adopt one of us.

I remember, it was early fall. The three of us pups were lying on the cool vinyl floor when Mrs. Luna said, "A man's coming at one o'clock to adopt one of you girls, so look your best!"

Of course I wasn't going to settle for just anyone. The person I chose would have to have good breeding. After all, I am a Maltese, and the Maltese breed is over two thousand years old! We originated on the Isle of Malta, near Italy.

Without warning the lawn sprinklers came on, spraying water in every direction. Brad scooped Angel in his arms and raced back to the hotel. "I believe we've had enough of lounging on the grass," laughed Brad. "It's time for our petit dejeuner. I'm sure you're hungry too."

I'm starving!

After breakfast, a glance at his watch told him it was time for their taxi to arrive. As they walked toward the lobby Brad looked down at Angel prancing along beside him. He realized that something sounded different. Brad noticed that Angel's heart-shaped nametag and license were missing. It was strange not to hear the faint jingle of the city-issued license and the red nametag Angel wore on her collar.

"Where did you lose your license, Angel?"

I tried to tell you it was getting loose. I lost it yesterday at lunch, next to that plant with the big purple flowers.

Brad heard his name called. "Monsieur Kennedy, I have something for you." In the desk clerk's hand was a small package neatly wrapped in brown paper, tied with twine.

The Count instructed me to present this picture to you as a gift. You will find a card inside the package. May I wish you a pleasant trip to Paris." Brad turned to leave when the clerk continued, " Excuse me, monsieur, I have something else for you. I have a message from Count Beauchamp. I am to return your charge slip. Count Beauchamp has instructed me to tell you that you must always be his guest when you stay at any of his hotels." Brad was astonished by the Count's generosity.

The Count likes us a lot, doesn't he?

Brad tucked the package carefully under his arm and walked across the lobby, forgetting to tell the clerk about Angel's missing license.

A porter carried Brad's luggage across the lobby and through the revolving doors to the taxi waiting by the curb.

"I forgot something. Would you please ask the taxi to wait?" Brad walked back to speak to the desk clerk.

"Excuse me, could you recommend a hotel for us in Paris."

"Of course, monsieur." The clerk reached for a brochure from a rack on the counter. "Here is a list of our hotels in Paris. You will be pleased with any one of them. Perhaps you would like me to call ahead for a reservation?"

"No, I think I'll decide after checking the location of each hotel."

"Very well, monsieur, as you wish."

On the sidewalk, the cab driver took the package from Brad and placed it carefully alongside the luggage already in the trunk. Turning, he reached for Angel. Seeing the cab driver's hands coming toward her, Angel began to growl. Startled, the cab driver jumped back.

"Thank you, I'll see to the dog," Brad said apologetically. "She's very protective when I'm carrying her. I guess the word is possessive."

"We're on our way back to Paris, Angel. Are you excited?"

Sure, I'm excited, but I have to tell you – the view from the seat is terrible! I can't see anything but the tops of the trees and a piece of the sky from here.

"There you are. Now you can see better sitting on the backpack." Brad left the château with a feeling of satisfaction. His interviews with the hotel staff and guests, as well as the photos of the château's gardens, lake and historic architecture, convinced him that his readers would include this château as one of their must-see locations.

"Perhaps I can interview Count Beauchamp when we get to Paris. He might have an extraordinary story to tell about the château."

The taxi arrived at the Massignac train station just as the train was about to leave. Grabbing the luggage, Brad ran to the platform and onto the train as the automatic doors closed behind them. "That was close, Angel."

It sure was. I almost got my tail caught in the door. You're the one wearing a watch. You should look at it once in a while.

After placing Angel on the seat next to him, Brad pushed his luggage in the overhead compartment and dropped into his seat. He pulled the brochure from his pocket and read the descriptions of the hotels in Paris. "The Moulin Rouge is in my budget and I like the location near the Seine."

Across the aisle, a young child was eating candy. Seated beside her was an elderly man. Brad assumed he was her grandfather. Brad smiled and politely nodded. "Are you going to Paris, monsieur?"

"Oh, no, we are going to Massignac, I'm taking her to her mother," the man replied with pride resonating in his voice.

"But, monsieur, that was Massignac. You should have gotten off when the train stopped." Brad could speak French fluently, but the man's French dialect was difficult to understand, nothing like the French Brad had learned at school. "Where are you from monsieur?"

"We are from Saint-Germain-en-Laye,"

"That is a great distance from here. I'll speak with one of the employees on the train." Brad made his way to the end of the car and spoke with the conductor. As he returned to his seat, he was surprised to see Angel lying between the elderly man and the young girl, licking her bonbon.

This is terrific stuff. Kids get the best treats.

"Angel, I don't think you should be eating the little girl's bonbon" Brad said as he returned Angel to her seat.

"Monsieur, I have spoken with the conductor and he can help you at the next station, although you'll have to take another train to reach your destination."

The rhythmic motion of the train, lulled Brad and Angel to sleep. When next Brad looked at his watch, the train was pulling into Gare Saint-Lazare.

With his luggage rolling along and Angel walking closely behind, Brad approached the nearest taxi.

"Monsieur, do you know where the Moulin Rouge Hotel is located?" Brad inquired.

Pulling out a small leather notebook from his shirt pocket, the cab driver leaned against the roof of his taxi and thumbed through the pages listing all the hotels of Paris. "Eh bien. Here you are. This is the hotel you are looking for," the driver said in heavily accented English. "Très bien. Are you here on business, monsieur?"

"Yes, I'm here on assignment to discover the true essence of France for the American tourist."

As the taxi merged into the traffic, the driver accelerated, nearly hitting the side of an oncoming car. From a block away Brad could see a traffic light turn yellow and then red. Anticipating that the driver would stop, Brad was surprised when they sped through the intersection. Bracing himself, he grabbed the handle over the window, preparing for a collision.

"Hey, that light was red!"

"Pardonnez moi Monsieur, I can't always tell the yellow from the red with these sunglasses. I should get new ones." The cab driver veered away from an on-coming bus.

"Yes, I think that would be an excellent idea."

Relieved to have reached their destination, Brad and Angel were let off in front of the Hotel Moulin Rouge. The driver jumped from his taxi, dashed around to the back of his cab, removed the luggage from the trunk, and placed it beside Brad.

"Voilà! monsieur, my name is Père Masquer and here is my card. I would be happy to have you call this number and ask for me when you need my service."

"Yes, of course, merci, but you must promise to change your glasses," Brad laughed.

"Oui, monsieur. That's a good idea. It should improve my driving, n'est-ce pas?"

Make that a course in driver's education while you're at it.

"What do I owe you, my friend?" Brad asked.

"Nothing, please. Consider it a favor."

Père held his hands up. Even though Brad was surprised, he pressed a five-euro note into the cab driver's hand.

"I insist. Merci."

Père tipped his hat, jumped behind the wheel and maneuvered his way around the parked cars, driving over the curb, continuing to press his horn and shouting from his window. "Mouvoir!"

When Brad reached the door of the hotel, he heard the loud screeching of brakes. Turning around he saw the cab squeeze between two vehicles as it collided into a truck. The man jumped out to look at his fender while the cab driver stood on his bumper, jumping up and down to dislodge the truck's fender. Brad shook his head in amusement. "We just made it here in time, Angel."

I like his chutzpah. Every day would be an adventure riding in his cab.

The little hotel, almost on the back doorstep of the Cathedral of Saint Sulpice, was tucked into one of those tiny streets untouched by the passage of time. Brad knew it would have the perfect atmosphere and be an ideal addition to his book.

As he approached the large glass doors leading into the hotel, Brad saw two porters, one on either side of the doorway holding the doors for the guests. He was surprised that the porters were women dressed in bright blue sailor's uniforms. Distracted by the porters, Brad failed to notice the large urn directly in his path. Preoccupied, he fell into the center of a large palm dropping Angel in the entryway. As she tumbled across the walkway, three ladies watched in amazement.

Whoa! What the heck is happening?

Through the fronds Brad could see Angel lying on the carpet. Several people hurried to comfort her and formed a concerned circle of sympathy. A lady began to pet her gently. "My little darling, are you all right?"

Two young girls leaned over Angel, each one speaking over the other. "Ma petite chérie, ça va?" "What happened to the little white dog?" "Elle va bien." "I don't think she's hurt."

I'm all right – what about Brad?

The two women porters pushed aside the fronds and each took one of Brad's arms, pulling him from the large palm. "Merci, madame. Oh, I mean, merci, mademoiselles."

Scooping up Angel from the carpet, Brad looked directly ahead ignoring several people who were glancing his way. As he walked through the lobby, he could see his embarrassed red face in the mirror.

"Bonjour, monsieur," he greeted the desk clerk, trying to regain his composure. "My name is Brad Kennedy. I don't have a reservation, but I've just arrived from one of your hotels, the Château Domaine, outside the village of Massignac. They assured me that you would have a room."

"Of course, monsieur. Once you have been a guest at any one of our hotels, you will always receive preferential service," the desk clerk bowed slightly. Having registered, the clerk handed a room card to Brad.

"Here is the access card for your room, monsieur. Your bags will be upstairs by the time you get there. You will even find a special bed for your dog."

Angel, tired of seeing only feet and carpet, scraped her front paws on Brad's leg. Brad picked up Angel and placed her on the counter. "So, you want to see what's going on?"

Of course I do. I want to see what you see. By the way, what was the reason for your little acrobatic trick outside the hotel?

Brad pushed some stray hair out of her normally well-groomed eyes, the only evidence of her spill. "So, do you think you and I should run off and join the circus, my agile gymnast?"

I'm ready. Is the Barnum and Bailey circus in town?

As Brad opened the door to their room, his Maltese detective noticed that the hotel staff had been especially attentive. A blue velvet dog cushion, a crystal water bowl, and a miniature pillow embroidered with "The Princess is Sleeping" on one side and "The Prince is Resting" on the other, greeted her. Next to the water bowl was a brochure, entitled, "For Our Canine Guests.

Chapter 16

Let It Rain

*B*rad spent the next couple of hours copying his notes and transferring them to the laptop while Angel lounged contentedly on her plush bed. Glancing lovingly toward her, Brad experienced a warm feeling. Having her with him made a noticeable difference. He felt calmer, more at home, in the unfamiliar surroundings. "This is my family," he thought. "And our home is wherever we are."

Like a thistle seed drifting slowly in the wind, a distant memory came to Brad. "I've said that before, a long time ago." Brad recalled the image of a girl sitting by a café window. Her hair was dark brown with several strands carelessly drifting across her forehead. "I know... her name... was...Adeline," he murmured. Then the memory disappeared.

Anxious to be outside in the invigorating atmosphere of Paris, Brad completed his notes and closed the cover of his laptop.

Brad would often write about the unusual, out-of-the-way places in the cities he visited. He felt it added a level of interest that few writers attempt. He would also include pictures of unusual events as well as the casual conversations with the locals. The people he interviewed would receive a copy of his book in gratitude for their contribution. Back in the States, Brad would receive letters and e-mail from all over Europe from the people he had met in his travels.

Attaching his digital camera to his belt, he looked at Angel who was sitting by the door waiting patiently for her walk with that special, amused smile that all dogs project.

So, Brad, are we going to be able to get out of the hotel without taking another dive into one of the palms?

"You're laughing at me, aren't you, Angel?" Brad smiled as

they walked toward the hotel exit, pushed through the hotel's revolving doors and out onto the covered entranceway.

The Paris sidewalks were crowded on this beautiful July afternoon. People were hurrying in every direction as the traffic sped by on the Boulevard Saint-Germain. Brad had always noticed a casual panache in Paris, a style that was uniquely French. The architecture, clothing, landscape and, above all, food were all part of the magic. His insatiable interest in every detail of France and his ability to speak the language gave him a decided advantage with the Parisians he would meet each day.

With Angel leading the way, Brad paused at each lamppost while she checked them and left her messages. Spotting a bakery on the corner, he decided to sample a French pastry in the country where they had been first created. Brad knelt down near the shop entrance and slid Angel into her travel bag, as he often had in the States before going into a shop where food was sold.

After he had chosen two croissants, a lovely young woman at the cash register pointed at the black bag hanging from Brad's shoulder. "Do you have a little doggie in there?" she inquired politely.

"Mais oui," Brad answered apprehensively.

"Is it a boy or a girl?"

"It's a girl."

"You must take her out. Je veux la voir. I want to see her," she said excitedly. Brad unzipped the bag and Angel popped her head up. "Ah, elle est si belle! I have never seen a dog like that before!"

The mirror behind the young lady reflected an array of delicious French pastries that attracted Angel's attention. Raising her chin, she tilted her head a little to the left so she could view her reflection beside the chocolate croissants and cream puffs. She liked what she saw.

I'll have one of the cream puffs, s'il vous plait. Just kidding. I know it wouldn't be good for me.

"Au revoir, mademoiselle. Merci beaucoup." Brad walked toward the door with Angel prancing beside him.

What a relief. It looks like I won't have to hide in a travel bag every time we go into a store.

"Angel, you certainly have more rights here than back in the States."

Two blocks beyond the bakery, they passed an outdoor café with tables that dotted the sidewalk. As they strolled by, several people turned to admire the little white dog waving her tail from side to side. Every time Angel heard a compliment, she would lift her featherlike tail and swagger as if she were a champion.

Did you hear the bakery lady? She said she had never seen a 'doggie' like me before.

"It seems you have a great many admirers here."

They stood on the corner waiting for the light to change when Brad heard the sound of dog's paws clicking on the sidewalk approaching from behind. Turning around, he saw a man and woman with a beige cocker spaniel walking toward them. "Bonjour, monsieur," the man said. "What kind of dog do you have there?" Brad was quick to take the opportunity to chat. The light turned green, but the dogs and their human companions were in no hurry to cross.

Angel walked over to greet the Parisian spaniel.

Hello, did you just take a bath?

We Parisian dogs get more than just a bath. We get a coiffure, and our nails are clipped. We even get a breath mint.

Upon returning to their hotel room, Brad transferred his notes into his laptop and finished the rough draft for the second chapter of what he'd decided to call, "Angel Discovers France," one of a series.

He glanced out his hotel window through which he could see distant rain clouds rolling across the sky. "Let it rain," he thought to himself. "Paris takes on a special beauty in the rain. And Angel has a raincoat," Brad remembered.

Looking around the room, he realized that his umbrella was missing. "I remember leaving it in the restaurant this morning."

Angel looked so peaceful curled up on the couch against a soft pillow that Brad was reluctant to disturb her, this being her favorite position for serious napping.

"Angel, you look so comfortable, I'll leave you here for a minute while I run down to get my umbrella. I won't be a minute."

Brad could have called housekeeping to have the umbrella brought to him. Instead, he decided to retrieve the umbrella himself.

More sleepy than curious, Angel raised her head only slightly as Brad pulled the door closed. She heard the lock engage automatically behind him. Before deciding to doze into dreamland, she was alerted by a peculiar smell. It was a strange odor that she had smelled only once before.

While still a puppy in Mrs. Luna's home, Angel's special talents were called into action. A man who had come to repair the fence came running from the house holding Mrs. Luna's purse with Angel close at his heels. Her barking alerted Mrs. Luna who appeared at the kitchen window. As he made his way to his truck Angel grabbed his pant leg with her teeth. From the kitchen window came a loud voice, " Drop it or I'll shoot your head off." The thief threw the purse into the driveway, shook free from Angel, jumped into his truck, and sped away. The strong odor remained in Angel's memory. A similar odor was now coming from under the threshold of the door.

I smell a dangerous person.

Chapter 17

A Kidnapping

T he room became very quiet. Angel looked around, sampling the air with curiosity. The odor she had detected coming from the adjoining room was becoming suspiciously more intense.

I know that my sense of smell is two hundred times more powerful than Brad's. And right now – I smell a human nearby who doesn't belong.

Angel jumped down from the chair and walked toward the door, but the bright green bedspread distracted her. The vibrant color reminded her of grass, and that in turn reminded her of an event that occurred the year before. Resting her head on the carpet Angel relived that warm summer day...

The green bedspread reminds me of the lawn where I won first place for "Best Trick" in the Portsmouth Dog Show on Pierce Island.

I remember how excited I was. There were more dogs than I ever saw before. A Great Dane did his trick just before I did. Imagine a dog carrying a tire between his teeth. I couldn't carry a bagel in my mouth.

I was only supposed to do one trick, but I got so excited when my name was called that I ran to the center of the lawn and waited for Brad to give me the signal to start. Brad suspended a biscuit over my head and I went into my tricks. I did a sit up, a roll over, a give-me-five, a walking backwards, and I jumped through my hoop. I did them all a second time, one after another, twice as fast. The crowd cheered. I was a smash hit.

It was time for a nap and I was anxious to go home, so we started to leave. We were almost out of the park when we heard my name called. "Would Angel please come to the judge's stand to receive her first place blue ribbon?"

Angel slowly opened her eyes, looked toward the door then closed them once again and went to sleep.

Angel was jolted awake as she felt two hands lift her from the carpet and carry her into the bathroom of the room next door. Cold, white ceramic tile surrounded her. She seemed to dissolve into the background with her alabaster white fur. Only her large brown eyes and black nose provided a hint of her presence.

This is the biggest bathtub I've ever seen. Who was that woman in the black and white uniform who put me in here? I took my bath last week.

Although the thick mahogany bathroom door was closed, Angel's howls, coming in a series of two long, contrasting notes, made their way into the plush sitting room on the other side. A woman was speaking on the telephone. "Oui, oui, oui," she kept repeating in quick succession. Slamming the receiver down, she pushed a laundry cart toward the bathroom door. "Venez avec moi, ma petite chérie," the woman purred as she gave Angel a nibble of French pastry. With the other hand she lifted Angel from the tub, dropping her into the bottom of a deep, empty laundry cart. Tossing the rest of the French pastry into the cart, she began to wheel it out the door and into the hall.

I'm not supposed to have food with sugar. Is this a bribe?

As she ate the last crumbs of her treat, Angel looked up to see several large, billowy white sheets cascading down on her, each one pressing her closer to the bottom. Angel, frightened, her heart racing, clawed at the sheets that enveloped her.

Hey, it's dark in here. I don't like this game you're playing!

Suddenly the cart was in motion. A high-pitched squeak from its wheels covered Angel's whimpering as the thief made her way hurriedly toward the elevator.

"I went down stairs to get my umbrella." Brad shouted into the telephone. "When I returned she was gone! I've looked everywhere. The door and windows were locked. Someone has stolen my dog and you have to find her!" Brad's voice was shaking.

He slammed the phone down and ran from the room. Just as he reached the elevator he heard a loud squeaking sound coming from the end of the hall. He turned to see a woman in a black and white uniform pushing a laundry cart toward him. When the doors slid open, he stood aside to allow the woman to push the cart into the elevator. "I'll wait for the next one." Brad spoke politely to the woman, stifling his frustration.

Just as the doors closed, Brad heard a familiar sound coming from inside the elevator. His brain raced to decide if what he had heard was fact or wishful thinking.

"Angel," he thought to himself. "It was the day I closed the door of the linen closet and I didn't know she was inside. She made a sound just like that!" An overwhelming feeling of apprehension ran through his body as he jabbed at the elevator button repeatedly.

"Come on, move!"

The laundry cart reached the basement of the hotel and was now traveling rapidly toward the open door of a grey, four-door sedan with a Parisian license plate parked in the loading bay.

Entangled in the sheets, Angel felt herself being lifted from the cart and pushed into the back seat. Upon hearing the car door slam shut she became desperate. Clawing and pushing with her head and feet, she tried to free herself from the twisted linen. As she squeezed her head between the sheets, she saw a chrome door handle.

All right, lady, you are making a big mistake. I'm getting angry. I have a friend who's a police dog and you don't want to connect with that gal's teeth.

Angel squirmed free of the last sheet, then quickly pushed through the space that separated the two front seats. Stretching her body to its full length, she lifted her head to reach the open window.

I can bark and I can bite. I may not be very big, but my brothers taught me how to clamp my teeth down, really hard.

Angel's barking echoed through the opened window and into the hotel's parking garage. With a constant, repeated cadence she barked louder than she had ever done before.

A rush of cold air blew through the car and past Angel as the woman slid into the driver's seat beside her. The thief shoved the key into the ignition and started the motor while pressing the button that swiftly closed Angel's window, silencing her calls for help.

Chapter 18

A Narrow Escape

*B*rad had just reached the lobby and was speaking with the desk clerk when he heard Angel's familiar bark. "Did you hear that?" he asked the clerk. "That's my dog!"

"Oui, je l'ai entendu. I think it's coming from the hallway that leads to the parking garage." The clerk dashed from behind the counter, but was quickly passed by Brad as they both ran to the rear of the hotel. His heart pounding, he pushed open the glass doors at the end of the hallway just in time to see a woman in a maid's uniform get into a car and drive away. The grey Renault with a yellow license plate sped around the corner and into the crowded street. They could see the back of a woman's head in the driver's seat.

"Did you see that woman? Was she carrying a dog," Brad asked the clerk. "I heard barking."

"I saw something white in the window," the clerk reported.

"I'm sure that was Angel."

Brad was overwhelmed with a sense of hopelessness.

As the grey Renault raced through the maze of Paris traffic, the driver continued to glance in the rear view mirror to see if anyone were following.

"I have a customer who is waiting for you my little pretty." The thief made repeated glances to the curled-up ball of white fur lying beside her on the front seat. Angel looked up sadly at this strange woman with the bright pink nose.

She smells like whiskey, cigarettes and dust. I'm allergic to all three.

With her two front paws now extended toward the top of the passenger window, Angel watched the Paris shops rush by. Her heart, heavy with sadness, created a prayer, a mantra, which she repeated over and over again.

I want to go home, I want to go home.

Looking at the crowds of people whiz by, Angel tried to look for Brad, realizing the distance between them was ever widening.

"Tu seras bientôt chez toi, ma chérie. It will be a new home for you, of course," the thief said sarcastically.

This woman was a thief and by the way she smelled and dressed, Angel knew she could not afford to keep her.

She's going to sell me. A Maltese is not an item you can pick up at K-Mart. I'll wait for my chance to escape.

Angel learned very quickly after her adoption that if she did what was expected of her, then she could get what she wanted. She decided to give the appearance of cooperation.

The car turned into the driveway of a large, grey stone mansion off the Avenue Charles de Gaulle, the gravel making a pinging sound as the stones hit the undercarriage of the grey sedan. The car lurched forward as the thief jammed on the brakes.

"Where's that box?" She picked up a box from under her legs. It was the box that held the leash, and collar she had purchased at Madame Duberry's Pet Boutique. Pulling out the contents, she tossed the box on the floor in front of Angel.

From the glove compartment, she grabbed a piece of dried meat, tempting Angel to come to her.

"Un morceau de viande, ma chérie," As she held the collar in one hand and the meat in the other, the thief was poised to act quickly. "Viens ici." Angel chose to cooperate for two reasons: one, she was very hungry, and two, she was waiting for the best opportunity to escape.

With the expert precision of an experienced dog thief, the woman slipped the collar over Angel's head and fastened the buckle while the leash hung loosely on the seat. Then, scooping Angel into her arms, she pushed herself toward the open door.

Angel quickly swallowed the meat while waiting for the right opportunity to make her move.

As the woman placed one foot on the gravel driveway, Angel sprang forward like a coiled spring. Squirming and twisting in a circular motion, Angel forced the woman to lose her grip. The thief tried desperately to regain control by holding onto Angel's tail.

With a surge of strength, Angel pushed forward and slid from the hands of the thief onto the ground.

The woman lunged for the leash that now lay at her feet. Angel sensed the urgency to use these few seconds to make her escape. Impersonating a fastball thrown by the best of the Red Sox pitchers, Brad and Angel's favorite team, Angel raced down the driveway toward the sidewalk and into the dense crowd of shoes and legs passing in both directions.

Au revoir, smelly woman! Phew!

A gravel driveway offers insufficient traction for sprinting after an agile, nine-pound dog. After three steps, the woman tripped over the leash trailing behind Angel and fell onto the gravel, ripping her dress from the hem to her waist. Kneeling in the driveway with the palms of her hands cut and bleeding, the thief watched Angel dash around the corner and out of sight.

"Viens ici, you little white rat!"

Angel had always encouraged Brad to get down on the carpet and play chasing games with her. She would dash under the dining room table, around the chairs, and leap onto the couch. He never could catch her unless she wanted to be caught.

"Viens ici!" the woman shouted once again. She struggled to get to her feet, shoes pressing into the gravel, and sprinted toward the sidewalk.

"Arretez la chienne!" the woman pleaded, maneuvering through the crowd of people as they passed by with determined looks of indifference. "Hey, watch where you're going lady!" A man shouted as she pushed by him, his newspaper falling from his hands and taking flight.

As the crowd of pedestrians dodged the scattered papers, Angel paused for a moment, looking about for a place to hide. She had no idea if she was running away from the hotel or toward it.

Darting past a newsstand, she smelled grass and trees and took a skidding turn into a park where she crouched down under a boxwood hedge. She scooted under the tangled branches as far as she could, hidden in the cool darkness panting with exhaustion. Her eyes wide, ears lifted and nostrils distended, she sharpened her senses in an effort to detect the proximity of the thief.

I'll know if she comes near. She's easy to smell.

Angel turned her head toward the park entrance as she huddled deep within the shadows of the hedge, her heart pounding. She lay silent, even as a large ant crawled across her head and down the edge of her nose.

Get off of my nose, monsieur ant! Move on to your ant nest, s'il vous plait. I don't need any more problems.

As she lifted her head, she felt a warm breeze that carried the scent of the thief. Looking through passing legs, Angel heard the thief's voice nearby talking to a police officer at the park's entrance.

"Monsieur, have you seen a white dog come through this gate?" the woman asked breathlessly, holding her hand to her waist, trying to keep her torn dress from separating. The officer had been preoccupied, helping a little boy untangle his kite from a tree directly over their heads. Angel had dashed past the officer just as he was looking up.

"Non, non, non, madame. No dogs are permitted in the Parc de la Folie without special permission." He adjusted his hat forward to shade his eyes. "And what may I ask are you doing here, madame? May I see some identification?"

"Identification?" the woman stammered.

"This is not a public park, madame. It is a restricted area. See that sign? This is Embassy Row. The park is only for the residents who live on this street. Do you have some identification?"

"I have no identification, monsieur, I did not bring my purse. Defeated, the woman raised her arms to the skies and shouted, "Je suis hors de la chance."

"You are out of luck, yes," said the policeman. "And now, you will move out of the park, s'il vous plaît." He pulled the kite from the tree and held it by the string. "Young man, here you are. Unlike madame, you are in luck."

Angel watched the thief, as she grew smaller and smaller,

disappearing into the pedestrian traffic.

They don't allow dogs. I'll make a quick dash for the sidewalk, no, I'll crawl toward the bench where I can see better and then decide.

Crouching low, Angel crept toward the sunlight as the patterns of leaves moved across her back. When she reached the edge of the path, she rested quietly under a park bench, planning her next move.

Suddenly Angel recoiled as she felt herself being lifted from the ground, then her body quickly relaxed. It was a friendly, gentle touch. A voice inside told her not to be afraid.

"Mother, look what I found. A dog!" announced the boy whose kite had been caught in the tree and now lay forgotten on the path. "Puis-je la garder?" the boy pleaded. "Can I keep her?"

You can't keep me! I belong to Brad.

"How do you know the dog is a girl?"

"Because she's beautiful. Like you, mother."

"Thank you, darling, for the compliment but I think the dog must belong to someone. She's wearing a collar and leash."

Madame Marguerite Revier, lived across from the park with her son, George, who was feeling much older, having celebrated his birthday a week ago. As a result of the change in his age, he started a new custom. He now began all introductions with, "My name is George, and I'm nine years old." With his coarse, straight brown hair and a small cowlick in the crown of his head, he looked a lot like Dennis the Menace.

Despondent, Brad sat in the hotel lobby looking alternately at his wristwatch and at the clock hanging over the front desk. He had been waiting for two hours for a report from the hotel manager for news about Angel's disappearance. As the hotel guests crisscrossed the lobby, he barely noticed the medley of orderly confusion they created. Finally the manager emerged from the elevator, his expression mirroring Brad's distress.

"Monsieur Kennedy, I want to assure you that we have done

everything possible to find your dog. We have identified the thief. She is not an employee of our hotel," the manager hurriedly explained. "She is an acquaintance of an employee. We have determined that the thief posed as a housekeeper. After gaining the confidence of one of our staff, she stole a housekeeper's uniform. Also, she stole a passkey and entered your room. She must have hidden your dog in a laundry cart. We have just found one at the garage service entrance. And please be assured, we will continue to make inquiries"

"A laundry cart!" Brad interrupted. "I saw a woman in a maid's uniform get into the elevator with a laundry cart, and I thought I heard Angel's bark after the door closed, but I had no way of knowing that the sound came from the... I'm sorry to interrupt. Please, go on."

"I understand, believe me. I have given the woman's name to the police. This is their phone number. We have also posted a reward in the employee's lounge for any information that will result in the return of your dog.

The manager placed a dog's collar and leash into Brad's outstretched hand." "This was found in a wastebasket next to the service entrance."

"You've been very helpful and I appreciate all you've done."

"I see you have your luggage. Where are you going?"

"I've made arrangements to stay in a small rooming house. I've made inquires and I hope to use this information to find the person who stole my dog. I won't leave Paris without Angel! Here's the address and phone number where I'm staying. Please contact me as soon as you hear anything." Brad wheeled his luggage toward the exit.

The hotel manager read the address: 13, Sacré-Coeur. Waving his hand, he shouted, "Monsieur Kennedy, arretez! Wait!"

The manager's voice quickly vanished into the lobby as he shook his head in disbelief. He continued to watch Brad through the glass doors as he disappeared in the distance. "How could Monsieur Kennedy stay in a section of Paris with such a notorious reputation?" he thought.

Chapter 19

A Practical Man

*B*rad called the same cab driver he had hired at the train station. He explained his situation to him and was assured that a room could be found in a part of Paris that was known as a place where anyone could buy and sell anything. Stealing and selling pedigreed dogs was just one of the many crimes that originate in the minds of the criminals that make their deals in the streets of Sacré-Coeur.

Waiting by the entrance of the hotel, the cab driver saw Brad and waved to him. He took Brad's bags, tossed them into his trunk, and slipped a pair of sunglasses from his vest pocket.

"See, I've changed my glasses. I can now see the red lights."

"Thanks for sharing the good news. I feel much better. I don't need any more to worry about."

"Do you remember my name?" the driver asked.

"Oui. I believe you said it was Père."

"Très bien! Père, very simple, one syllable. You speak very good French, so I suppose you know what my name means in French?" Père asked, flipping his cigarette into the gutter.

"It means father".

"You are correct. I was christened Père because my mother wanted me to become a priest. Obviously, I have a very disappointed mother. Maybe when I'm sixty-five I'll make her happy. I'll go to confession. I'll have all my sins forgiven at one time and then… I'll become a priest. This is a good plan since a cab driver has no retirement fund. You will find I'm a practical man, as every one knows." Père made the sign of the cross, opened the back door for Brad, and jumped into the driver's seat. Touching his two fingers to his lips, he pressed them against the St. Christopher magnet attached to the dashboard and started the motor.

He eased his taxi into a narrow space between two towering tour buses, pressing his horn repeatedly. As he dashed ahead, his cab lurched over the double yellow line and stopped in the middle of the intersection as the traffic maneuvered around him.

While turning his wheel sharply to the right, Père lurched forward just missing a motorcycle. "Hey, stay in your own lane or park that thing!" the cyclist shouted.

Brad's confidence in Père's driving was diminishing rapidly. "Père, slow down! I'm not in a hurry."

"Monsieur, you must relax. We drivers in Paris have our own unique way of showing our 'assertive personality.' I have that printed on a t-shirt," he laughed.

"I would like to help you find your dog. Are you surprised to hear me say this? I know how the criminal mind works. I've been in prison myself, but don't get alarmed. I have, as you say, kicked the habit. Now, I earn money with honest labor. You must want to get this dog very much to stay in a place like the Sacre-Coeur." Père took both hands from the wheel to light his cigarette, steering with the top of his knee.

"Is it so bad? I thought I could make contact with someone who would be willing to make a deal, money for information."

Père twisted and turned through the traffic, avoiding pedestrians and other cabs that were forcing their way into his lane. He played his horn like a musical instrument.

"My friend, I'll be your contact person. We can be Sherlock Holmes and Dr. Watson. I'll help you find your dog. If you have the money to hire me, I am at your service."

"I'll think about it, but first I want to place an ad in the paper and offer a reward." Brad was anxious to create a plan of action, although he was reluctant to form a partnership with an admitted convicted felon.

The tall buildings began to squeeze out the sunlight as Père continued to navigate the narrow back streets of Paris.

The people on the sidewalks grew increasingly somber as they grew nearer their destination. Darting eyes turned to look at the cab with suspicion. Men crouched together on street corners, gesturing in slow motion, while holding up fingers to indicate the price of an unseen product as clandestine deals were being made.

Père pulled up in front of an old dilapidated mansion that long ago had been the home of a wealthy and well-known family. Now only wrought iron posts and marble stairs remained as reminders of its former grandeur. The building had been a boarding house for over one hundred years. Forty years ago, partitioned into tiny one-bedroom flats, it became one of Paris' first city-subsidized housing.

Today, a woman, known as Madame Noblesse owned the derelict building, which she had purchased from the city for a ridiculously low price. The city government was anxious to rid itself of the responsibility of dealing with the criminal element the area attracted. At first, she was subjected to intimidation and extortion, but eventually madame would gain the respect of her unsavory neighbors. Her reputation as a shrewd negotiator and a force to be feared kept the criminals at a distance.

It was common knowledge that she offered her rooms only to those who could prove they were not on drugs, dealing in drugs or involved in any criminal activity. She would always say, "I only rent to people who want a cheap place to live and won't cause any trouble."

Madame Noblesse, a woman of substantial girth, lived in three of the rooms on the first floor, the rest were rented by the week. With her bedroom in the back of the building, she avoided the noise of the street. The sitting room, next to the front door, was her command post. Anyone passing the house could be seen and examined with her probing eyes.

All of her tenants had keys to their own rooms, but the front door of the building was always locked, and madame had the only key.

"Bonjour, Monsieur Kennedy," madame greeted a surprised Brad in a matter-of-fact manner as she opened the door. Adjusting her glasses to survey her new boarder with more certainty, Madame Noblesse quickly formed her opinion that was decidedly in Brad's favor.

"A bientôt. See you later!" Père shouted from his cab window as he turned the wheel toward the street. Brad waved as the taxi began to accelerate. Just then Père held up his thumb and pointing finger in a gesture Brad didn't understand.

Madame Noblesse observed the puzzled expression on Brad's face.

"Monsieur, your friend is telling you that he has a gun, if you need one."

"A gun? A gun." Brad repeated incredulous.

Picking up his luggage, Brad noticed the intricately designed mosaic tile in the entryway and the fleur-de-lis pattern encircling it. "This hallway must have seen far grander times," he reflected.

"I suppose you would like to see your room, monsieur,"

Without waiting for an answer, madame began to climb the stairs while Brad followed. With his suitcase in one hand and Angel's empty travel case in the other, he followed madame's footsteps.

The travel bag had always held Angel safely inside, her big brown eyes looking about, her floppy white ears framing her face making her look like a small child with white fur earmuffs. Its emptiness seemed heavier now than with Angel inside.

"Fifteen euros is what I charge, in advance, weekly. You get one key to your room. The bath is down the hall, over there to the right. Don't use too much water. There is a sink in your room. No cooking. The front door is locked at all times. Just ring the bell when you arrive. I will be here to unlock it for you. After 11:30 p.m. I go to bed and no one gets in. No visitors are permitted unless you come down and give your approval. A week ago a mademoiselle arrived saying she wanted to visit her brother. When he came down he peeked through the glass, turned around and ran up the stairs. I told the woman to "beat it," as you say. The man told me she had threatened to kill him, and he wasn't her brother. We have a safe house here," madame said, trying to catch her breath as they reached the top of the landing.

In the dimly lit hallway, they stopped in front of the first door at the top of the stairs. She put her hand into her dress pocket, pulled out a collection of keys attached to a long metal chain and selected one.

"You shouldn't be on the street after 11:30 at night. That's when the trouble starts. No one can help you. The police never come down here. We are on our own. You'll be safe here until you find your dog."

"How did you know I was...?"

"Looking for your dog?" Madame Noblesse interrupted. "I have my ways. Vous êtes Américain. You write travel books. You came to France to write a book about your travels with your dog. You were staying at the Hôtel Moulin Rouge when your dog was stolen."

Brad's mouth opened in astonishment. "How can you know all this?"

"In this neighborhood I have connections. We exchange information," madame said matter-of-factly. "I must be certain of the kind of people who become part of our little family here at the Villa Dumoit. This building has not seen high society for many years, but I do have my standards. We will get along, if you behave yourself and, of course, pay your rent on time."

As she handed a key to Brad, she ran her finger across the top of a hall table, inspecting the results with exasperation. Wiping the dust on her apron, she descended the stairs and disappeared behind her door, just like a friendly spider might retreat into her web.

Chapter 20

Embassy Row

A crisp afternoon breeze blew playfully through the chestnut trees of Embassy Row Park as Madame Marguerite Revier sat quietly with her son, George.

Gently holding the white dog in his arms, George looked at his mother, smiled and continued petting his new friend. "Mother, don't you think she's beautiful? She's so soft to touch, like your cashmere sweater."

Marguerite leaned to one side, raised Angel's face and stroked her. "Yes, George you're right she has both of those attributes."

Marguerite knew her answer did not sound enthusiastic, but she was concerned that George was becoming attached to the lost dog.

Sitting on the park bench, Marguerite adjusted her sweater, opened her book and began to read. The book was a gift. It represented the next step toward the fulfillment of her wish to return to the United States for a visit.

Noticing the author's photo, she adjusted her glasses and read the title, "Your First Trip to New England" by Brad Kennedy. Looking at the picture printed on the back cover she said, "His face looks familiar."

As she continued to read, she brushed a few strands of her hair from her forehead revealing a perfectly proportioned face, every feature regal: a delicate nose, turned up slightly, complimented her petite ears. Her eyes, the color of jade, projected a look of distinguished elegance.

She closed the book, pressing her hand slowly across the smooth cover and looked at her son as he sat talking to the dog.

"I'll take care of you. You'll be safe with me."

I miss Brad. I want to go home.

Off in the distance, a carrousel transported the playful passengers on their imaginary journey while the music played a familiar tune, "The evening breeze caressed the trees, tenderly."

Marguerite shaded her eyes from the sun, and looked towards the drifting clouds, catching a glimpse of a fading moon. She remembered a time and a place long hidden in her past that now was calling to her. Collecting her memories, as one might gather photos from an old album, she could see a young man holding a brooch and placing it in her palm.

"What is it?" she remembered saying.

"It's a wishing well." He said. "There used to be a well on every farm in America many years ago. It's considered a gesture of good luck to toss in a penny and make a wish." The young man pinned the brooch on her school uniform.

The music coming from the carrousel was comforting. Marguerite began to hum, catching part of a phrase as it floated by her.

'I'll be seeing you, I'll be seeing you," she repeated. "I can't remember the rest." The carrousel melody, with missing lyrics, continued to drift through the trees as the bright sun pushed the disappearing moon from the sky. The comforting memories she wanted to recapture slowly faded.

"George, Why don't you walk through the park and ask the people if they recognize the dog?"

"Yes, Mother but what if the dog was abandoned?"

"She has more likely become separated from her owner, and they're probably looking for her at this very moment. There's a lady over there. Go over and ask her."

Holding Angel in his arms, George walked over to the woman in a bright print dress who was feeding a chipmunk sitting beside her.

"Bonsoir, madame. Savez-vous à qui cette chienne appartient?" he said, wishing the answer to be no. "I have never seen that dog in this neighborhood before and I've lived here for over forty years, right there next to the chestnut tree that is in bloom."

Marguerite waved to her son. "George, ask those boys over

there if they've seen the dog before?" his mother encouraged, overhearing the woman's comment.

George approached the boys. "Bonjour. Avez - vous….Tenez, regardez cette chienne blanche?"

"Did you just give her a bath?" the tallest boy asked.

"Does your dog play chase? I have a ball," announced the boy with his hat on backwards.

"Why don't you put the dog down? Can't the dog walk?"

"Wait a minute. That sign says no dogs without permission," the boy with the missing front tooth said pointing toward the park entrance. The young lads began to form a tight circle around George, but suddenly they hesitated.

Back off.

Angel narrowed her eyes as the edges of her mouth curled, revealing four, very sharp canine teeth.

A smelly thief has stolen me. I was chased through the streets of Paris. I don't know where I am. I'm hungry. And I'm angry enough to bite someone.

Angel was alert and ready to defend.

The tallest boy, looking directly at Angel, grabbed George's sleeve. His threatening gesture provoked her to lunge forward with two piercing high pitched barks, followed by a low snarling growl. Startled, the boys jumped back and ran from the park.

Angel continued to growl and bark until they were out of sight. George's mother had watched the disturbance, but she didn't want to interfere. She waited to see how George would handle the boys who were trying to intimidate him. Only when she heard Angel barking and growling did she make her way toward the group.

"Maman, ils ne savent rien. They thought the dog was mine. Did you hear how loud the dog barked at them? She even scared me. At first I didn't know where the bark had come from because it was so loud for such a small dog. I'm sure she would have bitten the tall boy if he hadn't pulled away. Don't you think so mother? You should have seen her teeth. She had her mouth curled up on both sides." George was out of breath with excitement.

Angel, remembering her last meal, looked about for anything that had the slightest resemblance to food.

J'ai faim. Even people food would do.

"George, It is time for us to go. I have a two o'clock appointment at the American Embassy. Monique will prepare a late lunch for you. Do finish your lessons before I arrive home at 6 o'clock, d' accord?"

"Oui, maman, d' accord."

Marguerite encouraged George, her only child, to be self-reliant and to offer his opinions on most matters discussed in the home. Both she and her late husband were in agreement on the way George would be raised. They realized that their wealth and political status in France offered unlimited advantages to their son, and therefore, they had agreed that he would be taught civic responsibility by working in the Paris Youth Corps when he reached the age of sixteen. Since his father's death from a heart attack a year ago, Marguerite had made every effort to be both father and mother to her son. She felt the necessity to be firmer with him on many issues in which she had previously been more lenient, and she felt it was imperative to be consistent in her decisions.

"We will not make any decisions about the dog now. Marie will prepare a place for the dog in the laundry room while you are doing your homework."

Marie, their housekeeper, had continued her employment with Marguerite after she inherited the home from her late parents.

Her home stood directly across from the park. There were a row of six large, white, three-story town houses, each one displaying various architectural elements that conveyed the impression of wealth and social position. Two uniformed guards, one standing on each corner of the small street, provided security. This area of Paris, known as Embassy Row, and the street and park were restricted to the residence and their guests. To drive or walk into the area required a special identification card.

There were cameras located at several strategic points on the street; all were on a twenty-four hour monitoring schedule. Five Embassies had been located here for two hundred years. The only home that did not have an Ambassador in residence at present was Madame Revier's home, whose father was the ambassador to the United States many years ago when Marguerite was in high school.

Angel began to squirm free from the boy's arms.

Hey, I have to use that grass over there.

"Maman, je crois que la chienne doit faire pipi. May I put her down on the grass next to the curb?"

"Oui mon cher, but hurry. I can't be late for my appointment."

Marguerite and George crossed the sun-speckled street and went up the granite stairs that elevated the entrance and emphasized the beveled glass door, trimmed in polished brass and mahogany.

George pressed a large bronze buzzer next to the enormous front doors. After a few seconds a matronly woman in a black and white uniform greeted them.

The cool, tropical scent of gardenias floated through the air while the interior gave reassurance and protection for Angel.

I can smell flowers, but I also smell food. When he puts me down I'll do some investigating.

"Good afternoon, Madame Revier," Marie, the housekeeper, cheerfully inquired.

"Est ce que vous vous êtes bien amusée au parc?"

"Yes, Marie, it was a very eventful day."

"Madame, avez – vous une chienne? Marie posed a statement that was presented as a question.

"Yes, Marie, a very hungry one. Would you tell the chef to prepare some chicken for the dog from the roast chicken we are having for lunch?"

"Yes, madame." Marie took the leash from George and led Angel toward the kitchen.

Chapter 21

A Dangerous Place

F ar into the interior of the East Bank of Paris stood the Villa Dumoit. It was a destination where no tourist or respectable Parisian would venture. Brad stood in front of the open window of his bleak room. The smell of damp aging wood and wet concrete swirled through the narrow streets. As he leaned forward, his palms resting on the windowsill, he looked down onto the sidewalk below. Distracted by the faint sound of a pigeon resting on the window ledge of the building across the street, he wondered why the bird would choose to rest in a place such as this when there were so many beautiful parks in Paris?

"Maybe he's looking for a loved one," Brad thought.

There was a stark contrast between Brad's room and the opulence that surrounded Angel. He had no way of knowing that Angel was safe and protected in the surroundings of privilege and security. If only he knew that Angel was safe and well cared for, away from the thief who had stolen her, he could have at least found some peace of mind.

"How long will it be until I can find Angel and leave this place? Was it a mistake to come here? I'll probably be mugged before I can find her."

Looking around the room, he surveyed his comforts. A single bed, covered by a threadbare quilt of some age was shoved in the corner of the room. A small nightstand, barely large enough for a bedside lamp, had the good fortune of being made at a time when it held a necessary item for all bedrooms — the chamber pot.

A dresser, with four drawers and only three knobs, stood next to the door. Above the door was a large transom window. Forty years ago it could have been unlocked by inserting a hook into the hasp at the top and tilted downward, allowing the air to circulate throughout the room. Now, with the rust from years of neglect, it was permanently closed.

Brad sat in front of a small table in the center of the room, printing his advertisement on a piece of writing paper he had taken from the lobby at the Moulin Rouge Hotel. He decided to offer a large enough reward to gain as much attention as possible.

It read, "One thousand Euros when you provide the information that will lead to the return of my dog, Angel, a white Maltese." After placing the completed notice in his pocket, Brad looked at his watch. It was 1:30 p.m. and he would have to get his advertisement to the newspaper as soon as possible if he hoped to have it printed in tomorrow's paper.

With his coat slung over one shoulder and his key in his right hand, he prepared to lock the door, but first he glanced over toward the chair where he had been sitting. There, draped over the back was Angel's carrying case. Brad lowered his eyes and held back a lump in his throat as he closed the door and locked it.

At the bottom of the stairs, next to Madame Noblesse's apartment door, a black pay phone hung on the wall. Wetting his finger, Brad cleaned off the plastic surface in the center of the phone so he could read the number. He pressed the piece of paper with the newspaper advertisement to the wall, and added the phone number.

Brad stood outside Madame Noblesse's apartment door, reluctant to intrude upon her privacy, but if he was to find Angel, he must use every means and act quickly. After all, this was France and not America. "I can be more assertive in my own country but here I don't want to offend. I have no alternative but to forge ahead and keep asking for help."

After a quick succession of tapping on the aged mahogany door, a sliver of light began to appear through the doorway. First a hand and then a dimly lit face peered through the space. "Oui, monsieur?

"I was hoping you might know where I could place an advertisement? I would like a newspaper with the most circulation."

"Oui, monsieur, je comprends. You are advertising for the

return of your dog? It's funny that you should ask me. I haven't read a newspaper since Charles De Gaulle was president. There is nothing but bad news, and I can tell you young man that I have seen too many terrible things during my lifetime. I'm tired of reading about the world's troubles. The newspapers and the television keep repeating the same stories: war, famine, crime and poverty.

"Do you know what I do? I watch old movies and read books. That's what I do. Forgive me, you were asking for an opinion and directions, and I have given you neither. I'm just an old woman who has seen too much of life."

"You should speak with Monsieur Baudelaire. He occupies the room across the hall from you. He has worked for a newspaper. For a long time he would leave one by my door each evening. I couldn't tell him that I don't read the newspaper because he was being kind. Besides, I would wrap my garbage in it and, therefore, it served a purpose. He's here most days around this time. He works at night for the Rospier Café. Good luck monsieur." Madame Noblesse slowly closed the door.

After several knocks at Maurice's door, a tall heavyset bearded man wearing large wire rimmed spectacles appeared and asked, "Are you the new boarder? My name is Maurice Baudelaire, and yours is Brad Kennedy. Would you like me to help you find your dog?" Brad was surprised once again that someone knew of his problem.

"Yes monsieur, you're right, but how did you know about me?"

"Père Masquer, the cab driver who brought you here is my brother-in-law. He helped me find this place and persuaded Madame Noblesse to rent a room to me. What can I do for you, monsieur?"

"The landlady said that you had worked for a newspaper and I wonder if you would know which paper is the most popular in Paris." Brad pulled the written advertisement from his pocket and showed it to Monsieur Baudelaire.

"I worked at *Le Figaro* for six years and they have the most circulation. I can take you there myself. I am going that way. I should be able to get a very good price for you." Maurice took the advertisement from Brad. He glanced at the paper, placed it in his pocket, swung his coat over his shoulder, and gestured for Brad to follow him.

Standing at the top of the stairs, he turned to Brad. "You must call me Maurice, easy name, only two syllables."

As the two men made their way down the steep flight of stairs, Maurice continued giving advice to Brad.

"I think it would be best if we took the underground metro. It's only a few blocks from here and at this time of day the traffic in Paris crawls at a turtle's pace. Believe me, this will get us to our destination faster."

Standing with his back to the front door and leaning against the wall next to Madame Noblesse's apartment door, he whispered to Brad. "Before we depart, I'll give you some advise. If anyone speaks to us on the way to the metro, don't answer. I'll do the talking." Satisfied that he had prepared Brad, they began their journey.

A light mist began to moisten the street as larger droplets collected and fell from the brim of Brad's cap. Maurice pulled his coat tighter around his chest while glancing suspiciously from side to side.

Both men walked shoulder to shoulder as Maurice continued to lead the way. While dodging around men with shoulders hunched forward, fragments of conversations drifted by them, each one sounding aggressive and threatening.

Suddenly, a man appeared from an alleyway. With legs spread apart, he stood in front of them. Brad noticed the man had a tattoo on his forehead that read, décevoir. Startled by the man's appearance, Brad looked toward his new friend wondering what he should do.

Maurice placed his left fist in front of the face of the intruder, and pushed Brad aside. Then with his right hand, he pulled an object from his pocket. Holding his fist close to the face of the intruder, he threw the object on the sidewalk and then placed his hand back into his pocket. The intruder glanced down and upon seeing the object his eyes opened wide in shock. He gave Maurice a quick glance and bolted toward the dark recesses of a nearby alley just as the object rolled into the gutter. Maurice pulled Brad's sleeve and gestured for them to continue.

As they made their way toward the Metro entrance, Brad asked Maurice, "Did you throw money?"

"No, my friend, in this neighborhood you never want to give money to anyone. I threw a bullet. My gun is in my pocket. On this side of Paris we have our own ways of communicating. If a man throws a bullet, the message is that he has a gun and is ready to shoot. I was prepared and he knew it."

The force of air coming from the cavernous opening of the subway blew against their clothing as they stepped onto the escalator, and descended into a dark cavern-like hole. The sign overhead read: Rester à droite.

Musty air from a thousand moving bodies rushed toward them as they dodged around the crowds of people. Brad looked around the platform as he waited for the train. He noticed a man standing beside him holding a white cane in one hand and the harness of his seeing-eye dog in the other. Brad resisted the urge to reach down and pet the man's companion, knowing he should not pet the working dog of a sight-impaired person. Watching the dog, Brad inaudibly asked the golden retriever, "Have you seen Angel?" The Golden Retriever glanced up at Brad and then refocused on the train coming to a stop before them.

Upon entering the newsroom, Brad and Maurice were greeted by the sounds of clicking computers as young, energetic employees wearing headphones silently communicated with the outside world. A large counter created a formidable barrier as the creative energy of the news staff enveloped the room.

"Can I help you, monsieur? It's you, Baudelaire! I didn't recognize you. Have you found work on another newspaper?"

"I have an interview tomorrow with your competition." Baudelaire was enthusiastic.

"For now, I'm still working the night shift at the Rospier Café. My friend, here, Monsieur Brad Kennedy, would like to place an ad in the personal column. He's trying to locate his dog."

"Brad, this is my old newspaper buddy, Duval Nouvelles. We worked together before I was fired. I'm afraid I took journalistic freedom too seriously. Maurice smiled.

"Hey, Baudelaire, that's a good way of putting it. You managed to make the boss pretty sore at you. Why didn't you just let him edit your work before it went to press?"

"He wanted to censor my work, so we shouldn't offend the government. I can't work that way."

Maurice pulled Brad's ad from his pocket, and leaned over the counter toward Duval. Grasping his old friend's shoulder, he whispered, "Could you do me a favor and put this ad in the paper for old times sake?"

"Don't worry, I'll take care of everything. Just fill in the form, place it in the basket on the counter and I'll make sure that it gets into tomorrow's paper. Call me next week so we can have a glass of wine at the café around the corner. Remember Lottie? She asked me to tell you she misses your jokes. I'm sorry. I have to go now. I must attend to my work. Do you see my desk? It's filling up with requests that have to be completed before the paper goes to press. Goodbye, Monsieur Kennedy. If you are a friend of Baudelaire, then you are a friend of mine. See you next week." Duval called over his shoulder as he walked toward his desk near the window.

Maurice completed the form and gave it to Brad: "White Maltese dog, named Angel. Taken from Hotel Moulin Rouge. Reward. Call: 42.13.0488. Leave message."

"Do you agree with my changes?" Maurice asked.

Brad shook his head. "But you left out the amount of the reward?"

"If the amount of euros is more than ten, you'll have every swindler in Paris calling you. Without knowing the amount, the thief will call you for the price, and then you can bargain. My brother-in-law, Père will help you when the time comes."

Brad placed the form carefully in the basket, knowing he had done all he could. He imagined the thief reading the paper and calling with the instructions of where to make the exchange. "Maurice, I hope this ad gets some response soon."

"We'll hope for the best. I must leave you now, and see to my appointment. It's quite a distance from here. Do you know what subway trains to take?"

"Yes, I've written down the route we took so I'll just retrace my steps."

"Good, I'll check with you later this evening before I go to work at the cafe. Goodbye for now." Maurice waved over his shoulder. After a short distance, he returned to Brad. Maurice spoke softly. "After you get off the metro walk quickly to the apartment and remember, don't speak to anyone."

Brad stood in front of the newspaper building and looked at his new friend crossing the street. As Maurice reached the curb he turned and waved to Brad through the stopped traffic.

The door to the rooming house opened slowly as Brad reached the top step. "Bonjour, Monsieur Kennedy. I hope everything has gone well for you." Madame Noblesse closed the door and bolted it.

"You have a visitor. He's waiting in your room.

Chapter 22

If Dogs Could Cry

*T*he town house at 61 Rue du Cirque, Embassy Row, stands formidably among the other five homes of the privileged and wealthy of Paris, yet there is one distinction that elevates this home above all others. A mystical living being is in residence, and her name is Angel.

After Angel had completed a dish of chicken she was placed on a pillow in the laundry room next to the kitchen. This would be her resting place for tonight.

Angel had been taken from everything and everyone that represented her world. Her strength and endurance had been tested, and she had persevered. With the uncertainty of her future before her, she had an unwavering faith that she and Brad would be reunited. She was one tough lady, a thoroughbred and a survivor.

I don't know where I am or where Brad is, and I'm very tired. I'll just have to think about it tomorrow, for tomorrow is another day.

Curling into her familiar bagel shaped position, she closed her eyes and went to sleep dreaming of the first days of her life. The vision of Mrs. Luna's house came drifting through the curtains of her early memories. She could see the large courtyard where her brothers and sisters played in the sunshine, protected from the road on the other side of the fence...

There's mum lying on her side in the shade of the dogwood tree with my sister trying to get some milk.

Won't she ever grow up? She's too old to nurse. We have been on solid food for weeks.

Good old dad, twelve years old and still trying to boss everyone, growling when people pick up one of us. There I am sitting next to the food bowl, my favorite place. I hope I get something different to eat when

I get adopted.

There are only three of us left from the litter, my brother, my sister and me. I would like to have a home and a companion of my own one day."

Angel was startled by the washing machine that went into its spin cycle.

Where am I?

As she looked at the snow-white appliances and walls that surrounded her, she was reminded of the bathtub where the thief had put her after taking her from the hotel room. Recalling all that had happened, a deep longing to go home overwhelmed her. Where was her customary caress that Brad would give her so many times throughout the day, and the daily scratch under the chin? And the sound of Brad's voice telling her, "Good girl."

Instinctively, Angel began a primeval howl, communicating her loneliness. It echoed throughout the laundry room, traveled down the hallway, up the stairs and into George's bedroom.

Just as instinctively, George's ears were alerted to Angel's distress call. A universal and primitive bond between a boy and his companion, repeated ever since the first domesticated dog bonded with humans.

George pushed aside his computer keyboard, knocking over his chair, and within seconds he was turning the handle on the laundry room door. With his heart pounding, George flipped the light switch, and Angel appeared. She stood erect on a pillow with dark brown eyes shinning.

Where am I? Who are you?

I'm hungry and lonely.

George took the leash from the hall table, attached it to Angel's collar, and led her through the breakfast room toward the walled garden. The housekeeper called out. "Ou vas-tu avec la chienne? As-tu fini tes leçons?"

George shouted over his shoulder, "Yes, I've finished my homework and I'm taking the dog outside to do her business. When I return, would you please have some food ready for her?"

The sound of the fountain, the coolness of the grass on her

paws, and the smell of the flowers were all reminders of her garden back in the United States. Each feature added to her feeling of longing for home.

I wish I were home with Brad. I know he wouldn't leave Paris without me. Please take me to Brad. My heart is breaking.

If dogs could cry, Angel would have been sobbing, but all she could do was lie on the grass and look up at George with great sadness.

"I know you're sad and I know that you belong to someone who is also unhappy. I wish I could keep you." George picked up Angel and stroked her fur as she looked into his eyes, continuing to communicate her longing to go home.

The lights in the garden shed a golden glow along the flagstone walkway that led to the French doors.

Several sparrows, darting about the fountain, drank and then flew off to the top of the ivy-covered wall that encircled the garden. Pale orange-pink clouds brushed across the sky reflecting the light from the sharp rays of the setting sun.

George's mother arrived home and was standing in the doorway that led into the garden. As she looked over the landscape she felt an inner calm. With thoughts of life's problems momentarily fading, she gazed at the wonder of the irradiant sunset that gave a surrealistic quality to the flowers and trees. There, near the fountain, sat her son holding his white treasure.

Marguerite's eyes caressed her son. Her responsibility to care for him, as a single parent, weighed heavily upon her. She knew, deep in her heart, that George must have his own dog. A dog would soften the loneliness he felt since his father's death.

She didn't want to intrude or to interrupt the nurturing moment that her son was experiencing with his furry companion.

"Yes, we shall find to whom the dog belongs and after we do, George, you shall have a dog of your own," his mother whispered to herself.

"George! Mon cher, it is getting dark and it's time to feed the little dog."

Madame Revier had made arrangements for a week at a hotel in the countryside of Charentes, situated on eight hundred beautiful acres of woodland and lakes. The Château Domaine Hotel looked like a storybook castle, only a few miles from the little village of Massignac where Pierre-August Renoir had painted the people of the village. The owner of the hotel had purchased a copy of one of Renoir's paintings that now hung in the grand lobby. Painted in 1873, it is titled, "Confidences". The most distinctive part of the painting is found in the far right corner of the portrait. Renoir had painted a Maltese lying on the woman's dress.

The Château Domaine was where George was conceived and later where the Reviers had spent many happy days when they were a family of three.

"Who will take care of the little white dog while we are away, mother?"

"I've given Marie the responsibility of caring for her. Marie will be taking the dog home with her for the week."

"But mother, Marie has so many cats in her house. Will they get along with the dog?"

"My darling, you worry too much. Let Marie deal with the arrangements.

"Why can't we take the dog with us?"

"No, George, I've already given Marie instructions to look after the dog and to check the newspaper each day to see if there's an advertisement for a lost dog. Hopefully the family will be found before we return home."

"Yes, mother, I understand."

Marie was looking forward to her week away from the responsibilities of coordinating madame's household. There would only be Monique, the chef, to answer the phone and make excuses for madame's absence. Marie had never denied any request from her employer. When madame asked Marie to look after the white dog, Marie agreed reluctantly. She could not anticipate how her 12 cats would react to having a dog in their home. "I will hope for the best," Marie said to herself.

Angel was lying at the top of the stairs looking down at the suitcases in the entryway and pondered the meaning of another change in her life. With her head resting on her two front paws, she sighed.

The lady and the boy are going away and I'm to stay here. I'm sure that's the plan.

Angel saw Marie coming toward her.

"Tu me bloques," Marie said as she scooped Angel from the carpet, carried her down stairs and gently positioned her on the chair next to the wall.

"You sit right here and we'll say goodbye to madame when she leaves."

You mean I'm not going on vacation too? I'm really a lot of fun on holiday trips and at parties. Everyone says so.

Marguerite appeared in the downstairs hallway followed by George. Walking over to the chair where Angel was lying, he kissed the top of her forehead.

"Au revoir, fille mystérieuse, we will be returning soon." George gave a reluctant wave.

A man in a black uniform opened the door as Marguerite and George entered the back seat of the car and made themselves comfortable for the trip to the countryside of France.

Madame Revier needed some time away from Paris to think about her future. As Chief Administrative Speech Writer for the President of France, her extraordinary writing talent was well known in the diplomatic circles. The most important speech of the year was nearly complete and would be ready for the July 14, Bastille Day, celebration.

She especially wanted some time with George, away from all responsibilities. There was also a more personal reason — a reason she could never discuss with anyone. His name was Monsieur René Bordeaux. He had been her husband's best friend and partner in their law firm. Since her husband's death, René had given a great deal of attention to both her and her son. Even though she found his attention comforting, she could not return his affection. On several occasions René had told Marguerite that she would learn to love him in time.

Marguerite felt comfortable with René and grateful for his compassion and kindness. Was he not the one who had insisted on taking care of the funeral arrangements and the transfer of accounts that pertained to her trust? She knew nothing of paying bills and signing checks. Her husband, Lamar, had taken care of all financial matters. She was never denied any amount of money for herself or for George. She had never shown an interest in the corporate law firm that had been inherited through her husband's family. In fact, she resented the amount of time the business had consumed, time that she and her husband would never be able to recapture.

René had always been her husband's best friend, and his appearance at family gatherings was taken for granted. Now that Marguerite was widowed, René felt no hindrance in asking her to marry him. He pleaded that it was one year since her husband had gone and George needed a father. He argued persuasively, after all, he was an attorney. Every excuse she shared with René would be gently erased with his logic and charm. What defense did she have? All of her friends had agreed that René was the kind of man that women desire.

Marguerite was trying desperately to think rationally for George's sake. Only it was difficult to concentrate here in Paris. Somehow finding the lost dog had taken the pressure off making a decision, and it was improving George's mood.

The moment Angel entered their home she had brought a sense of peace. George seemed more jovial and mischievous, as he once was when his father was alive. She had begun to think of her days in America when she was young and in love for the first time. She must find the owner of the little dog, for she knew George was growing very fond of his little companion.

The black Mercedes drove through the streets of Paris and on toward the highway that eventually would take them to their destination. Marguerite gazed at the large poplar trees that lined the highway as splashes of sunlight streaked through the car and across George's face as he looked out of his window.

Marguerite pushed the back of her shoes with her toes, one at a time, until each shoe fell to the floor. She began to rub her feet on the carpet. "Finally, I am beginning to relax," she thought. Resting her head against the leather upholstery, she closed her eyes. The soft hum of the road soon lulled Marguerite into a peaceful sleep where unshared dreams lay saved in time.

After finding the dog in the park she felt a sense of peace intertwined with memories from her past. Her dream revisited a time recent in her memory.

Everyone had retired for the evening. She had been sitting alone by the fireplace in her living room staring into the flames. This was the room where she shared many intimate moments with her husband, his arms around her, protecting her from all adversity.

"I was like a child. Why didn't he encourage me to become independent?" she thought. "I never wrote a check, never drove a car or went shopping for groceries. Now, I'm not only grieving for my husband but I feel as though my father has died as well."

Leaning toward the coffee table, she poured another glass of wine and then noticed that the small, white, furry dog had snuggled up next to her on the couch. Angel's head lay on Marguerite's leg, her brown eyes offering kindness. Marguerite's attention became preoccupied with Angel. "Why do I feel such a strong fondness for this small creature whom I barely know? When I look into her eyes, I sense that she could speak to me at any moment."

"What would you tell me, little one, if you were to speak? You see more deeply than I do. Is there something you see that no one else can?" Marguerite drew Angel's face toward hers.

This is a painful time in your life. There's a place of contentment within your reach. You'll find it soon, and I can help you if you let me.

A memory, wrapped in love, enveloped Marguerite in a single phrase, "I want to come home."

"Why does this phrase haunt me? For years I've heard these

words whispered in my mind. What do they mean? They comfort me, I know, but who is sending them?

Brad is my companion and we should find him. He wants to come home. When we are together, we are home. It will be a home for you too.

"This little one is looking into my soul. You see my pain. I know... I feel it. You want to help me. That is what you are saying."

Marguerite began to sob uncontrollably. Tears, suppressed by strained emotions, finally welled up from deep within.

Ever since the death of her husband she had kept her composure for George's sake. She didn't want to frighten him. When Marguerite was just a child, no older than George, she had arrived home from school one afternoon and heard her mother's screams. They were coming from inside the house. Her mother had received the news of her parent's death in an automobile accident. Marguerite ran to her room, confused and frightened. George would never be subjected to such a sight. She had promised herself that she would always be strong for George's sake.

As she picked up Angel and held her in her arms, close to her heart, she thought, "This furry white creation of God has come to comfort me. Of that, I am certain."

"Mother, Mother, we're here at the Château Domaine. You fell asleep with your head on my shoulder. I'm a little sore but I didn't want to wake you. You looked so tired. Can I help the porter with the luggage?"

"Oui mon cher, just tell the clerk at the desk we're here. And tell him we'll have our meal on the outside terrace near the garden."

The clerk at the desk leaned forward and smiled at the young man looking up at him. "My mother, Madame Marguerite Revier, has reserved a suite for one week. She wants the suite we have always occupied. Please check your records for the suite number."

"Oui, monsieur, j'ai déjà tout arrangé. Will you be having lunch on the terrace as usual?" The clerk responded with amusement.

"Yes, we shall. Please make our reservation for 1:00, and have the luggage taken to our rooms. Mother, I mean, Madame Revier would like to freshen up as soon as possible." He had spoken just as his father had always done.

George felt much older since his father had died. Life was becoming more serious, first his grandparents and now his father were gone.

On many occasions George would listen as his father gave instructions to the staff, not only at hotels, but also to their chef and housekeeper at their home in Paris. He had memorized every word that his father had said, and he imagined that his father was standing next to him as he spoke to the desk clerk a few moments ago.

As George walked away from the counter, he glanced over his shoulder to see a large painting. Hanging over the fireplace in the lounge was a portrait of a man and woman. Something in the painting looked familiar to George, only he could not determine what it was.

Walking across the lobby, George stopped a few feet away from the painting and realized what had intrigued him. "That dog, lying on the woman's dress looks like the little white dog that we found in the park," George said to himself.

Assuming his mother had already gone to their rooms, George made his way to the elevator, pressed the button, and as the doors slid open he entered. He imagined his mother relaxing in her bath, the scent of her gardenia bath salts drifting through the room.

The elevator stopped, and the two panels slid back. George ran toward the door at the end of the hall as he had done so many times before. "I shouldn't be running down the hall like a child," George said to himself. He slid the plastic card into the slot, and the door opened.

"George, did you make reservations for lunch?" Marguerite called from the bathroom as she heard him close the door.

"Yes, mother, it's for 1:00 o'clock as usual.

"Merci. You did very well."

Chapter 23

A Distant Memory

*M*arguerite Revier's father had been the French Ambassador to the United States for several years. This was an impressionable time for Marguerite. While attending Georgetown Academy she learned to speak English fluently and later many of her friends in Paris would say she spoke French with an American accent, which amused her.

While living in Washington, D.C., she learned many American customs that seemed to fit her personality. Her fondness for Americans and many traditions of the country brought back warm memories. There was one person in particular tucked away on her shelf-of-memories. Thinking of him brought a comfort that no other person could evoke. She enjoyed this collection of mystic memories, which languished between what was real and what was exaggerated over the years.

Marguerite and George arrived at the terrace café shortly before the time of their reservation. A waiter recognized them as they approached. "Bonjour, madame and monsieur. It is a pleasure to see you again."

"Bonjour, Luis. Do you have a table for us?"

"Yes, of course Madame Revier, right this way. Following the waiter, Marguerite was distracted by the view of the lake and the passing boats as they drifted across the water.

The café tables were decorated with colorful blue and white-striped umbrellas. Dark blue napkins were placed on each table, complimenting the stark white of the tablecloths. A small vase with a pink carnation was centered on each table with one sprig of fern carefully placed to one side. George held his mother's chair as she arranged herself comfortably at the table that had been set to accommodate three people.

"Merci, George, tu es bien gentil."

"Thank you, mother."

George started to sit in the chair across from his mother but then decided to move to the chair next to her, realizing that it would not be proper to sit in the chair his father had always occupied. The waiter, noticing the empty chair, looked toward the hotel entrance, expecting to see Monsieur Revier.

"Will monsieur be joining you this afternoon?"

George looked at his mother's face, waiting for her to speak. A hot, piercing reality stabbed at his young heart. Perspiration began to moisten the back of his neck. He saw his mother look toward the fountain in the center of the terrace, her eyes fixed as though on a distant memory.

Looking at the waiter, George could see that he was waiting for an answer, an answer that his mother could not provide.

"There will only be two of us for lunch. Please inform the maître d' to place us at a table for two for every meal for the rest of our vacation."

The waiter looked at George with an expression of surprise and quickly disappeared.

They sat in silence for a few moments. Feeling uneasy, George knew he had to do something. Reaching for his mother's hand, he began rotating her wedding ring in a circle.

"Mother, remember when I was a baby I would play with your gold ring like this and you would tell me that it was given to you before I was born? You said an angel took it from his finger and gave it to you and told you that as long as you wore the ring I would grow up to be handsome and strong."

George wanted desperately to reach his mother, to bring her back from her distant gaze.

"Oui, chéri, je me souviens," she said as she turned toward George, trying to smile. "And the angel's promise has been fulfilled. You are handsome and strong, but the angel forgot to tell me one thing. He forgot to tell me how intelligent, kind and thoughtful you would be. George, you are forever an amazement to me."

Marguerite reached over and gently brushed the strands of

dark brown hair from her son's forehead. Her eyes were smiling yet filled with tears.

"Mother, I would like to go sailing on the lake. I know how to use the rudder and the sail by myself. I'll wear the life jacket if you insist."

"Yes, I do insist. I may even go with you."

At the end of the meal the chocolate mousse was placed on the table. The waiter seemed embarrassed. In confiding with the maître d' he had been told of the death of Madame Revier's husband. He wished he could take back his earlier comment. He felt responsible for the awkwardness he had caused Madame Revier.

George had just completed his dessert when he noticed a red and yellow object lying at the base of the purple hydrangea bush near their table. Pushing his seat aside, he walked over to investigate. Curiosity was the most intense part of George's personality, always wanting to know the reason why things were the way they were. George had a question for every comment made to him. Now, he was curious to determine what the red and gold object under the bush could be.

"Mother, excuse me, but I want to see what that yellow thing is over there." George walked across the terrace, leaned down with his outstretched hand and grasped the object. "Mother, this looks like a dog's license."

He placed the object in his mother's hand, both examining it carefully.

"Look, it's shaped like a heart. There's a word on it and some numbers.

"George, can you read it? I can't read anything this small with out my glasses."

George held out his hand as his mother placed the heart shaped object in his palm. As he turned it over, he could see the letters printed on one side and numbers on the other. Taking it between his two fingers, he squinted.

He read, A-N-G-E-L. 437-298-2882

"Mother, *it is* a dog's license."

Chapter 24

The Gardenia

The waiter brought the bill with a gardenia. "Madame, les employés du café sont tristes á cause de votre chienne perdue."

"You are very kind, thank you. Monsieur Revier has often spoken of the wonderful service we have received. He would have been pleased to know of your sympathies. To remember my favorite flower warms my heart. Merci."

After George and his mother discussed their sailing plans, she caught the attention of the waiter. When he approached the table she asked him to look at the heart-shaped pet license.

"My son found this over there under those bushes. One of your guests must have lost it."

"Oui, madame, I can see it is a dog license with the name Angelique. Just recently we had a guest with a dog and I think he called her Angel. They left about a week ago. She was a small dog, about this size." The waiter brought his hands apart showing the approximate size.

"She had long white fur with big round eyes that would stare at you."

George turned quickly to his mother and took her hand, squeezing it tightly. "Mother, do you think this dog named Angel could be the dog we found in the park?" He leaned toward the waiter and looked at the license in his palm.

"Thank you for the information, Luis."

"George, you could be right. It is possible that Angelique is the dog we found in the park."

Marguerite walked toward the lobby, followed closely by George. Stopping at the front desk, she asked to speak to the manager.

"Excuse me, my son found this dog license on the terrace. The waiter said it belonged to one of your previous guest's dog, named Angelique.

"Of course, Madame Revier. I will check our registration." The manager typed the request for information into the hotel's computer.

"Yes, I see there was a gentleman with a dog. It was very recent."

"Do you have a forwarding address for the gentleman? Marguerite asked.

"I'm sorry, madame, we are not permitted to give personal information concerning our guests. I am sure you understand. I can tell you that the man was an American and his destination was Paris. He asked one of our desk clerks to recommend a hotel."

"Well, can you tell me what hotel was recommended? I would like to return the dog's license."

"No, madame, I don't know where he made his reservation. We always give our guest this brochure with the list of hotels that we recommend. I see here a note from the desk clerk that he did not ask for a reservation for any specific hotel. I'm very sorry I do not have more information." He placed a white and gold brochure on the counter in front of Marguerite. She tilted it toward George so he could see the extent of the recommended hotels.

"George, there are so many hotels listed on this brochure. I'll contact Marie today and ask her to call every hotel listed on the brochure. She can ask about the man with the white dog. That's all I can think of to do. Do you have any ideas, George?"

"I can telephone for you."

"Thank you, darling, but this is our time together. It's been a very sad year for us, and we've spent too much time apart. You've been very understanding and helpful. I want these days to be special. Marie will do a good job for us, you will see." Marguerite put her arm around George as they walked toward the elevator.

"I'll press the elevator button from now on mother." Marguerite bent over, and lifting his chin, kissed him gently on the cheek. He reminded her of Lamar, her late husband.

Chapter 25

Such A Menagerie

The street that Marie lived on had changed very little since her childhood. She took the same way from the metro to her home as she had when she was a girl of ten. The Sycamore trees still formed a canopy of delicious shade just as they had long ago. With a bag of groceries in one hand and Angel in a carrying case in the other, she hurried along anxious to get home to her cats.

Marie could hear the phone ringing as she put the key into the lock of her front door. Nervously she pushed the key into the lock and then reversed it while the phone rang again and again. Angel sat patiently in her blue plastic carrying kennel by the front door as Marie continued to apply more pressure. "What is wrong with this key? I know I have the correct one," she mumbled to herself.

Marie was a very hefty woman who had spent many years in the French military. She was direct, opinionated and reliable. She had been the housekeeper for Marguerite's parents before Marguerite inherited the house on Embassy Row. She was retained in service, as was Monique, the chef.

Most importantly, Monique and Marie were like family to Marguerite. George especially liked Marie. He occasionally complained of her gruff ways, but he was convinced of her loyalty. He asked Marie to help him get a bicycle on his sixth birthday. They devised a plan to persuade his parents.

On that special day, while everyone sang Happy Birthday, Marie brought his new bike into the living room. She promised his parents that she would be responsible for seeing that George rode his bicycle only on the restricted street in front of their home. This collaborative effort would bind them together in friendship.

With a burst of strength, reminiscent of her days as a drill sergeant in the South of France, Marie leaned her full weight against the solid oak door and it flew open. The key was left swinging in the lock as she dashed toward the small table in the hall and picked up the receiver. "Allô, Allô." Marie shouted into the phone.

"Marie, I knew you must be home. This is Madame Revier. Yes, I am still at the château with George. La petite chienne blanche s'entend bien avec les chats." Just as Marguerite finished asking about the white dog's reaction to meeting Marie's cats, Marie looked at the open door where she had left Angel.

The kennel was gone.

Marie felt a rush of desperation. Dropping the phone on the table, she stood for a few seconds in shock. With her years of experience as a Black Belt still fresh in her mind, she lunged toward the front door and down the short flight of stairs to the sidewalk. Using her military training she formulated a plan of action. As she looked in every direction, scanning the terrain for the enemy she saw a man running down the sidewalk carrying a dog's kennel.

"Ah-ha, le voilà." Marie resembled a tank as she ran after a stout man in a grey overcoat. The thief, not aware of his pursuer, lumbered down the sidewalk carrying the blue kennel that held Angel prisoner. Stopping momentarily, he looked about, choosing what he thought to be the best escape route. Not taking the time to look back to see if he was being pursued, he thrust forward, jostling Angel from front to back in her carrying case.

I miss those quiet days resting in the garden.

Is this guy related to the lady who put me into a laundry cart?

Two women standing on the street corner waiting for the light to change were pushed aside by the thief. Just as he stepped off the curb, Marie appeared beside him. She wrenched the kennel from his hand and pushed it safely to one side. Pushing him onto the concrete, she jumped into the air landing on the thief's back in the middle of the street. The traffic came to a halt as horns honked, piercing the surrounding buildings and echoing off the walls.

With her right knee in the middle of the man's back, she shouted, "You pig!" She proceeded to use every curse word she'd learned during her military career. Pulling the man from the street, she pushed him toward the street lamp next to the curb where Angel lay in her blue kennel.

Let him have it, Marie.

As the traffic resumed, Marie twisted the man's collar tightly around his throat, pointed toward the boulevard in the distance and shouted in the thief's face, "If I ever see you on this street again, I'll throw you into the river." The thief rubbed his nose, examined the blood that dripped from his fingers, and limped away.

Exhausted, Marie took Angel from her case and carried her back to the house. "I'm sorry little one for the upset you've had. You'll have a pleasant meal and a good night's sleep, I'll see to that, you can be sure."

Although scrupulously clean, Marie's house had deteriorated over the years from the use of hundreds of children. Certainly not her own, she had never married. She considered her cats as her children. Her home had been an orphanage for over one hundred years before Marie's family purchased it. The peeling wallpaper and the frayed rugs had become familiar pieces of her surroundings, and there were no plans to alter anything. Of course, if there were ever any additional money, Marie would like some changes, if only for her babies, the feline variety.

Marie sat Angel on the couch as she called her twelve cats from the various rooms of the house.

"Come my little darlings and meet our new houseguest."

The tinkling of bells was heard coming from throughout the rooms and halls, each cat wearing a bell that made a distinctly different sound. One very large cat made a steady, consistent ding, ding, ding, as she wiggled her overweight frame up and down. A calico kitten sounded like a doorbell chime playing a vigorous tune.

It sounds like Santa's reindeer.

Marie had named each cat and although several looked very

similar, she could tell them apart by the sound of their bell.

Shopping one day for Marguerite, she found a store near the train station of Porte de Saint Cloud that sold very unusual antique collections. She was surprised and delighted to discover that a beautiful fur-lined box, sitting in the window, held twelve miniature bells, each the size of a large thimble. She asked the shopkeeper if each made the same sound...

"Madame, each bell has a distinctly different sound. This collection was used as a musical instrument by one of the most famous musicians in France, Cleo de Merode. Surely madame, you've heard of him? He played these bells throughout Europe. Of course that was over one hundred years ago."

When Marie saw the price, she knew it would take her a long time to save the money to purchase such a collection. Surprisingly, when Marguerite learned of Marie's desire to have the collection for her cats, she purchased them for a Christmas gift.

The concert of bells continued to float through the air as the twelve cats hopped, walked, crawled, leaped, and climbed about the house playing and annoying one another.

Angel had never experienced such a menagerie of feline musicians. Looking down from the couch, she was intrigued by the spectacle.

This reminds me of Cirque du Soleil.

Marie walked into the kitchen to prepare a meal for her cats and for Angel while her frozen Mexican dinner was thawing in the microwave oven.

Five of her cats were meandering about the room making pleading sounds for their dinner. The other seven were missing, and so was Angel.

Marie finished separating the chicken mixture into 13 bowls and made her familiar call-to-dinner sound she had always made. "Venez chatons, kitties, kitties," Marie repeated.

It was most unusual to have the meals ready, and not to have all 12 cats waiting.

She searched through the house, opening every door, calling out their names. On her way back to the kitchen she looked at the table that had been shoved in the corner. Leaning forward, she looked under and saw Angel with an odd look on her face.

"Do you know where my babies have gone?"

Angel looked toward the kitchen door that led to the back garden. The focus of Angel's attention was a pet door with the usual plastic flap that gave access to the outside. As Marie approached the door, she could see that the safety latch had been pushed down. Outside, crowded around the entrance to the pet door, were the seven missing cats. "How did this opening become locked?" Marie asked herself.

I did it. These cats are driving me crazy. I needed a rest. Please take off the bells.

Marie pressed the latching device and the frosted plastic door slid up allowing the cats to enter.

"Voilà," Marie said as she placed the 12 cat bowls next to the kitchen wall.

"And this one is for our guest, mademoiselle doggy." Marie gently shoved the bowl under the kitchen table where Angel sat, making her separation from the cats obvious.

"You will soon get acquainted with my 12 babies. They are adorable. Jacques, you did not finish your food. Are you not feeling well? Georgette, don't eat Colette's food. Finish your own."

Marie walked about the kitchen picking up one cat after another, as a mother cat would examine her kittens. When the cats completed their meal, she placed each bowl in the sink.

Glancing over at Angel with her head resting on the floor, she noticed that Angel had placed her paws close to her ears.

"You've never had a cat friend, have you? I never had a cat friend either until one night someone dropped a kitten over my fence. I heard the poor thing crying. It was cold that night. I couldn't leave her outside all alone in the dark. That was Colette. She is still very shy and allows the others to steal her food. She is my own sweet Colette, so affectionate and caring. It was not long before another cat was left in my yard. Why do people throw away their pets like old shoes? How cruel. Now I have 12 cats and they depend on me for a warm home and some food."

Marie looked at Angel as she told her story and Angel responded with a sympathetic look.

You have a kind heart. God bless you Marie. And thanks for the meal, too. And by the way, my stomach is not used to cat food.

When Angel completed her meal, Marie picked her up and carried her to the dining room where she laid a soft afghan under the credenza.

"This is where you'll spend the evening, in privacy and quiet."

She knew what I wanted.

Marie closed the door that connected the dining room with the kitchen and walked toward the stairs leading to her bedroom. As she climbed each step, her 12 cats followed, each one hopping over the other to gain the lead. With bells ringing, they talked to each other in their familiar meowing sounds.

In her bedroom, Marie could see the lights of the busy street below. She brushed the curtains aside and looked up above the rooftops. Off in the distance, the sky was growing darker and more threatening with impending rain. Lightning began to streak across the sky as the sound of thunder followed quickly after.

The cats dashed around the room excitedly until Marie gathered them up in her arms in twos and threes and carried them to her bedroom closet where a large quilt had been mounded in one corner.

"This will be your own safe place away from the noise until the storm passes, just as we have always done before."

Marie took her nightgown from the hook and walked toward the bathroom down the hall. Just as she reached the door, the phone began to ring. Returning to her bedroom, she reached over toward the nightstand, and picked up the receiver. "Allô. Allô. Oui Madame Revier."

"Bonjour…c'est vous?" Madame questioned.

"Oui, c'est moi," Marie answered with apprehension, realizing that the last time they spoke she dropped the phone abruptly to chase the thief.

"Marie, what on earth happened? One minute we were talking

and then I heard a loud crash and you were gone."

Marie decided to be evasive and not to explain what really happened, fearing that Marguerite would not trust her in the future.

"Madame, I am terribly sorry. There was an emergency. A neighbor wanted me to help her with her invalid sister who had fallen in a hole outside my home. It was a very big hole and I had to borrow a rope to tie around her waist and..."

"Marie, never mind telling me the story. I haven't much time. I'm just glad that you're all right. How is the little white puppy doing with so many cats in your house?"

"She is asleep in the dining room, alone. She's very comfortable. Quite happy I would say."

"Marie, I have a project for you. I would like you to call a list of hotels I'm going to give to you. Do you have a pencil and paper?"

"Je serai de retour à tout à l'heure," Marie paused. "I have the paper and pencil, please go on."

"You are to ask for the manager of the hotel. Now here are the questions you must ask.

Number one, has an American with a white dog stayed at their hotel in the last two weeks?

Number two, is he still there? If he is, call me and give me the name of the hotel. If he has left, ask if they know where he's gone.

Est-ce que je parle trop vite?," Marguerite inquired.

"No, madame. You are not speaking too fast."

"Now, I will give you the names and phone numbers of the hotels. Are you ready?"

"Oui, madame."

Marguerite read the list slowly as Marie wrote the names of the hotels and the phone numbers.

"We will be arriving home on Friday, no later than one o'clock in the afternoon. If there is any information about the American you must call me at once. Thank you for helping me, Marie."

"I'm very happy to help, but why am I asking about an American and his dog?"

"I'm sorry Marie. In my excitement, I didn't tell you what

happened at the Château Domaine today. George found a license for a dog named Angelique, and there was an American who stayed here a week ago, just before we found the white dog in the park. He left the Château and we think he has gone to Paris. It could be that Angel and the white dog that is staying in your house are one and the same. So you see, we must find the American."

"And Marie, do look in the newspaper every day to see if there is an ad in the personal column for a lost dog that fits the description of our dog. I'm hoping that the one we've found is Angelique and that we can find the American and re-unite them."

The thunder and lightning that occurred earlier in the evening interrupted the quiet of Marie's bedroom.

"What was that noise, Marie?"

"We are having a summer storm. The cats are frightened but the dog seems to be able to sleep through the noise. At least, I haven't heard her bark."

"Would you make sure she is comfortable before you retire? She must miss her friend very much and we do want to look after her as best we can."

"Oui, madame. Je le ferai," Marie assured her.

"Bonne nuit, Marie."

"Bonne nuit, madame. Ne vous inquiétez pas! I will take charge of everything and report to you directly."

As soon as Marie put the receiver down, she wrapped her robe around her shoulders and walked barefoot down the carpeted stairs toward the dining room. The twelve panels of glass in the doors that led into the dining room were covered with a sheer white curtain that softened the age of the doors and made them appear newer, with little evidence of the chipped paint. Marie gently pushed the curtain aside and looked toward the credenza, under which Angel was lying, now very much asleep, or so it appeared to Marie.

This house is noisy; with all the banging and pounding, how can anyone sleep? What's she doing up there?

Angel didn't realize that the noise was coming from outside the house.

Marie, reassured that Angel was not frightened, climbed the

stairs to her room, and placing her bathrobe on the footstool by her bed, she prepared herself for a long-needed rest from the exhausting activities of the day. As she adjusted the covers around her legs she felt the soreness in her knee, the knee that landed on the thief's back while he was lying in the street. "It feels good to know that I'm still able to take down the enemy." Marie massaged her bruise and smiled with satisfaction.

The hallway was empty of all sounds except the ticking of the intricately carved grandfather clock that dominated the wall by the dining room door.

Soon the storm had passed over Paris. In the silence of her bedroom, Marie was breathing deeply with an occasional snore that sounded very much like water going down the drain of a bathtub. This was an odd characteristic that had been a source of teasing during her tour in the French Army.

There was a soft, continuous sound coming from the bedroom closet, where Marie's 12 cats were purring with satisfaction. Her babies had full stomachs and a secure resting place for the evening.

Outside her bedroom, the narrow hallway, the carpeted stairs and the old heavily carved furniture created a restful atmosphere.

At the top of the stairs two glowing eyes appeared, slowly and mysteriously, looking down between the banisters in the direction of the dining room.

A dim light spread up the stairs from the hallway table and illuminated the restless creature that had been observing every one since Marie had entered her home. The creature knew the 12 cats very well but didn't understand the new arrival. The white one with the long tail looked very strange and smelled as dangerous as the cats.

Chapter 26

She Is An Angel

Silently, the strange being descended the stairs, step by step, until it reached the hallway leading to the front door. With the cunning instinct of the evolutionary genes that are unique to this creature, he bolted toward the wall and disappeared. The elusive being was now hidden within the recesses of the wall, running through the dark passageway toward the item he had been working on for several nights.

The electrical wires of the old house had deteriorated with age and now he was going to finish the task. He continued to chew vigorously, pausing only when he heard a clicking sound coming from the wire. Suddenly, sparks flew toward the dry and brittle papers that someone had stuffed into the walls for insulation ninety years before. A bright light illuminated the interior space. Instinctively the rat dashed down the wall toward one of his many escape routes, leaving the smoldering fire far behind.

I know I heard something in the hall. And I smell a strange odor. It smells like something that doesn't belong.

Angel left her comfortable enclosure under the credenza to investigate. She sniffed the crack between the pocket doors for a clue as to the creature's identity. Before Angel could determine its species, the odor began to fade. After a few minutes her eyes grew heavy and her body relaxed. Soon, her breathing became more regular as she fell asleep by the door.

Sensing danger, Angel was awakened by an odor. The smell of the rat was now replaced by a stronger odor that was life threatening.

Angel responded by taking action. Placing her two paws in the small space between the dining room pocket doors, she forced them apart, pushing her head through. Smoke drifted into the dining room. Angel spread her body flat on the carpet and began to crawl toward the stairs.

I know this smoke is coming from a fire and that means danger.

Angel knew what she must do…escape. But her instinct told her that her first responsibility was to help the rest of her pack which was, even if temporarily, Marie and her twelve cats.

Angel climbed the stairs, stopping periodically to rub the smoke from her eyes and nose. When she reached Marie's bedroom, she began to scratch vigorously on the door. With no response, Angel barked loudly.

Marie appeared in the doorway holding her dressing gown to her nose.

"My God, there's a fire in the house!" Marie shouted. She pulled Angel into the room, and quickly closed the door. Grabbing the phone, she dialed the operator, reported the fire and gave her address. Marie ran to the closet, and flung the door open. With the determination of a mother lion, Marie picked up two of her cats from the closet and ran to the window of her bedroom that overlooked the lawn. With two quick movements the window was opened and the cats went sailing toward the soft grass below. Marie didn't wait to see them land on their feet with stunned looks of surprise but returned to the closet to retrieve two more and out the window they flew, again and again, until the last two were safely outside.

A siren was heard coming from the distance, growing louder as it approached. Bright red lights, flashing from the emergency vehicles, were reflected off the windows of the buildings across the street. Standing at the window with Angel in her arms, she saw a fireman on the end of a ladder balanced on the window ledge.

"Turn around madame, and back down the ladder. Is that a cat you're holding? You can throw her to the four men holding the net. She'll not be hurt. You must do as I say. You cannot grasp the ladder safely if you're carrying an animal."

"I'm sorry my little Angelique, I must do as I'm told." Marie kissed Angel on the forehead and threw her toward the men who were holding the net.

What the heck is going on? Wait a minute can we discuss this firsttttttt?

After Marie's feet touched the grass, she ran to the fireman who was holding Angel in his arms. "Thank you monsieur, I will take the dog." She began to circulate through the crowd asking people to help find her cats.

"Pourriez vous m'aider à trouver mes chats," she pleaded several times. The neighbors responded by searching the yard, calling for the cats. "Here kitty, kitty, kitty!"

A fireman, with three cats in his arms, appeared from the bushes, and placed them in an empty container that held additional fire equipment.

"Tenez, les voilà, madame," The fireman said proudly.

"No, no, there are nine more of my babies. We must continue looking."

"Encore, neuf?" He walked toward the back of the house shaking his head in disbelief.

Placing Angel on the lawn, Marie was startled to see her dash toward the large magnolia tree next to the corner of the house. Fearful that Angel was running away, Marie ran after her. She stopped at the foot of the tree, and saw Angel looking up.

There they are, up in the tree branches.

"Good girl, you've found them."

The fireman placed a ladder at the base of the tree and climbed up while two others held a net. Wearing heavy leather gloves, the fireman grabbed each cat, one by one, and tossed them into the safety net.

A young man who had followed the fire trucks to the burning house ran toward Marie, and began taking pictures.

"What are you doing, monsieur?"

Pardonnez – moi, madame, I am a reporter for L' Humanite newspaper. Could I have a statement from you? What caused the fire."

"I'm very sorry, monsieur, I have no idea what started the fire, but I can tell you who saved our lives."

"There was more than one person saved from the fire?"

"No, I mean my twelve babies. They were saved also."

"Twelve babies!" the reporter shouted with growing interest.

"My twelve cats. They are my babies."

"Well, then, who saved you from the fire?" The reporter asked with disappointment.

"This little white dog saved us. C'etait un miracle, I tell you, a miracle. She is an angel. That's what she is, an angel."

"Tell me what happened?"

As Marie began to tell her story, a large woman with a red scarf tied around her head, wearing pink fuzzy house slippers came running toward her.

"Marie, Marie, I heard about the fire and I ran right over."

Claudis, Marie's friend, was breathing heavily as she placed her arm over Marie's shoulder. "Who is this man?"

"He's a newspaper reporter. He wants to know about the fire."

"Well, I'm taking you home with me. You can't go back in there. Bring your cats with you. Où avez–vous trouvé cette chienne blanche?"

"Monsieur reporter, I need time to think. Follow us and I'll tell you what I know, but first I must have a strong cup of coffee."

Chapter 27

A Mature Woman

The following morning a stack of complimentary *L' Humanite'* newspapers lay on the round table in the lobby of the Château Domaine.

Madame Revier was coming from her morning bath when George called from the other room. "Mother, do you want me to order room service or would you rather eat at the outside café this morning?"

"Would you mind if we ate on our own terrace, chéri?"

"No, I'd rather have breakfast here and get an early start sailing on the lake."

"All right George, I'll have my usual American style breakfast. Please order for us."

Sitting at her dressing table Marguerite looked into the mirror studying the lines that seemed to appear overnight. A mature woman, she felt herself rushing toward middle age much faster than she anticipated. It comforted her to remember her late husband's compliments. "You look stunning, darling. I'm so fortunate to have your love."

Startled, she heard a voice on the other side of the door. "Room service."

"Entrez vous, s'il vous plaît," George called from the terrace.

Marguerite pushed aside the curtains that led to the terrace and walked to the breakfast table. George began laughing as he saw his mother. "Mother, what are you wearing?"

"Why, a dress, of course."

Continuing to laugh, George walked around his mother, examining her closely.

"You can't wear a dress sailing. And you have on high heels too."

The waiter entered the room.

"This way please. We will have breakfast on the terrace." George pointed the way.

After the waiter arranged the items on the table, he walked toward the door. George continued his comments on his mother's clothing, but was interrupted.

"Shh, George, wait until the man leaves." George nodded, and the door closed silently behind the waiter.

"So, you think your mother is over-dressed?"

"Yes, mother, I do. I know this will be your first time on a sailboat but you've seen movies where the ladies are wearing tennis shoes and slacks and their hair is covered with a baseball cap. There's going to be wind and I'm afraid you're going to get a bit wet. After all, we're going to be on a sailboat with water spraying in our faces."

"Oh, I guess you're right. I'll change after we've had breakfast. I suppose if you are going to teach me to sail, I'll have to be a cooperative student."

"Yes, mother, you should."

"Oui, monsieur teacher."

They both laughed.

Colorful boats glided by in the distance while they enjoyed their breakfast.

"One of those sailboats could be the one we reserved for today's outing." George passed the butter to his mother.

"Just perfect, George, perfect. You ordered everything I like for our American breakfast, two eggs, sunny side up, and one strip of bacon."

After eating a portion of her eggs, she opened the newspaper that came on the tray with their meal.

Folding back the front page, she noticed a picture of a white dog surrounded by cats.

"George. Look at this picture!"

Standing behind his mother, he read the caption under the picture.

"Maltese Dog Saves Woman and Her 12 Cats."

"George, would you read the article to me? My glasses are in the other room?"

"Of course mother. Let's see. It says that: Marie Laturea, awakened by her little white dog some time after 11:00 o'clock last night, was saved from her burning home along with her twelve cats. Madame Laturea said that the dog was found last week in the Grand Park Rue de la Paix, near Embassy Row. The dog is in Madame Laturea's temporary care until the person who has lost her can be found. Madame Laturea said she thinks the dog's name is Angelique. It is suspected that the fire was started by a rodent that had been chewing on the electrical wires inside the wall."

"Mother, I think we should leave today for home!"

"But, George, you wanted to go sailing. We could leave early tomorrow morning or even later today. Marie is probably at our home safe with the dog. I'll get in touch with her and see what plans she has for herself in the meantime."

"Yes, I suppose that would work." George was concerned. "We should be leaving for our sailing date right after you call Marie."

George brought the phone to his mother on the terrace and sat beside her as she instructed the operator to connect her with Paris.

"Allô, Allô, is that you Marie?"

"Yes, madame, I'm here and the dog is with me. I will be staying here until you return. My friend is taking care of my little ones and my house is being taken care of by the insurance company. Maybe now I'll have some new carpets and wallpaper."

Angel sat by Marie as she spoke into the phone.

Tell her that I want George to hurry back so I can have someone to play with.

Angel began tugging on Marie's shoelace, unraveling the bow.

Tell her my picture is in the paper.

Angel continued to pull on Marie's shoelace and making growling sounds.

"Yes, madame, we saw the paper. It came this morning. I'll have everything ready when you arrive. No, I haven't looked at the personal ads yet. I'll do that right after I feed Angélique, and I'll tell the cook that you'll be here by early evening. Thank you, madame, for saying so. I'm happy to do what I can. Don't worry about us, we are perfectly well," Marie reassured Marguerite as she hung up the phone.

I'm not perfectly well. I'm starving. A steak would be nice.

Angel sat staring, wagging her tail.

George and Marguerite ran to the pier as the cool wind blew over the lake. "This wind will fill our sail with speed, mother." George ran toward the pier to untie the rope of their rented sailboat.

"Wait, I'll hold on to the boat while you untie the rope!"

Marguerite told George to reserve the bright red sailboat because it stood out among the array of white ones. With little persuasion, George put on his life jacket and helped Marguerite with hers. Marguerite was given the job of tightening and loosening the sail while George took charge of the rudder.

With the wind pushing against the bright red sail, the boat glided easily through the water. Marguerite was surprised to discover how much she enjoyed the quiet strength of the azure blue lake. Letting her hand float upon the surface, she felt the coolness of another time, another lake.

There was a young man walking beside her, tossing pebbles. They laughed as the stones skipped across the water and disappeared. Several miniature sailboats moved about the lake, remote controlled by children seated along the water's edge. She laughed when she remembered they had paid a child to use his controls to move the boat around the lake.

"Mother, why are you laughing?"

"I was remembering when I was in high school and a friend and I sailed one of those battery controlled miniature sailboats."

"What is funny about that?"

"Well, George, a big wind came up very suddenly and blew the boat over. My friend had to wade out to get it with all of his clothes on."

Marguerite continued to laugh.

Chapter 28

Life Is Pure Gold

*A*s he reached the top of the stairs, Brad could see light coming from the space under the bottom of the door to his room. Père Masquer, the cab driver, was sitting by the window in a chair leaning back on the two legs while resting his feet on the ledge of the window. He jumped up quickly as Brad entered, "Bonjour, Monsieur Kennedy. I have some information for you which will put a smile on your face."

Brad sat on the edge of the bed as Père picked up the chair, turned it around and straddled it, leaning his arms on the back of the chair.

"I have made several inquires about the woman who posed as a housekeeper at the hotel. She has done this many times before, but I can handle her." Père pushed his hat to the back of his head.

"Are you saying that you've made contact with the thief?"

"My connections have assured me that she will call this evening by eight o'clock tonight. It's five now. Have you eaten?"

"No, but I'm not very hungry. I would like to know more about this thief." Père stood up, and pushed the chair aside.

"There is no more to tell, my friend. I'll be leaving now and return with something to eat. When I come back we can talk about my fee. Don't worry, I charge the same rates as when I drive the tourists around Paris."

"What about the money for the thief? How much will she want for the return of my dog?"

"Ne vous inquiétez pas au sujet de cette femme. I will take care of everything."

Père placed his hand on Brad's shoulder. "I want to tell you something I learned in prison. When we worry, we waste time. Remember, life is pure gold and time a thief, oui?"

Père pressed Brad's shoulder reassuringly, and walked toward the door. "Get some rest. You look worse than me when I have to see my parole officer."

The door closed behind Père just as Brad reached for one of the pillows, pushed it under his head, and fell into a deep sleep.

Chapter 29

In Competition With Each Other

*A*s Marie and Angel entered 61 Rue du Cirque the cool interior was filled with the fragrance of gardenias, a flower that would always hold the memory of a lost love for Marguerite.

Monique, the family chef and Marie, the housekeeper, were considered more family than servants. They were a great comfort to Marguerite since her parents' and husband's death. They provided the familiarity and security for both George and Marguerite.

"Viens avec moi ma chérie Angélique, I have a surprise for you in the kitchen." Marie led Angel down the hall and into the brightly lit black and white tiled kitchen. It was natural for Marie to include her celebrated friend, Angel, as a new member of the family on Embassy Row. After all, she saved the lives of her twelve cats.

Monique stood four inches shorter than Marie although in circumference they were equal. Each had learned to tolerate the other in what became an ongoing competitive tradition of insults.

Marie was proud of her military service in the French Army and made references to it on a daily basis. Monique, on the other hand, took every opportunity to boast of her invented six years in the French Foreign Legion, "riding over the sand dunes of Africa." Each one, in competition with the other, created the persona of efficiency, while camouflaging the fondness they felt for one another. Even though the rivalry was constant, each one would extol the virtues of the other if either one was criticized by Madame Revier.

Marie opened the refrigerator, took out a piece of filet mignon and placed it on the granite cutting board.

That's my favorite cut of meat.

Angel's tail continued to wag while she pranced about the black and white squares.

Monique leaned over the cutting board.

"What are you doing with that piece of meat? C'est pour le diner de madame," Monique ordered.

Is there going to be a fight?

Marie took a carving knife from the drawer and stabbed the filet mignon. Extending her arm toward Monique, she displayed the piece of steak suspended on the end of the carving knife. "Madame can eat something else for dinner! This little Angelique saved my babies. She will be rewarded this day for her bravery! If there were a French medal for dogs, she would be wearing it around her neck." Marie spoke as though she were addressing a crowd. "There should be a statue in her honor in the Palais de la Justice aux Champs Elysées."

Would someone just please put the meat down where I can eat it?

Marie continued to speak in French, rapidly extolling all the virtues she could conjure to describe how she felt about Angel. Turning toward the stove she dropped the meat into the frying pan creating a sizzling sound as the succulent aroma filled the kitchen and Angel's nose.

Chapter 30

The King And The Dove

George and his mother lingered for a while in the hotel lobby after they returned from sailing on the lake. One of the popular additions to the Château Domaine was the large aviary in the solarium off the lobby. As Marguerite paused to admire the white doves she noticed that one of the birds was sitting on a nest.

"George, do you remember the story I read to you when you were five years old? It was called the "The King and the Dove." The king wanted a chestnut tree to complete his collection and so he sent his guard to remove the tree from a farmer's garden. Remember, the farmer told the king's guard that he could take the chestnut tree but what should he tell her when she comes each year to build her nest in its branches?" Marguerite glanced at her son wistfully.

"Yes, mother, I remember. I also recall the ending. It went like this…The king said, 'Take this message to the farmer. He may keep the chestnut tree, for a home is important to every living being and not even a king should dishonor this trust.'"

The hotel manager came over to George and his mother as they stood in front of the aviary.

"Madame Revier, your driver is ready to take you to Paris. Your bags have already been placed in the car. Would you please accept this gift on behalf of the staff?" The hotel manager bowed slightly.

"It's kind of you to remember my fondness for gardenias." Marguerite smelled the fragrant blossoms and smiled.

"Au revoir, madame." "Au revoir monsieur." Marguerite's chauffeur placed the luggage in the trunk of the car and held the door open for Marguerite and George who took their places in the quiet luxury of its leather interior. "Mother, I had a good time sailing this afternoon. You stayed dry until the very end." George laughed.

"Yes George I did, only I rather liked the cold water on my face. It reminded me of the last part of my facial at the Dufont Salon."

"Mother, you're a good sport. You had fun today, didn't you?"

"Of course, I did. We'll do it again before the weather changes."

As the car pulled onto the highway, they noticed a barrier placed in front of the main road.

"What's wrong? Why have you stopped? And why is there a barrier in the road?"

"I don't know," said the driver. "There's a sign next to the road that is pointing the other way. I'll see what it says, madame."

The driver returned to the car with a troubled look on his face. "Madame, there's a problem on the main road. The Tour de France cycling race began today. I didn't know it would begin this soon. I knew we were near Carcassonne, where the race begins, but I thought it was starting tomorrow. I am terribly sorry. You must not concern yourself. I know the back roads to Paris. It will take longer, of course but I can do it. I'll have you in Paris by tonight."

"Well, all you can do is your best. We'll make it an adventure, won't we, George?"

"Right. Are you going to call Marie and tell her we'll be late?"

"Here's the phone George, you can make the call. Tell her to put some soup aside for us.

Marguerite leaned forward and tapped the driver's shoulder. "What time will we arrive in Paris, taking the back roads?"

"It's hard to say, but I would guess we should arrive in Paris no later than midnight."

"Oh, dear, that long?"

Chapter 31

Cimetière du Père-Lachaise

*P*ère drove away from Madame Noblesse's rooming house leaving Brad alone in his room to wonder about the events that would take place. Tonight they would receive a call from the thief.

Brad found it difficult to close out the events of the day so that sleep could enter. He was exhausted, yet anxious for Angel's return. In the darkened room Brad was at last asleep, drifting further and further into a world that emerged from his childhood. His disturbing dream would once again revisit him…

"Do not make me call you one more time, young man! We're leaving right now!" Brad's father's angry voice ascended the stairs from the front door of the vacation cottage in the White Mountains of New Hampshire. "Thirty seconds. And I mean thirty seconds."

Brad crawled from under his bed. Tiny wasn't there. He raced into his parents' room and dove under their bed. He and Tiny had passed several rainy afternoons playing hide and seek, surely the little terrier was hiding.

Now desperate, Brad shouted. "This isn't a game, Tiny. Come!" He heard the engine of the family station wagon in the driveway. They had finished loading the car almost an hour earlier. He continued to call. "Tiny! Tiny, come on, we have to go!"

Tiny didn't come.

Racing down the stairs he pushed the front door aside and ran to his mother who stood anxiously by the open door. Throwing his arms around her, he pleaded, "We can't leave without Tiny! Please, Mom, make Dad wait." His mother stood with her arms to her side, feeling helpless.

"Get in the car, right now. We're leaving," his father ordered, leaning out of the window as he slipped the car into gear. Resigned, Brad took one final glance at the cabin and called, "Tiny!" The dog's name caught in his throat as he uttered the word.

With little hope of success, he turned and trudged to the car's back door, pulled it open and, after one final, desperate look he forced himself to climb into the back seat. The car pulled away.

Brad fastened his seat belt and then looked out the window hoping to catch a glimpse of Tiny.

The car bounced down the rutted driveway and out onto the highway. Brad unbuckled his seat belt and knelt backwards on the seat. Looking out the window, and not seeing Tiny, Brad was struck by the terror of their separation. "Mom, Dad, we can't go without Tiny. We just can't! We have to find him." As he said the words he spotted a small black and white shape, off in the distance, racing along the shoulder of the road. "Dad, Dad, stop! Stop! I see Tiny! Stop!" The little terrier was trying to catch up to the car as it sped down the highway.

"That dog is too much trouble," said his father. "I've had it with that animal. It's time somebody else takes care of him."

His mother sighed, and said gently, "Somebody will find him. He'll find a home on one of the farms. Wouldn't that be nice? He'd love it on a farm."

"Stop! Stop! Tiny can't run that fast," he pleaded through sobs of anguish. "Mom, make Dad stop! We have to go back!" He kept begging them to turn the car around. However, both sat silently in the front seat, a world away from their son.

Several hours later, they arrived home to a dark and unwelcoming house. The boy sat in silence, his eyes aged with sadness. His parents looked at each other, shrugged, and entered the house.

Twenty minutes later, his mother came back out to the garage and opened the back door of the van.

"Why are you still in the car? Come in and have some supper." Sitting alone in despair, he would not speak a word for days. It would be years before light would penetrate the darkness of that day.

No one mentioned Tiny again.

Each day, for the rest of that year, the young boy rode his bike to the edge of town. There, he would stand by the roadside looking off in the distance as the sun disappeared behind the foothills. The wind pushed against his tears as his words disappeared into the darkness.

"Come home. Tiny, please come home."

In his darkened room, Brad awakened hearing a voice calling in the distance. "Angel come home…Angel come home."

A knock at the door extinguished his nightmare as he sat up and called out, "Come in!"

Père entered, turning on the ceiling florescent light that illuminated the room with its harsh glow.

"Monsieur, I have brought the newspaper with your ad and something for you to eat."

Brad opened the newspaper and turned to the personals section looking for his advertisement. "Thank you, Père, I really appreciate all that you're doing for me and I'm deeply grateful."

Père placed a cup of coffee and a croissant on the table. "Eat! The phone call should come at any moment."

"Phone call?"

"Yes, a call from the thief." Père stood by the foot of the bed unbuttoning his black leather jacket.

Brad finished one half of the sandwich and most of the coffee when the phone rang in the downstairs hall. Both men left the room and were soon at the bottom of the stairs where Madame Noblesse stood holding the phone.

"I think this is the call you were expecting." She handed the phone to Père as Brad leaned on the wall with his hand on the top of the coin slot.

Père spoke rapidly in French while Brad pieced together what he could, hearing only half of the conversation.

The conversation concluded, a look of determination came over Père's face. "We have her. She wants to make a deal. We'll meet her at the Cimetère du Père-Lachaise. She'll be at the tomb of Chopin in one hour. Let's go!"

The cab moved through the darkening streets of Paris, around the Arc de Triomphe, toward the Place de la Nation and on to the Boulevard de Menilmoitant where they stopped in front of the most famous cemetery in all of Europe. Most of the celebrated French writers, musicians and people of wealth from many nations are buried here. The two men walked toward the enormous ornamental iron gates. A metal chain restricted their entry into this formidable depository of the dead.

"But the gates are locked." Brad was disappointed.

Père took a flashlight from his pocket and shone it through the iron bars, turning it off and on four times in succession. In a few minutes a tall man in a wrinkled grey uniform appeared from behind a tree. He slowly unwound the chain and pushed the gate open.

The darkness of the cemetery was intensified by the silence. Only the crunching sound of the gravel beneath their feet was evidence of the two intruders. Brad turned and looked back at the gate where only a few minutes earlier he had been standing. The chain had been secured, locking him in the cemetery. The guard had disappeared.

"Are you wondering where the guard has gone?" Père asked Brad. "Malersh is a strange man. He has been guarding the Cimetière du Père-Lachaise for over thirty years and his father before him. He keeps his own council, does not speak with anyone and no one knows where he lives. He may even live here in one of these stone mausoleums."

"Did the thief say she was bringing Angel?'

"Everything is arranged. She wants 1,000 Euro and Angel is yours."

Walking past the burial headstones, they paused in front of a monument dedicated to a martyred young French girl of the Resistance Movement during the Second World War. An oval picture of an attractive girl in a peasant's dress was attached to the monument.

Père made the sign of the cross. "Look at her pretty face, so young. She had the heart of a lion and the faith of an angel. Now, we go to meet a woman with neither a heart nor faith."

Brad looked at the picture of the young girl that adorned the stone monument and his eyes grew sad.

"How much further are we going?" He was anxious to complete the evening and be reunited with Angel.

"Do you see that large tree in the distance? Chopin's tomb is there. You must not say anything to the woman. I will deal with her."

A crow flew across their path and alighted on an ornate marble headstone, causing both men to notice the sudden movement of a dark shadow in the distance. Père whispered, "Wait." Putting his hand in his trouser pocket, he removed a small object and placed into his front shirt pocket. "Stay here and don't leave this spot no matter what you hear or see."

Père pulled Brad toward the marble edifice, pressing his back to the cold stone.

Watching Père fade into the darkness, Brad noticed the elaborate carving of the headstone in front of him. Two angels were holding a book on which these words were carved; She Died So Others Might Live, Madame Duprey, May 12, 1885.

The crow had flown to a tree branch above Brad. Sensing that someone was watching him, he heard a woman's voice. "Monsieur Kennedy, I am over here. Come."

Chapter 32

His Own Companion

As Marguerite's car made its way through the Provence countryside, on its way to Paris, George was completing his call to Marie.

"Mother, Marie said she will have some chicken sandwiches waiting in the kitchen for us. She said the newspaper was delivered this morning, but when she went to the foyer to get it, it was not there. She asked Monique if she had seen it, and Monique told Marie that she had wrapped the garbage in the newspaper because you told her not to save the newspapers when we are away on a holiday because you never have time to read old newspapers.

"Marie told Monique to get the newspaper from the garbage and clean it off so she could look at the personals section, but Monique said, 'I was hired as a chef, not a garbage collector,' and then locked the kitchen door. I think they are acting childish, don't you, mother? Marie was able to call five Paris hotels, and none of them had a guest named Brad Kennedy. She will continue calling tomorrow morning."

"Thank you for making the call, darling. It was amusing to hear you tell what happened. I think I shall hire you to make all my calls in the future. Maybe life will seem more amusing for both of us."

"Mother, I forgot, there is one thing more."

"More, oh, no," Marguerite laughed."

"Marie wanted to reward Angel for saving her twelve cats from the fire so she cooked one of your special steaks. Angel loved it. She said you could take the price of the steak from her wages, but mother, I told her that was not necessary because we were very relieved that she was safe and that Angel deserved a reward for saving someone so dear to us. And mother, I think she was crying when she said goodbye."

Marguerite embraced George, squeezing him tightly.

"Mother, that's child abuse when you squeeze that hard," George giggled.

"Why, you little scoundrel. You definitely have your father's sense of humor."

Since her husband's death Marguerite had made many decisions for herself and there would be many more to come. She knew that George should have his own companion once Angel was reunited with her family — and she decided to accept René's proposal.

The beautiful French countryside, with its picturesque villages hugging the hills, brought a sense of peace to George and his mother as their car maneuvered the back roads to Paris.

Chapter 33

A Cruel Joke

The marble gravestones were formidable and cold, much like the thief who stood facing Brad in the darkness.

"Yes, I am Monsieur Kennedy." Brad spoke gruffly.

The woman's face was covered with a flowing crimson veil that hid her features.

"I have your dog, do you have the money?"

Where was Père? Brad wondered.

"Yes, but first bring Angel to me. Well, what are you waiting for? I have the money and you have my dog."

The thief raised her hand and pointed. "Place the money at the foot of that cross over there. After I have counted it, I'll give the dog to you. That's the way it must be."

Being this close to the source of all his pain, Brad thought of nothing but getting Angel away from this vile woman.

"I'm putting the money, one thousand Euro, next to the cross." He placed the white envelope on the ground, and retreated. Looking about like an animal stalking its prey, she bent down and picked up the ransom.

"The money is correct. Here's your dog, monsieur," She placed something white where the money had been and faded into the darkness.

"Angel! Angel! Brad called. Come, Angel come. Angel come!"

When Angel didn't move, Brad ran toward the white dog and picked it up.

"Oh, my God! It's a stuffed animal!"

The woman reappeared from the shadows, held tightly by Père who was shoving her along the path toward Brad.

"Where's my dog!" Brad made an aggressive move toward the

woman standing four feet away.

"Wait, Monsieur Kennedy, I will take over from here. Here's your money," Père inserted the money into Brad's top shirt pocket.

"I don't understand, where did you go? Where's Angel?"

"Be patient and we'll soon have the answers."

The woman turned her head in each direction like a trapped animal desperate to escape.

"You do not have monsieur's dog, do you?" Père spat the words, still holding tightly to the woman's arm, his fingers pressing into her flesh.

"No. And let go of my arm." The woman grabbed Père's hand, thrusting her nails into his flesh.

"Sit down." Père pushed the woman onto the granite sarcophagus.

"No, it's bad luck to sit on the dead." The thief raised herself, only to be forced down once again. Finally, she submitted.

"You will sit there and you will tell us where monsieur's dog has been taken." Père was now standing over the woman, looking down at her right hand as she continued to rub the inside of her left arm.

"I do not know where the dog is and that is final."

"I think we should take her to the police. They'll make her tell us."

"No, she'll never tell them. I know this woman."

Looking at Père, her eyes filled with hatred, she spit at the ground. Père raised his fist toward the woman's face as if to strike her. Taking a step backward, he relaxed his hand, reached into his shirt pocket and pulled out a small object. This was the same object Brad had seen earlier when they arrived at the cemetery.

"Colette, I think this belongs to you. Would you like to have it?" Père let the object dangle from his fingers.

The woman has a name, Brad thought.

Colette squinted her eyes and moved her head from side to side like a cobra ready to strike. The gold object swaying in front of her looked familiar.

With a startled look of recognition, Colette thrust out her hand for the object only to have it swiftly disappear into Père's pocket.

"I'll tell you all that I know if you'll give it to me." Colette lowered her head in defeat.

"We are listening. Begin." Père looked down at her.

"Yes, I took your dog from the hotel. I was going to sell it to a man who has connections. But when I got to his house, your dog ran away as I was taking her out of the car. Your dog is as fast as a white rabbit. I couldn't catch her."

"Where did this happen?" Brad demanded.

"It was near a park."

"What is the name of the park?" Père asked.

"I don't know. I've never been there before. There are guards on each corner and they check everyone who goes down the street."

"That sounds like the Embassy Row area. There's a park across the street from the homes of the ambassadors." Père pulled his black address finder from his pocket and with a small flashlight began to turn the pages. "Here it is. Parc De La Folie St. James. This is the one we want."

Colette extended her arm with her palm up as she moved her fingers in a gesture of expectation. "Now, I'll take what is mine and leave you."

Père swung the object around his finger, the string winding itself tightly as Colette continued to hold out her hand in anticipation. Bringing his face close to hers, he threw out his words like daggers. "Didn't you say those same words to me five years ago?" Suddenly, Père stepped back, unraveled the string with the object dangling from it and thrust it into the woman's hand. Lifting herself from the cold slab, Colette brought the object quickly to her chest. Standing only a few inches apart, they stared into each other's eyes. Père grabbed the thief's hand and pressed the object she was holding to his lips, mumbled a few words in French, and then released her hand.

"You have your trinket! Now, you can go!"

Père was remembering the woman he had trusted. He envisioned her looking at the locket of their two children who were taken away from them five years ago. She was a woman he never understood and hoped he would never see again, but he knew that love dies a slow death.

The cab pulled up in front of the rooming house with not a word having been spoken by Père or Brad all the way from the cemetery. Brad felt a throbbing in his head. Stunned by his disappointment, he sat motionless, his body refusing to move. Père opened the car door for Brad.

"Don't despair, my friend, tomorrow we'll go to the Park and ask some questions. Maybe the person who found your dog has seen your advertisement. I'll pick you up at nine o'clock tomorrow morning." Père pushed the brim of his cap away from his forehead, and jumped behind the wheel.

"I'll be ready."

As Père began to pull away from the curb, Brad, awakening from his numbness, shouted, "Wait! I want to pay you!"

Père put his cab in reverse, maneuvered to the curb, and leaned toward the passenger side window. "Monsieur Kennedy," he said in a low voice. "You do not shout that you have money in this neighborhood. If you will turn around, you'll see Madame Noblesse standing in front of her window. It's past midnight, her lock up time, but I know she'll make allowances. We'll discuss my bill tomorrow. Bonsoir, monsieur."

Brad pressed the bell just as the door swung open.

"Good evening, monsieur. Is that your dog you're holding?"

"No, madame, it is a joke someone played on me at the cemetery, a very cruel joke."

As Brad climbed the stairs to his room, his feet grew heavier with each step. The glaring light from the naked light bulb on the landing illuminated the white stuffed animal that he held in his hand, casting a shadow that followed Brad up the stairs.

Chapter 34

The Ambasssdor's Luncheon

*A*t 61 Rue du Cirque, Embassy Row, Marie finished dressing and straightening her room. She noticed that Angel was still at the foot of her bed curled up in her robe. Lifting her head to see over the folds, Angel could see Marie looking sternly at her.

Is it time to get up? What time is it?

"Angélique, we have much to accomplish today, so I am ordering you to vacate my bed and to get prepared for a brisk march around the park. That is an order." Marie lifted Angel swiftly from the bed and set her onto the carpet. From the doorway, Marie looked back at the room. She was pleased to see everything in its proper place. The discipline and order she had learned while in the military contributed to her efficiency in Madame Revier's household. Marie was proud of the status she had acquired by working in Marguerite's home. She knew madame held an important rank in the diplomatic corps and that few applicants for her position could pass the government's scrutiny. She held the highest security clearance for any employee working for a governmental official.

"Angelique, you look beautiful now that I've given you a good brushing." Marie purred as she placed the brush into the hall drawer.

Thank you, Marie; you look – uniformly presentable yourself.

As Marie opened the door, she held Angel's leash, placing the loop around her wrist. "You are my responsibility and I'll take good care of you." Marie leaned down and patted Angel's head.

And you are my responsibility as long as I live with you. I'll keep all of the other dogs away, and if anyone comes too close, I'll growl. It's my job.

Across the street, Marie recognized a security guard. He was wearing a blue uniform with a gold insignia on each shoulder. "Good morning, Jacques." Marie waved.

"Hello, I read that your house was on fire," he shouted.

"I'm all right! This is Angelique. She saved me and my babies."

"Yes! I saw her picture in the newspaper! Wonderful friend you have, Marie."

Marie was now at the front entrance of the park. Angel continued to sniff at the base of every Chestnut tree bordering the sidewalk.

Wait a minute! I don't want to go in there!

Angel began barking, and pulled back on her leash. She remembered being frightened and confused, and resisted Marie's efforts to take her into the park.

As Marie struggled, Père and Brad were sitting in the cab waiting at a stop light only a few blocks away from the park. After several minutes waiting in traffic, Père began to press on his horn. He leaned out of his window to see what was causing the traffic to stop. The light had turned green and no one was moving.

"It must be a government caravan, maybe the President." Père wondered aloud.

In the distance, Père and Brad saw a series of black limousines with national flags waving from each fender. The caravan turned the corner several cars in front of the stopped traffic and continued in the direction of the park.

"They're probably going to Embassy Row. We'll have to park as close as we can and walk the rest of the way," Père explained.

Marie and Angel stared at the procession of flags as they came toward them. One limousine, with a French flag encircled by a gold olive branch on the door, stopped at a building four houses from Madame Revier's town house. Several men in dark suits encircled the car as the door opened.

"Angelique, that man getting out of the car is the President of France," Marie said proudly.

I knew that. I can't read but I look at the pictures. Brad has a lot of books on France.

Making her way through the crowd that had gathered along

the curb, Marie waved to Jacques who was standing by the house where the President was about to enter. She pointed to the President and waved at him again.

Jacques lifted his arm and waved in Marie's direction. Startled, she felt a hand on her shoulder. A man wearing a dark blue suit and sunglasses that covered half of his face stood beside her. "Madame, will you please come with me."

"Yes, monsieur, of course, but… but where are we going?"

Photographers were everywhere, clicking their cameras at the occupants exiting from the cars. Marie and Angel were escorted to the side of the street where Jacques was standing. "I have a few questions to ask both of you. I will start with you, madame. Why were you waving at this guard?"

"We are friends. I'm employed at Madame Revier's home over there, number 61. My name is Marie Duval," Marie spoke very quickly and nervously, waving her arm in the direction of madame's town house.

A woman in a dark lavender jacket and white slacks came over to where Marie and Jacques were being questioned.

"What is going on here, Bontey?"

"Madame Rousseau, I'm having a discussion concerning an unusual movement that I observed while the President was leaving his car for the Ambassador's luncheon. This woman has told me that she is employed by Madame Revier."

"Are you Marie?" the lady inquired.

"Yes, my name is Marie Duval."

"I know who you are. I'm a friend of Madame Marguerite Revier. I came to her wedding and spilled wine on my dress and you were so kind to help me. Do you remember? Bontey, these people have security clearances. I see no need to question them further. I'll take over from here."

"Yes, Madame Rousseau." The security officer bowed and walked briskly away to his post.

"Let me introduce myself. My name is Madame Lydia Rousseau. I'm the adviser to the President, actually his secretary, but the appearance of official titles in the government is very important. I am pleased to see you once again."

"This is my friend, Jacques, who is one of the security guards for our little neighborhood."

"And who is this lovely creature relaxing on the grass?" Madame Rousseau inquired.

"This is Angelique." Marie picked up Angel and held her toward Madame Rousseau.

"This little white Angel saved my cats from a horrible fire," Marie said proudly.

Yes, I did, just as she said. I did save them all. It's my job. That's what we companions do, save people from burning buildings. We find people and other living beings trapped. We ward off dangerous predators. That's our job.

"Wasn't there an article in the newspaper and a picture of you and Angel?" Madame Rousseau asked.

"Yes, it was in yesterday's newspaper. Oh, I just remembered, I have work to do. I'm to look in the personal column for an ad. Madame is trying to find the person who is looking for Angel."

"I thought the dog was yours. Wait a moment. I have an idea that is formulating in this head of mine as we speak."

Lydia was always dramatic when speaking. She would wave her hands gracefully in the air to make her point. Known for her charm and intelligence, she was liked by all of the ambassadors and their wives who often spoke of her generous and infectious spirit.

"You may not know this, but the President has a dog, and he was very interested in the article about you and Angelique that was printed in the newspapers. I feel certain that if I were to ask him, he would want to help in any way that he could. I don't mean he will do it personally, of course. He will have someone on his staff help you, someone who does things of this sort. How does that sound?"

Sounds good to me. I want to get back to Brad before he replaces me with a stuffed animal.

"Yes, I think madame would be most grateful. I know I am."

"Well, let's go into the house and catch the President before he goes into the dining room. Once he sits down to eat, there will be no interrupting him. He eats ravenously. If I can speak with the President for just a few minutes, we should have his permission to proceed."

Chapter 35

Angel! Angel! Angel!

*B*rad and Père parked the cab several blocks from Embassy Row and weaved their way through the crowd. They could see the line of limousines and photographers taking pictures of the dignitaries leaving their cars and entering one of the houses.

As they approached the barrier that separated the spectators from the invited guests, Brad noticed a woman in a lavender jacket walking up the steps with another woman who had a white dog on a leash. Just as they entered the house, Brad heard himself shout, "Angel! Angel! Angel!" Growing louder each time he called her name. "Père, did you see those ladies enter that house over there? I'm certain that dog is Angel. I know it's Angel. And this is where Colette said she chased her. That park over there!" Brad pushed between two people standing in front of a security officer.

"I'm sorry, monsieur, no one is permitted beyond this barrier. The President is visiting one of the ambassadors."

"I don't want to see the President. I want to get my dog from that house over there."

"It's no use, my friend," Père consoled. You would need a friend in a very high place to get into that building."

Brad frantically searched his memory for an answer. He remembered his meeting with the Count and the invitation to visit.

"Père, I know someone who could help us! His name is Count Charles Beauchamp. I met him at the Château Domaine. He gave us an open invitation to lunch with him when we arrived in Paris. I know he'll want to help us. I know it, I know it." Brad tried to convince himself.

Chapter 36

The Angry Stranger

Marguerite and George had returned home as the hall clock struck midnight. After a light meal, they retired.

Like most children and roosters, George was up with the sun. Knocking on his mother's bedroom door, he burst into the room excitedly announcing, "Mother, come to the window and see what's in the street. Over there, see, it's the President's limousine. Mother, come quickly."

"George, you've seen the President before. I could use a little more sleep this morning. I'm still on my vacation darling."

"Mother, come look. There's Marie and Angelique walking into the house where all the men and women are going." George pushed the window open and leaned out so he could see clearly.

"How do you know it is Marie and Angelique?"

"Mother, there is no other woman in Paris who looks like Marie."

Marguerite picked up her robe and placed it around her shoulders as she slowly opened her eyes and yawned. "All right George, I'm coming. I shouldn't be doing this without my morning coffee." Standing by George, Marguerite leaned out the window.

"Over there, mother, over there. That's the house." George pointed to the line of people entering the Ambassador's home.

"That's the American Ambassador's home, remember, we were there last Christmas? He gave you a present. What was it. Do you remember?"

"It was a pair of cowboy boots with a picture of the President of the United States painted on each boot." Marguerite and George laughed.

People stood behind the barriers, waving large political signs, protesting the war. Those who lived on the street, in the security of the guarded homes, were used to the activities of the government officials and usually ignored the dignitaries that crowded their street.

Marguerite watched the unfamiliar faces of the people behind the barrier close to the park and noticed an odd-looking man in a taxi driver's hat standing next to a taller man who seemed to be arguing with one of the security guards. "I wonder why he is so upset?" she thought. "So many people seem to be angry with the President, or maybe he is an American who is angry with his own President."

"He is very good looking. He must be unhappy from the look on his face." Marguerite seemed preoccupied with the angry stranger, and didn't understand why she had allowed herself to fantasize about him. She felt embarrassed to be staring at a total stranger, making up a scenario for his presence.

"George, go see if you can find Marie somewhere in the house. If you can't locate her, ask Monique if she knows where she's gone. Maybe she's taken Angélique for a walk."

"Aye, aye, captain, I will be back with a full report."

"You take me on one sailing trip and now I'm the captain? You're very generous, George. If I'm the captain, then I'm promoting you to Admiral, how's that?"

"Admiral will do nicely." George closed the bedroom door, walked across the landing, straddled the curved railing on the staircase and glided to the bottom in the quickest and most enjoyable way any nine-year-old would.

"Marie! Marie! Angélique, Monique," George shouted, as he walked across the foyer to the kitchen. Peering through the open door, he surveyed the immaculate space. "Look at the shine on that checkerboard floor. The black squares look as shiny as the white ones. I could cross the way I usually do, using only the black ones," he thought to himself. Taking slow, measured steps, George walked across the kitchen floor that led to the back garden.

"Young man, why are you walking on my clean floor?"

Monique demanded, stepping from the pantry.

"I...I'm looking for Marie and Angélique."

Opening a new sack of flour, she measured the amount needed for her pie curst. "They went over to the park fifteen minutes ago. I suspect they'll be returning soon. The dog's breakfast is on the counter. She's probably hungry by now."

"Thank you, Monique." George tiptoed out of the kitchen.

"Mother!" George leaned on the railing and shouted from the bottom of the stairs, tilting his head back so his voice would travel up to the second floor. "I told you that Marie and Angelique went into the American Ambassador's house! I'm going over to get Angélique so she can have her breakfast!"

"All right darling. That's nice. You do that." Hearing only a part of the message, Marguerite assumed George was going to give Angel her breakfast.

George turned the large brass doorknob, pulled the heavy door open and jumped down the granite steps to the sidewalk. As he walked along, he picked up a tree branch from the sidewalk. Dragging it across the wrought iron railings that bordered each town house, the branch made a rat-ta-ta-tat sound that alerted two security men standing in front of the American Ambassador's house.

The two men followed George as he ran up the stairs and squeezed between a distinguished-looking couple.

"Good afternoon, your Excellency and Madame Excellency." The American Ambassador greeted the Ambassador of Spain and his wife.

"I see you have brought your grandson to the reception. How do you do, young man?" The ambassador reached down and took George's right hand, shaking it firmly as the Spanish Ambassador and his wife looked at each other in surprise. As they were about to speak, they were guided politely along the reception line that led into the ballroom. Just as the Ambassador was about to explain that George was not his grandson, he was introduced to the American Ambassador's wife.

George looked quickly about the room but could not see

Marie or Angel. "Did I make a mistake?" he thought. " I can see better if I crouch down very low to the floor or if I get up higher I can see over all these people." The two security men separated, each one going in a different direction, looking for George.

George maneuvered around and in between the state representatives of the different countries until he reached the bottom of a long, winding staircase that was identical to the one in his home. Racing to the top of the stairs, he stood on the landing and looked out over the enormous room filled with impeccably dressed dignitaries.

"There, that's Marie and Angelique. They're talking with the President," George said to himself.

Chapter 37

Her Secret Rendezvous

B rad and Père drove to the address that was printed on the card.

"Père, I should have phoned the Count before going to his home, but I'm sure he'll want to help us. He's very fond of Angel."

The taxi arrived at the gate. A pole stood by the driveway with an intercom attached. "I'll see if he's home." Brad jumped from the cab and pressed the button on the box.

After several buzzing sounds, he heard a voice.

"Hello, who is speaking?" a man's voice answered.

"I'm Brad Kennedy and my companion's name is Angel. I must speak with Count Charles Beauchamp."

"Do you have an appointment, monsieur?"

"No, but it's an emergency, and if you'll tell him that I'm waiting, I'm sure he'll speak with me."

"Just a moment, monsieur."

For Brad, the time seemed to pass slowly, but in a short while the voice came on once again.

"Monsieur, the Count said he would be delighted to speak with you and Angélique. When you hear the buzzer, the gate will retract and you will have three minutes to enter. I will be waiting at the front door to greet you."

Brad and Père stood in the entryway of one of the oldest homes in Paris. Once occupied by Maria Antoinette for her secret rendezvous. Her entourage would often stay on for weeks, enjoying the food and the wine while one party evolved into another. During the French revolution the mobs of peasants removed everything of value until only the bare marble floors and flocked wallpaper were left as evidence of the opulence of a rejected aristocracy. How ironic that the aristocracy would once again take residence.

"Brad!" Count Charles Beauchamp joyfully announced as he approached them.

"I thought Broderick said Angelique was with you."

"Count," Brad began.

"No Brad, you must remember to call me Charles. Formal titles get in the way."

"Of course, Charles. I'm here because of Angelique. I need your help.

"Of course, of course, I'll do everything I can. First we should have some refreshments and then we will talk. Follow me into the library and tell me how I can help you."

Back at Embassy Row the President of France, in preparation for the celebration of Bastille Day, was holding a reception at the American Ambassador's home. George made his way up the stairs and was now looking down at the gathering of government officials hoping to see Marie and Angelique.

In the reception hall below, the President's secretary was about to speak on behalf of Marie.

"Monsieur le Président, may I introduce Marie Duvall and our heroine, Angelique. You recently read about them in the newspaper."

"Of course. So this is the little lady who saved the twelve cats and their mistress. I congratulate you both," the President lowered his head in recognition.

I've never met a president before. I'd like to tell him I enjoy going into stores and restaurants with Brad.

Madame Rousseau leaned toward the President and whispered her message.

"Yes Lydia, I think we can solve the problem. Tell Philip to look into the matter and to give his report directly to you. He's very good at this sort of thing. Now, if you will excuse me, I must speak to the Japanese Ambassador before he's seated."

Marie was so overwhelmed with being in the presence of the President that she couldn't move. She barely spoke above a whisper during the entire time the President was being introduced.

It's always best to go to the top when you're in trouble... I smell food.

Marie felt a tug on the leash.

"What is it you want, Angelique?"

I'm starving and there's food over there under the table.

"Excuse me, Madame Rousseau, Angélique wants something."

It was George who was responsible for the food under the table. George had noticed a waiter who had just sat his tray of hors d' œuvres on the upstairs hall table. Taking several pâte on crackers from the tray, he tossed two of them down into the lower foyer, near Marie and Angel. George knew Angel didn't have her breakfast and would go for the food.

"Marie, tell Madame Revier that I should have some information for her by the end of the week, maybe sooner."

"Yes, madame, excuse me, Angélique is pulling on her leash again."

With a burst of strength, Angel sent Marie hurtling through the assembled guests and into the Chinese Ambassador's wife, causing her wine glass to pop out of her hand. As it slid across the marble floor, it miraculously landed with the wine undisturbed at the foot of the Canadian Ambassador.

Marie continued to restrain Angel by grabbing the corner of one of the buffet tables laden with desserts. Bracing her foot against the table leg, she stopped Angel for a moment, only to lose her grip. She reached out to grab another section of the table, but her fingers were caught in the lace tablecloth, which pulled the display of elaborate desserts onto the highly polished floor.

Dishes, cakes, pies, and fruit compote laden with whipped cream slid in every direction while the women lifted their dresses and the men jumped to one side, trying to avoid the hurtling missiles.

Angel, determined to reach the food thrown by George, crawled under the marble table to reach her objective.

Food! What falls on the floor is mine.

While waiters dashed about the room repairing the damage, George descended the stairs and stood behind one of the green velvet drapes near the table where Angel was eating the food. Reaching from behind the drapes, George pulled on Marie's elbow.

"What are you doing here?" Marie gasped.

"My mother wants you to bring Angelique home so she can have her breakfast."

Good idea, George, I consider this liver and crackers only an appetizer.

The three intruders made their retreat. The once, dignified and quiet assembly of government officials were left milling about in confusion.

"Excuse me. I'm sorry. Pardonnez-moi, s'il vous plait," Marie and George repeated as they stepped over a large terrine of chocolate mousse and several slices of banana cream pie on their way to the door.

Chapter 38

You Belong To Someone Else

"**M**other, we're back," George shouted from the bottom of the stairs.

"Your mother is on the terrace having her breakfast. Here, give me the little dog so I can feed her." Monique took the leash from Marie's hand and led Angel to the kitchen.

Monique, you're a real friend.

"I'll bring your food young man after you are seated and Marie if you want something to eat, you'll have to get it for yourself. I have enough to do." Monique finished her sentence as she walked toward the kitchen.

"Don't worry about me, Monique. I was in charge of an entire battalion. We never missed a meal." Turning around, Monique pushed the door open. "And did you get a medal for that?"

Angel completed her meal, ran out into the garden and jumped on the chair between George and Marguerite.

Hello, everybody, anything you want to share with me?

"George, don't eat so fast. Where did you go?"

"Mother, I told you I saw Marie and Angelique go into the American Ambassador's house. I went there to get them. I told you before I left, and you said all right."

"I did? All I heard you say was that you were going to give Angelique her breakfast. George, the next time you're going out, come to me and ask before you leave. I can't hear every thing you're saying in this cavernous house."

"What did you say mother? Is the house too big?"

"Never mind George." Marguerite reached over and scratched Angelique under the chin."

Now, I'm getting some attention. Can someone find Brad? When am I going home? I know he wouldn't leave France without me. Scratch my back please.

"Look at Angelique. She looks so worried. She's misses her family."

Marguerite and George had grown very fond of Angel, but unlike George, who loved his new friend and playmate because she helped fill the emptiness left by his father's death, Marguerite felt love for the little dog because of a mystical connection with her past. Like the embers left from a crackling fire, a spark of love was there, always glowing, never to be extinguished.

"I wonder if Marie has finished calling the hotels for the American? Did she look in the newspaper, George?

"I don't think so, mother."

"George, bring the paper to me. We'll look in the personal column together."

Finally, we're doing something to find Brad. He's the one who's lost. I know where I am.

"We'll find your American." George picked up Angel and placed her on his lap.

"Mother, Marie has already found the advertisement in the paper. Here, she's circled it. There it is, right here." George pointed to the ad that read:

White Female Maltese, named Angel, Reward.

Call: 22-432-7685, ask for Monsieur Kennedy.

"Mother, we found Angelique's friend! May I call the number?"

"No, darling. I'll handle it."

"It won't be long now, Angelique" George held her close to his face, kissing her on each check. "I wish I could keep you, but you belong to someone else."

Chapter 39

A Friend Of A Friend

Madame Noblesse opened the medicine cabinet when she heard the phone ring in the hall. It was time for her medication. The doctor had prescribed two tablets, twice a day for her arrhythmia; a condition she knew could be fatal.

As the phone continued to ring she tipped the bottle and two tablets dropped into her palm. Reaching for the glass that always sat on the table beside the sink, she realized that it was no longer there.

"I must have left it in the kitchen." Madame Noblesse mumbled to herself as she shuffled down the hall.

The phone kept ringing, echoing through the hall outside madame's apartment door.

After filling the glass with water, she laid the two pills on the counter. As she reached for the tablets, the sleeve of her bathrobe brushed them forward and onto the floor, rolling out of sight.

"Why is that phone ringing?"

Supporting herself on the back of a chair, she knelt on the floor, bending over to look under the kitchen table.

"Oh, I'll just go and get two more from the cabinet! That phone is a nuisance. Stop ringing! Stop!"

Half way to the bathroom she changed her mind, and walked toward the door leading into the hall. Putting the receiver to her ear, she shouted, "What do you want?"

"Hello, is this Monsieur Kennedy's residence? May I speak with him?"

"No, this is not his residence, he rents a room here. I don't know if he's here or not. Call back later." She started to hang up the phone.

"Wait, please Madame. I must speak with him. It's about his lost dog. Would you see if he's at home?"

"Home, this is not his home." Madame Noblesse mumbled as she let the phone hang from the cord and walked to the bottom of the stairs. Leaning her head back she shouted, "Monsieur Kennedy! Monsieur Kennedy! There's someone on the phone who's found your dog!" As Madame Noblesse looked toward the top of the stairs, listening for a response, small beads of perspiration formed above her eyes.

The light fixture on the landing at the top of the stairs appeared to be swaying. She squeezed her eyelids together several times while a thumping sound grew louder from somewhere deep inside. Grasping the newel post with her left hand she leaned toward the bottom step. With her other hand folded into a fist, Madame Noblesse pressed the center of her chest where the pain stabbed into her like a hot coal. She wanted to rip it out and throw it away but it was too late. "Help me," she gasped. Making an effort to speak into the phone, she fell back against the wall, pulling the cord with her as she fell to the floor.

"Allô, Allô, madame. Is Monsieur Kennedy there? May I speak with him? I'm calling about his lost dog. Allô, Allô!"

Brad was emotionally drained as he finished explaining to Charles what occurred since they last saw each other.

"Brad, I'm sure we can resolve this matter in time. From what you've said, we at least know that Angelique is safe and with people who are undoubtedly giving her the best of care. I'll make the necessary contacts within the Protocol Department of the French Embassy and make inquiries as to the identity of the family that has found Angelique. It may take a day or two, but rest assured we will make contact with the family. For now, this is all we can do. It's too late to make any contacts, but I promise you it will have my full attention the first thing in the morning.

"Count, I'm so thankful for your help.

"No, you must call me Charles."

"Charles, I hope I'm not imposing."

"Not at all. I am embarrassed this could happen in my country and to my little Angelique, too. She has become my confidant. Where are you staying? Which hotel?"

"I am staying at a rooming house in the Sacre-Coeur."

"No, you can not be staying there. It's not the place for you. I insist you stay here. We have a lot of work to do and I'll need you here to help with the decisions after we find Angelique."

"Of course, if you think it's best." Brad was relieved. Looking around the room, he noticed for the first time that Père was no longer with him. "My friend seems to have slipped away."

"Did you say he is a taxi driver? He probably had to go to work."

"Yes, I suppose so." Brad was disappointed.

"I'll send my driver for your luggage tomorrow morning. I cannot send him now because it's not safe in that part of Paris, especially after dark."

"Of course, Charles, tomorrow will be fine."

"Now, about this evening, I'm afraid I must attend the musical, Les Miserables at the Paris Opera House. I would like you to join me. I have a box at the theater that my wife and I use occasionally. Unfortunately she is no longer with me. It seems I've promised to escort a friend of a friend to the theater. She's very entertaining; at least she has that reputation." Charles smiled knowingly.

"I have nothing to wear for this evening." Brad raised his arms, displaying his wrinkled clothes.

"That shouldn't be a problem."

Pulling a cord that hung next to the fireplace, Charles reached for a bottle of wine that sat in an ice bucket. He poured two glasses, handing one to Brad.

"You wanted to speak with me, monsieur?"

"Yes, Broderick, you know the wardrobe situation. Is there something in one of the guest rooms you could find to fit my friend. Possibly a black tie and suit?"

"Of course, that will be no trouble at all. Would monsieur be ready to accompany me upstairs at this time?"

Brad looked at Charles who nodded in agreement.

"I'll meet you down here in two hours. We can leave with plenty of time to pick up the mademoiselle and be at the theater before the curtain goes up."

Madame Nobleese lay motionless at the bottom of the stairs with the phone slowly swinging from its cord. A mouse dashed across the hall. Startled, to find madame in his path, he retreated to the space between the stairs leaving behind the few crumbs that had fallen from her pocket.

Marguerite, held the phone to her ear, and listened intently, waiting for someone to respond. There was only silence.

"I don't understand, I heard a woman calling Monsieur Kennedy but no one came to the phone. This is most frustrating."

"Mother, is there an address given for Monsieur Kennedy in the advertisement?"

"No, just the phone number. I'm sorry, Angelique, I tried. We won't give up though. We'll find him." Marguerite stroked Angel sympathetically.

He isn't at the place you've been calling. I know I can find him if only I could get outside to smell the wind.

"Mother, I'll bet Angelique could find him. Dogs have a powerful detecting device inside their nose. They can detect smells two-hundred times stronger than any human."

He's right, I can.

Marie entered the room and walked over to the breakfast table, leaned over madame, and whispered into her ear.

"Oh yes, thank you. I'll take the call upstairs in my room, Marie."

"George, take Angelique into the garden and play with her. She must be disappointed that we weren't able to contact Monsieur Kennedy." Marguerite walked toward the stairs as

George placed Angel on the brick path.

Finally, I can exercise. I need some grass under me.

Angel bounded toward the fountain, looking back to see if George was following.

Marguerite closed the door to her bedroom, picked up the phone on her bedside table and pressed one of the five black buttons. She knew why René was calling. Although she had decided to accept his proposal, she had yet to discuss her decision with George.

"Hello, René. I'm happy to hear your voice, too. No, I haven't forgotten this evening. I wasn't sure you could make it. I know your schedule has often extended into the evenings. Yes, I'll expect you at six. The restaurant near the theater will be fine. I enjoy their Chicken Cordon Bleu very much. Yes, René, I've given a great deal of thought to what you've said. You're a very persuasive man. You do present a very good case and René… René. Please, let me explain!"

Marguerite turned toward the window, holding the phone away from her ear, not speaking. She was beginning to feel pressured by René's insistent attitude.

"Yes, I'm still here."

In the reflection of her bedroom window, she could see a vague image of herself, George and a man, not as tall as her husband nor as tall as René. She turned her head to one side, looking closely to see the face of the man looking back at her in the window. The sound of René's voice brought her back from her imaginary journey.

"Allô, Allô, are you there darling?" René repeated.

"Yes, René, I'm here. I just noticed something that needed my attention." Marguerite glanced at the bridal photo that sat on her beside table. "René, I have come to a decision. After the theater I'll give you my answer. Yes, I'll see you at six o'clock this evening.

René felt certain that by the end of the evening Marguerite

would finally consent to marry him. She was the prize he had always hoped to win. Being her late husband's business partner, best friend and confidant, he made the most of his opportunities to be in the company of the woman he desired more than any other. Over the years before her husband's death, he had fantasized that one day he would be Marguerite's husband. There was no force that could stop him. She was his obsession.

René had not been the friend that he appeared to be. He purposely kept Marguerite separated from Lamar by encouraging him to take more responsibility in the firm. When he learned of Lamar's life-threatening heart condition he pushed him further. Although René felt guilty about insisting Lamar spend more time at the business, his compulsion to possess Marguerite overrode his conscience.

He would often say, "Lamar, how do you expect us to occupy the top spot in Corporate Law if you aren't willing to make some sacrifices?" The sacrifices he was alluding to often resulted in taking even more of Lamar's family time away from George and Marguerite. She had no way of knowing of René's deception and blamed Lamar for causing the distance in their relationship. Many people have addictions that influence their decisions. René's addiction was Marguerite.

George ran toward the far wall of the patio garden with Angel close behind. Both were out of breath as George swooped Angel up in his arms and kissed her on the forehead while Angel began to lick his chin.

"Angelique, that tickles." George laughed and turned his head from side to side.

I know it tickles. That's why I do it. You have fun and I have fun. That's another one of my jobs. I make children and grown-ups laugh and for a while they are as happy as I am. Except that now, I'm not very happy. I miss Brad and that leaves a big empty spot in my heart that won't go away.

Angel cried, without shedding a tear.

Turning the corner near Embassy Row Park, René's headlights illuminated the security guard at the main entrance.

Jacques was on duty this evening and recognized René when he pulled up beside him.

"Good evening, Monsieur Gullemont," said Jacques.

Jacques held out his hand to receive René's card.

"Good evening Jacques." René kept his photo-thumbprint-identification card in the console of his car where he could access it quickly.

Jacques inserted the identification card into his security-monitoring device attached to the center of his belt. The red light turned green and a voice responded, "Security clearance identified. Admit one René Gullemont, if he appears on your guest registry." The voice concluded.

"Monsieur, here is your card. I have one more task to perform before I can admit you. Excuse me I will be with you in one minute."

Jacques pressed a number code on his phone and in a few seconds he began to speak.

"Marie, I have René Gullemont at the entrance. Are you expecting monsieur this evening? You are? May I respectfully remind you that someone from the house should notify the security guard at least two hours before the guest's arrival? You can dial your code on the computer next to your front door and then type your guest's name. It saves time. That's quite all right. We're only too happy to assist you. Good night Marie."

"I am terribly sorry for the delay, Monsieur Gullemont. You may proceed."

George stood in the open doorway with Angel in his arms as René's headlights lit up the front entrance to Madame Revier's town house.

"Who is your friend, George?" René followed them into the living room.

Ignoring his question, George turned around and positioned himself in the doorway of the living room.

"Monsieur Gullemont, my mother said I should greet you at the front door and offer you a glass of wine or a cup of coffee if you prefer."

"George, is that the dog you found in the park?"

George was in the habit of ignoring René's questions when his mother was not in the room. Angel examined René very carefully from George's arms. She felt him become tense when René had entered the house. Angel stared suspiciously.

George picked up an afghan from the couch and created a nest for Angel on the chair near the fireplace while Angel continued to probe René with her eyes.

"Would you prefer wine or coffee, monsieur?"

"I think coffee for now. There will be plenty of wine later to toast the event. What's the dog's name?"

"Excuse me, I think I hear Marie calling. It's my dinner time." George made his way to the kitchen followed by Angel.

Yes, it's our dinnertime.

Stopping at the kitchen entrance, Angel hesitated while George held the door open. She looked back to where René was seated with his feet propped up on the coffee table and began to emit a low growl followed by a loud bark that startled René.

I don't like that guy. He looks like he's getting ready to move in.

"I don't like him either, Angel." George closed the door.

"Marie, Monsieur Gullemont would like a cup of coffee. He's in the living room. I'm supposed to eat my dinner now. Can I have mine with Angel in the breakfast room?" George placed Angel on the chair closest to him. "Here you are my little Angelique. He patted the cushion next to him. "You sit right next to me and our 'wonder chef' will bring you a delicious meal." George spoke loud enough for Monique to hear the compliment.

"I know what you're doing young man. You're spreading whipped cream on my ego so you'll get your favorite brownie dessert. You're correct. I'm a wonderful chef, the best on Embassy Row. I've heard your mother's guest say so many times. I like cooking and I like to see people eat what I cook."

I like your cooking too, Monique.

"Even your little dog likes my cooking. Look at those brown eyes staring at me. She is waiting for a warm plate of chicken. Am I right little doggy?" Monique opened the refrigerator door and took out a bottle of milk.

Yes, you're right. You make the best meals.

Chapter 40

I Wish George Had Been My Son

Upstairs, the door to Marguerite's bedroom was left open so that she might hear René when he arrived.

Seated at her dressing table, she chose a pair of diamond earrings that suited the outfit she had chosen for the evening. Placing the black velvet case in front of her, she noticed that one of the earrings had fallen on the carpet. As she bent over to pick up the earring, she hesitated. Looking down at the glittering diamond on the lavender floral design, she remembered the day she received them. René had given them to her the same day George was baptized into the Catholic Church. Marguerite and Lamar had asked René to be George's godfather.

She pushed the small gold pin through her ear lobe remembering how surprised she was to receive the gift. It was not customary for the mother to receive a gift on such occasions. She also remembered René saying, "I wish George had been my son." At the time, Marguerite felt embarrassed, not knowing what to say, questioning the appropriateness of the remark.

She returned the earrings to the case, selecting another pair given to her by her husband on their last wedding anniversary. Marguerite paused at the bottom of the stairs and looked across the entryway into the living room where René sat with his back to her.

"I wish I was certain that I'm making the right decision."

"Good evening René, I'm sorry to keep you waiting. I apologize for Marie forgetting to call the security access. She never forgets to do anything I ask her to do. But it has been a very difficult week for her." Marguerite poured herself a glass of wine.

"You have nothing to apologize for. I'm just excited that you're back in Paris and that we'll be together all evening." René took Marguerite's glass from her hand and turned the glass to the side from which she drank. He kissed the edge softly then returned the glass to Marguerite. Placing the wine on the table without drinking from the glass, Marguerite said, "Before we get on our way I must say good night to George. I won't be long." Marguerite walked toward the kitchen as René followed her with his eyes. Aware that his romantic gesture wasn't acknowledged, he regained his enthusiasm by telling himself that Marguerite would love him, one day. René lived and loved with passion and without reservation, never measuring what he received with what he was willing to give.

The dinner was superb as planned, for René had chosen one of the most renowned restaurants in Paris. Located four blocks from the Champs-Elysées, patrons would make reservation a month in advance. He had given the maitre d' and the waiter explicit instructions along with a large tip. A gardenia was to be brought to the table in a crystal bowl at the beginning of the meal.

"René, you are very thoughtful. I'm overwhelmed by your kindness. You have been so helpful since Lamar was taken from me. I can't thank you enough for what you've done." Marguerite turned away, facing the palm that separated their table from the others. She took a handkerchief from her purse.

"Marguerite, I love you. I've loved you from the first day I saw you."

René knew he had declared too much from the expression on Marguerite's face. His enthusiasm had caused him to divulge what he hadn't meant to say. He could see from her questioning expression that she did not welcome his confession.

Marguerite pushed her chair from the table and excused herself. "I'll be right back. I want to powder my nose." She felt embarrassed to say something as old-fashioned and feminine, but she had not been accustomed to having to explain her departure to her husband, and she felt awkward to consider herself on a date.

As she crossed the dining room, looking for the sign marked phone, she told herself that if George did not agree with her decision to marry René, then she would not go forward with her plans. Closing the door to the booth, Marguerite dialed her residence. "Hello, this is the Revier residence, Marie speaking."

"Marie, this is Marguerite, would you please put George on the phone?"

"I'm sorry. George and Angelique have gone to bed, madame."

"Would you peek into his room to see if he's still awake? I would like to speak with him."

"One moment madame, I'll see." Marie crossed the hall from her room and standing at George's bedroom door, she pushed it open, allowing a stream of light from the hall to cross over George's bed. She could see that he was breathing evenly with his eyes closed.

Angel lifted her head and looked toward Marie.

Is something wrong? Have you found Brad?

"Shh, Angelique. Everything is fine, go back to sleep."

"No, madame, George is asleep. Do you want me to wake him?"

"That won't be necessary. I'll speak with him tomorrow morning. Thank you Marie. Don't wait up for me. I can let myself in."

As she closed the door of the booth and stood looking toward the dining room, she could see René glancing at his watch. Marguerite didn't want to make a final decision without asking George. But it was her decision. She must do what is best for both of them.

Chapter 41

Merely An Actor

*A*long stream of taxis were lining up at the Paris Opera House. Doors were opened as ladies and gentlemen were helped to the carpeted walkway. Politely maneuvering through the crowd of theatergoers, women glanced at the gowns of others while the men pondered the bets that were made on the French soccer team.

The Paris Opera House is one of the most beautifully designed buildings in Paris. It was completed in 1887 under the direction of Emperor Louis Napoléon Bonaparte as a place to display his wife's beauty and her jewels.

Changing the plans for the evening, the Count's "friend of a friend" informed him of an earlier engagement and decided to meet him at the theater. "There's my young one for this evening. She's coming this way." The Count held out his hand toward the brightly dressed woman walking toward him.

"Bernice." The woman kissed Charles on each cheek.

"Brad, I would like you to meet Bernice. Bernice, this is my American friend who is looking for his lost dog who is also my friend."

A murmur of conversation flowed throughout the lobby of the theater growing louder as the number of people increased. With his young "friend of a friend" on his arm, the count moved past several distinguished looking people as Brad followed closely behind.

"It's hard for me to hear in this crowd. You'll have to stand to my left because I lost most of the hearing in my right ear from a blow I received as a child." Charles raised his voice over the sounds of the crowd.

Looking detached and preoccupied, Bernice, was rehearsing in her mind the arrangements that were made for the latter part of the evening.

Brad leaned toward Charles' left ear.

"Charles, are you familiar with tonight's performance? Have you read any reviews?"

"No, I haven't." He looked at Bernice.

"Are you familiar with the musical that is playing this evening?"

" What did you say?" Bernice turned toward Charles, startled by the question.

"Brad was asking if you knew anything about the performance this evening?"

"I don't go to the theater much. I usually go to the movies." Bernice yawned. "How long will this thing last?"

Brad looked at Charles, waiting to hear his answer, but there was no indication he was going to recognize the question.

From the corner of the lobby, a man and woman approached them. The woman moved gracefully in front of her escort smiling as she tapped Bernice on the shoulder to gain space for them to pass. Bernice turned quickly and stepped aside, while the Count bowed his head smiling in recognition. "Good evening, Marguerite."

After the couple passed and began to climb the broad, gilded staircase that led to the private boxes, Charles leaned toward Brad and said: "That was Madame Marguerite Revier. She lives on the same street where you saw Angelique enter the ambassador's house."

Brad looked interested. "Could you ask her if she knows anything about Angelique?"

"It wouldn't be polite to intrude on her evening. We must respect her privacy."

"I understand."

Brad was disappointed.

"Now, I don't want you to worry about this matter. I have promised to take care of everything tomorrow. You must relax and enjoy the show."

Brad watched Marguerite and her escort as they climbed the stairs, imagining himself walking beside her. She seemed familiar as though he had known her before. Why would this woman draw his attention? He continued to follow her with his eyes until they disappeared beyond the top of the landing. Mental images of her face and body were frozen in his mind even though her presence was fleeting. He reviewed her features, looking for a match from his past. The feeling of fondness and familiarity for this woman was inexplicable.

"Brad, please sit here. This seat offers the best view of the performers." Charles gestured for Brad to take the chair on his left, while Bernice sat on the Count's right.

As Brad turned the pages of his program he noticed that the same couple who passed them earlier was now occupying the box to his left. He tried to remember the name. Was her name Marguerite Bovier or Revier? Yes, he was certain it was Revier.

Looking out over the audience, Brad observed the late arrivals squeezing by those already getting comfortable in their seats. A grey-haired couple opened their programs as they looked up to the boxes above. Brad imagined himself sitting in the last section of the theatre looking up at the boxes as the couple was doing now.

The box seats had always represented a separation between the haves and have-more. He suddenly felt like an imposter. As he smiled with amusement at his old-fashioned class distinction, he looked across at the row of box seats on the other side of the theatre. There were forty-five on either side, all furnished with red velvet chairs. Gilded cherubs, tucked away in the corners of the vaulted ceiling, looked down on those fortunate to be among the advantaged patrons seated in the private boxes. With a flurry of manicured hands, they tenderly adjusted their elegant clothing and jewelry.

The entire gathering was like a theatrical production with Brad merely an actor playing his part. Tilting his head, he rubbed his forehead nonchalantly, trying not to be obvious while glancing over toward Marguerite as she sat only a few feet away in the adjoining box.

Brad felt a familiarity, forming a bridge to a distant memory. There was a tender emotional connection with Marguerite that he could not explain. "This is embarrassing. She's probably going to think I'm flirting with her."

René adjusted Marguerite's chair, allowing her the favored location on the right for viewing the stage. This position was the closest point between the Count's box and their own. Marguerite had a clear view of Brad only a few feet from where she was seated. Turning to the right, she adjusted the pillow that René had placed behind her and casually let her eyes drift to where Brad was seated. Feeling he was being observed, he tried not to look in Marguerite's direction.

"Are you comfortable, Marguerite, " René asked as he reached for her hand.

"Yes, I am." Marguerite felt a strange sensation she had never felt before. Was this a feeling of apprehension because of her decision to accept René's proposal or was she apprehensive about George's reaction to her decision to marry René?"

Looking over at Brad was at first a distraction, but then she found herself gazing at him as if he were a celebrity. "He looks familiar. He looks like someone I knew. He speaks French with an American accent." She began to laugh at herself.

"Why am I doing this?"

"What is amusing, Marguerite? " René asked.

"I was thinking of the time I lived in America. My father was the French Ambassador. We lived in Washington, D.C., and I went to school there for a few years. I was only seventeen. When I returned to France, everyone said I spoke with an American accent."

"I wonder if she's laughing at me for being so obvious. She must have seen me looking at her." Brad felt awkward.

"I feel like I'm writing a screen play in which this woman will perform the starring role. Why am I playing this juvenile game when I'm sitting here with two sophisticated people who are so proper."

Bernice leaned over toward Charles and then pointed at her

watch. Her lips moved silently to pronounce the words that he couldn't hear. "How long is the show? When can we go?" Looking directly ahead, Charles put his right hand in front of Bernice and snapped his fingers, then placing his finger to his lips, he looked toward the stage as the curtain went up.

Both Marguerite and Brad found it difficult to enjoy the performance. Each felt a strong attraction for the other. After the final curtain they expressed their anxiety by enthusiastically applauding the performance.

The applause continued to reverberate throughout the theater as waves of affection poured from the audience. Soon everyone was standing as the final curtain descended. The excitement, which the audience experienced earlier, was beginning to dissolve into a quiet satisfaction. Some even had plans for additional entertainment. They were more anxious than others to exit the theater; at least Bernice appeared to give that impression.

Marguerite took René's arm as he guided her through the crowd, making their way toward the grand staircase. He was anxious to be alone with Marguerite and could barely enjoy the performance anticipating her decision.

Marguerite glanced toward the carved, gilded ceiling, her eyes resting on the two cherubs that held back a curtain of clouds as rays of sunlight cascaded down the walls. Just as they reached the top of the stairs, Marguerite looked over toward the two gentlemen who were hesitating at the point where the crowds were not moving. She noticed that one of the men was the same man she observed from her townhouse window and as they approached she could see that he was also the man whom she had been glancing at throughout the evening. The closer Marguerite came to the trio, the more nervous she became.

"He seems so familiar. Now that I have seen both sides of his face and the back of his head, I'm certain he's someone I've known."

Brad didn't know that Marguerite was walking toward him and she was now directly behind Charles. Just then the crowd began to move once again, allowing for the people at the top of the stairs to make their descent. Brad looked over to his left toward Charles to comment on the performance when, as he began to speak, his attention was drawn immediately to Marguerite who had been staring at his profile.

"I enjoyed the performance very much, Charles." Brad spoke slowly as he looked toward Marguerite. "You were very kind to include me." Brad continued speaking without making any attempt to divert his eyes from Marguerite. As the crowd began to move once again down the stairs, Brad gradually maneuvered himself so that he was next to Marguerite. He purposely brushed her arm as they reached the last step.

"Pardonnez-moi, sil vous plait, madame," Brad bowed slightly and smiled. When Marguerite heard Brad speak she was even more certain of her recognition.

René presented his ticket to the valet who matched the card with the appropriate key. The young man ran through the darkness, dodging around the cars as their headlamps illuminated his white uniform. A red Alfa Romeo soon appeared by the curb. Marguerite and René slid into their seats as two valets, one on either side of the car, gently closed their doors, their voices chiming in unison, "Bonsoir, monsieur et madame."

Marguerite's thoughts were beginning to replay the events of the evening as they entered the Paris traffic. She wanted to recapture the emotions she felt when she saw the stranger for the third time. She knew she should be making conversation or René might think something was wrong. But there was something wrong and she had no idea what to do about it.

"Marguerite, darling, did you enjoy the performance this evening?"

"I'm sorry René, what did you say?" Marguerite turned to look at René in the dim light of the dashboard.

"I asked, if you enjoyed the musical this evening?'

"Oh, yes, very much, although I was a little tired during the last act."

"Did you notice the accent of the gentleman who bumped into you this evening?"

"Yes, he said excuse me if you please."

"No, I mean the way he said it. He spoke French with an American accent, similar to yours." René smiled as he turned the wheel of the car and entered Embassy Row. After the security guard had checked their identification, they drove on to Marguerite's townhouse. René turned off the motor and started to open his door.

"Wait, René, I'm very tired, exhausted in fact, could we talk tomorrow? I think I would like to take a hot bath and retire. It's very late."

"Of course. I'm disappointed, but I understand. Haven't I always put your happiness before my own, and I always will." René leaned over and kissed Marguerite, holding the moment as long as he could.

"Let me walk you to the door," René reached for the door handle.

"Thank you René, not this evening. I'll just dash right in. Good night. You've been wonderful, as usual."

Marguerite turned the key in the lock and entered the softly lit foyer. As she closed the door she heard the sound of René's car drive away. Throwing her keys on the hall table, she took off her coat and dragged it behind her toward the large winding staircase. Half way up the stairs Marguerite paused. Looking at her left hand as it gripped the railing, she saw her wedding ring through moist eyes. She continued to climb once again, each step requiring more effort than the last.

At the top of the landing she saw a light at the end of hall coming from her bedroom. A faint sound, which she imagined to be Lamar's voice, but she knew it couldn't, came from the end of the hall. As she gently pushed the door open, the light from the closet spread across her empty bed. Tears welled in her eyes as she looked at the covers folded back on one side.

She was alone.

Chapter 42

I Know Who You Are

*B*roderick approached the Count as the party of three reached the side entrance of the theater. "Monsieur, the car is only a few feet this way." Broderick pointed in the direction of the Count's silver Mercedes limousine.

Seated across from the young lady, Brad noticed that she appeared preoccupied with her watch. He felt it would be polite to make some attempt at conversation but decided that it wouldn't be welcome since she had been distant all evening and evidently felt comfortable sitting in silence.

"Count, excuse me, I mean Charles, can I ask you a question about Madame Marguerite Revier, the lady you greeted this evening?"

"Of course Brad, What did you want to know?"

"Was that her husband?"

"No, he is René Gullemont, a very famous attorney as well as a partner in her late husband's business."

"Do you know what her name was before she married Monsieur Revier?"

"No, my wife and I met them about three years ago at a charity auction which was held in their home. My wife knew Marguerite when they attended the Sorbonne. They remained friends, mostly lunching together with other friends from college. We husbands were never invited. I'm afraid that's all I know. Are you interested in being introduced to Madame Revier?" Charles was hiding his amusement.

"Yes, if you could arrange the meeting. It would have to be something casual. I wouldn't want to give her the wrong impression, even though I may have already done so."

"How can that be, you haven't even met her."

"Well, I might as well tell you that I'm attracted to Marguerite. I know it sounds strange but I feel I know her. I've no idea why I'm being drawn to her. Possibly my emotions are clouding my reason. I shouldn't allow myself to be distracted. To find Angel is my primary concern." Brad lowered the car window, letting the night air bathe his face with coolness.

The limousine crossed the Pont des Arts and turned left away from the direction of the Count's residence. Continuing past the Arc de Triomphe toward the Av. des Champs Elysees, it stopped in front of the Hotel De Marc Dumente.

"Brad, Bernice and I will be spending some time here. Broderick will drive you to my home where I will expect you to get a good night's sleep. I assure you that we will have some answers tomorrow." After Charles helped Bernice from the car, Broderick listened attentively to the instructions the Count whispered in his ear.

As the car drove through the streets of Paris crossing the wide boulevards that parallel the Seine, Brad found it difficult to think of anything except the extraordinary woman. He felt her presence just thinking about her. As the car paused at the traffic light, Brad heard a guitar strumming a familiar song coming from a nearby nightclub. He was drawn to the melody, so familiar, yet he couldn't recognize it with certainty.

Broderick drove through the enormous gates toward the mansion that for centuries witnessed countless historical events. With its secrets hidden in the past, it stood in formidable silence.

Unlocking the door, Broderick held it open for Brad to enter.

"Monsieur, after I've parked the car I'll be retiring for the evening. There is a petite meal on the dining room table. You'll find a white napkin spread over it. There is a bottle of white wine also. I shall not see you until tomorrow morning. You may sleep as long as you wish. Breakfast will be ready fifteen minutes after you request it. Simply press the button next to your bedside. Good night monsieur."

"Goodnight, Broderick. Thank you for all your attention." As he watched Broderick close the front door and disappear, Brad felt more alone in this enormous house than he did in the small rooming house. He was grateful for several chandeliers that cast light throughout the dining room, bringing warmth to the surroundings. Brad removed the napkin to reveal the contents of his evening meal: cheese, salmon pate, quartered toast and a bottle of uncorked wine.

Alone in the dim light he began to recall all that had occurred during the evening. His thoughts of Marguerite were hazy at first, but with concentration he was able to sketch her features in his mind as he poured a second glass of wine. The small meal gave him comfort and provided the energy needed to make the journey through his past, constructing a time and place where he may have known Madame Marguerite Revier.

Reaching for his glass, Brad's ring caught the edge of the tablecloth, spilling the wine. "I've worn this ring for so many years. I've forgotten that the setting can easily catch material," Brad reminded himself.

Twisting and turning his ring, he felt drawn to the window. A sculptured fountain in the corner of a private seating area, obviously for two people, caught his attention. As soon as Brad opened the window, the soft sound of cascading water came pouring in.

The enormous room with its high ceiling and baroque molding reminded Brad of his high school library.

The water's melodic sound became musical notes that danced around the room. Brad's memories began to converge, recalling a melody, vague at first, and then growing more familiar. He continued to pace around the room, sensing that moving forward would bring the memories closer.

Allowing his instinct to dictate his movements, Brad's attention was drawn toward the dimly lit ceiling. He could see a fresco consisting of blue sky, white clouds and sculptured tree branches. Something caught his attention; only he could not see it clearly.

"Where are the light switches?" Brad wondered.

He walked around the room turning on all the lights. The room was soon brilliant with light, transforming it into a theater, where Brad's life was being reenacted.

A melody, off in the distance, grew more pronounced as he continued to walk around the room humming the tune again and again.

The words came streaming into his consciousness, infused with a feeling of love rising from deep within. Brad heard himself singing the lyrics to a song he could vaguely remember.

"I'll be seeing you in all the old familiar places, that this heart of mine embraces all day through."

The melody and the words gained clarity as Brad continued pacing around the room, humming and reciting the first two phrases of the song.

"...That this heart of mine embraces all day through."

"The lights, the lights, they're too bright."

Swiftly he went around the room turning off the lights. Each illumination faded away until the room was in complete darkness except for one ray of light. The one light that needed no earthly power was spreading like cream-colored silk across the floor. It poured in from the window like liquid gold.

Brad had suspended all reasoning on his journey through this unknown dimension, relying on his inner strength as encouragement to press on. Following his instincts to continue moving, he walked slowly toward the light.

The moonlight pierced its way through the branches of the chestnut tree and into the room. Brad pushed the window open, allowing the curtain to sway like a flapping sail. The fluttering of the leaves brought the answer. A sound in the breeze whispered, "Marguerite is..."

"I know who you are! Brad called out as he raced toward the front door and out into the driveway. Stopping under a towering Chestnut tree he reached for a small branch that hung a few inches above his head and sang,

"I'll find you in the morning sun and when the night is new; I'll be looking at the moon but I'll be seeing you."

Chapter 43

Ole Joe

George's night light spread a warm glow across his bed while he and Angel breathed deeply, tired from a full day of games of chase and story telling. With her nose close to George's hand, she went to sleep with his scent comforting her longing to be home.

The bond between them had become stronger, and even though Angel was devoted to Brad, her instinct told her that she could include other loving human beings in her "pack."

Tonight, George was dreaming of his new family and Angel was dreaming of hers. Each counting the number four in their "pack."

Yes, dogs dream too, and Angel is no exception. George opened his eyes and looked at Angel lying beside him. He could see her furry chest rising rhythmically while she made soft wolfing sounds mixed with murmurs and snorts. He suspected she was chasing a squirrel. Angel was dreaming but it was not a squirrel. It was something white.

…Angel raced through the white, cold and wet substance. "It's snow, Angel," Brad called out. She pressed her face into its unknown strangeness.

It's cold on my teeth. I can't taste anything.

Here in the White Mountains of New Hampshire, on a wintry December afternoon, Brad and Angel were experiencing their first communion with snow, and the crisp winter air, all interconnected with the sheer pleasure of nature's moments of joy.

"Come on let's run," Brad prodded, turning back to see if Angel was following.

What do you mean let's run? The snow is up to my chest. Walking is my limit.

As the dream ended the snow disappeared and so did Brad. Angel looked at George and noticed his heavy breathing.

It was a dream. I'm still here in this big house. When will Brad come for me?

Angel saw a light coming from the hall and jumped from George's bed. Pushing her nose through the opening, she entered the hall. The crystal chandelier over the stairs cast muted light through the railing, creating elongated black shadows. Angel hesitated at the top of the stairs, looking through the black and white lines that were spread across each step.

I have to find Monique. She has something to share with me.

The clock's heavy pendulum swung back and forth creating the heartbeat of the house.

Angel hopped down each step pausing to listen and smell.

When she reached the bottom of the stairs, she walked slowly toward the kitchen, and pushed through the door. The room was dark except for a small nightlight that fanned out along the black and white tiled floor.

Looking down the hallway leading to the servant's quarters, Angel saw an opened door at the end of the hall. In the distance, a light led the way to Monique's room. As she looked through the opening, she saw Monique reading, seated in a plush upholstered chair, her legs pulled under her robe. Even though Monique couldn't see Angel on the other side of the door, she could feel her presence.

"Hello, Angelique. You've come for a little chat, haven't you? Monique continued turning the pages of her Gourmet magazine. "I know you aren't happy. You miss your family. You may not be able to speak, but you have your own special way of communicating. Only you and I know the truth. I think we should have a little talk, don't you? Come over here my little sprite and sit close to me." Monique tapped the arm of the chair.

Angel entered the room and placed her paws on the edge of the chair and waited. Monique leaned over, picked up Angel and tucked her into the folds of her robe.

"Where shall I begin? I know, I'll tell you the story of Ole Joe.

"My first childhood friendship was with one of our two horses, Ole Joe. I always knew Joe wasn't happy, but I didn't know why. One day when we were alone in the field, his thoughts came to me, and I put them into words. You know, Ole Joe didn't want to plow the fields. He wanted to pull our wagon, the one my father made into a surrey. I told my dad about Ole Joe and he laughed.

"Summer came and went and then one day he wouldn't eat his oats. He looked sick after the first week and he lay down in the barn and wouldn't get up. Nothing we did would make him move. He was getting so skinny, I thought he might die.

"One night I went into the barn and snuggled up to Ole Joe. I looked up into his big brown eyes and I asked him, 'If I promise to hitch you up to the surrey, will you eat and not die?' And you know what Ole Joe did? He licked my face, and he got right up.

"When the sun was about to rise over the foothills and the fields were all wet with dew, I hitched Ole Joe up to our surrey and we went down the road apiece to the railroad tracks and then we came back. When my dad came out of the house and saw Ole Joe hitched to our surrey, he stood on the porch and laughed. Then he came over to Ole Joe and rubbed his nose. He said, 'You knew what Ole Joe wanted all the time. You're a horse-whisperer, that's what you are.'

"Ole Joe never pulled the plow again."

Monique told her story with all her heart wrapped up in the telling. But she left something out, and Angel knew it.

Walking toward the bathroom door, Angel looked back at Monique.

"Would you like some water?" Monique asked.

Angel waged her tail.

Returning from the bathroom, Monique placed the bowl in front of Angel, "There you are, one bowl of water for Angelique."

After Angel drank only a small amount of the water, Monique noticed an envelope under Angel's paw. "What is that you have, little one?"

Angel knew Monique was a kind and thoughtful person who was also very lonely. And more importantly, Angel knew the reason why.

"You're up to something, aren't you? You didn't come down here just for a drink of water. There's a water bowl in the upstairs hall, I know because I put it there. So, my little white dust mop, are you going to tell me the reason for your visit?" Reaching down, she slid the envelope from under Angel's paw.

Monique felt a tightening across her chest as she looked at the letter. One of many she had received from her mother and refused to answer. She hadn't questioned why she kept them and never opened them.

Yes, the letter is from your family. The family you left behind when you changed into someone else.

Angel knew that Monique would soon understand what she was trying to tell her, she just needed more time and concentration for the message to come through.

It's time to change back to the person you were, Monique.

Looking under the bed, Angel crawled toward the far corner. With her nose, she pushed a brown shoebox full of letters toward Monique.

Slowly and methodically, Monique read each letter for the first time. The last letter, dated some twenty years ago, reinforced her deep sense of longing to return to her home and to reclaim the identity she had left behind.

She leaned back, her eyes gazing toward the ceiling, as tears flowed, releasing her pain. Closing her eyes, she imagined her family in front of a thatched roof home in Saint-Louis, French Guiana.

You are still a part of your family. They are waiting for you.

Angel put her head on Monique's lap and nudged the hand that held the letters.

"I'm going home. I'm going home." Monique repeated, wiping her moist cheeks with the edge of her nightgown.

Chapter 44

Monique's Confession

*A*fter a restless night Marguerite awoke feeling tired. The drapes in her bedroom were still closed which meant George was still sleeping.

George felt responsible for helping his mother smile and laugh. Since she loved the sound of the sparrows singing their collective songs in the garden, he kept the bird feeder full of seeds and the drapes opened in his mother's room each morning. "I suppose I should be getting up," Marguerite mumbled from under the sheet.

George had awakened earlier than usual and was distracted from his normal routine. Angel was not at the foot of his bed and this concerned him very much. He dashed about the room looking for her. Satisfied that she wasn't there, he ran towards the top of the stairs, placed his leg over the curved banister and slid down to the bottom. Running toward the kitchen, he pushed the door open as he called out. "Angelique, Angelique, where are you?"

Monique came from the pantry carrying a jar of peaches and a two pound sack of flour. "If you're looking for Angelique, she's out in the garden. She has already eaten, had her toilet and is now playing with a very large black beetle, at least she was when I last saw her. Is your mother up yet?"

"No, I don't think so, but she will be as soon as I turn on the bird alarm."

"The bird alarm, what's that?"

"I pull back the drapes and open my mother's bedroom window and the sparrows sing her awake. I do it every morning unless it's too cold to open the window, and then I stand by her bed and whistle."

He opened the door that led to the garden, jumped down each step and ran to Angel who was indeed preoccupied with a black beetle. George lay beside her, eye to eye with both the beetle and Angel.

"What do you make of it Angelique? Will you make it your pet? I know children in Japan do."

I'm amusing myself until lunchtime. I wonder what beetles taste like?

"Don't eat it Angelique, it will make you sick. I can persuade Marie to give you another steak. She thinks you're special." George picked Angel up, and carried her into the house.

"George, would you tell your mother I would like to speak with her when she has the time?"

"Of course. Where's Marie?"

"She went home to meet with the carpenters and to visit her cats that are staying with a friend. She'll be returning by dinnertime. Why aren't you in school?"

"I'm on vacation. This is July, remember?"

George raced up the stairs as Angel followed closely behind. Entering his mother's room, he told her of Monique's request to speak with her.

"Have you been annoying her?"

"No, of course not. I stay out of her way in the morning so she can get her work done just as you asked. I'm bored, mother. I would rather be back in school with my friends. There's no one to play with in this neighborhood."

George pulled the cord that separated the drapes and pushed both French doors open onto the balcony as the sounds from the birds filled the room.

"I think you may be wrong, George. Remember the boys you met in the park? Weren't they about your age?"

"They weren't very friendly when I asked them about Angelique."

"Yes, that's true, but haven't you found that boys seem to bully each other until they find out if the new boy can play the same games?"

"I never thought about it that way."

"Let's go over to the park and give them another chance. We'll leave Angelique with Monique until Marie returns. How does that sound?"

"Yes, that sounds all right. Can I ride the carousel?"

"Darling, if you remember, when we were there last it was being repaired. I think they were changing the music or something."

Pressing a red button on the telephone that summoned Monique, she waved George to the door.

"Now, you run along and get dressed while I talk with Monique. Take Angelique with you."

Tucking the last strands of her hair into a circle on the back of her head, Marguerite smiled into her mirror at her son's reflection.

"Mother, that looks like a halo you're wearing."

"Is that a compliment, George?" she laughed.

"Come, Angelique, come." George clapped his hands together. "Mother, she isn't moving."

"Just pick her up and carry her."

George reached for Angel, only to see her dash under the chair beside the bed.

It's important that I be here for Monique. She has a message for your mother.

"I think Angelique wants to be with you, Mother."

"That's fine George, I'll keep her with me until Monique and I are finished talking. Now, run along and get ready. We'll be leaving for the park in one hour, mon chér."

Crawling from under the chair, Angel made herself comfortable, waiting for Monique to arrive. Marguerite heard a soft rapping on the door and turned from her closet. "Come in Monique. What is it that you wanted to see me about, something to do with the menu for next week?"

Marguerite took a seat on the chaise and tapped her hand on the cushion beside her, indicating for Monique to join her.

"No, madame. It's a personal matter. I... I, have to leave... tomorrow. I'm flying to Guiana. I'm sorry madame, but I must go." Monique pulled a handkerchief from the pocket of her apron.

"Monique, you're crying. Has something upset you? Why do you feel you have to go? Whom do you know in Guiana?"

Marguerite could feel her heart pounding. She was confused by Monique's announcement, and she needed time to sort out what was happening. Her late husband, Lamar, handled all crises. He even made decisions without consulting her. She accepted this arrangement, but now, faced with Monique's announcement, Marguerite needed time to compose herself and decide what to do.

"Monique, I can see you're upset. Let's sit here calmly and sort this out together." Marguerite put her arm across Monique's shoulder.

"Now, you must tell me everything."

Her hands clasped tightly in her lap, Monique took a deep breath and, in a proud voice, announced, "I was born in French Guiana, South America. My real name is Malisha. I know I have white skin, but my family members were sharecroppers, descendents of slaves. My parents were both black. We had ten children in our family. My mother was not well. I took care of her because I was the oldest." Monique stopped speaking. She stared at the curtains as they fluttered against the yellow carnations that dotted the wallpaper.

Yes, Monique, go on, I'm listening.

"Our family made artificial flowers from sugar cane stalks that grew on our small farm. The sharp strands would cut our hands. My brothers and sisters, all of us, would sit for hours on little stools, hunched over the wooden buckets of chopped cane stalks. When I wasn't working with the cane, I helped my mother cook the meals.

"The white lady who owned the farm loaned us two horses so that we could plow more fields. My father was proud of his two horses, one for the plowing and Ole Joe for the surrey. Some days I felt like Ole Joe. I knew he would rather die than pull the plow. Every Saturday, I would hitch up Ole Joe and we'd go into the village and trade our flowers and sugar cane for food and cash from the white-man's store."

Marguerite pulled a tissue from a small drawer and handed it to Monique.

"Take your time. I'm here to help you," said Marguerite.

"One Saturday, I saw the storeowner put a television on the counter with these two funny wires on top of it. I never saw a television before and I stood by the counter as though I was hypnotized. I remember hearing the storeowner laugh at me.

"He said, 'You ain't never seen a television before, have you?'

"No sir, I haven't. Could I watch it for awhile?"

"He was nicer than most white folks. He gave me and my sisters and brothers a piece of candy each time we came. If they didn't come, he knew how many pieces to give me to take home.

"The television was showing a white lady cooking. She explained what she was doing and I started memorizing everything.

"I stayed a long time that day and the man didn't chase me out of his store or anything. Finally, he said, 'You better go on home. Your dad will be wondering where you are.' I started for home with our groceries and as Ole Joe and I went down the road, I began praying. I prayed…. I prayed harder than I've ever prayed. Joe turned around and he looked at me. He was listening to my prayers. I said, 'Lord, let me be a cook in a restaurant or maybe even a chef. Me and Joe, we don't want to pull a plow.'

"They called the lady on the television, Chef Melinda. She was beautiful and she made delicious looking food. I didn't tell anyone about my dream to become a chef. Every week after that, when I went to the store to get the groceries, I would take notes while I watched Chef Melinda. I misspelled a lot of words, but I could understand the recipes when I got home.

"The next year I was eighteen and I rode the bus to the city to get a job as a cook in some white person's house. I got a job real fast when I told the white family that if I didn't fix a good meal, then I would leave and they didn't owe me anything. I cooked one meal and they told me I was hired. They asked me how I learned to cook white peoples' food. I never told them. I thought it might get the store man in trouble.

"I saved my money and went home every month to check up on my mother and to give my family some of my pay. My little sister took over for me and got the groceries each week. One day she told me that the white man at the grocery store saw a sign about a chef school in the same town where I was working as a family cook. I had enough money saved for the tuition, so I sent in my application.

"When my application was returned, I asked the lady I was cooking for if she could find out the reason. She said she would call for me, but she already knew the reason. I asked her why, and she said, 'Malisha, those people know you're black, even if you look white. They have all the names of every black family in the county and they probably looked up your name on their list. The chef school is only for white students. Didn't you know that?'

"I left that day and never came back to cook for that white lady. I didn't cry. I told myself they would never make me cry. I was going to become a chef some way; I just knew it.

"I saw an ad in the paper one day when I was getting groceries. The store man let me look at the paper as long as I folded it back real neat so that it didn't look like it had been used. This ad was asking for a maid to help with a white lady in a wheelchair who was going on a cruise to Europe and she needed someone to do for her. I was interviewed and got the job. That was the last time I saw my family.

"When the ship got to France, I left with the lady in the wheelchair and I just walked away in the crowd. I never went back to the boat. I got a job washing dishes in a restaurant and I saved my money and enrolled in a chef school. I never told anyone about my family. After I graduated I made up a story for my first interview. I said I'd been in the French Foreign Legion. I don't think anyone believed me, and it didn't seem to matter because my scores at the chef's school were the highest in the graduating class.

"When I applied for work with your family, twenty years ago, I was told I had to pass a clearance check, I thought I might not get the job.

"I was happy when they told me that I got my clearance. It also made me scared though. I thought that if they ever found out that I was lying, I would be fired or even deported. I went to your father and told him everything. He told me that he would check into it. Later he told me that the name I had chosen to replace my real name was the same as a woman chef who lived in Bordeaux and the authorities thought I was she.

"My dream came true on the day I began to work as chef for your family. But now I keep hearing in my heart, 'You must go home to Guiana. Your family wants you.'"

Marguerite looked up at Monique with tears in her eyes. "You're part of our family too."

Shocked by Monique's confession, Marguerite sat quietly, staring at her hands, trying to compose herself.

"Monique, if you must go, then I'll purchase your airline ticket to Guiana; it will be a round-trip ticket though. We'll be here waiting for you." Marguerite embraced Monique.

"Now, go pack your things and I'll take care of all of the arrangements after I return from the park." Marguerite walked with Monique to the door of her bedroom, followed by Angel. Both women embraced and exchanged kisses on each cheek.

"I have prepared lunch and dinner for everyone," Monique cleared her throat. She walked toward the stairs as Angel followed. Picking up Angel, Monique whispered into her ear. "It will be your turn to go home soon, my little one."

I never lose hope. Dogs never lose hope. I have faith in tomorrow. I always have. I'll miss you Monique.

Angel licked Monique under her chin.

Passing Monique and Angel coming down the stairs, George noticed that Monique looked upset.

When he entered his mother's room, he saw her standing in front of the window. "Mother, are you crying?"

"Yes, mon cher, Monique is leaving us. I'm going to miss her terribly."

"But why? Where is she going?"

"I'm sorry darling, I just can't discuss it now. Could we talk about it later? I'm trying to compose myself so that we can enjoy our time in the park. I promise to explain everything this evening."

"All right, but will you answer one question, now?" George

and his mother walked to the top of the stairs.

"Yes, if I can."

"Are you ready to go to the park?"

"Yes, of course, have I ever kept anyone waiting?"

"Yes, mother, millions of times." George slid down the banister just as he had done many times before, only this time his mother was watching.

Chapter 45

Sharing Confidences

B rad pressed the button on the nightstand notifying Broderick he would be down for breakfast.

"I have fifteen minutes. Is that what Broderick said?," he asked himself.

Before Brad opened his bedroom door he went to the dresser and picked up the Chestnut tree blossom he had left there. Even though elated to know the identity of Madame Revier, and to discover the emotional connection he felt, he was not completely happy. He longed for some news concerning Angel.

Brad found comfort knowing Angel was probably in a caring home on Embassy Row, although he had no idea that Angel was with Marguerite.

As Brad entered the dining room, he looked at the table where he had been sitting alone the night before.

Broderick entered from the corner of the dining room and placed Brad's breakfast in front of him.

"Good morning, monsieur. I trust you've slept well? I sent for your luggage this morning and everything is in your room. The Count will not be joining you for breakfast. He said he will have the information concerning Angel's disappearance by this evening."

"Thank you, Broderick."

"I see you have a blossom from the chestnut tree. "Perhaps you know the history of our tree?"

"No, I'm afraid I don't. Could you enlighten me?"

"Of course, although there is a book in the library that can explain it much better than I." Broderick left the dining room and returned with a red leather-bound book.

"Thank you Broderick. I'll read it while I'm having breakfast."

Brad's reverence for books had grown over the years. He knew that his attitude was shared with many educators whose collection of books represented their life interests. As he picked up the book, he was conscious of its weight, so heavy for such a small book. Turning back the cover, he was surprised to find a large space that had been carved out, making it appear like a box. Inside was a smaller book entitled, The Chestnut Tree's Mysterious History, by Charles Anthony Fleck, written in 1774.

Taking the book gently from its enclosure, Brad glanced through the pages. One page had been creased at the corner. Dark with the imprint of many fingers, he suspected there was more interest in this one page than the rest of the book.

Brad began to read.

"…For centuries the chestnut tree has held a mysterious secret that has only recently been recorded. In remote villages of France, the peasants would use the herbs from their gardens and leaves from their trees for medicinal and spiritual purposes.

"It was also believed that the chestnut tree, when planted near the home, would spread its branches to protect all those who dwelt within. The chestnut blossom, when placed in the window, would bring a loved one home safely from their journey."

Brad held the weathered text in one hand, and the chestnut blossom in the other. Walking across the room, he placed them both on the windowsill, confident that the legend would come true.

"Come home, Angel."

Broderick saw Brad standing by the opened window as he entered the room. "Monsieur, your taxi driver friend is waiting for you in the hall."

Since there was nothing more that could be done to find Angel, Brad felt drawn to the location where he had last seen her, Embassy Row.

"Père, How are you? I wasn't certain that you were available. Would you take me to the park where I saw Angel?"

"Absolument. We will go now, oui?"

The cab hesitated at the end of the driveway as two ornate, wrought-iron gates parted, allowing Père to drive through.

"I came over to deliver a package that you left in your room at Madame Noblesse's place. I have sad news for you. Madame Noblesse is in the hospital. She had a heart problem. I moved into your room so I can help her with her business until she returns. I gave everybody a key to the front door because I can't be there to open the door and drive a cab too. You understand?"

"Of course. I'm sorry to hear about Madame Noblesse."

As the car raced through the Paris traffic, Père pressed his horn several times. Turning the corner he swerved around two startled pedestrians crossing the street. The traffic light turned red just as Père pumped his brakes to stop his cab. Shouting out of the window, Père called out to the driver that lingered in front of him as the light turned green.

"What are you waiting for? Look at that man! He's talking on his cell, smoking a cigarette, and drinking coffee. He must be steering with his knees."

Père continued to weave through the narrow streets, exceeding the speed limit. As he jammed on his brakes, Brad shouted. "Be careful! Take your time, Père! I want to go to the park, not the hospital."

The cab screeched to a stop a block from the park. "Should I wait for you?"

"No, Père, I have no idea how long I'll be here. I'll call you when I'm ready to leave." Brad pulled his wallet from his pocket and took several euros out.

"No, I've already been paid. Broderick has given me a check from the Count and I'm to give him a bill at the end of each week."

Brad looked at Père in disbelief. As the cab pulled away from the curb, he walked toward the ivy-covered fence that surrounded the park. Noticing a section of the park that bordered the sidewalk in the non-restricted area, he walked up and peered through the bars.

Brad imagined Angel, frightened and alone, running into the park and hiding from the thief who had kidnapped her.

George stood outside on the front landing of their home in Embassy Row with the door opened to the street. "Hurry Mother!"

"The park is not going anywhere, George. It will be there when we arrive."

Since George had not ridden the park carousel for several weeks, he was impatient to see if it was repaired. As they crossed the street, sounds of children's laughter could be heard coming from the park. George ran ahead through the shaded entrance. Turning around, he waved to Marguerite. "I'm going to be over at the carousel."

Marguerite looked up through the branches of the chestnut trees that bordered the walkway leading to the carousel, noticing the sharp pointed leaves and the cluster of white blossoms for the first time.

"They are so fragrant, why haven't I noticed them before?" she thought.

Taking a seat on the park bench nearest the beautifully painted collection of moving horses, she became conscious of the absence of the traditional carousel music, the music that every one remembers from their childhood.

George came running toward his mother and sat on the bench beside her.

"There's a new man operating the horses. I asked him when the music would be fixed and he said it's working fine now. I'm going to go for a ride. I have money."

George ran to his favorite black-stallion, the one with the gold saddle. As he jumped onto the platform, next to the horse, a blond-haired blue-eyed boy around George's age, grabbed onto the reigns of the horse George had chosen.

"Hey, I was here first." George shouted. "Oh, you can ride him. I rode him a million times. I guess it's your turn." Lifting himself onto a white-stallion, George waved to his mother. While the two boys sat waiting for the ride to begin, George looked over at the boy seated on his favorite horse.

"I've never seen you here before, did you just move in?"

"Yes, my dad is the ambassador from Cooba."

"Did you say Cuba?"

"No, not Cuba, we pronounce our country's name like this, Coo-ba."

"Oh, Cooba. Yes, I get it. What's your name?" George asked.

"Cory Martinez."

"Cory is not a Spanish name."

"My mother is Canadian and my father's Cuban so they made a deal. He got to give me my last name and my mom got to give me my first. What's yours?"

"George Revier. That's my mom sitting over there."

"Is George a French name?"

"I suppose so. I never thought about it."

The carousel made its first revolution and then stopped. After a few seconds it began to move once again. While the horses went up and down, the two friends smiled at each other. Side by side they shared their imaginary ride, taking them to a place where there were no boundaries or limitations. Holding on to their childhood fantasy for a little while longer, the two boys rode the carousel, pretending their horses were real.

Music came from the center of the carousel, soft at first, and then increasing in volume. George and Cory waved to Marguerite as the horses made their rotations. Marguerite began to hum along with the music. The lyrics drifted across her mind as she began to form the words.

"...And now the purple dusk of twilight time, Steals across the meadows of my heart. High up in the sky the little stars climb, Always reminding me that we're apart."

"I know that song. I've heard it before, a long time ago." As the music played, Marguerite looked up through the trees at the sky, as a small yellow finch flew over to the fountain. As the music continued she felt a feeling deep within her. Her memories began to travel back, back like the pages in a calendar, blown by the winds of time. She could see herself and her family traveling on her first ocean voyage to America. Her father had accepted the position of Ambassador. They would soon be in Washington, D.C.

Her first week at the High School was frightening. Convinced that her English was not adequate, she rarely spoke to anyone. She knew from past encounters with new acquaintances that she had little choice who she could invite to her home. Her mother, being uncompromisingly set in her ways, would always dictate her friendships.

Marguerite was a shy, attractive young girl, not aware of her many talents, that is until the day she met a young man in her music class.

The instructor paired them because the boy could speak French. As the months passed, they were soon sharing confidences and personal jokes. They enjoyed drawing cartoons and writing short stories about their teachers. Sitting in the cafeteria at lunchtime, they would compose limericks about the pretentious students who chose their friends based on the "Washington, D.C. Curve." This was a term they had created. It meant choosing friends whose parents were from the favored positions, closest to the President.

Both Marguerite and her friend qualified, but refused to associate with what they called, "the whipped cream crowd," meaning sweet and full of the cold air of superiority.

Their infatuation for each other progressed into love. Sharing confidences, they were soon inseparable which alarmed Marguerite's mother.

Just as the carousel began to slow, Marguerite heard her name being called. As she looked over at George she saw him running toward her with his new friend.

"Did you call me, George?"

"No mother."

"Someone called my name."

"The only time I call you Marguerite is when I'm angry with you. Mother, I want you to meet my new friend. He's from "Cooba" and his name is Cory Martinez. Can he come over to our house?"

Threatening clouds fulfilled the promise of rain just as the carousel began to move. Suddenly drops appeared on the sidewalk, causing Marguerite to grab George's hand. "Say goodbye to your friend. We better hurry because I didn't bring an umbrella."

The intensity of the rain increased, forcing them to race toward the park gate and into the street now filled with water. With her arm around George, she forged through the drenching rain toward the golden glow of the welcoming lamps on either side of their front entrance.

"Marguerite, Marguerite, I'm over here!" Brad called.

Marguerite heard Brad's distorted words, muffled by the pouring rain. As they reached the shelter of their front door, she glanced back toward the park — but saw no one.

"We're both soaked, George." Marguerite inserted the key into the lock and pushed the door open. She tossed her wet shoes aside, and slid into a pair of slippers taken from the hall closet while George ran upstairs to change his clothes,

"Bring my bathrobe George! It's hanging on the back of my dressing room door!"

"Madame," Monique called from the kitchen doorway. "You had a phone call while you were out. I wrote the number and placed it on your desk. I don't have any luggage. May I borrow one of yours? I can send it back after I arrive in Guiana."

"Of course you can. You don't have to send it back. Go to my room and take one from the closet. No, wait, I'll get it for you. I have a few items I want to place in it first.

"Thank you madame."

"Monique, I've made your airline reservation. You are to leave from the Roissy-Charles de Gaulle airport, at 11:a.m. on Flight 166, gate 12. I've placed a copy of the reservation on the hall table. It's in the blue envelope with your name on the outside."

Marguerite was gaining confidence in her ability to take charge of her life. She had never made an airline or hotel reservation before. Since Lamar's death she drew upon all her accomplishments to give her the encouragement to persevere.

Seated at her desk, she glanced down at the completed speech she had written for the President of France. There were only a few revisions to be made: first, the length of the speech and second, the insertion of several amusing stories that had become part of her writing style. Her speechwriting career began when her father asked her to take the place of his assistant who had been taken ill just before he was to give a major speech at the United Nations in New York City.

Her work for *Regards*, a major magazine in France, ended when her father was given acclamations for his speech at the U.N., which she had written. She began to devote more of her time writing speeches for her father and eventually left *Regards*.

Realizing that she would have a couple more hours of work on the President's speech, Marguerite read the note left by Monique. Just as she reached for the phone to return the call, it began to ring.

"Good evening, Madame Marguerite Revier speaking,"

"Hello, Marguerite, this is Charles Beauchamp. I hope I'm not interrupting your schedule? May I have a little of your time to discuss an important matter?"

"Of course, I was just preparing to return your call. My chef gave me your message when I returned a few minutes ago." Marguerite held the phone tightly between her head and shoulder while opening a card from René that had been on her desk for three days.

"Marguerite, did you notice the gentleman who was with me last night?

"Yes, I did."

"He is an American who is now a guest in my home. His dog was stolen a week ago from the hotel where he had been staying. Her name is Angelique. Your housekeeper was seen with a white dog going into the United States Ambassador's home yesterday and from my inquiries, you are the one who found the dog in the park. The American is very anxious to have her returned, and I have promised to take care of all the arrangements."

"Yes, of course, Angelique is upstairs with George. We can bring her to your home this evening. I'm so relieved to know Angelique will be reunited with her family. I have a couple of hours left to work on the President's speech, and then I can deliver Angelique."

"That won't be necessary Marguerite. I would prefer not to interrupt your schedule. You must be fresh for the ceremony tomorrow at the Colonnade near the Eiffel Tower. I'll be with the presentation party, seated next to the Prime Minister of Great Britain. Do you have the itinerary for the celebration?"

"Yes, I do, but I haven't read it as yet."

Charles continued, "I've spoken to the President's secretary and asked her to place you, Brad Kennedy and myself in the same seating area. There is a space for George, should you decide to bring him. We can talk before the ceremony begins. Please bring Angelique with you. It will be quite a surprise for Brad."

"I think that is a splendid idea. George will be coming with me. He thinks he's old enough to attend and I agree."

They continued to discuss the events that had occurred since the theft of Angel and the political situation that had been of some concern to Charles.

"I should conclude our conversation and let you get to work, Marguerite. You have been very helpful. Say hello to George for me. Goodnight."

Marguerite went to her room to get a suitcase for Monique. After placing several of her personal embroidery handkerchiefs along with one of her personal travel kits into the opening, she closed the case. The finality of what was happening pressed against her heart. A family member was leaving.

Unfastening the luggage once again, she went to her writing desk and opened the middle drawer. She pushed the pearl rosary beads aside and took out a small white prayer book decorated in semi-precious pearls. Her mother had given her both items on her First Communion. Marguerite was only six years old. How proud she was, all dressed in white with a veil and gloves, stroking her prayer book.

Marguerite held the book tightly as she carried the family heirloom over to her bed and placed it into the inner side pocket of Monique's luggage.

"Faith and hope will sustain all of us until Monique comes back."

Chapter 46

Monsieur le Présidènt

*B*rad held tightly to the wrought-iron bars while his eyes followed Marguerite as she and her son ran through the rain and disappeared into the house. His words were muffled by the sound of the pounding rain. With his head lowered, he pushed against the cool metal. Numb from disappointment, Brad took little notice of the rain that soaked his clothes.

Alone in the rain, his energy melting, he felt defeated. "This park is like a prison, shutting out the rest of Paris." With his hands deep in his pockets, his head lowered, Brad walked to the nearest phone booth and dialed Père.

Slumped in the back seat of the cab, Brad saw the Count's home appear at the end of the street. Père pulled off the road, and stopped at the gate. With the rain pounding the roof of the taxi, Brad stepped out of the cab and pressed the buzzer on the intercom.

"Hello, Count Beauchamp's residence. Broderick speaking."

"Broderick, it's Brad." After a series of clicking sounds, the gate opened.

"Thanks Père, I'll walk to the house." Despondent, Brad trudged through the drenching rain as water poured down his face and neck. Just as he reached for the knob, the front door swung open.

"Monsieur, I took the liberty to have this ready for you." Broderick handed a bathrobe to Brad. "If you will turn left through the archway you will find a toilet at the end of the hall where you can change from your wet clothes. Please leave them on the chair by the door. I have some dry things hanging in your room. The Count will be dining with you in one hour." Bowing slightly, Broderick gestured in the direction Brad should go.

Exhausted from his afternoon of frustration and disillusionment, Brad lay on his bed thinking of a time in his life when his family was experiencing the same emotions. He began to recite a rhyme that appeared in the *Washington Post* when his father's reputation in the federal government was at its lowest.

"…Humpty Dumpy sat on a wall. Humpty Dumpy had a great fall. All the King's Horses and all the King's Men couldn't put Humpty Dumpty together again." He had heard his father referring to himself as Humpty Dumpty, and the President as the King. Now, he could appreciate the comparison in the nursery rhyme. It described his feelings this evening.

The last years in the Federal Agency were devastating for his father. Coming home from high school one Friday, Brad was told that his mother was on a vacation, only to discover that she had left for a rehab clinic.

After he had prepared a pizza from the refrigerator and sat down in the kitchen to eat, he heard loud voices coming from his father's office. Walking down the hall he stood at the door and listened. He recognized the man's voice who was arguing with his father.

"…First the nuclear accident at 3 Mile Island, and now this failed rescue attempt to save the hostages in Tehran. Richard, I can't help you this time. I have to stay distant from all of this. You and I know the King approved the operation but no one else does. He's concerned about the reelection. Did you send your wife to the place I suggested?"

Startled, Brad heard a knock on his door. "Come in."

"The Count will be expecting you in a few minutes if it is convenient, monsieur."

"I'll be right down. Thank you, Broderick for reminding me."

"Well, my friend, I have some very good news for you. I have been on the phone all morning with the President's office. There is so much bureaucratic insecurity and red tape since the terrorist situation that it was beginning to appear that I might not be able to get any information about Angelique. But their cooperation was suddenly forthcoming when I reminded them of their need for more financial support in the next presidential election and where they might find it. Fortunately, I received the answers to my questions."

Charles motioned for Brad to follow him into his library. "Have a seat over there." Charles picked up a cut glass decanter, removed the crystal stopper and poured a glass of port wine. He raised the glass, nodding his head in reference to Brad's acceptance, pouring a second glass, he handed it to Brad.

Taking the seat opposite Brad, he sat back, placed his feet on the cushion and said; "I think we're both comfortable and prepared for some good news, don't you? First, and most important, I want to assure you that Angelique is safe and extremely well cared for by Madame Marguerite Revier and her son, George. I have been informed that Angelique is being fed filet mignon and sleeps on George's bed." Charles laughed. Brad began to smile for the first time since Angel had been kidnapped.

Charles continued, "Marguerite is anxious for you to be reunited with Angelique. She tried to phone you on the day Madame Nobleese had her heart attack. She has been searching for you ever since her recent visit to my hotel near the lake. She has a wealth of information for you. I told her it was best if she waited to share everything with you personally."

"Are we meeting this evening?"

"Unfortunately, Marguerite has a crisis. Her chef is leaving for Guiana, and she also has the responsibility of completing the President's speech for tomorrow's national celebration."

"There's a celebration tomorrow?"

"Of course, it will be the 14th of July."

Brad appeared uncertain of the significance of the date and then with a surprised look, announced, "That's Bastille Day. Correct? We celebrate the 4th of July and you celebrate the 14th of July."

Charles smiled at Brad's remark and continued to share the

plans for the next day's activities.

"There will be a lengthy program of speeches, some music, a little marching, a great deal of singing and at the conclusion, fireworks. You will be my guest, of course. I've arranged for you to meet Madame Marguerite Revier and her son. They will have Angelique with them."

"Charles. I'm so relieved. I feel like I've come out of a fog and now I can see where I'm going. The journey to locate Angel has been a great strain on me. I've made many generous new friends, like you, who have helped me. I'm so grateful."

With his glass of wine, Brad walked toward the fireplace. Leaning his arm on the mantle, he looked up at the portrait of an ocean scene that brought a memory he would never forget.

"The anxiety of this past week reminds me of one of the most trying days of my life, a day I will never forget. After I tell you, I think you'll understand how deeply this kidnapping has affected me. May I tell you the story?"

"Of course." Charles filled their wine glasses and sat back in his chair.

"It was early July and I was sailing on the Piscataqua River in my home town of Portsmouth, New Hampshire. I remember it was late in the afternoon and the current kept pulling my skiff out toward Whale Back Light House. I began to pull my sails in just as a fog bank suddenly enveloped me. I couldn't see beyond the bow of my boat. The only comfort I had was the foghorn's repeated warning, and with each pulsating tone, I sent out my "faith message", a kind of prayer. Off in the distance I could see the vague outline of something yellow. As I drew closer I could see what it was. A kayak was lodged in the rock. There was a woman inside.

"I threw my lifeline in an effort to keep us from drifting apart. We were both scared of being pushed out to sea by one of the fastest currents of any river in the United States. We wouldn't have much of a chance to survive out in the open ocean. I held her hand for a few seconds to give her comfort, but I knew I was also asking for encouragement.

"Finally the wind started to pick up and we caught the on-coming current just as the fog began to lift. Wet and tired, we decided to use our oars to push free of the rock. We separated near Pierce Island and I put sail for the pier.

"There is a big difference between my story and Angel's kidnapping. In Portsmouth, two people were clinging together for survival, no one to call for help. Here in Paris, so many kind and caring people have helped me and for that I'll be eternally grateful. Charles, you have answered my prayers. I can't thank you enough. The fog has lifted. And I can see Angel on the shore." Brad and Charles raised their glasses in a toast."

After returning from a tearful goodbye to Monique at the airport, Marguerite stood in front of her desk, looking down at the gold Presidential Seal embossed on a bright red, blue and white folder. The completed speech was inside. She was certain it was the best speech she had ever written and she knew the reason. Her fondness for America and the memories of her youth were a promise of a life of self-confidence and independence. A gift she treasured.

"This speech will rekindle the friendship between France and the United States."

As she opened the folder she turned to the third section of the speech and read the last paragraph. She had included many of the allies of France; the first country to be mentioned would be the United States of America.

It began...

"The English may have been the first settlers in the new world, but the French provided the assistance at a crucial time during the American Revolutionary War. We were proud to help you fulfill your destiny as a sovereign nation where democracy could flourish.

"The Statue of Liberty in the New York harbor is not only our gift to the United States, it is France's symbol of our two countries' promise to protect Liberty and Justice for All."

Marguerite closed the folder and dialed the private number to the presidential estate. "Hello, this is Madame Marguerite Revier speaking. Would you inform Monsieur President that his speech is ready to be picked up? Tell Monsieur President that I'll be arriving at the ceremony at six o'clock. And would you...Yes, I'll wait." Interrupted by the secretary, Marguerite was told the President would like to speak with her.

"Yes, Monsieur President. You're welcome Monsieur President. Oh yes, I'm certain the American Ambassador will be pleased with the speech. The speech expresses your deep commitment to support the documents on which America has been founded. Yes, I have implied, without stating, that we do not arbitrarily support the various military adventures of administrations that appear every four to eight years. Yes, Monsieur President, it will be well received. If you stay within the text, even the newspapers cannot fault you for any undiplomatic remarks, I can assure you.

"Yes, I will be there as arranged. You are very welcome, Monsieur President, au revoir." Marguerite took the folder from her desk, walked to the foyer and placed it in a brown leather valise that was kept on top of the baroque side table. Taking the key from the drawer, she secured the contents and took the key with her, expecting the President's currier to retrieve it within the hour.

Marie had returned from her home earlier in the day and was seated in the kitchen interviewing a replacement for Monique. Angel had been lying next to Marie's chair when the interview began. Angel sat up and listened.

"The customary three meals will be cooked for the household before any decision will be made pertaining to your employment. You may begin tomorrow morning with breakfast. You should be prepared and ready to serve by eight o'clock."

Tell her I like steak once in a while besides my usual chicken.

"Here is the menu for the three meals. You may replace any of the suggested items if there is an entree you feel would be more appropriate or more delectable. I'll notify you of Madame's decision after your trial period is complete." Marie stood up and shook the applicant's hand. Angel stood up also and looked at the new trial chef.

You haven't introduced me.

"Oh, yes, this little girl is Angelique and there are small steaks in the refrigerator with her name on them. You may cook half of one for her dinner."

Only half?

George's voice came from the upstairs hall, "Angelique!"

Hearing her name, she dashed up the stairs. George, who had been standing at the top of the stairs, was now crouching down in the dog-play position. "Want to play, Angelique?" George took a blue rubber ball from his pocket and threw it down the stairs. The ball tumbled down every other step and landed underneath the round table in the center of the foyer. Angel, accepting the challenge, ran down the stairs. George threw his leg over the banister and slid down, meeting Angel as she reached the last step.

"Come Angelique, bring the ball to me!"

Angel grabbed the ball in her teeth but instead of running toward George, she ran in a large circle. "Come back here!" George continued chasing her as she dashed down the hall and through the open door to his mother's office.

No one has ever caught me.

Angel looked back over her shoulder at George, teasing him.

You're panting harder than I am.

Angel ran around the office and squeezed under Marguerite's desk. The wispy white sprite, that was just beyond his grasp, sat smugly in triumph.

After having accompanied the applicant to her car, Marie was coming down the hall toward the office when she heard George calling Angel.

"Madame, I've interviewed the last candidate for the chef's position. George, what are you doing in here, take Angelique into the garden so your mother can finish her work." Marie reached under the desk and gently retrieved Angel. "How are you today, my little Angelique of the kitty-cats?"

Marguerite rose from her desk and walked over to Marie.

Placing her arm around George, she stroked Angelique and scratched her under her chin.

"Marie, this evening is a very special occasion for Angelique as you know, as well as for all of us. She will finally be reunited with her family. I think Angelique should look her very best, don't you? I would like you to take Angelique to the laundry room and give her a bath? George, would you like to help?

What, I don't want a bath. I don't need a bath. Look how white I am.

Angel defended herself by pushing her head under Marie's arm.

"George, when you are finished helping Marie with Angelique's bath, I want you to bathe yourself and get dressed for this evening. You'll be wearing your black suit. Marie has placed it on your bed. Remember now, bathed, dressed and ready to go by five o'clock. I have a great many arrangements to make before we leave for the celebration and I want you to be ready by five o'clock.

"I'll see to everything, madame."

Marie carried her little treasure from the room, followed closely by George.

The sink in the laundry room had been used for cleaning a great many garments over the years, but it had never held a more celebrated dog, at least that was Marie's opinion. As the water and suds cascaded over the edge of the sink, the yellow rubber ducky bumped into Angel's nose for the second time.

I could do a better job by myself in less time.

In spite of all their good intentions, Angel was not amused.

"I'm holding her as tight as I can, Marie, but I don't think she wants to cooperate."

I told you I'm not dirty!

"I didn't know she was so dirty. Look at the color of the water!"

It looks pretty clean to me.

"Doesn't she look like a big white rat when she's wet?" George laughed.

And what do you look like when you're wet?

With the rubber ducky lying in the bottom of the drain, Angel was lifted from the sink and wrapped in a yellow and blue beach towel. "Let me dry her, Marie." George held out his arms.

With much exertion, George enfolded Angel in a towel. Twisting and turning, Angel resisted being confined until she slid down and onto the floor. Feeling no restraints, she ran for the doorway, dragging the end of the towel across the laundry room floor. Marie and George lunged after her, only to see her dash down the hall and bound up the stairs. As she gained speed, her confidence increased. Avoiding being caught was a talent she perfected having played the "chase game" with Brad throughout their home.

As she gained distance from the cleaning brigade of Embassy Row, Angel paused at the top of the stairs and looked back at the exhausted Maltese hunters. With a large pool of water collecting around her, she looked in each direction and made a choice.

"Catch her before she runs into your mother's bedroom!" Marie shouted.

The door to Marguerite's room was rarely closed except during her naptime or when she retired for the evening. This was not one of those times.

"What is this?" Marguerite saw a trail of water staining the carpet as a very wet, skinny- looking dog ran under the chaise lounge.

"Angelique, is that you? When you're wet you look five pounds lighter. You're all fur." Marguerite laughed.

Why does everyone think I look strange when I'm wet?

George and Marie came tripping into the room, both trying to enter through the doorway at the same time, forming a human logjam.

Marguerite laughed as George and Marie slid down onto the carpet. "Which of you three had the bath? You all look equally wet."

I'm glad everyone is having a good time, but could I have a towel? I'm starting to shake.

Angel jumped on the chaise and rubbed herself against the brocade cushions.

George was happy to see his mother laughing. It had been a

very long time since he'd seen her laugh as much. He wanted his mother to come back — the mother who could always make each day a time of sunshine and rainbows. "We need Angel to make my mother happy again," George said to himself.

That was a lot of fun. I hope we can play this game again.

George retrieved the towel from the hallway and wrapped it around Angel, rubbing her vigorously. After drying her off, he made a nest for her from his mother's terrycloth bathrobe. Angel snuggled her nose under the folds. Closing her eyes, she drifted away to a place with no measure of time or distance — a place where everything is as it should be, a place where Brad is waiting to be found, for he is the one who's lost — at least Angel thought so.

Chapter 47

Bastille Day

*I*t was Bastille Day, July 14th at Embassy Row. The ornate mahogany wall clock in the hall struck 4:30 as the phone began to ring. "Hello, Yes, I'll see if she's at home monsieur." Marie stood by the upstairs master phone that was one of the three that communicated with every room in the house. Pressing one of the five multicolored buttons, she rang Marguerite's room. " Madame, René Gullemont would like to speak with you."

Marguerite hadn't spoken to René since she left him abruptly on the evening of the musical at the Paris Opera House. She knew why he was calling and she knew she couldn't give him a truthful answer. She wanted to be alone with Brad sometime before the evening was over, and René would not understand. She had always known the luxury of telling the truth and having no fear of anyone. But surely this lie would not be out of fear, she told herself.

"I don't want to hurt a friend who has shown me kindness and consideration," Marguerite whispered to herself as she walked toward the phone.

"Hello, René. Yes, I'm going to the celebration. We're leaving in a few minutes. I'm sorry René I've been given only two tickets in the presidential section. Yes, I know that, but this year the security is even more restrictive. We must all bring our identification cards even though every security officer knows me. No, I won't be able to meet with you after the event. The President has asked me to attend the Ambassador's Dinner and I cannot refuse. I'm afraid it will be quite late before I get home. That is very thoughtful of you René, but Marie will be escorting George home after the fireworks. I promise to call you in a couple of days. Yes, I did receive the card and flowers. They were lovely. You are so kind and thoughtful. Yes, René, I miss you too. I must go now. I don't want to be late. Good night René."

Marguerite hung up the phone and called out for George as she hurried down the stairs and into her office. There, on the desk was her copy of the President's speech. Placing it under her arm she walked quickly toward the foyer where Marie, George and Angel were waiting. She stopped in front of the hall mirror and looked at her reflection. Marguerite sensed that something was missing from her dress. "Why are we waiting? Let's go mother."

"Marie, you and George go out to the car. The driver should be outside waiting. I'll be along in a minute." She placed her purse and the speech on the hall table, raced up the stairs, rushed into her room and walked over to her dressing table. Pressing a corner piece of molding, a spring device opened a miniature-hidden door. Several items were moved aside to reveal a small object. She held it tenderly in her hand as she pushed the door closed. Making her way down the stairs, she stopped in front of the mirror once again. The object was carefully pinned to her lapel. "There, now I'm ready."

The driver was standing by the car as Marguerite entered and took her seat facing George. "Mother, I've never seen that brooch before. Did father give it to you?"

"No, mon chéri, it was a friendship gift that I received a long time ago, long before I met your father." Marguerite looked out the window, imagining the moment when it was first pinned to her dress. "What is it?" George leaned forward to look at the design.

"It's a wishing well. See the little bucket and handle?"

"I've never seen one of those." George placed his finger on the delicate chain.

"There was one inside the patio of a small cafe in Georgetown where I would often meet a school friend. Your grandfather was the ambassador to the United States at that time and we lived in Mount Vernon, Virginia. It was a small community and not far from where I attended school."

"You never told me that before, mother."

"I think we're coming near the presidential viewing colonnade. I'll tell you all about my life in America tomorrow, but for now, prepare yourself for a great deal of excitement."

"Mother, can I hold Angelique while we are seated on the colonnade? She's very well behaved."

"I was going to suggest that you hold her even before you mentioned it. I've a surprise for you George. The man who's been looking for Angelique will be coming to the celebration and he will be sitting near us. I thought you would like to be the one who will place Angelique into his arms. You might even want to tell him how fond you have become of her. I think he would like to hear this from you." Marguerite pulled a tissue from her handbag and gently touched her nose.

Are you crying because I'm leaving? Did you find Brad? Something's going to happen.

"Marie, you'll be in the same place as last year. The driver will escort you to the location. After the fireworks you'll accompany George home. Prepare a light supper for yourselves. I should be home before eleven thirty."

"George, I'll expect you to be in bed and very much asleep before I get home."

"Yes, mother, I will. I suppose this will be the last time we will see Angelique." Stroking Angelique, his eyes grew moist.

I'm going to miss you too.

"George, that may not be true. I have a feeling that we may be seeing a great deal of Angelique in the future."

George smiled broadly as Angelique raised her ears, tilted her head and looked over at Marguerite.

What do you know that I should know?

Chapter 48

Noblesse Oblige

*B*rad had a restless night. Standing at his bedroom window, he looked at the rising sun that would give him the strength he needed for another day.

The bright orange glow slowly began to paint the room with hope. A breeze blew the curtains against the window frame as it traveled though the room bringing the promise of a new beginning.

Brad dressed quickly and went into the garden. He found that his days in a garden were as necessary for him as food. He was reminded of a poem that Marguerite had given him.

"If I had but two loaves of bread,
I would sell one and buy a rose,
For it would feed my soul."

A light mist of dew covering every leaf and petal created a fragrance reminiscent of a flower shop. As he strolled under the chestnut tree, he stopped near the fountain. Taking a coin from his pocket, he tossed it into the air in the direction of the marble statue of a boy and girl resting back to back. They held the handle of a bucket, their hands touching. The water poured from the bucket filling the large basin. Resting on the bottom of the fountain, his coin glittered and reflected toward the surface.

Off in the distance cathedral bells were chiming a melody from his past. He looked up through the branches and then down toward the coin in the water, and began to recite…

"The chestnut tree, the wishing well."

Repeating the phrase several times, he tried to recall other lyrics from the song.

"Monsieur Kennedy, Broderick called from the terrace. "Breakfast is now being served."

"I'm coming, Broderick, thank you."

"I would like to do some writing. I haven't done much in the last few days. I think I should be able to concentrate now that everything is almost back to normal," Brad told himself.

As he climbed the granite steps that led to the terrace, Brad noticed the rays of the morning sun reflecting off of the French doors. Like mirrors, he saw the trees, fountain, garden and a few scattered clouds in the distance behind him. Staring in the glass, he saw an image reflected. There were three people: a man, a woman and a child. They were looking at a portrait. The beginning of a song could be heard inside his head.

"I'll find you in the morning sun and…"

Concentrating, he tried to recall the next phrase, only it wouldn't appear.

"I'll find you in the morning sun and."

"I'll find you in the morning sun and when the night…"

"Good morning." Charles took a seat at the breakfast table. "You look miles away from Paris. I guess you miss your New England country."

"Good Morning." Brad leaned over the table and picked up his glass of orange juice.

"Yes, I was trying to recall the words to a song I once knew. Don't you think our memories are the most treasured and often the least appreciated gift we give ourselves?"

"I agree. We can play them over and over again in privacy. But I wonder if the memory of an event is ever exactly the same as the original."

When Brad met Charles, during his short stay at the Château Domaine, he looked very old. Today, he looked surprisingly much younger. Only Angel and Charles knew the reason for this remarkable transformation. Fate would one day give Brad the opportunity to write about Charles' life, and the mystery from his past would be known to everyone.

"Charles, staying in your home has brought contentment into my life. Every day I'm more grateful for your hospitality."

"I'm delighted to have you as my guest. This house is too large for one person. It's almost as big as the Château Domaine. I will share an amusing story with you. Last summer a relative, a charming woman, came for a visit. She was once a very famous actress. After three weeks, I thought she must have left without saying goodbye, then to my surprise I saw her one afternoon in the library looking for a book on watercolor paintings. I asked if she had left and then returned.

She said, 'I've been leaving the house early each day, walking through Paris, painting with my watercolors, and eating my meals at the sidewalk cafes.' She laughed and walked through that doorway over there. Our paths never seemed to cross. Isn't that extraordinary?"

Broderick moved about the dining room taking away the dishes as they became empty.

"Thank you Brad for expressing your appreciation. We are a family with very old traditions handed down for centuries. There was a time when the aristocracy helped rule France with each succession of kings. Of course your government has never had a monarch."

"Not officially. Though we did have two presidents who projected royal delusions during their administrations." Both men laughed as Charles continued his explanation.

"Many traditions were built around our hospitality and the service we performed for the monarch. In French we say, noblesse oblige, meaning, 'we of noble birth must oblige those who seek shelter.' Of course, I have a special and more personal reason for offering my home. Besides my fondness for you, there is also my affection for Angelique. I'm afraid she has captured my heart."

Chapter 49

The Linden Tree

*T*he desk in Brad's room was covered with papers, notes and clippings. As he typed his travel story on his laptop, he paused to remember his college professor at the University of New Hampshire. He followed the professor's advice and created his own writing technique. The professor would say, 'Brad, just put the story on paper. Don't be concerned with the spelling or grammar. You will have to revisit the manuscript many times to add, delete, modify, and elaborate. Practice this and your unique style of writing will blossom.'

After two transatlantic calls from his editor Ryan Hadlock, Brad raised his arms, stretching his shoulders, squeezing his writer's tension away.

"I can now work with enthusiasm, knowing I will be reunited with Angel."

Brad walked toward the window and looked down at the driveway where a silver Mercedes was parked in the shade. The driver was leaning against the car smoking a cigarette.

"If the driver's here, then I should get ready." Brad looked at his watch and saw the time was 4:00 o'clock. "We should be leaving at 5:00 o'clock," Brad remembered.

After a quick shower Brad reached for his robe when he heard a light tapping on his bedroom door. "Come in."

Broderick entered the room carrying a tray covered with a white napkin and placed it on the round table by the window.

"The Count suggested I bring a light meal for you. The banquet will not begin until sometime after 8:00 p.m.. The car will be leaving at 5:00 p.m. for the ceremony. There will be some delays since we will be going through several security checks. Leaving at five should give us plenty of time." Broderick bowed slightly and left the room.

As if rehearsed, Brad and Charles met at the top of the stairs. "Bonsoir." They both greeted one another as they descended the stairs in conversation. "I hope Broderick gave you something to eat, I had something myself. These political ceremonies can seem much longer if one has an empty stomach." Charles smiled.

Broderick opened the door and stepped aside as Charles and Brad walked toward the waiting car. All four men were dressed in black tie attire.

Hesitating for a moment, Charles stood by the car. "Broderick, you and the chauffeur will go to the same location as last year after you drop us at the colonnade."

The Count continued to give instructions as Brad looked back at the large estate, the long winding driveway and the limousine. He realized there was more similarity between himself, Broderick and the driver than there was between himself and Charles. It would not seem unusual if Charles were giving Brad instructions also. Brad was not an aristocrat. He was of the working class. If it were not for Angel, their paths would never have crossed.

Completing his conversation with Broderick, they entered the car. Brad looked at the two men in the front seat, his smile turning into laughter.

"Why are you laughing? Are you thinking of an amusing story?" Charles looked surprised.

"Yes, I suppose you could call it amusing. I was imagining myself writing a book about the improbable events that have occurred since my arrival in France. If I were to write about everything that has happened over the last week, no one would believe it." Both men laughed. Brad had regained his sense of humor and was relieved to know that in a short while he would once again be reunited with Angel.

"When we bring a companion into our lives, whether a dog, cat or any other pet, we love them and we hurt when they are taken from us," Brad thought.

The driver skillfully maneuvered the silver Mercedes onto the wide boulevard, slowly inching into the Paris holiday traffic. Brad lowered his window to get a clearer view of the Linden trees that spread their branches over the Quai de Grevelle. The aroma of their mimosa-like fragrance filled the car, reminding him of the day he had seen two Linden trees at the Château Domaine. The tree planted near the wine cellar especially intrigued him. He had wanted to ask Charles for an explanation of the enormous difference in the size of the two trees, and this was his opportunity.

"Charles, you have two Linden trees planted in the gardens at your château. I noticed that one tree was twice the size of the other. Were they planted the same year?"

"Yes, Brad, they were actually planted on the same day. Did you notice the plaque that was on the circular bench surrounding the larger tree?"

Brad nodded.

"Do you recall the words that were engraved on the plaque?"

"Yes, it read, 'In Memory of all French People who have resisted tyranny, August 31, 1944."

"That's essentially correct, except the date is inscribed before the dedication." Charles lowered his window and looked at the crowds of people, many carrying small flags of France as they crossed in front of the car in the stopped traffic.

"Why is one of the trees twice as big as the other?" Brad repeated his question.

Charles continued to look out the window, preoccupied with the people passing along the sidewalk. As the car waited for the traffic to move,

Brad waited for an answer. Maybe Charles didn't want to discuss the topic, although he couldn't understand why.

After a few minutes, Charles closed his window, pushing the sounds of the crowds and traffic away. The two men sat in silence. Finally, Charles turned toward Brad, his eyes narrowing.

"Brad, my father and I planted those two trees on the same day. The occupation of France was at an end. Paris had been liberated. On the day my father planted the trees, we stood over the hole that was dug for the tree closest to the wine cellar and my father said a prayer. Before we put the tree in the ground, he said,

"Je suis désole.

"Are you saying, that a prayer is what caused one tree to be twice as large as the other?"

"No Brad, I'm not suggesting the prayer made the tree grow taller. The tree grew larger as a result of the — Nazi fertilizer we placed in the hole before we planted the tree," Charles smiled knowingly.

Chapter 50

Adeline And Kevin

Marguerite, George and Marie arrived at the Place de Fontenoy Colonnade fifteen minutes before the Count's car stopped at the first security check point, a mile from the Eiffel Tower.

Marie waited in the car to be transported to her viewing area while Marguerite, George and Angel were escorted to the V.I.P. checkpoint.

After their identification cards were scanned, they walked to the colonnade viewing area where they located their reserved seats. Marguerite, noticing their names attached to the back of two seats, looked at the seats next to hers, and read the names; "Brad Kennedy," and to the right, the name, "Count Charles Beauchamp."

"Mother, can I walk to that railing? I want to have a closer look at the Eiffel Tower through the telescope. I have a coin. Can I take Angel with me?"

"Yes, but don't go any further. Let me attach her leash around your wrist. Now, you've been united forever." She laughed.

"Why did I say that?" she wondered.

Echoing in the distance she could hear the bells of the Cathedral of Notre Dame. "Why are the chimes so comforting? It's as if I'm hearing each toll for the first time."

The Bastille celebration was a common event in Marguerite's life, yet she felt her heart racing. The anticipation of the event could not have been the reason. It was something else. A mixture of emotions, familiar, yet exhilaratingly new, enveloped her. She could see herself standing along the railing of the Andréa Doria cruise ship, sailing for the United States. She was very young. The rush of the strong ocean wind against her youthful body was recaptured.

Marguerite let the memory fade as she became conscious of the two energetic playmates running toward the ornate stone barrier to look at the Eiffel Tower. George, pressing his arms on the cool marble, looked down at the crowd and the Tower beyond while Angel peered through the narrow columns.

If I could only see as well as I could smell.

Suddenly, Angel's ears arched as she sniffed the air, her senses heightened by an unseen force. Turning to the left and then to the right in quick succession, she began to pull on her leash causing George to tighten his grip. "What's the matter, Angelique?"

With her head strained upward, she sniffed the air and whimpered.

"Angelique, what's wrong? Stop! We have to wait here!"

You can stay here, but Brad is nearby, and I have to go find him.

Her attention focused on the limousines waiting at the bottom of the stairs. Angel barked several times, and then began to howl as she continued to pull on her leash.

Let's go. He's coming.

"She sounds like a wolf," George thought. The leash tightened around his wrist, cutting off his circulation. Angel's halter, now strained to its limits, broke at the buckle. George fell back against the railing and slid to the ground.

With a clear view of what was happening, Marguerite pushed aside the seat in front of her and sprinted toward her son.

"George, what happened? Which way did she go?" Marguerite looked down in the direction of the security checkpoint.

"Mother! I couldn't help it, Angel kept pulling and pulling, and then her halter broke! I thought she was going to pull my hand off!" George rubbed his wrist, trying to get the circulation to return.

"George, stay with me, I think Angel went this way. Oh my God, this can't be happening." Marguerite dashed down the steps toward the red carpet where a long line of limousines were pulling up to the yellow line.

Like a deer bounding through the forest, Angel leapt down the steps leading from the colonnade to the reception area. With her ears blown back by the wind, she made a curious sight as several couples ascending the stairs, moved aside.

"Where did that dog come from?" the Canadian Ambassador's wife remarked, as Angel dashed around the legs of several people gathered in small groups. The line of people grew longer as the impeccably dressed couples waited to have their identification cards scanned.

"I don't see her, do you George?"

"Yes, mother, I do. I just saw her tail go by the leg of the American Ambassador's wife.

"Oh, dear, this is terrible. Excuse me. Pardon me. Did you see a little white dog go by here?"

"Angelique! Angelique! Here Angelique! Come Angelique!" Marguerite and George repeated the same desperate chant.

The Count's car finally reached the Boulevard de Grenelle where the barricades had been placed across the intersection. An identification card was handed to the security officers who stood by the car holding an electronic scanning device. Both officers touched the brim of their hats and gestured the car forward.

Entering the restricted area, Brad saw the red carpet that extended from the curb up to the viewing colonnade. Each car stopped at the yellow line as a valet opened the doors for the occupants to exit. Brad had lowered the darkened windows of the limousine to view the pageantry and hopefully catch a glimpse of Marguerite and Angel. What he saw was a continuous line of well-dressed dignitaries, climbing the broad granite steps. At the top of the stairs, Brad saw a woman turn and glance down toward the line of people. "She looks as though she's been frightened by a mouse," Brad thought.

Finally their car reached the yellow line just as he closed his window.

Brad and Charles turned toward the door, waiting for the valet.

Angel sat, panting with excitement on the curb, sniffing the government officials as they were helped from the limousines. The women, decorated with expensive jewels that glistened in the sunlight, held out their hands while white-gloved valets gently helped them from their cars. Gentlemen with graying hair and black shoes, shined to a mirror-like finish, offered their arms to the ladies as the doors closed behind them.

Looking much like an ornamental alabaster statue, Angel sat motionless staring at the silver Mercedes that had just reached the edge of the yellow stripe.

A valet, surprised to see a dog, called out, "Come here doggy. Come away from there!"

I'm not moving. I'm waiting for Brad.

Angel growled a warning for the valet to stay away. Just as he reached down to scoop her up, the silver Mercedes' rear door opened and Angel leaped into the car.

Pushing their way through the crowd, Marguerite and George saw Angel disappear into the limousine.

Determined that Angel would not escape, George gathered all his strength for a boy of nine, and pushed his way past the valet who was reaching into the car to help the people inside. George's full weight fell against the valet's shoulder, causing him to lose his balance. The valet slid backward against the Russian Ambassador who was standing next to the curb tying his shoelace.

Triumphantly, George bounded into the silver limousine. From inside, Marguerite heard George calling, "Mother, come look!"

As she looked in the back seat she saw Angel vigorously licking Brad's face, as her long white tail waived excitedly in a circle.

"Angel, Angel, let me catch my breath." Brad gasped as she continued to jump about licking his face. Everyone was laughing, relieved to see Angel and Brad reunited. It was truly a holiday of emotions.

Marguerite felt complete satisfaction seeing Angel united with Brad. This happy event revealed another important piece of the puzzle. Now, she understood Brad's true identity and how much a part of her life he'd always been. He had never left her heart.

"Kevin. It's you, isn't it?" she asked,

"Yes, Adeline. It's me."

OK, can we go home now?

"Angel, I hope you won't mind if we stay in Paris a while longer. Brad looked into Angel's eyes, seeing his reflection mirrored in her devotion."

As long as we stay together, it's all right with me. No — more — laundry — carts!

"George darling, would you mind going ahead with Charles? We'll follow along in a minute."

Charles nodded in agreement, placing his hand on George's shoulder. "Come along young man, you can show me where I'll be sitting."

"Yes, monsieur, follow me."

As George and Charles walked up the stairs toward the colonnade, Marguerite attached the leash to Angel's collar. Angel pranced between them as they ascended the stairs.

"We have so much to talk about," Marguerite said nervously stumbling over her words.

"But first, I want to tell you something," Brad confided.

"All right, what would that be?" Marguerite's warm smile came toward Brad with all the affection she had stored away in her heart for so many years.

"I have to whisper it into your ear because long ago when you left America, I told myself that when we met again, the first thing I would say to you would be…"

Brad turned Marguerite toward him and slid his cheek slowly across hers. Pressing his lips to her ear, he embraced her and whispered; "I love you, Adeline. I've never stopped loving you."

The music from the military band playing *"La Marseillaise"* was heard off in the distance as the sound of cannon fire echoed thoughout the city. As the last note was heard, the President of France took his place at the podium and began to speak.

"To the People of France, honored guests and every citizen on this planet. We are here today to celebrate a New France, for each year on July 14th we renew our solemn vow to all those who have made France the jewel that it is today.

"We will continue to release the dove of peace each year so that everyone in the world will have the opportunity to stand with their family and watch the sunrise over a world of peace and hope."

Hundreds of white doves took flight and circled above the crowds. In a short while they faded into the setting sun.

The red carpet was void of everyone except the two people who mattered the most; the two lovers who could hear each other's heart beat. Brad and Marguerite were transformed back in time. They were once again, Adeline and Kevin.

Chapter 51

Quai De Grenelle Colonnade

When the speeches, music and singing had come to an end, Charles leaned over toward Brad and said, "Why don't you go to the banquet in Marguerite's car? It will give you a chance to talk. I'll follow in my car and meet you there."

"Thank you Charles, I would like that very much."

Sitting beside one another with Angel seated on Brad's lap, Marguerite gazed at Brad.

"I overheard what Charles said. Can we assume that he has arranged for us to be seated together at the banquet, also?"

"Charles arranges everything. He has even planned a dinner in honor of Angel's return. He's already given Broderick the seating arrangement." Brad laughed.

The sound of muffled laughter came from Brad and Marguerite as George looked disapprovingly at his mother. "Shh, mother, you two should behave yourselves."

Angel climbed over Brad and lay on Charles' lap, and then she raised her head to look at him.

Thank you for finding Brad.

Charles leaned forward, and Angel licked his cheek.

"You have a wet kiss, Angelique, but we're good friends, so I guess it's all right."

The sun was beginning to rest on the horizon as the Victorian streetlamps of Paris spread their magical glow. Each gilded building and statue began to reflect its golden rays toward the cheering holiday crowds below.

Several squadrons of jet airplanes spread vapor trails across the dark blue sky, signaling the beginning of the extravaganza of lights and fireworks.

George sat impatiently, anticipating the fireworks. "Mother, when does it start?"

"There are the planes. Now it will begin." Marguerite felt a warm hand envelope hers. She was reluctant to look at Brad's face. Would she awaken to discover it had been a dream?

Placing her other hand over his, she caressed it, as one would hold a small bird that had fallen from its nest. "It's I who have fallen from my nest. I want to love and be loved," Marguerite said to herself.

Off in the distance, the Eiffel Tower faded to a silhouette against the darkening grey-blue sky. George looked over toward Angel who was lying across Brad and Marguerite's lap. He smiled, hoping this was a glimpse of his future.

Suddenly, George's attention was turned toward the top of the Eiffel Tower. As he stared, the excitement he felt throughout his body was like nothing he had ever experienced.

A collective gasp spread throughout the viewing stand.

First one, then another, bright, piercing laser beam of light tore through the darkness, rocketing toward the sky, each one emanating from the tallest point of the Eiffel Tower. Several more, shooting in horizontal directions, lit the tallest buildings across the Seine. A dozen more thrust downward, illuminating the crowds with circles of lights as small as coins.

George was spellbound in his chair, his eyes darting about the city below. It was magical, unreal, he thought. Suddenly all the hundreds of lights began to revolve, spinning like a giant disco ball, flashing, pulsating, and growing smaller, then larger with beams of light shooting in every direction.

Marguerite squeezed Brad's hand as he moved closer to her. "You can look at me now, it's not a dream. We're home. The four of us, we're home."

As Brad spoke the word home, music was heard off in the distance, growing stronger and more pronounced as the lights from the tower continued to revolve, shooting beams of light all over Paris.

A shower of musical notes, never heard before, came from everywhere. Was it a hundred violins recorded over and over to produce the music of thousands, playing each note perfectly? Were there harps, playing harmoniously within the strands of the violins? The music was not definable nor the instruments clearly discernable.

No one in the entire city of Paris had ever seen or heard the sights and sounds that had been created for this celebration of Bastille Day.

Charles looked around and noticed that the people seated in the Quai de Grenelle Colonnade area looked astonished and immensely impressed. Waves of cheering, whistling and shouting grew louder, from the colonnade to the Eiffel Tower.

As suddenly as the lights appeared, they were extinguished. The darkness absorbed every flicker of light, leaving only a velvet, black curtain over the city. Tonight, only the stars of the universe lit Paris. This was a sight never seen before. The city of lights had been silenced as everyone looked up at the stars. A bright shooting star tore across the sky, as if orchestrated for the event. Then a tremendous sound, louder than the sound of thunder, startled George, causing him to lean forward. A high-pitched sound followed and a silver missile was seen piercing the darkness over the Eiffel Tower. Bursting apart, it scattered silver and gold sparkles in all directions. They hoverd for a moment before they began their long descent, slowly evaporating, before they reached the ground.

"Mother, Angelique, the fireworks are beginning!" George stood, holding on to the back of the chair in front of him like a ride on a rollercoaster.

Three silver rockets streaked toward the sky, each one spinning in different directions, bursting into a shower of red, blue and white. Angel, sitting erect on Marguerite's lap, gazed up at the extravaganza of exploding colors. Brad reached over to stroke Angel while he looked toward Marguerite. "Do you suppose the city of Paris is celebrating Angel's homecoming?"

"Of course, there can be no other reason, except the possibility that the city of Paris has heard that Kevin and Adeline have come home. Our last day together we both agreed that home would always be wherever we are."

Marguerite placed her hand over Brad's.

I have two new companions to protect. But it's my job.

Chapter 52

Mussee De Louvre Banquet

W hile being driven to the Louvre, Brad and Marguerite leaned back in each other's arms. They had much to say to one another after so many years had passed between them, but they chose to express their passion for each other in a way other than conversation.

George, Angel and Marie were sleeping comfortably in their beds by the time Marguerite and Brad were seated at the Musée de Louvre banquet.

The decision to hold the banquet in the Musée de Louvre was made by the President's adviser, Lydia Rousseau. Choosing this location was an ingenious way to give the government officials an opportunity to appreciate the controversial new glass domed pyramid under which the banquet tables were placed.

As Brad helped Marguerite take her seat, an attractive lady waved from across the room. The tables were too broad for conversation, so she walked its length and was soon standing next to Marguerite. "Marguerite, how have you been? Is this the man who lost his dog?" The lady kissed Marguerite on each cheek.

"To answer your questions; I'm fine and yes, this is Brad. Brad, this is Lydia Rousseau, a close friend of mine who is responsible for this sumptuous banquet here in the Louvre."

Rising from his seat, Brad shook Madame Rousseau's hand. "Lydia, you were so kind to help locate Angel. Charles told me of your assistance getting through the bureaucratic red tape to locate the person who found her. That person of course, was Marguerite.

"Yes, and Marie told me you were very helpful when she was questioned by security. That was awfully kind and considerate. But then, I'm not surprised, we were always there for one another," Marguerite embraced her friend.

"Lydia, you're to be congratulated. You chose an extraordinary location for the banquet. How did you arrange it?" Brad questioned.

Pointing to the glass pyramid dome above the banquet tables, Lydia explained, "My darlings, the Louvre Trustees had so much bad publicity when they built this glass pyramid in the plaza of the Louvre that they jumped at the chance to please us. Well, I'd better return to my place before the food is served. I can see that the Chinese Ambassador who is occupying the seat next to mine is wondering where I've gone. It should be a very interesting evening. If he speaks Cantonese, we will have a chance, but if he speaks Mandarin, then I'll have to use sign language for the rest of the evening. Wish me luck." Lydia waved as she walked away.

Marguerite watched Lydia take her seat across from them. "Look Brad, she's signing the letter 'M,' poor Lydia."

Brad took Marguerite's hand in his. "You remind me of a girl I fell in love with. It was her first day of school. She was wearing a blue dress. She had these two pink cheeks, each one punctuated with a dimple, another gift she received from the gods of beauty. You were trying to ignore me in our chorus class but I was determined that you would be exposed to my charms." Brad laughed. "When the teacher introduced us, I was happy that I had paid attention in my French Language class. Being with you, speaking French and the other kids not understanding what we were saying, made each day special for me. Do you remember the first day we saw each other? It was in the café across from the park." Brad mused.

Marguerite added, "You got off the bus at the park across from the cafe and you stood there just looking up at the tree. I wondered what you were looking at and then I realized it must be the blossoms because you reached up and picked one."

Brad continued the story, "It was a chestnut tree. When I crossed the street, I saw you seated at the table by the window. You were looking down at your book."

Marguerite interjected, "I saw you coming, but I turned away because I didn't want you to see me staring at you. When you came in and sat at the counter, I was wondering who was going to receive the flower."

"And when I placed it on your book, you smiled. Do you remember the bell that hung over the café door that rang whenever someone came in? When you left for France that first Christmas vacation, I was so lonely. I would go to the café and sit at our table. When I heard the bell, I'd look up, expecting to see you come through the door. After awhile, I couldn't even pass the café because it hurt too much."

"Shh," Marguerite pressed her finger on Brad's lips. "Your heart is here now, safe with me. Remember, the morning chimes will always ring for us."

Everyone at the banquet was engaged in polite conversation as the waiters moved about serving each course, wine glasses refilled.

"Come with me, I have something to show you." Taking Brad's hand, she led him away from the table, across the hall and down a long dimly lit corridor. The sound of the silverware brushing against the dishes, mixed with conversations, grew fainter as they made their way past the marble sculptures by Rodin.

Brad didn't know why they left the banquet; however being alone with Marguerite was reason enough.

"Here's the gallery I wanted you to see. George and I were here a month ago and when we came upon a painting by Renoir, titled "Confidences", George noticed something in the painting that I want you to see. There is a copy of the portrait in the château where we stayed." Marguerite pressed the light switch next to the doorway, illuminating all the pictures that hung around the gallery. At the far end of the room, with a long bench placed in front, hung an oil painting in the impressionist style. "Sit here in front of the painting with me and tell me what you see."

"I've seen this painting before at Charles' Château Domaine. I glanced at it on my way through the lobby. Angel seemed very interested in it. Now, I have a chance to examine it more closely. This is intriguing.

Brad began, "I see a man reading the paper, and a lady leaning on his shoulder. She is wearing a straw hat with red flowers. The man has a beard and he is also wearing a straw hat. Oh, yes, I can see the tips of her shoes. They are red also. It looks like a park setting. I think of us when I look at this painting." Brad took Marguerite's hand.

"There's something else in the portrait. Actually, it is the most important subject in the picture," Marguerite teased.

With his eyes scanning the top, sides and center of the painting, Brad noticed the spots of light that were highlighted on the leaves. He could see the light brushstrokes of blue on the dress and the billowy folds of her gown. There was a black spot surrounded by something that looked like a feathery hat. As he stood and walked closer to the painting, he began to laugh.

"That looks like Angel. Renoir painted a Maltese. I knew Chopin had a Maltese who sat on his lap when he composed on his piano. I wonder if Renoir had a Maltese?" Brad and Marguerite stood in front of the painting, each with an arm around the waist of the other.

Brad reached for the light switch, and the room was in darkness. Not a word was spoken. Sun-drenched memories warmed their thoughts of spending the rest of their lives together. Just as a decision was about to be made to speak the words they both were thinking, the lights in the gallery came on, chasing the darkness from the room and with it the words that would have expressed their tomorrows.

"Monsieur and madame, I'm sorry but this part of the Louvre is closed for this evening. Only the pyramid concourse area is available to the guests. If you will follow me, I will escort you to that area," the museum guard instructed.

Walking a polite distance ahead, the guard moved the purple velvet cord that had barricaded the hall from which the intruders had journeyed to see the painting.

"You haven't changed, have you Marguerite? You are still breaking the rules," said Brad.

"No, Brad, I have changed a great deal since I've seen you last. With you, here in my life I feel myself becoming the person I used to be. I had to lock me away when we parted because I had to be someone else. I know that now. Don't you feel the same way that we felt the time we were caught sneaking into the theater?" Marguerite laughed.

"I remember. It was your idea." Brad laughed

"Yes, but you held the door for the three other students. That's why we got caught. You always were helping the other guy. That is one of the million things I love about you." Marguerite waited to see what Brad's reaction would be to the declaration of her feelings.

Brad faced Marguerite and raised both of her hands, turning them over so that the palms were extended, he leaned over and kissed each one. Then he placed them on his shoulders. "I have been waiting for you to tell me those words."

Brad and Marguerite stood in the alcove, away from the festivities, in the shadow of the sculpture entitled "Balzac" by Auguste Rodin.

"Brad, I have so many questions to ask you. There's so much I want to know. Can we meet tomorrow?"

"Yes, but Angel is in your home." She's with Marie and George, remember? If I go back to Charles' home, I will be separated from her once again. I don't think I want to do that. You don't want me to be unhappy, do you?" Brad had a coy smile.

"You are welcome to spend the evening, of course. We can leave now, if you want. I doubt whether anyone will miss us."

Chapter 53

Citizens Of Paris

P aris in July can be very hot, yet with an occasional shower, the mornings are often the most pleasant time of the day, and so it was on the morning of July 15th in the park across the street from Embassy Row.

Although the park entrance had been opened since eight o'clock in the morning, there was no one there to enjoy the sounds of the sparrows that darted about the fountain, nor the cool breeze which caused the damp leaves of the chestnut trees to flutter as they released the last rain droplets onto the grass. Some of the tree blossoms had prematurely fallen from their branches, like confetti thrown upon a wedding couple, giving the brick walkway a white, speckled look.

George had opened the windows on the second floor of Marguerite's town house in order to welcome the morning sounds and fragrances of the garden.

George and Angel had eaten and were in the garden before 7:00 a.m. looking at the squirrel that came every day to get his share of the birdseed.

"You seem especially interested in our squirrel, Angelique," George said, as Angel stood on the bench beside him, looking very much like a hunting dog.

I chase the squirrel that comes to our garden in Portsmouth. He's not allowed to eat the birdseed, and he doesn't when I'm in the garden.

"George!" Marguerite called down from her bedroom window.

"Yes, mother."

"Have you and Angelique had your breakfast?"

"Yes, I fixed it myself. The cook was sleeping. She has a hangover. I think that's what it's called."

"George don't announce your opinions to the entire

neighborhood. Lower your voice."

Pushing aside a tree branch that hung over the walkway, Brad strolled up the brick path to George and Angel.

"Good morning my two favorite people." Brad squeezed onto the bench next to George and picked up Angel.

Marguerite called from her window, "I heard that. Am I not included on your list?"

Brad looked up to see Marguerite leaning over her bedroom balcony and shouted to her. "Can we spend the entire day together, the four of us?"

Marguerite extended her arms into a large "V" shape as she raised her voice above the garden below.

"Citizens of Paris, today I will not accept any phone calls, nor will I accept any visitors. The entire day and evening will belong to me and my family."

Brad began to applaud as George leaned over and kissed Angel, providing her the opportunity to give him numerous wet ones.

The happiest days for me are when I am with my pack.

Angel jumped down and ran toward the squirrel as it dashed through the hedge and up the chestnut tree.

Brad, George and Angel were waiting for Marguerite to join them in the park across from Embassy Row.

Marguerite ignored the sound of the phone ringing as she picked up her sunglasses from the entryway table

"Madame, You have a phone call."

"I'm not at home. Tell whomever it is that I've gone out."

"But madame, he said to tell you it was René and that he must speak with you."

Marguerite was anxious to leave for the park and be with her new family. Placing her hand on the doorknob, she hesitated, then opened the door; after several seconds, she closed it.

Standing in the doorway to the kitchen, the cook watched Marguerite, expecting an answer.

"I'll take the call in my office. You may tell monsieur that I'll be with him shortly."

As she walked down the hall a memory came racing from her past. At her parent's home in Mount Vernon, Virginia Brad was standing outside her bedroom window, tapping the window pane to attract her attention.

"Brad, what are you doing here? You're going to get us both into trouble." Marguerite raised the sash, leaned forward and kissed him.

"We're leaving, my family and I. I can't tell you where because I don't know where we're going. My parents have already enrolled me in a school in another country. Brad leaned over the windowsill and kissed Marguerite again. "I'll call you in a couple of days."

"But why are you leaving?" Marguerite felt empty inside.

"It's a government thing. I told you my father worked for the government, but what I didn't mention was that he is being blamed for his involvement in a scandal that will hurt the administration. We have to leave tomorrow. I'll try to call you before we leave." Brad turned and disappeared through the hedges.

"Wait, come back!" Marguerite shouted, not caring if her parents heard.

Brad returned from the darkness looking like a lost puppy. Marguerite took the ring from her finger and pressed it into his palm. "One day you'll return this to me, until then — 'I'll see you in the morning sun and when the night is new, I'll be looking at the moon, but I'll be seeing you.'" They embraced, gaining strength from each other's love.

Marguerite entered her office. Once it had been her father's, and it was filled with memorabilia from his days in the French diplomatic service. Although she found the office comfortable for her work as a speechwriter, she felt she was ready for a decorator to take charge and make the room a reflection of her personality.

Pulling the chair away from the mahogany desk, Marguerite picked up the phone.

"This is the most difficult call of my life," she said to herself as she took a deep breath and pressed the talk button.

"René, hello, I was just going out."

"Marguerite, I miss you. It was difficult being alone and not celebrating Bastille Day with you as we did last year."

"I'm sorry, René, it couldn't be helped."

"I thought we might spend the day together."

"I can't do that René. I have a guest."

"Is the guest Brad Kennedy?" René's voice changed. He sounded bitter.

"Yes, René, we discovered that we were friends in the United States. We went to school together when my father was the ambassador. You remember, I told you." Marguerite wanted to conclude the conversation.

"Yes, I remember you telling me your father was the ambassador, but I don't remember your mentioning a Brad Kennedy."

"It's a long story and very difficult to explain on the phone, René. Can I call you in a few days? We can have lunch and I'll explain everything."

"Marguerite, I love you."

Marguerite stood up and walked away from her desk wanting to place the phone down and end the conversation. She felt like a bird trapped in a cage.

"I have waited for your love for a long time. I just can't give you up, Marguerite." Leaning forward with his head resting on his arm, René placed his hand over the phone, too emotional to speak.

Both Marguerite and René were trapped by their emotions, one wishing to possess, while the other wanted only to escape.

"René, I have to go now, I'll call you in a few days, I promise."

"All right, I'll be patient. I can wait. Good night."

A cold silence descended over the room. Suddenly, for the first time, she was afraid.

Marguerite walked quickly to the small lavatory connected to her office. The sound of running of water could be heard as Marguerite splashed the cool liquid over her face. She took an antacid tablet from the cabinet and brushed her hair back with her fingers.

As she walked across the street toward the park, each step brought her closer to a life she had always dreamed would be hers.

Chapter 54

I'll Be Seeing You

"Hello everybody, I'm sorry I took so long," Marguerite joined her new family on the park bench.

"Mother, I want to remind you of what you said a couple of days ago."

"And that is?"

"You said, 'When have I ever been late?' That is a quote." George and Marguerite laughed.

"He has you, Marguerite. Admit it."

Angel looked at Brad.

Your record isn't so good either. You're usually late for my vet appointments.

"Would you like to ride on the carrousel George? I want to talk to your mother. Here, this should be enough for a couple of rides."

Brad took Marguerite's hand in his. "You said last night you had some questions for me, and I have some for you, but I'll go second." Brad laughed. It was a nervous laugh. He still couldn't believe how fortunate he was to have found Marguerite. "I have enough love inside my heart for two more people," Brad thought. "I'm ready to answer your questions."

"Tell me why you had to leave school and disappear? And why do you have a different first and last name?" Marguerite leaned her head toward Brad.

"I'll tell you as much as I can," Brad said. There are some facts that are still wrapped in government secrets that I can never share. It wouldn't be safe.

"My father had a very important position in the government; even today I cannot give you his title. There were several scandals:

the nuclear accident at Three-Mile Island, the American hostages in Iran, and the failed attempt to rescue the hostages in Tehran.

"Each one became more damaging to my father's reputation. It was a complex and involved situation. I remember my father having meetings at home with the members of the cabinet. Some of it I overheard. My dad was the obvious person to blame for the inefficiency of his department. He was asked to turn in his resignation and we moved away. I wasn't allowed to say where. We actually moved to Vancouver, British Columbia. We lived in a high rise on the 21st floor at 1277 Nelson Street. I was so lonely for you. I promised my parents I wouldn't give my phone number to anyone or write. It felt like we were in the witness protection program. When it was time for me to enter college, I wanted to attend the University of New Hampshire because my grandfather graduated from there.

"When I enrolled in college, I called the French Embassy in Washington and asked for your address. They said your family moved back to France and they were not permitted to give more information.

"I wrote a letter to you every week, for a year, in care of the French Embassy in Washington, D.C. I have a few I didn't send. They're at home in Portsmouth."

Marguerite looked shocked. "I never received any of your letters. Mother must have thrown them away. My parents planned my entire life, schools, friends, even my husband was chosen for me. I'm sorry you thought that I didn't care about you or that I was ignoring your letters." Marguerite put her arms around Brad. "We have today, and tomorrow. This is my gift to you, Kevin Tracy." Marguerite embraced and gently kissed Brad.

"Mother, mother, I asked Poppy, the man who runs the carousel, if Angelique could ride. He said she could ride in one of the Swans. Is that all right?"

"Well, what do you say Brad? Do you think Angelique would like to go around and around on the back of a bird?"

"I took her on a miniature train in Naples, Florida, and she liked it. Angel, how do you feel about going on the carrousel?"

Looking up at Brad, Angel glanced toward George and ran with him to the carousel.

Let's go, I'll ride anything once. If I get sick, then it's adios carousel.

"You were going to tell me how your name evolved from Kevin Tracy to Brad Kennedy."

"Yes, my father, Richard Tracy, never returned to Washington. His friends in Vancouver, British Columbia, gave him a job at the University, researching orca whale migration.

"The newspapers continued to hound us for stories and interviews each time the Senate Investigative Committee held a hearing that concerned one of the scandals. I can't remember when there wasn't at least one reporter in our driveway or sitting on our front steps. I received a phone call at my dorm the first week I was at the University of New Hampshire. My dad told me that my mother started drinking heavily, and she had checked herself into a Palm Springs clinic. I loved my mom and dad very much. They weren't the best parents in the world, but they recognized their mistakes. I forgave them for abandoning my dog. They were always interested in my activities, always supportive of my choices. They knew about us and wanted to meet you.

"My dad was 65 when he went into the hospital; he never came home. I went back for the funeral. My mother wouldn't speak to anyone. The reporters were hovering at the edge of the entrance to Arlington cemetery as we walked to the gravesite. For the two weeks I was there, the reporters never left the front of our house. I had to get back to my classes, so I returned to New Hampshire.

"The first morning, upon my return to UNH I was walking to an early morning class when four reporters ran up to me asking questions. A Washington newspaper had gotten hold of some tapes that implicated my father in some governmental cover-up. There were a great many times that my friends stopped calling because their parents were concerned about my family's reputation. There were so many unsubstantiated rumors that after a while it didn't seem to matter whether they were true or not. It was still news and it sold papers.

"My father was in the process of writing a book when he died.

One evening my mother decided to unlock my father's files. She discovered that all the locks were missing. All his papers mysteriously disappeared from our home. Every file, letter, picture and note pad vanished. The day after it happened, my uncle called and said he had spoken to mom and they both agreed I should change my name rather than to carry the notorious title of the son of Richard Tracy. The judge did the rest."

"You were all alone?"

"Yes, but I had phone calls from my uncle, and he helped me financially while I was at the University.

"Once I had my name changed, I felt liberated. It was a new beginning for me. The reporters stopped coming around, mainly because I had created a successful strategy of avoiding them."

Distant cathedral bells rang in melodic waves, striking twelve times as George secured Angel in the Black Swan and took his place beside her. The time had come for the carrousel to begin its imaginary journey.

Hearing the first musical notes coming from the carousel and the cathedral bells, Marguerite and Brad looked at one another. Grasping hands they walked toward the colorful fantasy ride of make believe. Brad began to hum the tune as Marguerite sang the lyrics, slowly – softly. Brad joined her, halting at first and then the words came surely and clearly, drifting back from their past.

> *Cathedral bells were tolling*
> *And our hearts sang on.*
> *Was it the spell of Paris?*
> *Or the April dawn?*
> *Who knows,*
> *If we shall meet again?*
> *But when the morning chimes ring sweet again:*
>
> *I'll be seeing you*
> *In all the old familiar places*
> *That this heart of mine embraces all day thru:*
> *In that small café*

The park across the way,
The children's carrousel,
The chestnut trees, the wishing well.

I'll be seeing you
In every lovely summer's day,
In everything my heart can say,
I'll always think of you that way.
I'll find you in the morning sun;
And when the night is new,
I'll be looking at the moon
But I'll be seeing you!

George held firmly to Angel's halter. "I got my wish. Angelique is part of our family now."

"Brad, where will you be staying while you're here in Paris?"

"I've been staying with Charles, but I can't take advantage of his hospitality any longer. Do you know of a moderately priced hotel not too far away from here?"

"We'll do a search together after dinner. Or maybe tomorrow would be better. We should spend some time alone this evening. I haven't told you my story," Marguerite said, smiling with complete happiness.

"When we get back to your home, I'll call Broderick and leave a message for Charles." Brad was contented knowing that they would have more time together this evening.

Angel raced ahead pulling George along.

"It seems that Angelique is taking me for a walk, Brad!" Marguerite and Brad laughed as they continued to recapture the special relationship they shared long ago.

Before Brad and Marguerite left for the evening, they peeked into George's room. A small nightlight spread a protective, peaceful glow over the two friends. Two very contented soul mates lay cuddled together, sharing a Peter Pan evening of dreams.

As Brad and Marguerite walked in the warm July evening, the fragrance from the Linden trees brought a wonderful gift of remembrance of their days walking through Georgetown. The moon had almost decided to be full this evening, but still a welcome addition.

"Look at the moon. It's following us as we walk. There it is hanging over your head." Brad pointed.

"It stopped following me the day you left. You've brought it back." Marguerite looked up through the tree branches.

"The moon was never there for me either. It was the morning sun that gave me hope. I always had faith in tomorrow." Brad surrounded Marguerite with affection as they walked along the moonlit street.

The security guard, standing under the street lamp, recognized Marguerite as she and Brad approached the intersection.

"Good evening Madame Revier and Monsieur Kennedy."

"That's surprising, how did he know my name?" Brad asked as they past the secured area and continued along the Rue de Lafayette.

"I gave the security headquarters your name yesterday and informed them that you were to be admitted at any time. I have always found them very thorough. Do you know were we are going?"

"No, and do you know I don't care? I'm with you and that's all that matters."

"I knew you must be hungry, so we are walking to my favorite café. It's only a few blocks away.

As they walked together, each step in concert with one another, closely matched, both in temperament and in passion, they knew their love had never weakened. It only lay dormant like the mustard seed, buried deep in the earth. When the soil is tilled, it rises to the surface, growing tall and healthy, and finally it blooms.

Café Amour was renowned for its food and wine. With only six tables outside, they were usually occupied.

"This is very nice." Brad followed Marguerite to the wooden podium. The grey-haired man recognized Marguerite and guided her to the farthest outside table behind a potted palm.

"Madame Revier, I'm very pleased to see you this evening. Welcome, Monsieur Kennedy, to Café Amour." The matre d' handed them their menus.

Brad laughed and asked Marguerite, "Did you give the matre d' my name when you made the reservation?"

"Of course, Brad, that's how things are done here in Paris. "Noblesse Oblige."

"Yes, I've heard of it."

"We don't have a park across the way as we did in Georgetown." Brad reached across the table and took Marguerite's hand.

"No, we don't, but look at the light coming through those trees. That's not a street lamp. It's the moon. It may not be a full one, but almost." Marguerite leaned across the table and kissed Brad. "What is moonlight without one of those?"

Removing his hand from Marguerite's, he raised his little finger on his right hand so he could remove the ring. Holding the ring in the two fingers of his right hand, he held it so Marguerite could see it in the light. "Do you remember the last words you said to me on the day we parted? You said, "Keep this ring until we meet again, then place it on my finger once more." Brad raised Marguerite's right hand and slowly slid the ring on her finger. "Here it will stay until you ask me to move it to your left hand." Brad took Marguerite's hands in his, leaned forward and gently kissed her palms.

There was a comfort, a familiarity of connected energy that required no conversation, no expectations. Being alone and feeling each other's presence filled them with extreme pleasure.

The meal and wine were extraordinary; only the dessert was left to savor.

"And now, Madame Marguerite Revier, would you tell me why my lovely Adeline Caturia is now Marguerite? I know women change their last name when they get married, but they rarely change their first name too."

Marguerite dipped her spoon into the chocolate mousse, took a bite and began; "Remember when we discussed our future? You wanted to become a writer, maybe a screenwriter or playwright? Well, my passion was to be an actress."

"Yes, I remember."

"After we left Washington, D.C. and arrived in Paris, my father retired from the diplomatic service for a year. He wanted to write his memoirs. I was eighteen and they had already enrolled me at the Sorbonne. I refused to go, which shocked them. They were in a state of panic. I made a bargain. I would go to the University if I could attend the Ecole de Mime Corporeal in Paris, under the direction of the great French actor, Etienne Decroux, for one year. They had no choice but to agree. I was thrilled. My passion was finally realized.

When I attended my first class, I wrote my stage name, Marguerite, with no last name. From then on, I was known only as Marguerite. No one was to know our government connections. That is where I met Lydia. We came from similar backgrounds, and we've remained friends ever since.

Within five months my acting skills had improved greatly. I was very good. My performance became more focused, more natural. I shall never forget Monsieur Decroux's response to my performance in the improvisation class. "Marguerite, that was a perfect portrait of *wanton insolence.*"

"I went home singing. Most of the other students received a *pas mal* comment. I stood out from the crowd, and I cheered for weeks. I applauded myself every morning in front of the mirror. I was in heaven. But then, the year ended and I had to fulfill the commitment to my parents."

"When did you decide to marry? Did you finish the University?

"Yes, I finished with a degree in journalism. I married Lamar a few years after I graduated. His parents had a family law practice, and it was quite natural for Lamar to take over when his father retired. My parents treated him like a son. He even resembled my father, my mother would always remind me.

"I decided to use my degree in journalism by applying for a job with the *Regards* magazine, but then my father asked me to write a speech for him because his speechwriter was in the hospital. I did very well, and my father was complimented in the press for his wonderful words.

"After that, my father would have no one but me write his speeches. I enjoyed doing it very much. Even after George came along, I continued.

"Before my father's death he told a reporter from *Regards* magazine that his daughter had written all of his speeches. Soon I had numerous requests from every political office seeker for my services. I refused them all until the President called one day and asked me to consider a position on his staff. Of course, he meant I would write all of his speeches.

"Today, George and I have the two servants, who are like my family. My parents' home is mine now since the death of my parents five years ago."

"What about our future together?" Brad asked. "George wants to keep Angel, and Angel won't go without me. I want my days and nights to be filled with my family of four."

"You are making a very big leap after thirty years of separation to, "let's get married". So much has happened in such a short time."

"Marguerite, we may look different, but our hearts are still the same." Brad reached across the table and held Marguerite's hand tightly.

"Brad, let's pretend we've just met."

"Where are you going with this?" Brad asked.

"Be patient. I have a plan. You suggested that we should see each other exclusively. I've accepted. Of course, who wouldn't, a charming man like you? First we will date, and date, and date; the two of us and then the four of us, and then the two of us."

"Now, I understand your plan." Brad pushed his chair closer to Marguerite.

"In a little while we can make arrangements that are more

permanent. Agreed?" Marguerite asked. Tilting her head to one side, she smiled.

"Is that your best offer?"

"Yes." Marguerite responded.

"Madame Marguerite Revier, I accept the challenge. You're wearing my pin!" Brad touched the chain that hung from the golden wishing well attached to Marguerite's blouse.

"Shall we go home?" Brad asked.

"Mine or yours?" Marguerite laughed as they took hands and began their walk.

Just as they crossed the street from the café, Brad noticed a red Alfa Romeo sports car with a man behind the wheel looking their way. There was something about the car that seemed odd. It was parked in a no parking zone, which puzzled him. Pushing the thought away, Brad looked over at Marguerite. The moon, almost full now, followed the couple as they walked along the Rue de Lafayette, laughing and sharing. The streets and sidewalks were empty. No one else existed, at least, as far as they were concerned.

Chapter 55

The Guest Of Honor

T he phone next to Brad's bed made a soft buzzing sound. Reaching over the edge of the covers toward the nightstand, Brad put the phone to his ear. It was Broderick announcing that breakfast would be served in fifteen minutes. "Yes, Angel will be with me."

Brad looked toward the foot of the bed expecting to see Angel. She was not in her usual place. His heart raced as he glanced quickly around the room. Looking back at the bed, Brad noticed a large lump between the headboard and the extra pillow.

"So there you are." Brad sighed with relief.

"I wonder when I'll be able to leave you by yourself again without being anxious."

Brad sat on the edge of the bed, his head lowered, trying to compose himself. Angel's kidnapping and the abandonment of his best friend, Tiny, were the two tragic events in his life. His heart had not completely healed, and it was unlikely it ever would.

Angel pushed the pillow away and scooted over to Brad. Nuzzling between his arms, she stretched her neck to reach his chin, giving him a wet 'hello' lick.

"Good to have you back home, Angel."

Brad whisked her from the bed, cradling her in his arms as he circled around the room, singing.

"Hello Angel, well hello, Angel, it's so nice to have you back home where you belong. You're lookin' swell, Angel, I can tell, Angel, you're still glowin', you're still crowin' you're still goin' strong. I feel the room swayin' I hear the band playin', one of my old favorite songs from way back when, so, bridge that gap, fellas, find her an empty lap fellas, Angel'll never go away again."

Ready for the days adventure, a prospect to savor when two

friends are reunited, Angel and Brad began their journey. With the bedroom door wide open, Angel ran ahead and descended the stairs. Crossing the hall she ran out the front door as Brad followed closely behind.

When she reached the edge of the lawn, she began her morning sniffing. She would look at Brad every so often to assure herself that he was still there. Although satisfied she was back in her familiar world, her security had been shattered. It would be a very long time before she would trust strangers again.

"I wonder what Marguerite is doing now?" Brad knew his happiness would be complete with Marguerite and George standing beside him this morning.

Looking at the front gate, Brad noticed a red Alfa Romeo parked next to the curb, the same sports car he had seen parked in front of the café the night before when he dined with Marguerite. The driver was staring at him. As Brad walked closer to the gate he realized the man was the same person who escorted Marguerite to the Opera House. Just as he reached the gate, the car drove away.

Brad walked back to the house. Stopping at the entrance, he glanced into one of the side panels of glass on either side of the door. He could see the driveway and the gate's reflection. The red sports car had returned and was now parked across the street.

Brad continued into the house feeling uneasy about the incident. "I should talk to Marguerite about this guy."

Seeing Charles coming down the stairs, Brad waited near the last step. "Charles, good morning, have you had breakfast?"

"Broderick brought something to me earlier. Have you had yours?"

"Yes, I had a breakfast drink and Angel had her usual."

"Good morning, Angelique." Charles picked her up gently and cradled her in his arms.

"Brad, what are your plans for the day? I would like to discuss something with you."

"Angel and I were going to do some hotel shopping. I want to find a place close to Embassy Row."

Are we going to move in with George? I like the food there.

"I would like you stay longer if you could. Let's go into my office. I have something to show you that I've been working on since we met at Château Domaine."

Once in the office, Charles placed Angel on the leather sofa next to Brad and walked around his desk. Pulling a yellow file folder from his top drawer, he handed it to Brad. Brad pressed the switch on the lamp, and the light encircled the papers. After he read the first page, Brad hesitated and looked up at Charles. "Charles, this is very personal information. I don't know what to say."

Brad could not understand why he was being asked to read such a revealing manuscript. Both men sat in silence.

Angel got down from the couch, walked around the desk and jumped onto the high back chair near Charles. After a few seconds, she leaped onto the desk and placed her face next to a gold-framed photo of a grey-haired couple standing in front of the Château Domaine.

"Angelique, would you like to know who they are? They are my parents. The picture was taken in 1939, before the occupation. That's our dog with them."

He looks like a German shepherd.

"I'm sorry Brad. I should have explained before I gave you the folder. I've been writing my memoirs. After returning from the château, my energy improved a great deal as well as my overall health. Would you like some coffee or tea?"

"Yes, coffee would be fine," Brad watched Angel as she bounded from the desk to the chair and onto the carpet.

I think Charles has a proposition for you.

She sat at Brad's side, curled up with her head resting on his leg.

Don't you think Charles looks younger?

Charles summoned Broderick and requested coffee with brandy.

Sitting in the chair across from Brad, Charles leaned back and took a deep breath.

"Brad, your little friend has made a very important change in my life. Since the day she and I spent that afternoon together, my life has been transformed. If you remember when we last spoke, I was in a wheelchair. I was taking medication for depression and I never had more than a few hours of sleep each night. As you can see I'm walking, and my appetite has returned. I'm more active than I've been in years, and I haven't taken any medication since I left the château. Angelique was the one who made the difference. I don't question how it happened. I'm just thankful Angelique came into my life."

Broderick tapped on the door of the office and entered carrying a tray with the beverages. Placing it on the low table between the two men, he left the room.

"Charles, I'm delighted you've shared your happiness with me, and I know Angel is happy for you as well. Are you asking me to work for you as an editor? In other words, I'll be preparing your manuscript for publication?"

Brad noticed Angel looking very intently at Charles and then glancing back at him.

Say yes. You can use the work.

"Exactly, I want to employ you. I want you both to remain here, at least until the book is completed. If you will give me the amount of hours you wish to work each day, then I can schedule my time for our collaboration." Charles eyes lit brightly with enthusiasm. "Are you agreeable with this idea?" Charles looked hopeful as he handed Brad a cup of coffee.

"I would like very much to help you write your book. I'm honored you have confidence in my ability. Angel and I would be delighted to accept another helping of your "noblesse oblige." Both men laughed.

"Now for my surprise!" Charles stood up and pulled the cord for Broderick.

A surprise. I like surprises.

As Brad closed the folder and returned it to Charles, Broderick entered the room. "You rang monsieur?"

"Broderick, it is time to fulfill our promise to Angelique."

A promise? You promised me something?

Angel stood on the couch looking at Broderick as he began his speech.

"Angelique, Count Charles Beauchamp would like you to be

the guest of honor at a dinner party to be held on July 25th. You may give me the names and addresses of the guests you would like to invite. If I could receive the list by tomorrow, it will expedite the matter.. The guests will begin arriving at 6 p.m. It will be black tie." Broderick bowed slightly and scratched Angel under her chin.

"Thank you Broderick. Angel and I would be honored to attend." Brad took Broderick's hand and shook it vigorously as Broderick, surprised at the familiarity, looked away in embarrassment.

"Thank you Broderick, that was perfect," Charles said as he placed the yellow file folder into his desk drawer.

"Broderick, before you leave would you please pour a glass of wine for yourself? I think we should make a toast." With their glasses filled, Brad held Angel and raised his glass toward Charles and Broderick. "Our first toast is for Angelique and our second is for our collaborative efforts to complete the story of my life at the château during the war years." All three men touched their glasses and raised them to Angel.

This is a wonderful life. I feel special.

Broderick stood near the sofa waiting to see if there were any further requests.

"Broderick, I think Angel might like to meet your dog, Sophie. Where is she?"

"She's in her yard behind the garage." Broderick looked pleased.

"Brad, Broderick has a dog. I think she's a cocker spaniel. Is that correct Broderick?"

"Oui, monsieur."

"Charles leaned over to pet Angel as he directed his remarks to Brad. "Would you like Angelique to share a little time with Sophie. They may enjoy playing together."

"How would you like to play with a cocker spaniel, Angel?" Brad asked.

Yes, I would like to have some canine companionship.

Angel barked, and ran toward Broderick.

"I'll go with you to see how you get along with your new friend," Brad suggested.

Charles placed his wine glass on the table and turned to Brad. "So, my friend, we have settled the matter of your staying, and we can begin working on the book on Monday. Is that agreeable?"

"That's perfect." Brad extended his arm and the two men shook hands.

"Broderick, since Angelique will be with us for awhile, would you like Sophie to have the run of the house so they could be company for each other?"

Broderick looked shocked to hear the Count suggest such an idea. He had noticed a great many changes since they had returned from the château, including the Count's attitude. Broderick stood in silence.

"Well, Broderick, do you think that two dogs, running about will be a problem for you? I know I shall enjoy the sounds of happy paws running down the hallways." Charles waited in the doorway for Broderick's answer.

"Monsieur, yes, it would make me very happy to have Sophie about the house. She's very well behaved."

"I hope she won't be too well behaved. I would like to see a bit of play and merriment in this house. " Charles smiled broadly as he disappeared down the hall.

Broderick nervously began to pick up the wine glasses from the table. Holding the tray in one hand, his sleeve brushed against the bottle of wine causing one of the glasses to tip over and break, leaving the other teetering on the tray. Brad, who had been standing near the table, reached out quickly to prevent the remaining glass from falling to the floor.

"Merci monsieur. There have been so many changes that I…"

Setting the tray on a stand in the hallway, Broderick folded his hands together tightly while trying to compose himself. It was evident that Broderick would need time to grow accustomed to the changes in Count Beauchamp's personality.

Brad and Angel followed Broderick to the kitchen where he pulled off his black apron and placed it on the back of the door. "This way, Monsieur Kennedy."

Angel dashed ahead, barking as she ran toward the chain-link fence where Sophie had been lying in the shade.

Hello, hello, wake up. Come on. We have some exploring to do. This is a big house.

Angel ran into the gated area, as soon as Broderick released the latch, prompting Sophie to jump up. Nose to nose, they exchanged information about each other.

I know your name is Sophie. Mine is Angel. Let's get out of this cage and have some fun!

Running and jumping over one another, they tumbled on the lawn and into the shrubs. Brad and Broderick stood close by laughing. Brad had never seen Broderick so relaxed and full of humor. The change that had taken place in Charles was now affecting Broderick. When Brad first met Broderick, he seemed one-dimensional. He was there only to give service to others. Now, seeing him with his companion, his personality came alive.

"Come on, Broderick! Let's chase them across the lawn. I've never been able to come close to catching Angel. She's very proud of that fact." "Sophie's the same. She gets my heart racing trying to keep up with her."

Dashing from the edge of the lawn to the other side of the hedge, Broderick and Brad raced after the two new friends.

Slow down Sophie. We don't want to crush their egos.

Angel dashed under the garden bench with Sophie close behind.

Chapter 56

Extravagante Expresse Theatre

*A*ngel's special evening had arrived. The newspaper, *Le Figaro*, printed a two-column article with a photo of Angel in front of the Eiffel Tower.

"An American, and his Parisians friends, joined hands to find Angelique, the celebrated hero of Paris who saved the lives of twelve cats and their mistress. Count Charles Beauchamp will host a celebration in honor of Angel at his estate in Paris that will include celebrities, government officials and friends of the American, Brad Kennedy."

Parisians often speak of rain as if it were an old acquaintance. They welcome a visit now and then, but the length of the visit should be only two days at the most. So it was a cause for regret that the day before Angel's home coming celebration, the streets of Paris looked like miniature canals. Each day, the rain and wind usually an infrequent visitor, now threatened to become a constant companion.

Sitting alone in the window seat as the rain continued to collect in the streets of Embassy Row, George looked on, disappointed. Angel and George were looking forward to the big party at Charles' home; after all, it was the celebration of Angel's return. "All this rain. I wonder if the party will be cancelled."

Two miles away Angel stood in front of the closed French doors leading into the garden at the Count's home looking at the rain as it poured down the panes of glass.

If this continues, the party will be cancelled. There's something I can do and George can help me.

Placing her paws on the glass, Angel lowered her head.

At Embassy Row, a young boy sat in the window seat of his living room thinking of his friend, Angel. Folding his hands, he remembered his First Communion and the prayer he had learned to recite.

Both Angel and George, though in different parts of Paris, had assumed a position of reverence. As George knelt in his window seat, Angel pressed her head against the French door. The two friends exemplified hope, faith and perseverance.

As the clouds parted and the last drops of rain disappeared from the sidewalks, the two smiling friends began to think of each other, happy that their celebration would soon commence.

The large gates at the end of the driveway parted as several white vans drove up the drive to the Count's estate. A security guard, hired for the occasion, had instructions to admit only those with an invitation.

The decorators transported an array of colorful banners, balloons and floral arrangements through the open doors. Caterers emptied their vans of delectable gourmet delights, whisking them into the kitchen. Angel ran about excitedly sniffing the aroma that drifted from the bright silver trays.

This one's crabmeat and that's roast beef.

Following one caterer, she would change direction and follow yet another as she sampled each new smell.

"Is this dog taking inventory?" a server questioned.

When the kitchen door opened into the dining room, Angel slipped through. Seeing several ladies dressed in white and black uniforms, she dashed under the dining room table where her new canine friend, Sophie, was hiding.

Has anyone dropped any food yet?

The servers walked about the room decorating the tables with flowers. The four arrangements consisted of tulips, lavender, roses, and gardenias, each one accented with a red crystal candelabra in the center.

A waiter pushing a cart laden with hors d'oeuvres stopped in the dining room so that a waitress could cover it with a white tablecloth. Angel and Sophie crawled along the carpet and pushed themselves under the white linen.

Dashing from under the cart, they ran toward Charles, and snatched a slice of ham that dropped onto the carpet.

Charles stood in the doorway, enjoying the frenzied activity. "Angelique, have you seen Broderick?"

Angel and Sophie ran to the front door looking back toward Charles, barking as they ran.

Follow us. We'll take you to him.

They ran down the steps, across the driveway and stopped next to Broderick. Looking up, they saw him giving instructions to a young valet.

"Broderick, may I speak with you for a moment?"

"Of course monsieur, " Broderick finished his instructions and walked over to Charles who was standing on the landing.

"Broderick, as you know I'm expecting a delivery. It's the painting from the château. When it arrives, please have it hung in the ballroom over the fireplace. I will give you a signal at the end of the meal. Tell the orchestra to play the tune I have chosen. All of the guests will go into the ballroom where there will be dancing before and after the unveiling of the portrait.

I would like you to be standing next to the painting, and when I give you a nod, after my little speech, you will pull the cord and reveal the portrait. Do you have the red velvet curtain for the workmen to install?" Broderick nodded.

"Please test the mechanism a few times to be certain that it will not get stuck and ruin the desired affect. I know we haven't used the room for ten years and there is a lot that can go wrong. I'm relying on you to see that it will be ready. You've been doing a marvelous job coordinating all of the activities.

"It's been quite a challenge, monsieur."

Charles walked to the foyer, followed by Angel and Sophie. "Come along ladies." He motioned in the direction of the stairway.

Looking down from the top of the landing, Brad saw the two new friends and Charles walking across the central hall surrounded by caterers, waiters, waitresses, busboys and musicians. They were all dashing about carrying, pushing, and lifting items for the celebration.

Brad shouted to Charles. "Have you seen the article in the newspaper about Angel's celebration?"

"Yes, I read it this morning. I showed it to Angelique." Charles laughed as he jumped out of the way of two tall women dressed in black. They were moving about with clickers that made a sound like very loud crickets. As they went about the rooms directing the workers they would point and click. Pink ostrich feathers protruded from the front of the silver headbands of the two women as they twirled, pointing and clicking their way in and out of each room.

One of the musicians who had been pushing the piano through the entryway sat down on a stool and began to play a jazz tune. Two tap-dancing waitresses went about the room, each carrying a tray with crystal wine glasses that tinkled as they tapped their way into the ballroom.

A waiter picked up Angel and sat her on the stool by the man playing the piano. He placed her paws on the two lowest keys and continued to keep the beat as Sophie and Angel barked each time her paws connected with the piano keys.

A twelve-piece orchestra appeared in the entrance hall, playing Glen Miller's "In The Mood." The lady clickers continued their pirouettes as they pointed in the direction where the orchestra would be playing.

Opera music, coming from the outside, grew louder as two sopranos, in full costume, sang the last act from Carmen.

Laughing and turning in all directions, Charles was elated to see the montage of people weaving about the rooms. He was glad he'd taken Lydia's suggestion to hire the Extravagante Expresse Theatre Appovisionner to entertain as well as serve the dinner. He had been assured the evening would be an original with a succession of delightfully unpredictable events that would forever be in the memory of each guest.

From where Brad had been standing at the top of the stairs, he couldn't tell if the people were part of the evening's entertainment or the staff hired to prepare and serve the meal. "This looks like the opening scene of a Groucho Marx movie," Brad laughed.

"What's going on, Charles?" Brad shouted from the top of the stairs. Angel, hearing Brad's voice, ran to the stairs, jumping two steps at a time until she reached the top. Brad caught her on the final leap. "We need a little practice on our tricks if we are going to entertain the guests tonight, Angel."

I'm ready when you are. I have plenty of energy.

Angel licked Brad's ear.

"Brad, we'd better change! The guests will be arriving in a couple of hours. Did you call Marguerite today?" Charles dodged several workers who crisscrossed into the various rooms on the first floor.

"She and George will be arriving thirty minutes earlier than the other guests. I'll be ready by then!"

Charles walked down the hall followed by Sophie who bounced along at his heels.

"Sophie, we're having a lot of fun, aren't we? You certainly make this house come alive."

Brad finished dressing while Angel sat on the alpaca rug in the center of the room.

Anticipating the arrival of Marguerite and George, Brad thought of the man in the red sports car. He wondered how well Marguerite knew him.

Hearing a faint tapping sound, Angel ran to the door and returned with Marguerite and George.

"You arrived at the very moment I was planning the rest of my life." Brad reached for George, who held Angel. Pulling them close, Brad said, "Group hug."

George, pulling back slightly, looked up at Brad, "I missed Angelique. I hope you both come to live with us soon."

We're all going to be together, right Brad?

George knew he was being forward, but he had taken liberties before and survived. Hearing Brad and Marguerite laugh, George knew he had made the right decision.

"See, Marguerite, we must make George happy."

"Did you prompt George before we came over?" Marguerite continued to laugh.

I like the idea of moving in with George. He's closer to my size, and besides, I like being around kids. They know how to have fun.

"You look lovely, Marguerite, or should I say Elizabeth?" Brad teased.

"Elizabeth, you remember that too." Marguerite pulled Brad from the group and kissed him.

"Mother, I'm not following this very well. Are all adults 'twitsy'?"

George liked to coin new words and waited to see how long it would take before the kids at school began to use them. He kept a record in a special calendar on his desk at home.

"Be respectful, mon cher. Brad called me Elizabeth Browning, and I called him Henry David Thoreau in high school. They were secret names that we used when we talked to each other on the phone. We had a parent problem, and we felt it was best to devise ways of communicating that made life more interesting and less complicated at the same time. This is something you'll understand when you're older. Fortunately, you'll never have the difficulties we experienced." Marguerite held tightly onto Brad's hand.

"Mother, I think I understand about half of what you're saying. Can I take Angel out to play?"

Yeah, I would like to go outside and run. I'll introduce you to my new friend, Sophie. Let's go.

George placed Angel on the carpet and ran from the room. As they reached the top of the stairs, Sophie came running toward them.

"Wow, where did you come from? You're beautiful."

Two good friends were licking George as he sat at the top of the stairs.

Chapter 57

Welcome Home Angelique

B rad and Marguerite watched from the doorway of Brad's room as George ran down the stairs with his two companions. Marguerite took a seat in one of the two chairs while Brad laced his shoes. "Honey, who was that guy who escorted you to the Paris Opera House?"

Surprised by the question, Marguerite hesitated, wondering how much she should tell him.

"If you don't want to tell me, that's all right."

"No, I don't mind. He was my husband's business partner and friend of the family."

"He's in love with you, isn't he?" Brad reached for Marguerite's hand.

"How did you draw that conclusion?"

"Let's call it 'man's intuition', shall we?"

Brad's humor eased the anxiety she felt by his question.

"Yes, Brad, he is in love with me, but my heart has never been his. I'm fond of René. He's been a good friend. George doesn't like him though. I don't know why. Since you've come back into my life, I have no motivation to share my time with anyone else but you and George. I know that sounds selfish, but I don't want others making decisions for me. I want to start a new life with you. I don't want to consider anyone else. When Lamar died, I was devastated. I loved him very much, but we were never friends. He was a good husband and father. René never married, and he spent most holidays with us since he was Lamar's best friend. After Lamar died, René took over the business responsibilities and some of my personal financial affairs of which I knew nothing."

Marguerite stood up and walked toward the window; turning around she stared longingly at Brad, "I'm not the same person I was when I was Lamar's wife. I see everything differently now. I feel young and confident when I'm with you. I know I'll have to explain all this to René soon. I keep putting it off. I know it will hurt him. He wants us to get married."

Brad walked over to Marguerite and took her in his arms as tears fell on his shoulder. "We don't have to discuss this anymore today. We'll sort it all out later, together. After all, we're best friends. Best friends who fell in love." He took the handkerchief from his jacket pocket, touched the corners of her eyes and kissed her.

"Marguerite noticed a square package in brown paper lying on the dresser. It was wrapped tightly with string and from its size and shape it was obviously a picture.

"Just taking a wild guess Brad, is there a picture in here?"

"I forgot all about it. That package has been moving with me ever since Charles gave it to me when I stayed at his Château Domaine. It was a gift. It's probably a picture of the château. There was so much happening that I never thought to open it.

"Should we open it now?" Marguerite looked excited.

"I don't see why not." Brad began to pull on the string.

Downstairs, Charles, dressed impeccably in his black Windsor suit and black tie, suddenly felt uneasy. "The surprise will be ruined if he opens the package. I forgot to tell Broderick not to put the picture back in Brad's room after he picked it up from the framers. I wonder if it's too late." Charles rushed up the stairs to Brad's room. Appearing in the doorway, he saw Brad with a pair of scissors about to cut the string on the package. "Stop! I don't want you to do that."

Charles walked swiftly toward Marguerite and Brad and eased the painting from his hands. Brad and Marguerite stood in disbelief, as Charles walked out of the room. "I'll explain later!" Charles shouted from the top of the stairs.

Brad and Marguerite looked at each other. "What was that all about?" Brad stood with his arms extended as though the package was still in his hands.

Outside the guests were arriving. Each car stopped at the gate to have their invitation examined by the guard. Examining the invitations with a flashlight, the security guard looked surprised to see someone he recognized. This was also a person he shared a cell with while in prison.

"Père, is this your cab? "

"No, I stole it so I could make my grand entrance in a 1988 Citroen? Of course it's my cab. Maxie, how are you?"

"Never mind how I am, what are you doing here? Where did you get this invitation?" The security guard was suspicious. "Wait a minute while I call the house."

After a brief conversation on his remote phone, he leaned inside the car and tapped Père on his shoulder.

"Glad to see you're going straight, Père. How's Claudel?"

"Every things fine, Maxie, just fine. Call me if you want to go first class. Here's my card." Irritated by his friend's attitude, Père tossed his card toward Maxie as he drove up toward the house, the card fluttering to the ground.

Père parked his cab away from the other cars. He felt embarrassed parking close to so many expensive new cars and limousines that crowded the driveway. Reluctant to get out of his cab, he noticed several chauffeurs leaning on the sides of their cars, smoking and talking in groups of two.

"Hi, Père. What are you doing here, did someone call a cab?"

"Hey, Père, the guy I'm driving for doesn't trust your driving. Did you get new glasses yet?" Laughter rippled through the parked limos as the drivers watched Père walk toward the opened double doors of the entrance.

Presenting his personalized invitation with Brad's signature to the doorman, Père hesitated. Feeling uncomfortable, he looked around at the drivers who were staring at him from the parking area. Just as he was about to walk away, the doorman smiled.

"Good evening Monsieur Père Mesquer, I have instructions to take you to Monsieur Brad Kennedy as soon as you arrive." He held out his hand in a welcoming gesture. "Please follow me monsieur."

Standing on a mosaic tile pictorial scene of the Roman Coliseum dated, 850 AD, Brad, Marguerite, George and Angel were waiting to greet the guests in the center of the grand entry hall. As Père approached, Brad extended his hand, bringing him closer. "Here is my good friend, Père, who helped me find Angel. He's a great guy."

"If you are a friend of Brad's, then you are my friend also." Marguerite leaned over to Père and kissed him on each cheek. Père, embarrassed, explained, "I do what I can to atone for my past. It's what I have to do if I want to be a priest one day." Brad laughed as two jugglers dressed in green, red and white-striped pantaloons walked between Père and the other guests.

"Mother, can Angel and I follow the jugglers?" George pleaded. Angel wagged her tail in agreement as she and Sophie pranced around George.

"Yes, but keep Angel on her leash and don't let her out of your sight. Do you know where you are to sit in the dining room? Angelique and Sophie will be on your left. They have their own chairs. Remember to look at your watch. We are being seated for dinner at 7:00 o'clock." Marguerite looked to Brad for approval. Shaking his head in agreement, they both smiled as George, Angel and Sophie ran after the jugglers.

A six-piece jazz band marched around the landing at the top of the stairs, as everyone applauded. They were playing the song, "Don't Get Around Much Any More." The trumpet player led the group, followed by the saxophone and trombone players. All were moving their gold-plated instruments up and down to the beat of the music.

Stopping at the top of the landing, a man and woman joined in singing the lyrics.

"Missed the Saturday dance. Heard they crowded the floor, couldn't bear it without you. Don't get around much any more…"

Marguerite and Brad strolled about talking to the guests. Lydia caught their attention and walked over to greet them. "Where is our guest of honor, little Angelique? Lydia looked around the room.

"She went off with George. When last I saw them they had joined the marching jugglers. We'll join them in the dining room later." Marguerite saw Marie approaching.

"Madame, I'm sorry to be late, but my friend who looks after my cats is not well and I had to go home to feed them. After changing my clothes I went through the mail and started on my way here. I took the Metro, which wasn't a good idea because there was an electrical failure and everyone had to get out of the cars and walk. It was so dark that we had to hold hands like a chain to get out of the Metro. Everyone was trying to get a cab, and two men were fighting over one."

"Marie, Marie! Stop! You've told me enough. My, you do go on with your stories," Marguerite began to laugh. "Now, tell me, is that letter you're holding for me?"

"Oh, I forgot the letter… yes, it's a letter from Monique. It arrived after you left for the party." Marie handed the envelope to Marguerite as the sound of trumpets played in unison. Two vocalists at the top of the stairs announced in perfect harmony, "Dinner is served."

The guests began to take their seats according to their place cards; each name in gold and black lettering was positioned near the wine and the water glass.

Thirty-five guests were seated at the elegantly decorated table, and after introductions were made, the conversations continued.

"Hello, my name is Maurice. I helped Brad locate Angelique. We placed an advertisement in the *Le Figaro* newspaper for Angelique's return. We lived in the same rooming house for awhile. I'm an unemployed newspaper reporter. How about you, what's your name? What do you do?"

"I'm Lydia Rousseau. I, too, helped to reunite Brad and Angelique. Marguerite's housekeeper, Marie, came to the American Ambassador's home with Angelique, and I introduced them to the President."

Astonished, Maurice thought she was kidding but then decided to take a chance on it being true.

"Are you the President's wife?"

"No, just one of his secretaries. Now why should you be unemployed? You seem to be an intelligent and energetic man."

"I believe in free speech, but my employer didn't. Now I'm an unemployed reporter."

"I have an idea." Lydia gestured dramatically in the air as she held her empty glass toward the waiter to be refilled. "There is a position open on the President's press secretary staff. Would you be interested?" Maurice and Lydia leaned toward one another in close confidence, both engrossed in the personality of the other as the first course was served.

George turned around in his chair, his attention riveted on several servers who were gliding around the room on roller skates placing the food gracefully in front of each guest. "Mother, this is most unusual. Those roller-skating waitresses must have practiced a lot to keep from spilling the food."

After the main course was completed, twelve actors, dressed in native American costumes, consisting of feathers, leather pants and colorful stripes painted on their faces, came bounding into the dining room, chanting and beating their drums. Each drum was encircled with several, long, white feathers that tossed about as they danced up and down from one end of the dining room to the other, lifting up one leg, hopping, and then repeating the movement with the other.

Marguerite and Brad were distracted by the colorful display of dancing which prevented them from seeing Charles tapping George on the shoulder as he whispered a message in his ear. George slowly eased out of his chair and picked up Angel as he followed Charles from the room.

Where are we going? I would rather see the dancers.

Charles returned to the dining room and leaned over Marguerite, "George has taken Angelique outside for a break, and they'll be back shortly." Charles walked over to the head of the table and raised his arms in the air. The actors disappeared through the doorway as the servers skated toward the kitchen.

Everyone's attention was directed toward the doorway where two men dressed in red and green Shakespearian costumes

brought elongated trumpets to their mouths and blew loudly, causing the room to grow quiet.

Raising his voice, Charles began to speak to everyone in the dining room. "As you know we are here tonight to celebrate the return of the most famous dog in Paris, Angelique. For this occasion a cake has been baked with the inscription, 'Welcome Home Angelique.' "

Just as Charles spoke the last word a five-foot tiered white cake came gliding, mysteriously, into the room as the guests began to applaud enthusiastically.

Marguerite pressed Brad's arm, looking anxious. "George should not be missing this." Brad pushed his chair back and started to walk from the table to look for George and Angel when the trumpets sounded once more. Startled by the loud sound, Brad turned toward Charles who directed the enormous cake to the end of the dining room.

Just as Brad began to leave to find George and Angel, he felt a tap on his shoulder. Broderick leaned over toward Brad and said, "Don't leave, Angel and George are here."

"But where are they?" Brad glanced around the room.

Charles was now standing by the gigantic cake holding a large, glittering sword. As he raised the sword to cut the first slice of the cake, the trumpets blared for the last time. Just as Charles began to lower the sword, the top of the cake suddenly shot straight up and landed beside the waiter next to the buffet table. Confetti sprayed in every direction like miniscule dots of multicolored snow, as a bright spotlight lit the guest of honor and her friend.

"Hi, everybody. I'm Angelique's friend!"

And I'm Angelique. We live in a cake.

George stood in the middle of the cake, holding Angelique in his arms.

After the initial shock of seeing Angel come out of the cake, Brad walked over and took Marguerite by the hand. With broad smiles, they hugged the two celebrities.

"We were wondering where you had gone. Brad was just going to go after you two when they brought the cake into the room. This was the biggest surprise I've ever had." Marguerite continued to laugh.

George assured his mother, "It was Charles' idea, and Angel wanted to go with me. She likes to play tricks."

He's right, that's one of the things I do best.

After the cake was served, the guests continued their conversations for a short while longer until the light from the chandeliers began to dim, signaling the next event.

After the cake was served, the guests began to leave the table and enter the ballroom for the unveiling of the portrait.

Marguerite, George and Brad approached Madame Noblesse and introduced her to Charles." Madame Nobelesse, this is our host, Count Charles Beauchamp."

"Welcome to my home, and thank you for helping my friend Brad by giving him a safe place to stay." Raising Madame Noblesse's hand, Charles gently kissed her fingertips.

Surprised at such an unaccustomed display of graciousness, Madame Noblesse turned her head shyly. She was remembering her eighteenth birthday dance. Her escort had pinned a corsage to her dress and kissed her gloved hand. Madam Noblesse's heart raced as she savored the moment.

"Thank you, monsieur. You are very kind."

"If you will take my arm, I'll explain a few of the portraits in the ballroom." Charles led Madame Noblesse across the parquet inlaid rosewood floor.

"Mother, you have been carrying that letter with you all evening. Who is it from?"

"It is from Monique? Marie brought it to me and I haven't had a chance to read it." Marguerite slid her finger between the edges of the flap and pulled out the contents. Looking over Brad's shoulder, she raised her arm, signaling for Marie to come join them. As George, Angel, Brad and Marie gathered around in their family group, Marguerite read the letter.

Chapter 58

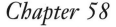

Confidences

*D*ear Madame,

When I arrived in Guiana I expected to find our little village, but it had disappeared. An office building and shopping center replaced all the small farms. I located my brothers by going to the city hall. They have a laundry business and are very successful.

My mother is now ninety-five years old and in the hospital. She has her own room on the same floor as the AIDS Ward. There are many AIDS patients and more coming every month. I've decided to stay and help. It seems the hospital's chef quit three days before I arrived. I think it was a sign from God that I should stay and cook for my people. My mother said to tell you, "God bless you for looking after my little girl."

Give my love to everyone and especially to Angelique.

Yours truly,

Monique [Malisha]

Marie's tear-filled eyes expressed sorrow for the loss of a good friend. Marguerite placed one arm around Marie and the other around George. Marguerite, wanting to give hope to her little family, confided. "I pray that Monique will come home to us...one day."

Everyone was now in the ballroom enjoying the music. Gradually, a few couples began to dance. A colorful band came through the doorway playing Latin music. When Lydia and Maurice heard the music they hurried to the center of the room gathering Madame Noblesse, the Cuban Ambassador and two other couples, joining the conga line that gradually encircled the room. More couples joined them as they shuffled and kicked their way around the ballroom. In the hallway and up the stairs, a majorette, twirled her baton, led by the colorful Leftist Marching Band that encircled the guests.

Broderick waved to Charles as he left the conga line for a glass of wine. "Yes, Broderick?"

"Monsieur, it is time to unveil the portrait. Shall I make the announcement to the guests?"

"Yes, I'll meet you in front of the portrait as soon as I have everyone's attention."

Broderick went to his position near the covered painting and took a small mechanical device from inside his vest pocket. Holding it toward the ceiling, he pressed a small button extinguishing every light in the room.

A gasp could be heard throughout the ballroom. The music stopped. Whispers traveled around the room until an amber light was seen shining on the covered portrait that hung on the wall above the fireplace.

The glow of the light grew brighter, revealing a red velvet drapery over the painting. Two men, dressed in white with gold braided uniforms took their positions on either side of the portrait and raised their French horns. As they began to play, the melodic sounds rippled throughout the room.

Broderick stood in front of the covered portrait. As he motioned for silence, the room grew quiet.

The waiters circled about the room serving each guest a glass of Champagne as Charles took Broderick's place and addressed his guests.

"My friends, we are here to celebrate the homecoming of an extraordinary friend of mine. If everyone will raise their glass we will make our toast."

In the corner of the room, Brad whispered in Angel's ear and placed her on the floor. Charles leaned forward, beckoning Angel to come to him. Picking her up, he kissed her on each cheek and held her in his arms facing the guests.

"Ladies and gentlemen, we raise our glasses this evening to Angelique, who has no equal. The President's secretary, Madame Lydia Rousseau, is here to present the certificate."

Lydia unrolled the parchment scroll, and read; "The President of France recognizes the bravery and devotion of our American cousin, Angelique. She will forever be an honorary Ambassador of Paris, France." Lydia leaned forward over Charles to kiss Angel on each cheek. Then she walked over to Brad to hand the certificate to him.

Charles announced, "As we drink our toast we shall announce to the world that Angelique will always be our Ambassador of Devotion and Love. L'amour toujours."

With a feeling of camaraderie, the guests intertwined their arms, listening with their hearts.

Taking their position at the end of the ballroom, on either side of the covered portrait, four of the band members raised their glockenspiels. With their padded mallets poised, they waited patiently for the portrait to be unveiled.

Charles approached Brad and Marguerite and led them in front of the covered portrait while George, holding Angel, stood between them. As the little family stood in the center of the ballroom, looking up at the bright red velvet cloth, Charles gave the signal for the band to play their glockenspiels. The sound they made was like the bells ringing on New Year's day.

With voices raised, everyone began to sing La Marseillaise, the French national anthem, filling the room with national pride.

As the last musical note echoed through the ballroom, Charles signaled Broderick to pull the cord that released the red velvet cover. The cloth slowly slid to the floor. A light from above the canvas cascaded down, illuminating the portrait, known as "Confidences", by Renoir.

Whispers circulated around the room in admiration as the guests approached Brad and Marguerite to congratulate them and to admire the famous Angelique.

Over in the corner of the room sat Sophie, listening and

looking at all the excitement. Angel walked over and sat next to her, licking her nose.

It's a lot of fuss for one dog, right Sophie?

As the guests began to depart, the orchestra moved onto the large veranda where they played the final song, "I'll Be Seeing You." Marguerite and Brad began humming the melody and singing the lyrics.

The glow of the early morning light extinguished every star in the sky as Charles and Brad stood by the front door saying goodbye to their last guest.

"Charles, I'm going to take Marguerite home. I will be returning later." Brad winked and shook his hand.

"Wait, I have a special present for you both, Charles said." Broderick appeared with the brown package tied with string. Taking a pair of scissors from his pocket, he cut the string, handing the package to Brad.

Marguerite looked over Brad's shoulder to see a copy, although much smaller, of the portrait hanging on the wall in the ballroom.

"This is the surprise I meant for you both. When you left my hotel, you left with a portrait of the château which I have given to many of my guests. When I decided to move the old portrait of "Confidences" to my home in Paris, I wanted to have a smaller copy made for your home to remind you of our friendship. But when I discovered your picture of the château had not been exchanged, I had to retrieve it from you so that I could present the correct portrait. I know this may sound a bit complicated, but it can't be any more complicated than the adventure we have had getting our adorable Angelique back where she belongs."

You can say that again.

"Thank you Charles. Your generosity and thoughtfulness surpass any experience I've ever had in my entire life." Brad put his arms around Charles and brushed both cheeks according to French custom. Marguerite repeated the gesture of friendship as Charles put his hand on George's shoulder. Picking up Angel, Charles received a lick on his nose.

"There go those wet kisses again," Charles laughed.

That's the only kind I can give. It's what I do best.

The last car in the driveway was waiting for Marguerite. As the driver opened the door, the security guard came over to the car with a bouquet of lavender flowers. Assuming they were for her, Marguerite held out her hand.

"These are for Monsieur Kennedy. There is a note attached." The guard placed the flowers in Brad's hand and quickly went back to his post.

With Angel on his lap, George curled up on the back seat and went to sleep.

Marguerite and Brad slid across the seat as the door closed. The car glided through the gate and on to the main road as Brad turned on the opera lights. Opening the envelope, he slid the folded letter onto his lap. Marguerite pushed closer to Brad, holding the lavender flowers in her lap, as she listened to him read the letter.

Monsieur Kennedy,

It was wrong of me to take your dog. I know you must love her very much and I'm sorry that I stole Angelique. When my children were taken from me, I knew it was for the best, but I want my children. I am now in a recovery program and each day I pray that my children will not forget me. Tell Angelique I'm sorry. Please pray for me.

Colette Baudelaire Masquer.

Brad looked over at Angel, asleep on George's lap. With Brad's arm around Marguerite, they sat in silence. No words could express the deep emotions they felt for each other and for Angel who's spiritual journey brought them together.

They had finally come home.

...Two sea gulls called to one another as they flew over Portsmouth South Cemetery. The setting sun cast shadows over the intimate gathering of new friends as the story drew to a close.

"Brad, what happened to Marguerite and George?" Karen asked.

Brad took Angel's leash and shook everyone's hand. "Thank you for your hospitality. We have only a few hours left until we catch our fight to Paris."

"But you haven't answered my question. What happened to Père, Charles, and all the others?"

Angel ran down the path as Brad followed close behind. Turning, he looked at the family seated on the lawn.

"That — my friends — is another story.

I'll be there too. It's my job.

Looking at the planet Earth from deep in space we see the intense blue of the ocean that appears as a tiny stream separating Europe from North America. Millions of years ago the continents were one. Even though the continents are now separate, there will always be a bridge of friendship between France and America.

Fini

A Portrait Of Angel

Painting and illustrations by Denise F. Brown

Acknowledgments

*M*y path to publish this novel has been fraught with emotions. Through it all there were many friends, business associates and acquaintances that offered their help. So many, that I always refer to this novel as, "our book."

It is with great affection that I thank those who have helped "our book" to become a quality artistic endeavor.

Ryan Hadlock, Mary Jackson, Kathleen Sullivan, Rosemary Hamilton, and Norbert Benecke, Adrienne Jahn, Sally Gray, Hillary Kang, Shirley Blanton, Luis Salvati, Pam Gharabally, Denise Brown, John O'Sullivan, Carol Adams, Marie-Michelle, Barbara Allen, John Boettjer, Sherry Brandsema. Senator Elaine Krasker, Irwin Bierhans, Don Speice, Stephanie Voss Nugent, Doreen, Mary Walker, Diane Stradling, Bert Eckert, Kathi Maher, Holly Lantinen, Rinda Hill, Dr. Anthony Guerino, Karen Penhale, Laurence Cioaba, Ce Ce Ann, Harway Jenni , Mundy Marion, Hendricks Chandra Sharp, John Simon, Walgreen executive Steve Forest, Dee Scott (Baby Angel's nana) and Governor John J. Lynch.

Author Stuart Wisong and Angel in the village of Massignac near Le Château Domaine

Reading Group Guide

1. Do you feel the author portrayed Angel as a spiritual being?
2. Who was the most amusing character in the story?
3. Are there any surprise endings you might project for Madame Noblesse and the Count or Maurice Baudelaire and Lydia Rousseau?
4. Is there one word or sentence that you would use to describe your feelings about the story?
5. Has this novel given you a new insight on the relationship we have with our companions?
6. What was so unique about Brad and Marguerite's early relationship?
7. What prevented Brad from adopting a dog sooner than he did?
8. How did adopting a dog change Brad's life?
9. How is Madame Noblesse's life different from that of Count Charles?
10. How did the abandonment of Brad's dog affect you as he relives the story in his dream?
11. Why did Marguerite's feelings change toward Rene?
12. Are there any emotional struggles in Marguerite's life that women can relate to?
13. Do you think it is possible to continue to love someone after thirty years of separation?
14. What are the mystical qualities that Angel possesses that are unique to her or do other dogs have a similar spirituality?
15. How did the author express his compassion for domestic animals?
16. What character in the story did you find most unusual? In what way? What is the theme expressed throughout the story?
17. Since the story does not have a traditional ending, what do you imagine will happen to each of the main characters if a sequel was written?

Recommended Books from our Animal Welfare Library

Our pets are members of our family. Their devotion is beyond description. They bring the joy of living to us each day. We grieve deeply when they leave us. It is our responsibility to do the best we can to care for them, that is why I am sharing these books with you.

The Bond, Our Kinship with Animals. Our Call to Demand Them.
By Wayne Pacelle, Presaident & CEO of the Humane Society of the U.S.

Kindred Spirits, by Stephanie Laland (Purchase on amazon books for less)
Peaceful Kingdom - Random Acts of Kindness by Animals, Stephanie Laland

Cat Stories by James Harriot (Plus) Dewey, A small town library cat.
by Vicki Myron

Homer's Odyssey, A Fearless Feline Tale, or How I Learned about Love and Life with a blind cat. By Gwen Cooper

Are You Poisoning Your Pet by Nina Anderson

Shock to the System, the facts about animal vaccinations, pet food and how to keep your pets healthy by Catherine O'Driscoll

Food Pets Die For, Shocking facts about Pet Food. By Ann N. Martin

The Ten Trusts - What we must do to Care for Animal Welfare. By Bernie Graham

Complete Guide to Natural Health for Dogs & Cats by Richard Pitcairn, DVM

It's Me or the Dog How to Have the Perfect Pet by Victoria Stilwell
(A Primer for Dog Training)

The complete Handbook of Dog Training by Thomas A. Knott

Creature Comfort - Animals That Heal by Bernie Graham

A Rare Breed of Love. The True Story of Baby and the Mission She inspired to help dogs everywhere, by Jana Kohl, Psy D.

Pets in America - A History by Katherine C. Grier

In Your Face - from actor to activist, by Chris De Rose

Why we Love Dogs - Eat Pigs and Wear Cows An introduction to Carnism by Melanie Joy Phd. World Speaker for Animal Welfare.

Even with four legs, Angel prefers an occasional ride.

Angel could never resist a carrousel ride.

Even in France, a trip to the country brings a restful repose.

Diamonds Are a Girls Best Friend.

Viande Boucherie (Angel's Favorite Shop in Paris.)